# KEEP HER FROM THEM

McRae Bodyguards - #4

Jolie Vines

WWW.JOLIEVINES.COM

Cover design – Natasha Snow

Formatting by Cleo Moran / Devoted Pages Designs

Cover photography – Emma Jane Photography

Cover model – Hayden

Editing – Emmy Ellis of Studio ENP

Proofreading – Lori Parks

*– Is it too much to want to be a princess and swept off my feet by a hot Scotsman? I think not.*

# BLURB

*A rebellious princess and the bodyguard who'll break every rule to keep her.*

## Alexandra

As a member of the royal family, my life is a spectacle. Every move I make ends up in the headlines. When a familiar face from my past joins my security team, his return brings more than just old memories. Raphael suspects someone close to me is leaking my whereabouts, putting me in danger.

I should be furious. Instead, I can't resist pushing his buttons. He wants me safe. I want to tease him. Besides, disappearing from the public eye isn't an option.

Until it becomes the only choice I have.

## Raphael

Guarding a princess wasn't in my plans, but the more time I spend around Alex, I mean Her Royal Highness, the more I realise she's in real danger. A series of close calls proves someone is selling her out, and it's my job to stop them.

But keeping her safe means getting too close. Too close to the way she fits against me, the way she looks at me like she remembers everything we almost had.

The princess is off-limits. I have too many secrets to hold onto someone like her.

But staying away? That might be the one order I can't follow.

--

*Keep Her from Them* is the final book in the *McRae Bodyguards* series, a lower drama-high romance series that follows our favourite crew of Scottish bodyguards. You can read this as a standalone.

# READER NOTE

Dear reader,

Thank you for picking up *Keep Her from Them*, the final book in my McRae Bodyguards series.

The audiobook featuring Lisa Zimmerman and Kale Williams is delicious.

These books are focused on romance and light on anything potentially triggering, but please note a warning for on page sex scenes and mild threat.

As with the previous books in this series, there's a hidden code in this story. Join my Jolie Vines Reader Group on Facebook or go to the acknowledgements at the end for answers.

Love hot Scottish heroes? I have five series of them. Once you're done reading this delicious story, check out the full works and reading order at the end of the book.

There's also a map of the McRae lands you can download for free here: https://www.jolievines.com/mcrae-estate-map

Love, Jolie x

# 1

## Raphael

If ever a building represented my relationship with a woman, it was this one. The royal palace sat back from the busy London street with armed guards at the gold-tipped gates. Tourists peered through high fences, their cameras capturing every moment.

Somewhere in the pale stone building, a princess waited.

Hostile, defensive, and out of reach to me.

Alexandra was cousin to King Philip and the prettiest lass who ever existed. Also my latest subject as a bodyguard, temporarily, at least. Ever since getting this assignment, I'd thought about her, wondering about her life and whether she remembered me.

Back at university when we'd met, I'd acted to protect her in a way that hadn't exactly pleased her. In fact, I'd caused Her Royal Highness no end of embarrassment.

Aye, she wasn't going to be happy to see me at all.

My taxi from the airport stopped, and I shouldered my

sports bag and exited to the warm summer afternoon. By force of habit, I was early, and not due to meet with the team manager for another hour to get my briefing ahead of an evening of work.

Through the throng of sightseers, I approached the main gate and held up my ID to the armed officer.

"Raphael Gordonson, reporting for duty. I'm due to meet Barrington Bray."

The woman took my ID, ran her gaze up and down me, then spoke into her comms. To my right, one of the tourists aimed their camera my way. I flinched and turned, a long-held automatic response to having my picture taken.

"Received and understood." Whatever the armed guard heard confirmed my case, and she returned my ID and unlocked the gate. "Walk directly to the archway. Someone will meet you."

On royal grounds, I crossed the wide-open frontage until I reached the towering building. I'd seen Ossington Palace any number of times on TV, for the king's lavish ceremonies or when they marched troops outside, but never visited.

Through the archway, a beefy Guardsman toting another deadly weapon queried my presence then had me follow him around the building and into a side entrance. He left me at a staff desk where another guard searched me and swabbed my shoes, then an administrator photographed me and made an ID for me. No one spoke more than they needed to. Not unfriendly, but with a quiet efficiency I appreciated.

I was taken to an office. Behind the closed door, a man spoke loudly on the phone, his tone haughty and posh. My escort rapped a knuckle on the glass then ushered me inside, closing me in.

The man, Barrington, I presumed, waved an arm in

exasperation then slammed the door of an inner room, continuing his call in private. I set down my bag and took in my surroundings.

This part of the palace was very different from the glamorous exterior. The offices looked like they were from the fifties and hadn't been refitted since. A rotary telephone with a curly cable perched on a desk. Paperwork teetered in a wire tray. A frame on the wall held rows of identical black radios, old-fashioned models but still the most modern piece of technology in my eyeline.

In the other room, the shouting ceased. I stood taller, waiting to be admitted.

I was here as a favour for a week maximum. Ben, my boss, had lent me out to another firm who held the private security contract for members of the royal family for when they weren't covered by the police. Barrington ran the team I was joining, and though I'd never met the man, I wanted to make a good impression.

Yet as I waited, I found myself thinking less about the job and more about the person I'd be guarding.

At twenty-three, the princess was the same age as me and often in the headlines. I never went looking for her but couldn't avoid occasionally seeing her latest scandal. On the short flight down to England, I'd read through articles with pictures of her stumbling out of nightclubs and laughing in the backs of limos. There were rumours of lovers, drunken nights, and even drug use. She had a reputation as a party girl, no matter how smart and formal she appeared when standing next to her older cousin, the regent of our realm.

She'd picked up the nickname Sexy Lexi in the tabloids.

It was a step on from the girl I'd known.

In my normal career, I protected Leo Banks, world-famous rock star and a good friend. I'd wanted to join his team, based in an aircraft hangar on the same Scottish estate where I lived, for as long as I'd known about it, and had signed up the minute I'd passed my helicopter training.

Would Alexandra be impressed that I could fly?

Would I even get the chance to show her?

I didn't want to examine too closely why I was obsessing over that.

The door flew open, and the man stomped out, his tie askew around his thick neck as if he'd yanked it loose. His cheeks glowed with the heat of anger. "You're early."

"Mr Bray. Glad to be here. I'm Raphael Gordonson." I offered out a hand.

He didn't take it, going to the exit instead, his posh accent sharpening. "Do I look like Bray? The name's Jared Jessop. Don't mistake me again. Now follow. We're leaving."

Now? Shite. I grabbed my bag, jogging after the man who'd set off down the corridor.

He shot me a glance, and a scowl darkened his lined brow. "Leave that. You can pick it up after the event."

I did an about-turn, snatching my suit jacket then tossing my bag back into the office. Had to trust nothing would go missing in a palace.

With clear impatience in every move, Jared checked the time and strode deeper into the interior of the building, griping about the delay.

I shrugged on my smart jacket. "We're heading straight into a briefing?"

"No time for that. You're hitting the ground running, sunshine. Shouldn't be a problem, right?"

That must've been what enraged him on his phone call, but damn. Mobilising without any preparation wasn't my favourite.

"It would help if I understood—"

Jared stopped abruptly. "Let's get one thing clear. You don't need to understand anything. All you need to do is follow orders and obey my every word. We're heading out unexpectedly early, and that means you need to do your fucking job and jump when I tell you to. Standard protocol can be discussed on the move."

We reached the end of the corridor that spat us out at a different part of the building's exterior. Three vehicles waited in a line, all black, shiny, and high-end. At a guess, I imagined they were modified to be bulletproof or maybe even bomb resistant, judging by the type of tyres needed for the additional weight.

That was as far as my thoughts got me. Jared threw himself into the first vehicle with a snap for me to climb in the last. I passed the central vehicle and stole a glance inside.

My heart beat out of time.

Princess Alexandra sat in the back, perfectly made up and regal, yet at the same time exactly like the girl I remembered. Her dress sparkled, and she had her dark hair up in a fancy style.

I recalled it loose and brushing over my bare skin.

The princess interlaced her fingers as if nervous, then her gaze rose to mine, locking on for the fraction of a second it took for me to pass by.

The too-short eye contact fried my brain.

Then the moment had gone, and I climbed into the last car, the convoy immediately starting out with a shout from a guard.

Next to me in the back, a solid bodyguard in his forties

regarded me. "Hey, new guy. We were expecting you. I'm Johnnie, that's Will," he indicated to the man in the front passenger seat, "and Riss is travelling in the car with our principal."

I remembered my name and introduced myself. The rapid turnaround of the afternoon had thrown me. Jared said I was early, but then we'd launched into a mission without a single word of where we were going or any plan. Had I been on time, I would've missed the assignment, not that I had a single fucking clue what was going on.

Jared had used the half a minute in the corridors to put me in my place where he could have given a shorthand explanation. I didn't like it. I was used to Ben's calm professionalism. Even in the midst of danger, our team had each other's backs entirely.

Above all that was another more potent thought.

Of exactly how Princess Alexandra's eyes had flared as they'd taken in mine. She'd recognised me. All I wished for was to go back in time and take another second to see how her expression resolved. In hatred or forgiveness.

For unknown reasons, that felt more important than I could say.

The busy streets of central London passed us by, and Johnnie handed me a radio.

"Familiar with the model?"

I inserted the earpiece, clipping the radio into my inside

pocket. "I've used a different version, but I assume they all work the same."

He performed basic checks with me, confirming I could hear the team. Johnnie had the weatherbeaten aspect of a man who spent his life working outdoors. His brown hair was greying at the temples and cut military neat, and thick biceps stretched his shirt.

Will was likewise stacked with lean muscle, but he wore a more sarcastic set to his mouth.

Like me, both men were outfitted in standard bodyguard wear for formal events. Black trousers and plain shirts covered by suit jackets, designed so we could blend in. We didn't carry guns—that was only for the royal protection officers who worked for the police, and the palace guards who were military. Our job was arguably more dangerous with how we'd put ourselves between our subject and danger. Our bodies were our weapons.

"Can ye fill me in on the event?" I asked.

Johnnie rolled his eyes. "Jared up to his usual self then? Boss isn't hot on briefings. Thinks they're beneath him."

I contained my annoyance. Not all team dynamics could work as well as mine. "Isn't Barrington the boss?"

The bodyguard held up his hand and the second much lower, as if to indicate levels. "Jared is our team lead. We don't see much of Barrington, more's the pity." He gestured between him and the man up front. "We usually carry out our own prep and risk assessments, but Jared did the advance work on this one. It's not such a big deal as it's a low-risk event."

"What does that mean?" I asked.

"The principal added the night to her calendar herself."

Our principal was Alexandra, the woman I couldn't

forget one car ahead.

I frowned. Why would that mean her security was lesser? It was as much based on the person as the place.

Johnnie continued, "I'll walk you through it. Don't worry, this one is pretty basic."

The tightness didn't ease in my chest. I could roll with the punches but I didn't enjoy being on the back foot, particularly in such a high-profile job as this.

Particularly under the scrutiny of a princess.

"It's an art exhibition with drinks. The principal, codenamed Penny Allen, will spend up to two hours at the venue then return home."

I held in my surprise. 'Penny Allen' was an alias the princess had used at university. Based on the initials of Princess Alexandra, the codename was used to refer to her by anyone who protected her. That she still used it years later was strange. If I knew it, dozens of others from the student body would, too.

Johnnie talked me through the venue and the risks, but all too soon, we arrived at a modern building with glass walls and a barrier holding back a small crowd.

Men with cameras lurked amongst them.

The princess had been haunted by photographers during her studies. Back then, she took measures to avoid them, and from mutual friends, I knew she hated having to do so.

I leapt from the car, falling into formation with the rest of the crew and watching Jared for orders.

Perhaps it was the air of unpreparedness I was riding, but I had a bad feeling about tonight, even if her team did this regularly. They'd kept her safe enough, though she was too often in the headlines.

Aye, that was what bothered me.

Princess Alexandra hated the press yet now seemed to court them. What caused that change of heart?

I locked down my intuition and fell in at the back of the diamond formation we assumed to get her into the building.

And the lass didn't look round at me once.

# 2

# Alexandra

Circulating through the art gallery's busy room was taking more effort than typical for a meet and greet. What I ought to do was wear a smile and ask each person who came to talk to me for their favourite painting from the exhibition.

I couldn't bring myself to voice the words.

For the first time in years, I was nervous.

The source of my anxiety? A painting across the room that panicked me when any of the glittering attendees went near. I wished I could hear what they said.

Not that I'd had a chance. I was mid-conversation with a fifty-something man who'd talked for several minutes about what kind of art I should enjoy. The fact I'd studied kept my tongue while he spoke.

To my right, broad-shouldered against the wall, my favourite bodyguard watched on. Riss was the only woman in the team, and her perfect no-nonsense attitude was exactly what I liked about her. She and I had an agreement for how to get me out of situations like this. One small gesture from me and she'd find a reason to interrupt and enable a quick escape.

My attention drifted back over the room. So much that I lost track of what the man was saying. Then my heart thumped as another of my bodyguards neared the artwork I had so much riding on.

Somehow, Raphael Gordonson was on my team and running his serious gaze over the art.

In the car, when my nerves had me rushing to be early for the event, I'd found myself looking into his eyes. A man I hadn't seen in the years since we'd been students at Edinburgh University. We'd never been in the same lectures, but mutual friends brought us into each other's orbit.

I'd liked him. Then after that single, damning photo of us had slammed onto the front pages, my hope of a normal student experience evaporated. It made sense that he'd be working in protective services, but why for me? The overprotective, jumped-up...

Fingers locked on to my arm and tightened.

I started and snapped my gaze to the man leaning into my space. He gripped my wrist. Pain shot up my arm.

He curled his lip. "Tell me, princess. What's caught your attention so intensely? Is it the nudes?"

Instantly, a figure appeared at my shoulder. In a single move, Raphael clamped the stranger's arm and twisted to break his hold on me.

"Get your hands off her," he snapped.

A moment later, Riss cupped my arm and swung me away. "No touching, sir," she advised, all before I'd had a chance to even react.

Riss guided me across the room. I peeked back to where Raphael and another of my team blocked the man so he couldn't follow.

A mixture of annoyance and outrage fizzed up my spine under my sparkling dress. "What on earth?"

"He'll be escorted from the venue." Riss directed me to the refreshments table. "My apologies for not intercepting. I shouldn't have ignored his overeagerness to keep talking to you. Are you okay, ma'am?"

"Fine, but it wasn't your fault. I should've moved on sooner. Did anyone see?" I rubbed the bare skin that still tingled with the unexpected contact. Red finger marks decorated my flesh.

"I think not. I'll stay close."

I scanned the room, relief following that Riss was right. The hosts, the gallery's owners, were holding court with a group around them. Two assistants talked others through the works on display. Of those looking at me, which people always did, none wore concern.

Taking a breath, I forced my expression to neutral, and ever the professional, Riss stepped back, murmuring quietly to her team over her comms and leaving me to continue my role. In my family, working royals considered themselves performers when on duty like this, and the optics of every event mattered. So I'd been told.

For a moment, I was free of conversation, and I allowed myself another glance to the left side of the gallery where two women regarded that certain painting which held me in its grip. Their conversation was animated.

My breath caught.

As subtly as I could in a sequinned evening gown, I moved closer, making polite small talk with a mingling group as I went, Riss never more than a few metres away. Finally, I was in earshot.

"...reminiscent of Beaux in terms of how the light falls," one of the women commented.

My heart pounded. I adored Cecilia Beaux. To be compared to her was a dream. The nude painting they examined was special to me, not just as a supporter of the arts, but because it was *mine*.

I'd secretly arranged with a gallery assistant to enter it into the event, though under an assumed name. My painting of a couple entwined in a tryst had been the first I'd had the confidence to share.

I needed to hear more. Two gentlemen appeared in my eyeline.

"Your Royal Highness, it's a pleasure," the much older of the two said, clutching the arm of his companion. "We were just saying how wonderful it is to attend an event promoting such a wealth of up-and-coming artists."

I smiled, one ear still trained on the judgement of my work. The exhibition was made up of young female artists in an industry where the vast majority of art sold was by men. "I'm honoured to be able to support such a good cause."

He answered my question about his favourite. I couldn't help the distraction as my brain leapt back to the women.

"Can't say I'm a fan of the colour choices," the second observed. "The use of light is admirable and the technique adequate, but the artist," she squinted at the label, "EC

Hunt, would do well to spend more time at the easel and less trying to imitate others."

Ouch.

"You're right, it's copycat and weak in the attempt," the first woman agreed. She beckoned over another couple.

I struggled to hear their conversation, though it was obvious what they were saying. The newcomers both peered at the painting, then *laughed*.

"That's the problem," a tall blonde woman advised. "You open events like this to amateurs and most buyers can't tell the difference. To the trained eye, this kind of trash has no place in an exhibition."

All four tittered over their wine glasses.

Shock cut through me. I used every bit of willpower I possessed so my wave of upset didn't show.

Riss appeared at my shoulder. "A moment, please, ma'am."

She'd picked up on my distress. I exhaled shakily and smiled again at the people I should've been talking to. "If you'll excuse me."

They let me go, and I made a beeline for the hallway at the back of the gallery. It wasn't the done thing for me to take a break while on the job, but the criticism of the painting I'd been so proud of hit me like I'd been punched. I couldn't stop the feelings.

"Comfort break," Riss explained to the team over her comms.

In the cool and empty corridor, I paused until Johnnie appeared, standard protocol to have him wait with me while Riss scoped out the bathroom. She gave the all-clear, and I slipped inside and locked myself in a stall.

Sweat pricked my brow. I sat on the closed toilet and

dropped my head to my fingertips, careful not to ruin my make-up.

Imitate others? That was how all artists learned, but I thought I'd got past that and into a style of my own. I'd been delusional. Thank God I hadn't put my real name to it, not that I'd ever truly considered doing so, considering the naked people I'd picked as my subject. The palace would not be impressed.

*This kind of trash.*

The dream I'd barely let myself entertain of becoming an established painter dissolved in front of me. And it hurt.

I allowed myself thirty seconds to feel the disappointment then fished out my phone from my clutch. There was only one person who would understand.

**Alex:** *Come over tonight? I need a drink.*

**Dori:** *Shit. Yes, I need it, too, but who do I need to kill? Can I borrow Riss for the dirty work? Wouldn't want to bloody my clothes.*

He'd understood instantly. A short laugh that was almost a sob flew from my lips.

**Alex:** *Be at my place by ten and ready for a night in.*

That was code for us going out. I didn't think my messages were monitored by security, but nearly always when I was clubbing with friends, some photographer found me, so I kept my movements out of messages.

Dori sent me a thumbs-up, and a small piece of my broken heart throbbed. All I needed now was to fix my expression and finish the job I was here to do.

Tonight, I'd dance and drink my feelings away in a dark club with my best friend. I just had to keep it all in until then.

# 3

## Raphael

A yawn came over my comms. "How much longer?" Will asked.

Johnnie's voice returned, "Ten minutes."

I hadn't seen anything of Jared since we got in the building, nor had he emerged when the arsehole attendee had grabbed hold of Alexandra.

Internally, I bristled, trying to keep my emotion off my face.

I was a stand-in. Will had filled me in on how the fourth member of their team, Toni, had needed emergency time off because his mother was ill in a hospital in another country. He'd made a joke about it.

It all added up to an increasingly negative view I had of Princess Alexandra's security.

From first impressions, they were sloppy as fuck. For starters, mostly absent Jared had treated me with disdain, though I made up a quarter of his protection unit. I knew nothing of their practices, how they communicated and the language used to alert to situations. The team had taken over handling the incident with the attendee, but once outside, the man had been released without a word. We didn't know his name. We didn't have a picture or anything to tie back to this event should we encounter him again.

And no one gave a fuck when I challenged them on it. I'd demanded an ID check, and Will had told me to stop worrying, though that activity was part of our job.

All of this was so different to how we looked after Leo, and he was arguably less vulnerable than a princess.

I was equally certain my feedback would not be well received, but I'd give it to Ben and he could talk to the owner of the business. To ignore it would be enabling a potential attack, and I couldn't allow that.

Princess Alexandra continued her steady circulation, mingling with a group of artists and smiling, though without the same energy from earlier. When we'd got here, she'd been bubbly and excited, but that had changed. Probably from the handsy attendee.

I didn't take my eyes off her. Not as she concluded her talks and signalled to Riss that it was time to leave, nor as she congratulated the gallery owners and stepped out into the hall, and certainly not as we readied to emerge into the street.

She shone. Even if her mood was blue, she radiated something compelling that commanded my attention and had my body on high alert. Aside from being gorgeous, with that luxurious brunette hair and brown eyes, high cheekbones, and expertly applied make-up emphasising her lips, she was magnetic. Every time she lowered her eyelashes, I got lost in the sweep back up. Every graceful move caught up in a spell.

She shimmered in a sparkly dress and tasteful jewellery, every inch the nation's treasure. The one they loved to see up to no good.

Through the art gallery's glass frontage, a selection of photographers were still visibly present, but the gallery staff who had been at the barrier and checking invitations were no longer there. The gap between the fences was wide open, and members of the public milled either side.

It meant the princess would need to walk straight through them to reach the vehicles at the road.

My pulse sped up, and I pulled up short and put a finger to my earpiece. "Insecure exit. Crowd control required."

"Negative. Just get in the fucking cars," Jared reported back.

I swore and hustled to keep my position in our formation. This time, I was on Alexandra's right, and she slid me a curious look.

It was strange being close to someone I knew but couldn't acknowledge. Maybe at the other end of the journey, she'd stop and say hi or ask me what the hell I was doing here.

There wasn't time to think about that. We emerged into the warm night, and cameras lifted.

My heart thumped faster.

I'd hoped to find Jared out here managing the crowd, but he was striding on ahead and ignoring the very obvious danger in his hurry to leave. Across the other side of Alexandra, Riss, a formidable and solid woman with black hair in a tight bun, held herself with lethal poise, muscles bunched like she was ready to throw down.

We descended the steps. At the front of our diamond, Johnnie called out for the people around to make way. Some did. Others ignored him, maybe wilfully, or maybe because they had no idea who was amongst them.

I scanned every face. Searched every hand.

We reached the barrier, tightening our formation to move through as one.

Suddenly, on the far side, a man lurched forward.

"Riss, hard left," I snapped.

The bodyguard spun to face the danger. I recognised the man. It was the guy from inside the gallery.

"Princess Lexi, how did you enjoy the naked portraits?" He stuck a phone in front of her face, but Riss instantly blocked his reach. "Tell us why you were so fascinated by the sexy pictures." He struggled to get past Riss.

I wanted to fucking deck him but kept going, and we adjusted our positions to cover the bodyguard left behind.

A few metres further and we reached the safety of the cars. The chauffeur had the doors open, and the princess climbed inside. He closed her in but hesitated.

"Is one of you accompanying her?" he asked.

Riss had travelled down in Alexandra's car but was still occupied in keeping the threat at bay. We needed to leave, immediately. Yet neither of the other men were moving, and Jared was already in the first vehicle.

It wasn't my place, but I took charge. "I can."

Johnnie shrugged. "Go for it."

Without further delay, I rounded the car and climbed in the other side. My action seemed to speed everyone else up. Riss gave up being a human blockade and joined the two others in the final car, and we set out.

It took several streets of distance before my heart calmed and I stopped scanning our surroundings, wondering what the ever-loving hell had just happened.

Then awareness gathered around me.

I was alone, mostly, in a plush car with a woman who was staring at me. I faced her.

"Hey, Alex." Why was I launching in with the informal? "I mean Your Highness."

Her expression slipped to incredulous. "Bodyguards usually stick with 'ma'am'. Only friends refer to me as Alex."

I blinked, annoyed, even if she was right. "Excuse me. We were friends, once."

"You are not excused. As I recall, you didn't act very friendly last I saw you, and that was a long time ago."

I let out a breath that was fifty percent irritation and the other part relief that she remembered me as much as I did her. "I was trying to help."

The cars merged onto a busy road, nose-to-tail evening traffic slowing our progress. Alexandra didn't reply.

"Your security is shite. Does that kind of thing happen often?"

She glanced at the driver. "Why are you on my team, Raphael?"

So she remembered my name. "I work for another crew and was borrowed as a favour to replace your fourth team member."

An expression crossed her face, too fast for me to pin it down, but it was something close to sadness. "Toni is with his dying mother. They weren't going to let him leave, but I insisted. Awfully random to have you appear in his place, but anyway, your criticism of my bodyguard team is noted. Now you've gifted me your so-valuable insight based on a few hours of experience, there's no reason to continue this conversation."

I stared back, open-mouthed. "You used to be nice."

She collected her phone from her wee bag, keeping it low and out of sight of the windows. "I used to be a lot of things until someone stripped his shirt and ruined it all."

Silence fell around us, thick and heavy.

Had to get my mind off the night in question. Of half-naked me and sweet, hot her. Of the fact she obviously blamed me for it.

"I should've tackled that man and left Riss to deal with ye." I just couldn't help the gripe.

She didn't even look up. "At least Riss would allow me some peace and quiet after a stressful evening."

Fucking hell.

None of this had been what I'd expected. I'd imagined reconnecting with Alex again. Getting a chance to apologise to her had been important to me, but I'd assumed she'd accept my explanation. That I'd work for her with extra diligence because of our shared history.

Only in the last part was I right. Princess Alexandra was still pissed off with me even years later, and any apology I could make would fall on deaf ears.

A short while later, we were back at the palace. Our car halted, and I readied myself to wish her a good evening, but someone opened her door and she swept out, her heels clicking on the cobblestones as she disappeared into the house.

I followed more slowly, seeking out Jared. The man reached the entrance. I called his name. He didn't stop.

A hand landed on my shoulder, and Johnnie turned me. "The boss asked me to show you our digs. Beer after?"

Adrenaline still coursed through me, but I agreed and let myself be managed. Though every instinct yelled at me to fix the things I knew were wrong.

*I*n a modern pub on Islington Avenue, with a football match blaring on a TV screen that took up most of one wall, I nursed a beer, the glass cool against the still-warm night.

Johnnie and Will watched the match and talked shite about the teams. I was stuck in my funk.

My phone buzzed, and I lifted it to find Ben's name on my screen.

"Got to take this," I said to the others, not that they were paying any attention to me.

Outside, I found a quiet spot against the wall and answered my boss. "Thank fuck. A rational person."

Ben chuffed a laugh. "Ye haven't found much of that there?"

"Understatement of the year."

"Talk to me."

In a rapid list, I gave him my thoughts, ending with, "If your friend, Barrington, wants a kidnapping on his hands, he's close to getting his wish. Their setup is the sloppiest shite I can imagine."

"He messaged me an hour ago with feedback. His team lead, Jared, took credit for a good evening's work, and advised Barry that his training enabled ye to act quickly when the photographer launched at your subject."

My mouth fell open in incredulity. "He has to be fucking kidding. Jared told me nothing. He didn't even stop when that happened."

"Yet took all the credit. Aye, he did. But there's more.

Have ye checked the headlines tonight?"

I frowned. "No. Was it reported?"

My phone vibrated with a link Ben had forwarded me from a gossip site. I opened it. The headline screamed: 'Sexy Lexi's Eye for Naked Ladies' and was accompanied by a shot of one of the portraits displayed in the gallery, the princess nearby. The article went into detail about how Alex had been enamoured with that specific painting and how that meant she had a kinkier side than the newspaper had guessed at.

I growled frustration. "That is gross."

"What's interesting to me is how unbothered Barry was. If this was Leo, his publicist would be up in arms."

I knew that to be true. Leo weathered an enormous amount of publicity. Rumours of the breakup of his marriage were frequently touted because it made money for the sites that gossip-seekers visited. The fact he and Viola were the perfect couple with two sons and a wonderful life together meant nothing.

"Ye can't stop them talking shite but ye can keep them away so they can't get the shot," Ben grumbled.

I closed the article. "The whole event was a shitshow. I'm gutted that I didn't see the guy taking pictures of her inside the place."

My brain refreshed the scene. It had to be the man who'd grabbed Alexandra. He was a chancer paparazzo who'd got onto the guest list somehow, and the phone in her face outside was his last-ditch attempt to get a reaction. We absolutely should've taken his details. There was nothing stopping the arsehole from trolling her next event as he clearly had access.

I scanned the article again then asked a question of my

boss. "How can I get hold of the photographer's name? The article didn't have an author or any credits."

He clucked his tongue. "Leave it with me." A pause followed. "You're only there a few days, but why do I get the impression you're going to turn that team on its head?"

I didn't have the right. Jared wouldn't listen to me, and a glance through the window showed me the two boozy bodyguards who I suspected wouldn't give a damn. Barrington might, though. Riss was another possibility. All I knew was I couldn't ignore the gaping holes in the protection they provided.

I said goodbye to my boss with a promise to catch up the following day. The tightness in my chest still hadn't gone. If a wannabe journalist or photographer was able to get as close to Alexandra as the man had today, a stalker or someone who meant her harm had equal chance.

It couldn't be allowed. I had to do something about it, even if they didn't like it.

Another message landed, this time from my best friend and in our team's group chat.

*Jackson: What do bodyguards and testicles have in common?*

I thumbed a reply of a sobbing emoji because his jokes were the worst, just as another of our team answered.

*Valentine: They're ugly and hairy?*

*Valentine: WAIT, they come in pairs? Tell me I've got this right.*

*Jackson: They're always behind a big dick. I actually like your answers better.*

Without planning it, I dialled my friend. Jackson and I had gone to Edinburgh Uni together. He knew a little of my history with the princess but not the full story.

Jackson picked up immediately. "Miss me that much,

huh? It's been one day."

I sighed. "Maybe a bit. I...just needed to run something by ye."

"Hit me."

How did I start? I didn't even know what I wanted to say. "I talked to Alex today."

"Ye mean Her Royal Highness Princess Alexandra?" He put on a posh voice. "Was she snarky with ye?"

"Aye, a little. I didn't expect it." Or maybe I had and I wasn't being honest with myself.

"I never got the full story of what happened. Tell me and I might be able to suggest a way to fix it."

In a rush of time, I was eighteen and reliving the scene. "It was a comedy of errors. I was studying when my phone started blowing up with messages from other aviation students who were at a house party. They go hard and were trashed. I gave up my books to join them. In the party, I spotted Alex."

She'd been dancing in the sweltering, sweaty living room in just a cropped top and booty shorts. I'd gotten a shot of lust so damning I was stunned. Then I took in the bigger picture and clocked the way some of the other men were looking at her. One in particular was trying to get close enough to rub up against her. I'd had a bad feeling about him.

"She was with another lass who I knew, and I took her friend aside and said I was worried about Alex getting felt up by this guy who was watching her. The friend listened and pulled Alex out, bringing her to me to explain. She was annoyed. Not at me, but at the fact she couldn't go anywhere without trouble. There was always someone wanting a piece of her. I told her she could dance closer to me and I'd make sure no one touched her."

Jackson made a funny sound. "No wonder ye ended up a bodyguard."

"Shame I didn't have the skill back then. She danced with me and her friend. When the other lass went to get a drink, Alex looped her hands around my neck and got right up close."

"Wait. I can't believe it's taken ye five years to tell me the story. Ye dirty danced with a princess?"

I swallowed, because what came next destroyed any of the good feeling from our minutes alone where I'd kept my touch on the curve of her waist but she'd grazed hers under my t-shirt. "Someone took a picture, not of us, but the flash brought me to my senses. I spun around to shield her from it. Alex's friend returned in that same second, and we jogged her arm so she spilled her revoltingly sweet cocktail over Alex. She was a sticky mess. Alex slipped into the bathroom to clean up, and I waited outside with no clue what to do. Then I had the bright idea to knock on the door and offer my shirt."

"Which she accepted?"

"She did." I'd never forgotten how hot she looked in my clothes when she emerged from the bathroom. "I still felt that overprotective vibe, so escorted her out."

She'd kissed me on the cheek, the heat and scent of her driving me wild again.

"I opened the door for her, and she nudged against me as she passed. It was the exact second a waiting paparazzo took a picture. It was all over the news the next day. My face was in shadow so couldn't be made out, but I was bare-chested, and the princess was in an oversized man's t-shirt in the doorway of a house, as if leaving a hookup. The gossip rags had a field day. They never identified me, but it was humiliating for Alex who had to endure asinine commentary on her letting loose in her student years and implying she was sleeping around."

Jackson swore low. "That's hardly your fault."

"I flew at the guy and threatened to break his camera. He took off running, and when I turned around, Alex had gone."

"Ah, with the assumption that you'd made it worse. She hasn't spoken to you since?"

"She was only in Edinburgh for a short time. She moved on without me ever getting a chance to clear my name."

"Why would ye need to?"

"I think she thought it was an act because I'd set her up."

There was a pause. "Like you were the one who called in the photographer? Why would she think that?"

"I don't know. Maybe because I'd sidelined her at the start? Her friend never spoke to me again, though, so it's just my assumption." Plus her attitude tonight doubled down on my hunch.

He made a sound of derision. "Ye were in hiding. Ye had even less reason than her to be splattered all over the tabloids."

"She didn't know that."

It was true. At age fifteen, I'd fled my Mafia-wannabe father with my younger sister in tow. Ariel was now dating Jackson, and the older brother we moved to live with, Gabe, was due a baby any day with his wife, Effie. Things had turned out good for us. Princess Alexandra's existence appeared not to have changed at all.

Jackson gave up words of comfort. "I know ye. Injustice bothers the fuck out of ye. Clear the air with her. Fix it and regain your peace of mind."

He was right. I'd find a way.

We said our goodbyes, and I breathed a little easier, the conversation having brought peace to my frazzled soul. That fell away when my gaze touched on a scene across the street.

Islington Avenue was home to dozens of bars, restaurants, and other busy venues. Directly across from where I stood was an exclusive nightclub, the name HELL lit up by neon-orange lights swirling in the summer night. It was after eleven, and a line formed with clubgoers to the right of the entrance, many of the crowd wearing masks of light scraps of lace or more elaborate designs of demons and angels.

To the other side was an unlit alley that led down the left of the building. A taxi had slid into it and stopped by the club's side door. My gaze locked on to a couple falling from the car, the light from the vehicle's interior highlighting their features.

Princess Alexandra giggled and stumbled on her sky-high heels, a wig covering her hair but not fooling me for more than a second. Her companion, a tall lad in expensive clothes and with floppy blond hair in his eyes appearing every bit like a European prince, threw an arm around her, an e-cigarette held between his lips. He was familiar, though I couldn't place where I knew him from, but he was rolling as much as she was.

The two of them tied masks to their faces and entered the club. I almost choked at the attempt at disguise. It wasn't enough.

My principal had snuck out without any security.

I was moving before I even registered what I intended to do.

# 4

# Alexandra

A throbbing beat pulsed through the club's VIP suite, and Dori threw back his whisky then scrambled up, dragging me with him.

"Dance. Immediately," he said.

I sagged onto his chest, the fine material of his shirt smooth under my hot hands, and my blonde Marilyn Monroe wig crushing against him. The multiple cocktails I'd consumed before we'd even left the palace were combining into a rolling head rush, so I muttered a complaint.

"The room is moving."

"Then match the rhythm and you'll feel normal."

Normal was a joke. When had I ever felt that? Out of our private booth, he tugged me towards the dance floor.

"No fair," I whined. "You're high. You can see straight."

"I can't see shit behind the mask."

"Don't take it off. I just can't with mine…"

He hugged me to him. "I won't. I know."

We passed booths full of well-dressed men and barely dressed women and then the darkened bar with a bartender setting a blow torch to a cocktail while dry ice smoke rose from another. Not everyone wore a mask, like the white lace one I'd kept on or Dori's black version. From those who clearly wanted to be seen, I recognised a few people, some more famous than me, but no one approached us or even slid us curious looks.

For once, I'd got away with coming out unnoticed.

Even the bouncer had let us into the VIP floor on Dori's name, not mine.

On our right, a barrier gave way to the drop down to the huge nightclub floor below. It was so packed with bodies that heat rose in a wave.

Dori lifted his chin. "Down there?"

I shook my head.

He gave me an incredulous stare. The thing about my best friend was no matter what he did, he was always stunning. Tomorrow, I'd roll out of bed dark-eyed and puffy-cheeked and it would take a solid hour for me to put my face back together. He'd sweep his fingers through his hair and would be artfully tousled and picture-perfect in an instant.

He bowed deeply then climbed onto the first rung of the railing. "Listen up, mortals," he yelled to the throng below.

No one could hear, I hoped.

I slid my fingers into his belt loops. "Geddown."

"My girl has decreed we will not be joining you this evening. You'll have to imagine your hands on my body. Cry your hearts out."

His designer trainers slipped on the rung. Dori teetered and clutched the rail. I swore and tackle-hugged his waist. The idiot burst out laughing.

"Darling girl, if I fall, let me go. It's no good me taking you with me. Your cousin would lop off my head."

My fit of the giggles returned. Dori might act the arrogant asshole, but that's exactly what it was: an act. Scratch the surface, and there was a deeply unsettled boy in the body of a beautiful man. Heartbroken, too, though he wouldn't tell me over what.

After arriving at the palace earlier, my friend had read something on his phone. An email, or perhaps a news article. Whatever the contents had been, the abject pain in his expression knocked my silly bout of sadness into the shade. I'd asked, but he'd refused to discuss it, merely locking his phone and taking on my mini bar.

He intended to drink to forget, and I was on board with that plan.

"We can dance up here," I ordered.

His easy smile returned, and we stumbled onto the exclusive dance floor. Despite being smaller, it was still packed, and in the middle of the bodies, I made an effort to lose myself. Dori matched the beat with effortlessly sexy moves. I attempted to keep up, but my mind kept wandering.

Back to the unhappy art exhibition.

Back to the bodyguard in my car.

Not that I'd ever confess it, but Raphael was the first real man I'd ever had a crush on. As a young teen, I'd fallen in and out of love with celebrities, same as anyone else. Except I had insight most others didn't. I'd met the objects of my affection, and each occasion neatly killed any attraction. Pop singers were typically jaded and whiny when the cameras were off them. Actors assumed they were the centre of attention and had little to say that wasn't a soundbite. None of them could be considered real, which meant my crushes weren't either.

I'd gone to an all-girls' school, so by the time I reached university, I was woefully inexperienced in the opposite sex and determined to learn. Then I'd seen this handsome Scotsman around my friendship group. I discovered his name and even found ways to talk to him. Raphael was funny and self-effacing. He made no attempt to big himself up to impress me.

One night, at a party, I'd danced with him.

A shiver ran through me at the memory. I'd felt safe with him in a way no one else had ever made me feel, and it had emboldened me enough to want to make a move. I'd pressed myself against him. I'd touched him and slid my fingers under his t-shirt, my eyes closed and my heart pounding so hard.

I'd been eighteen and scared out of my mind at where such a touch could lead, but I'd known instinctively that Raphael was a safe pair of hands.

It was ancient history, but nothing could take away the memory of that skin-on-skin contact and the sharp chemistry that had rushed in my veins. He'd squeezed me back. He'd felt it, too, at least I imagined he had.

I'd wanted to kiss him. I'd inhaled his scent, and it drove me crazy.

Five years on, and I knew exactly how he'd made me feel in that moment. He'd been my sexual awakening and the start of more than one change.

Through the dance floor crowd, I caught a glimpse of the top of the steps where a black-clad bouncer stood. An older man crept up and spoke in his ear.

I stilled, watching them.

The older man had the appearance of a photographer. But how on earth had they discovered me? My disguise was good.

The man slid something into the bouncer's hand, right as a spinning spotlight passed over them. Pale paper, suspiciously like folded notes.

My heart sank, and the memories of Raphael faded.

Too often, it went this way. I could enjoy a night out until the paparazzi arrived. Usually, they didn't get into clubs, instead just waiting to upskirt me outside. Candid photos were sometimes taken by other partygoers, though not normally in the VIP section like we were in now. I'd hoped so much to avoid that tonight. I needed an evening out.

Dori caught me by the hand and spun me around.

I peered over my shoulder to the stairs. The bouncer stood alone. Where had the man gone?

I leaned on Dori and spoke in his ear. "Did you see a guy?"

He whirled me. "Stop looking at other men when the best is in front of you."

"Idiot." I laughed and wobbled on my heels, my skirt riding high up my legs and my head rushing. By the time I got my vision back, there was no strange man in sight.

I hadn't imagined it, but the paranoia could've tainted what I saw. Besides, it didn't matter. I'd already been embarrassed in the press tonight, the palace comms team notifying me of an article appearing even before I'd taken off my shoes from the art gallery visit. It was a taunt, though the article writer didn't know it, on my precious painting. I'd been obsessed with it. It had been such a big deal to me, and the disappointment continued to crush me, even after I'd vowed to dedicate my night to making Dori happy.

I signalled to the hovering server waiting discreetly by the edge of the dance floor, and gestured between me and my friend for another round of drinks. She nodded and trotted off to the bar. If I couldn't force myself to forget, alcohol would have to do the job for me.

Then we'd dance until the world fell away.

# 5

# Raphael

My phone buzzed with a message from Ben.

*Ben: Your pap is named Malcolm Dennis. Prolific in London. Typically targets young female celebrities and sells the photos with suggestive headlines to trashy news sites.*

He followed with a couple of pictures of the man in question. I recognised him instantly as the person who'd confronted Alexandra at the art gallery.

In one, Malcolm had his beanie hat pulled low and collar up as if incognito. That would make no difference to me. I'd recognise him in a heartbeat.

I passed through the nightclub, the first room a wide space with a star-studded ceiling, orange-lit bars to the left and right, and masked yet elegant men and women in clusters of seating with champagne in ice buckets. Fake flames flickered up columns, giving the effect of entering Hell, the club's name played out in its decor.

I'd bypassed the queue with the help of my palace-issued ID. The princess might not have taken her team, but the club's security was clearly used to bodyguards pursuing their principals. They hadn't blinked an eye at me.

At the far end, an opening in the wall gave way to a dark cavern with a different vibe to the chill bar room. I entered, and a wall of noise slammed into me, red lights chasing along the perimeter and the black walls dripping with condensation from the packed-in bodies. Humidity stuck my black t-shirt to my body, and my senses scrambled from the all-out assault.

I scanned the crowd for a glimpse of her. Hundreds, maybe thousands, of people crammed together on the dance floor, a lot of flesh showing but too many pockets of shadow obscuring my ability to search. I scanned every masked face. I could blame the single pint of beer I'd drunk, but my heart raced like there was a reason to be afraid.

Alexandra's regular team was untroubled at her being in here, so why was I?

In my haste to reach her, I'd paused halfway across the road, then darted back to clue in Johnnie and Will. Both men had shrugged off my concern and had gone back to watching their match.

They were off the clock. She hadn't invited us along, which meant my presence here wouldn't be welcome, but I couldn't leave it alone.

Blame single-mindedness, but I was in this city to do a job, and it didn't matter to me what time of day or night my services might be required. I had nothing else to do and every instinct screaming that this was where I needed to be.

Red lights chased under my feet, and I prowled the perimeter of the floor, edged past two devils who were simulating sex against a wall, or maybe actually fucking, and finally reached a set of steps that ran up to a mezzanine level. A bouncer guarding them lifted his gaze at my approach.

"VIP only," he mouthed at me and tapped a discreet sign that said the same.

I held up my pass. This thing was a magic bullet, because he shone a penlight on it, nodded, and unclipped the velvet rope to allow me to proceed.

Up I climbed, the elevation providing a useful vantage point over the heaving club but giving me no joy in my hunt. The DJ switched up the tune, and all hands rose, obscuring the faces even more.

I could search this place for an hour and come up empty. There were side rooms. Hallways. Fuck knew how many hidden corners a lass could get lost in.

At the top, I emerged onto a broad platform with private booths and a barely lit bar at the back. If downstairs had the feel of exclusivity, this took it up a notch. None of the sticky floor and cheap beer I'd known from my student years— the last time I'd gone clubbing. Here was polished and high-end, with uniformed staff and subtle hints of luxury and concealed lighting. Judging by the wealth practically dripping from the clientele in the form of purposefully displayed watches and glittering jewellery, it was a rich kids' playground.

At the very far end was a smaller dance floor, and my pulse skipped at a glimpse of a woman in the centre of it. *Found her.*

Even in a lacy white mask that hid her features well, I knew her. Alexandra's pearl-coloured dress offset her tanned skin and rose dangerously high on her thighs. Her blonde wig hid the brunette locks I'd obsessed over, knowing just how they looked spilling down her back.

Heated thoughts bombarded me. Of winding her hair

around my fist. Guiding her mouth so I could taste her. I'd never kissed her, yet I'd been so close I almost knew the shape of her lips against mine.

The jackass with her, I assumed her boyfriend in a black mask that matched hers, plucked a glass from the tray of a waitress, threw back the drink, then wiped his mouth with the back of his hand. Alexandra did the same and giggled, stumbling as she tried to set the cocktail glass back on the tray. The waitress disappeared back to the bar. Alexandra fell on her friend, her laughter not stopping.

Damn. If I thought she was tipsy when she got here, she'd wandered merrily into drunk-skunk territory. Plus her man was the same, the two of them keeping each other standing. It was her business what she got up to, but it bothered me that she'd left herself so unprotected, especially knowing she was being hunted. Why not take her team? Even one person to watch over her?

Movement in my peripheral vision caught my attention.

A man emerged from a passage at the far end of the booths. A bathroom hallway, by the sign above the exit. My blood pumped faster as I identified Malcolm Dennis, the exact hunting paparazzo I'd worried about.

He slipped into an empty booth, his gaze locked on to Alexandra. Below the level of the table, he toyed with something. Had to be his phone, or maybe a small camera, but I wasn't taking any chances. I needed a plan and fast.

Backtracking, I returned to the bouncer at the top of the steps. "That guy in the end booth is a photographer. He should be kicked out."

The bouncer jumped his gaze to where I subtly indicated. He shrugged but didn't shift.

I stared at him. "He's going to take pictures of your clientele. Remove him."

"None of my business how a man puts food on his table."

"Ye know Princess Alexandra is over there?"

He folded his arms, confirmation that he'd clocked her yet didn't care.

For fuck's sake. "If ye don't remove him, I will."

The bouncer stood taller, his lip curled in obvious annoyance. "Start any fights, and it's you who'll be thrown out, whoever the fuck you think you are."

I glowered, but the man's position was clear. He wasn't going to help. He might even stand in my way, judging by how he'd defended the wrong person. Perhaps it was an accepted part of this club's scene, he'd been paid off, or maybe it was just the target in question who he didn't care to defend.

Throughout the conversation, I'd kept Malcolm in my eyeline. A drink had appeared on the table in front of him, but he hadn't moved, which meant he was waiting for the right moment to strike. For the princess to fall over or maybe be alone. If I took him on and failed, and the bouncer was good to his word, I'd be on the outside and unable to intervene.

Which left me one solution in my rapid risk assessment and strategy planning—to persuade her to leave with me.

My issues were that we weren't exactly friends, I wasn't supposed to be here, and most likely she'd laugh in my face if I made demands.

In the middle of the VIP dance floor, she whirled around, beautiful, chaotic, and with clumsy movements. My stomach sank. It was history repeating itself. Me trying to protect her, and with every chance this was going to go badly. Yet I couldn't walk away.

I brought out my phone and booked a taxi to pick us up

outside in a few minutes.

"Is there another set of steps leading away from here?" I asked the bouncer.

He grouched out that there wasn't and turned to a pair of women approaching.

With him distracted, I went on to stage two.

I made my way along the edge of the booths and up to Malcolm's. With a clumsy swipe, I neatly knocked his drink into his lap.

"Fucking shit." He leapt up, snatching his camera out of the way.

I kept my head down. I didn't expect him to have paid as much attention to me as I had him earlier but couldn't be sure. "Sorry," I slurred as if drunk.

Malcolm brushed down his sodden trousers, swore again, and made for the bathroom.

I had minutes to cinch the deal.

# 6

## Alexandra

Dori stilled at my side. With my eyes closed, I heard rather than saw the reason.

"I'm Raphael Gordonson, Alex's bodyguard. You're her boyfriend, aye? I need your help."

Dori choked. "Did you just call her Alex?"

"He does that," I slurred and cracked open an eye.

Raphael really was here. Tall, and dark, and stupidly handsome. My head swam. I missed what he said next.

Dori's voice pierced my consciousness. "Darling girl, stop sleeping on me. The bodyguard says there's a photographer."

I flushed cold. I hadn't been paranoid with the exchange I'd witnessed. "Where?"

Raphael answered. "He's been watching from a booth. Same guy as from the art gallery."

I peered through the crowd to the booths. Nope, no creep. Like earlier, he'd been seen then vanished like a ghost.

"I saw someone slip the bouncer money. The one who did this." I made a grabby hand, taking Dori's arm in a death grip.

My bodyguard's eyes darkened. "Ye don't deserve to have your night splashed over the tabloids tomorrow. Leave while he's out of the way. I have a car waiting outside."

Photographers followed me all the time. I'd made an art form out of evading them when needed but had come to accept it as part of my reality a long time ago—interestingly, right at the point the first scandalous headline appeared, with the man in front of me bare-chested in the picture.

That was the turning point in my life. The tabloids and scandal pages changed their tone. They'd always commented on my looks and fashion but shifted it up a notch to my love life. I'd been barely eighteen, yet my adulthood made me fair game for them to hunt. The types of sordid acts I'd read about myself apparently doing were so far from my timid reality it was laughable.

Raphael had been right in the middle of that crossroads of history.

Dori rolled an unsure glance down to where I leaned against him. "Your overfamiliar employee says we should go."

"He says a lot of things. Doesn't mean I'll obey. Who knows what his motivations are."

We were at the back of the dance floor and close to the rail. I straightened from Dori and wobbled backwards on my high heels. Raphael caught my waist, steadying and releasing me in one smooth move.

A lick of heat curled in my belly. If I ran, he'd chase me,

I was certain. That was a far hotter image than he had the right to claim.

I lifted my chin. "Why are you here?"

"I was nearby and saw ye come in. I worried."

"How did you even recognise me?"

He pursed his lips but didn't answer, as if it was obvious. Except it wasn't, because no one else had stared.

"Where were you?" If he'd followed me all evening, I'd riot.

"With Will and Johnnie in a bar across the road."

I squinted around. "Did they come with you?"

He shook his head, but I already knew the answer. They wouldn't bother if they weren't getting paid for it, and wraparound security cost more than the budget allocated to little old me.

"You've been on my team for five minutes. Why do you care?"

"I just want to get ye out of here safely."

Standing next to Dori, Raphael tightened his jaw. Between the two men, my blondie Euro aristocrat bestie and my dark and delicious bodyguard, I was a lucky lady for the view.

I also knew the second my friend made one of his infamous bad choices, as his mother had termed it when we were younger.

Dori's lips curved with interest. "We don't need your help. The worst that photographer could've got so far is us dancing with no clear sight of my girl's face. Fuck that guy. If he wants pictures, we'll give them to him. Point him out."

All three of us turned. From the bathroom hall, a bedraggled older man strode out, so out of place among the glittering elite that he was unmistakable. He passed the bouncer at the top of the steps, and the two men shared a look. That little interaction confirmed my suspicion that he'd paid good money to be told where I was.

My soul was heavy that there was yet another place I couldn't be left alone.

Dori laughed. "Never mind. Got him. Let's have some fun."

"What are we going to do?"

Ignoring me, he pushed through the people on the dance floor, temporarily clearing a path and providing direct line of sight to the man hunting me. I stood taller, and the photographer raised a small camera in his hand.

Instantly, Raphael stepped in front of me and blocked the shot. For some reason, that gesture amid everything else he was doing hit me in the feels. I peered around him.

Instead of going to the photographer, Dori veered to a clear part of the rail over the dance floor. In a pause in the music, while the crowd waited for the beat drop, Dori yelled at the top of his voice. "Oh my God. It's Elsie Sale!"

Screams followed, and faces swivelled as people tried to spot the celebrity musician who was the darling of the music scene.

I cackled and hugged onto my bodyguard's arm. The alcohol coursing through my veins made me bold. I wasn't going to miss Dori's show for the world, yet my attention caught and snagged on the feel of Raphael's hard muscles.

As the first person I'd ever touched in the romantic sense, he'd provided the blueprint for how a man ought to be built. I'd compared everyone who came after with him, and all had fallen short. Yet he'd been a teenager then, and this body was all man. The solid chest and the arms that had held me were thick with hard muscle. He'd been strong, but now he was something else.

It tantalised me.

It woke a deep female instinct that yearned to be protected. A matter of hours ago, when the photographer had grabbed my arm, I'd considered how no one ever touched me. That was a fact. Everyone was careful around me. The few boyfriends I'd had were the exceptions, but even they were hands-off most of the time. No lover had ever held me in public.

It was as if handling me was a treasonable offence, but it only boosted my sense of isolation. I clung to Raphael a little more.

Dori prowled the railing, his lips pouted as he no doubt enjoyed the chaos he'd created below.

Raphael twisted to keep Dori in sight while using his body to block me. The arm I was holding lightly curved around me, and his free hand gently cupped my shoulder. His almost-embrace had no reason to be so familiar. Once, we'd done this, and years ago. Maybe he'd been the first man I'd touched, but he was hardly the last. I snapped my brain back to the present and focused on my friend.

The photographer left the steps and slipped into an empty booth. Still at the rail, Dori eyed the man but signalled for a waitress. In an instant, a woman was at his side, a tray under her arm and her uniform the black and orange of the club.

Dori bent to whisper in her ear. Starry-eyed, she smiled at him then darted off.

My friend leant back on the barrier, the music thumping, his blond hair falling in his eyes and his posture the picture of elegant languor.

I wanted to join him. Whatever he was planning was going to be good. Yet at the same point, I was enjoying being right where I was.

The waitress appeared again, her steps brisk, and an ice bucket clutched in her hands. Inside it, a champagne bottle smoked. Oh God. I knew what Dori was going to do.

He accepted the bottle and took a swig, leaving the bucket by his feet.

The clueless photographer was still squinting my way, his camera in his hands and catching the light every now and again.

He had no idea what was coming.

Raphael put his lips to my ear. "We need to—"

He didn't finish that sentence as Dori moved into action. Putting his thumb to the end of the champagne bottle, he shook it.

White foam sprayed out in a torrent, soaking the photographer and the booth. The man leapt up. Dori shook the bottle again and doused him a second time, pure malice and delight in his expression.

He yelled something that didn't reach us. People in booths either side jumped from their seats and scuttled away, the waitress watching with her hands to her mouth. The furious photographer scrubbed down his face, and droplets of fizzy wine dripped off him. He held up his camera and yelled at my friend.

Ha. Screw him. I hoped it was broken.

Dori shouted something back then made a third attempt with the champagne bottle, but it was empty. He set it down and picked up the ice bucket instead.

"Fuck. Now we really need to leave," Raphael warned.

"Are you joking? The night has just become interesting."

I pushed against Raphael, but my bodyguard held firm.

"It'll become a headline about ye if we aren't careful."

"Still don't understand why you care so much," I muttered.

Dori leapt up onto the booth's table. He crowed something I couldn't hear and raised the ice bucket then upended it. Ice splattered down. I squealed at the fun, wide-eyed as Dori stooped to collect the camera from the table and use it to snap pictures of the soaked and frosted paparazzo instead.

People shrieked. Ice slid across the floor and tinkled down to the dance floor below. Partygoers neared to watch the drama, and another waiter ran for the bouncer who'd had his back to the antics and hadn't yet noticed. The photographer wiped his face and snatched for my friend.

Easily, Dori evaded the reaching hand, years of skiing paying off in his quick dodge. He slapped the hand away and took another photo, running his mouth the whole time. I needed to hear what he was saying because his taunts were clearly working. This was gold. Hilarious.

On the table, Dori twisted and presented his backside to the man. I giggled. Half the VIP dance floor was now watching, some subtly filming or taking pictures.

The photographer lunged at Dori and this time caught his wrist. He yanked hard, and Dori crashed down to the table. The two men wrestled for the camera, and a punch was thrown. Someone screamed. The bouncer rushed in and grabbed Dori by the ankle.

In an instant, this had turned ugly.

My heart skipped a beat. "We need to help him."

"We have to go."

He was right, except I couldn't just run. "I won't leave my

friend."

Raphael muttered a string of swear words then tore his gaze back to mine. "Listen to me. This is becoming a brawl, and we need to get out of here before it gets worse. We'll move fast and get ye to the car outside. Once in there, you'll lock the doors and I'll come back for your friend."

The photographer pulled an elbow back, his fist raised.

I squeaked in distress. "Dori had bad news tonight. He isn't thinking straight."

"I'll help him. I promise. Please, Alex. Come with me."

I put my hand in his and my faith in his direction. Raphael kept me close, body blocking me past the fight which now had two bouncers wading in. I couldn't see Dori to know that he was okay. I stumbled down the steps and nearly fell. Raphael tucked me under his arm to finish the descent. At the bottom of the steps, he half carried me, sprinting around the edge of the club so people had to move out of our way. It was chaos down here as well, with a hunt going on for the celebrity Dori claimed was present and people slipping on ice.

I closed my eyes and tapped my forehead to Raphael's shoulder. My mask was askew and my nerves on the very edge. What had started as funny had turned horrible. I was scared for Dori, and the warm hug of alcohol was quickly shifting into a headache and nausea.

Cool air ghosted over me, and I opened my eyes to the steps outside the club and the street. I wobbled down the first, clutching hard on my bodyguard's arm wrapped tight around me and under my breasts. A car waited. Raphael snapped open the door and guided me onto a leather seat, barking something at the driver. The man made a quick promise, his wide-eyed gaze skipping over me. Huddled in the seat, I shuffled my skirt down my thighs, straightened my wig, and watched Raphael run back inside.

Dori and I had been in escapades in the past. He was six feet tall and strong from all the sports he did, but he was a lover, not a fighter. Words he'd used to describe himself when provoked by punchy guys who didn't like his pretty style or expensive clothes.

If he got hurt because I'd decided that dancing and drinking our emotions away was a great idea, I'd never forgive myself.

Over all that was another concern.

That my bodyguard might get injured, too.

My thoughts were interrupted by a bright flash of light. A lens hit my window, the shutter clicking. Another photographer had been lying in wait. And I was caught in their trap.

# 7

# Raphael

Leaving Alex in the car went against every single one of my instincts, but when I made promises, I kept them. Inside the club, the scene had taken a shift to dark and dangerous. Still, the music played, but a fight had broken out near the DJ's stage, and a crowd formed a tight circle around it, clubgoers hooting at the action.

I threaded my way to the VIP area steps. Halfway down, Dori struggled under the grip of two bouncers, his arms restrained behind his back.

Fuck. I jogged the rest of the distance, spotting an older man in a suit waiting for the party to descend. Had to be the club's manager.

I whipped out my ID. "Bodyguard service. I'll take him from here."

The older man scowled. "Too little, too late. The police are on their way."

I resisted the urge to close my eyes in frustration. I wasn't sure who Alex's friend was, but it was a safe bet that he was of the same social set as her, and an arrest made bad headlines. I needed to resolve this fast. "I sincerely hope you don't mean to detain my client for defending himself?"

The man's eyes widened in incredulity. "Your client assaulted another patron and damaged my furniture."

"My client disarmed a photographer your staff took a bribe from. I'm happy to tell that to the police when they get here. I'm sure your patrons will love hearing how ye give zero fucks about their privacy."

The two bouncers escorting Dori reached the bottom of the steps. Alex's friend glared at them from under a floppy blond fringe. His shirt was torn and missing buttons, and sweat gleamed on his chest, his black mask around his throat. For fuck's sake. He was the very picture of a spoiled playboy. I needed another incentive.

Tightening my jaw, I came back to the club manager. "If the prince is arrested, ye can kiss goodbye to any of his friends or associates coming here again."

The man's hostile expression dialled back a degree. "He's a prince?"

For all I knew, he could be. "Aye. Hand him over and we'll go."

The manager stared at me for a beat longer then turned to his staff. "Release him." To me, he added, "Get him out of here, now. You can leave by the side exit."

It meant we'd be half a building away from Alex, but with the fight on the main dance floor, I'd take it. I nodded, and the bouncers released Dori with a shove. The young aristocrat swung around, but I neatly hooked an arm around him and towed him after the manager. A short hallway took us to an exit, and we spilled out into a dark and dirty alley, the door slamming behind us.

The second we were outside, Dori shoved me off. "I'm not a fucking prince."

I heaved a sigh of relief. "Then who the hell are ye?"

"Count Sonderburg."

"All the same to me. We need to get to Alex."

The count pulled his phone from his pocket, the screen lit. "She's calling me."

My stomach did a strange flip. "Answer her."

He curled his lip but obliged, putting her on loudspeaker.

"Are you out of the club?" Alex gasped.

"I am. You didn't need to send your attack dog in to fetch me."

She audibly exhaled then replied, "Is Raphael okay?"

"Ask him yourself."

"All good," I quickly said so she knew I could hear.

A tyre screech came from her end of the line. My heart thumped. It didn't come from nearby. I could hear the road at the end of our alley just fine.

"Alex, where are ye?" I asked.

"Someone tried to take pictures through the taxi window. I had to leave. I'm so sorry for abandoning you."

Dori paled and handed me the phone. Whatever was in my expression had infected him.

"You did the right thing," I told her. "Are they chasing ye?"

Her voice came out small. "I don't think so, but my driver is going fast just in case. I'm almost at the palace. Can you please bring Dori back?"

"Of course I will. Stay on the line."

I gave the phone back to Dori and fished out my own,

summoning the nearest taxi. It was only a minute away, but that felt too long. My strategy to separate them had been a sound one. I got my principal out and away safely. Had I been part of a team, she wouldn't be alone right now. But the shite setup designed for her protection was failing hard.

On my phone's app, the car neared, and we left the alley to find it. At the roadside, I scanned the crowd outside the club, anger brewing inside me all the more. This was a disaster from start to finish.

Dori rolled his shoulders, a bruise revealed on his collarbone.

"Are ye hurt?" I asked.

He shook his head. A black cab pulled up, and we climbed in, leaving Hell behind.

The cab moved out, and Alex's friend put his head in his hands and muttered something down his phone. I held my tongue. He'd made the night a hundred times more dangerous. Alex had encouraged him. Neither would want to hear what I had to say about it.

It was only Alex's quiet, "I'm safe," that finally let me take a deep breath.

A short while later, we rolled up to the palace gates, our driver stopping but the armed police keeping to their posts.

"They won't let the cab in," Dori informed me.

We made the rest of the trip on foot, our IDs checked and Dori weaving as we crossed the courtyard to the archway and through. He stumbled. I braced him with an arm around his back. This time, he allowed the support, even as a second guard checked our IDs at a side door.

I warred with myself over how to handle this. I'd have to tell Jared about intervening tonight, which didn't worry me as I assumed he couldn't care less, but more, I was afraid for

Alex. She was the one I needed to warn.

Dori led the way down a hall far more opulent than the ones I'd walked half a night ago with Jared. Huge paintings of pastoral scenes were interspersed with portraits of long-dead royals, the gold leaf on the frame glowing dully in the low light. There was no one else in sight, and our footsteps thudded on the floor.

"You're a real one for the help," he slurred.

"If you'd left when I asked instead of getting into a fight, it wouldn't have come to two bouncers strong-arming ye down the stairs."

Dori shrugged. "Fuck your judgement. If I hadn't doused that asshole and trashed his camera, he would've been sneaking more pictures."

"And the riling up of the crowd?"

"If they all took pictures, it'd devalue his."

We reached an entry hall. Any further questions I had died on my tongue at the image ahead.

At the foot of a marble staircase, and in a shaft of moonlight, Alex sat, her knees together and her arms wrapped around her white dress with her delicate lace mask in her fingers. The wig had vanished, and her brunette curls fell in waves. She was an angel from a grandmaster's painting. A vision. At our entry, she peeked up.

She looked so vulnerable I wanted to hug her.

That was never going to happen.

Dori pushed away from me and dropped to a sprawl next to her. "Your bodyguard is a grouch. He claims I made things worse tonight."

She sighed. "Didn't he have to pull you from a fight?"

"It was already over."

"I'm glad you're back in one piece. Can you wait upstairs for me?"

He grumbled agreement then shot me a glance, his lip curled in obvious dislike before he gave Alex his parting line. "See you in bed."

His disappearance left me alone with Her Royal Highness. I wasn't jealous. There was no way that emotion coursed through my veins at the thought of him stripping and waiting for her in a four-poster bed.

Alex twisted her fingers together. "Thanks for getting him out of there. You were off the clock. You didn't need to do any of that." Her gaze turned curious. "I still don't understand why you got involved."

I wasn't entirely sure either. I raised a shoulder. "If I hadn't, that could've ended badly."

She tilted her head in question.

I elaborated. "More than one photographer tracked down your location. Your friend decided to fight rather than just leave. We could've got out of there much easier without his escalation."

"It isn't his fault he got into a fight."

I gave her a sigh of disbelief.

"God, fine." Her voice cracked. "Then it's mine because tonight was my idea. I just hate that I can't go anywhere without things like this happening. But I can't and won't sit at home and do nothing for the rest of my life. They'll hunt me and write stories about me no matter what I do."

"I never said ye can't go out. Just take security."

She made a sound of frustration. "I can't. The team is only available to me for events when I'm representing my family. You won't get paid for what you did tonight."

"I don't care about that. But what are ye talking about,

only a few events?"

"The team is shared with other members of my family. You wouldn't know as you haven't been here long enough. If I'm working for the Crown, I get cover, but in a personal capacity, rarely is there the money, hence why I stay here when I'm in London. Ossington Palace is one of the most protected buildings in the country. Outside of that, I'm on my own."

That lack of service couldn't be right. "You're expected to take care of yourself the rest of the time? How is that fair?"

"It's my lonely reality. Why should I expect the princess treatment just because of an accident of birth? If I want it, I have to earn it." Alex stood, her bare feet on the polished floor. She picked up her heels by their straps and moved into my space.

Two soulful brown eyes peered up. "However things work in your regular job, it's different here. But just know I'm more than grateful for the assistance. Goodnight."

Like I was in some kind of dream, the princess pushed up on her toes and put her hand to my chest, gifting me the lace mask. She kissed my cheek.

Then she turned and disappeared, off to join her boyfriend in her bed.

# 8

# *Alexandra*

Inside my suite of rooms, I locked the door and tossed my shoes to a corner then entered my bedroom. A shirt flew through the air, thrown by Dori. I caught it, a favourite one I usually wore to bed. He smirked at me then rifled through his sports bag, extracting a pack of pills. He popped one and drained a bottle of water.

I wrinkled my nose. "What is that?"

"Something to knock me out. Can't sleep without the meds, won't function tomorrow without rinsing out my kidneys."

I entered the bathroom and stripped my clothes then slipped the long t-shirt over my head. For a moment, I studied myself in the mirror. Life had come full circle. The shirt was Raphael's, given to me on that fateful night we were photographed together.

I swallowed down a pang of emotion, maybe for the loss of the girl I'd been, or for some kind of regret for the evening. There was something in Raphael's manner that always made me feel...judged. It made me want to rebel against him, and that childish reaction allowed me to enable Dori. What a mess.

Methodically, I removed my make-up.

Images from the evening kept on coming in a fierce bombardment. The art gallery. The cutting words. Dori launching into a fight. Raphael rescuing me. The memory of his warmth almost batted away the icier ones, but not enough.

Back in my bedroom, Dori had already passed out face down on my big bed. I took a second to check he was still breathing then left him and entered the bedroom next door. I kept the lamps off.

Faint light from the windows gleamed over an easel which held a half-finished painting. Another portrait. On a table next to it, my paint-spattered tray held tubes and brushes.

Fuck my stupid dreams.

I marched to it and snatched the canvas free. Raising it, I cracked it down over my knee, splintering the frame, then repeating it on the other side. When it was broken beyond repair, I shoved the whole thing into the bin.

It did nothing for my upset, but at least I wouldn't have to look at my failure again tomorrow.

A toe poked my side, rousing me from a heavy sleep.

"What?" I opened an eye.

Dori held out a mug, which I assumed was coffee, and a packet of paracetamol.

"Drink me, eat me, then choose between the bad news or the badder news."

I struggled up, my head pounding in the worst way. Last night, I'd left the shutters of my bedroom closed, but strong daylight pierced them in streams, telling me it was late in the day. I accepted two pills and washed them down with a swig of Dori's drink.

"Badder isn't a word. And I don't want either. But tell me anyway."

"Despite my best efforts, a picture was sold."

I groaned and dropped my head back to the padded headboard. "I don't know if that's bad more than just expected. What's the rest?"

There was an interesting pause. I blinked my eyes open to find Dori giving me a quizzical look.

"The picture is of your overprotective bodyguard half carrying you from the club."

"Let me guess the headlines. I was too drunk to stand? Pulled from a fight?"

"They took another angle. A comparison to a previous scandal."

I stared at him. "What? Just spit it out."

Instead of speaking, he took back the coffee and held out his phone. Onscreen were two pictures, side by side. In the first, I was under Raphael's arm, my wig askew and the mask half off so it was clearly me. The photo cut off at Raphael's chin, so only displayed him in a partial view. The second was of me exiting the house party at age eighteen, a half-naked Raphael behind me.

The headline screamed: 'Sexy Lexi: Five Years of Hot Antics.' The article claimed once a party girl, always a party girl.

I grumbled and pushed it away. "It was the photographer outside who took that shot, then. Not the man you tackled, so you did help."

Still, Dori was regarding me with interest.

"What?" I asked.

He raised his phone again and enlarged the picture so it focused on Raphael's jawline and down to his broad shoulders. He then dragged the photo to show the same in the second shot. The parallels were obvious. It was the reason the editor had picked that photo as a pairing to last night's one—the framing was almost identical. Except they hadn't made the connection Dori was about to, only referencing an unidentified bodyguard in the more recent shot.

"I knew he was familiar," my friend drawled. "He's the same guy you moped over when you left Edinburgh. Tell me I'm right."

"I don't mope."

He snapped his fingers in utter delight. "He used your name like you were friends, because he knows you. Why didn't you say, darling girl?"

Why hadn't I? I spoke to Dori every day about all manner of trivial things, but maybe that was the point. Raphael wasn't trivial. He felt like a deeply buried secret, though that made no sense as I hardly knew him.

I stole back the coffee. "He's no one, and there's nothing to tell."

There really wasn't. At eighteen, I'd touched him, wanted him, and then I'd left him behind. When I saw him next,

I'd apologise and we'd move on. I could only blame my hangover for how everything about that felt off.

# 9

## Raphael

Across the desk in the antiquated fifties-style office, Jared's face mottled red as he tore me a new one, his screen displaying a tabloid picture of me and Alex last night.

"Look at that shit. You exposed the princess and the whole team to ridicule."

"What are you talking about?"

"The story implies she was drunk. The photo suggests she couldn't walk out under her own steam. That reflects on the Crown. What were you thinking?"

I stared at the image. Her pretty face. My arm around her, under her breasts. It looked like a boyfriend helping her more than a bodyguard, but that wasn't the point. "I was doing my job."

"You had no right to be there. You acted outside of your jurisdiction."

A rush of anger had me balling my hands into fists on my knees. "I went in to protect her, and it's lucky I was there. I pulled her out of a situation that could've turned ugly. One which your team refused to help with. Tell me how any of that is wrong."

He slammed his hand down on the desk, rattling the wire trays and his stained mug. "As a temporary member of my unit, you jump when I tell you to jump. You're on duty when I tell you you're on duty. You don't get to wade in whenever you choose."

I snorted in disdain, disgusted with his behaviour and his management of the service. "So in your world, I should have just left her to the wolves?"

"You shouldn't have been there. You didn't have the right." He held up a finger, stopping me as I was about to speak again. "I can't have someone like you in my unit, even just as cover. From the start, I didn't like you, and you only proved me right."

I was so infuriated I wanted to yell. He didn't know me and hadn't taken the time to try. "There is nothing bad in protecting our principal when she needed it. You're the one in the wrong. You need to find out how that photographer discovered her. You need to change everything you're doing before someone gets hurt."

Jared stood. "Don't presume to give me orders, kid. You're fired. Get the fuck out of my office."

Fired? For a second, I stayed in place, unable to speak.

Jared smiled, and his haughty tone only got haughtier. "Maybe you'll learn next time not to try to teach an old dog, you little punk. Now fuck off before I get the police in here to throw you off palace grounds. See if the press want *that* photo to add to their collection."

I forced myself to move. Him calling in the armed officers would see me ejected from the building, and I had to speak to Alex first.

Out of the office, I took a right rather than a left, heading deeper into the palace. I emerged at the base of the sweeping staircase where the princess had sat last night and waited for me to bring her friend home.

I had no clue what I was doing, only that I didn't have her number. I definitely didn't have the clearance to roam the building unchallenged, and even if I did, I had no idea where her apartment or rooms were.

If I accidentally stumbled in on the king, I could be shot.

A man in a suit and carrying a tray stepped from an ornate doorway across the hall. He looked me up and down. "Can I help you?"

"I'm Princess Alexandra's bodyguard. I need to speak to her."

He gave a professional smile. "The princess left the grounds half an hour ago. Though clearly without you. Perhaps you should take that up with your manager?"

I muttered thanks, and the man watched me go back the way I'd come. Beaten, I trudged away. I'd missed out and now had to leave without saying goodbye.

Maybe it was for the best. I didn't belong here. She hadn't liked my interference. When I got home, I'd talk to Ben about her safety then put this...whatever it was I had going on behind me.

My Inverness flight touched down at four p.m., and I drove straight from the airport to the McRae estate.

London was a buzzing city, but there was nothing like coming home to the Scottish mountains I loved.

The peacefulness was a balm over my rough edges.

The open road wound past the glistening loch surrounded by foothills and rolling heathland. Summer was in full bloom, and everything was green, with wee flowers studded in the landscape and the air clean and clear. Elsewhere, the Highlands would be thick with tourists, but we were tucked away in a remote spot that only locals knew.

It was secluded and private, yet in under an hour, I was nearly home.

With my car windows open, I drove past the two huge stone gateposts that marked the entrance to the estate, Castle McRae ahead of me on the other side of the bridge. I crossed it and swung left, taking the route through the woods and passing the second McRae castle, Braithar, the place I currently called home.

No time for stopping now. I'd already rung ahead to Ben, and when I finally reached the wide-open moor where the aircraft hangar was located, my boss was waiting for me. Leaning against a car, he chatted with another man, my older brother, Gabe, kitted out in a mountain rescue jumpsuit and backpack as if poised to head out onto the hill.

For days, I'd felt like a fish out of water. Being home and seeing familiar faces eased another degree of my tension. I leapt from the car, and Gabe's attention shifted to me.

As always, he spread out an arm to pull me into a hard hug. "Glad you're back."

I hugged him. "Any news?" His wife was due to have their bairn any day. My first niece or nephew.

"Not yet. Effie's bored out of her mind, but the midwife

said another week or two yet."

"If you're heading out, tell her I'm here if she needs anything," I said.

Despite there being almost no snow, the mountain rescue teams were busy, and my older brother flew the rescue helicopter. Summer brought long hours of daylight, and hikers took the opportunity to get lost or injured in the mountains with alarming regularity.

"Ariel's with her this afternoon," he referenced our younger sister, "but I'll take ye up on that this evening if I'm still out."

Further members of the rescue team exited the hangar, led by Lochinvar, the leader of the mountain rescue service. Gabe saluted us and strode away to join them, leaving me and Ben alone.

My boss, a solid man more than a decade older than me, watched me with a more serious expression.

I matched it. "We need to talk."

He pushed off the car. "Aye. Let's take it inside."

I followed Ben into the hangar. The open frontage gave way to a stunning view of the landscape. Inside, mechanics worked on helicopters, and a collection of studious cadets listened to an instructor in the flight school I'd once attended.

We bypassed it all and entered the bodyguard office, a freestanding structure built at the back.

Ben parked himself behind his desk. I didn't sit. Unlike with Jared, I trusted my boss with my life and needed to pace to get the words out.

"I sent the news article. Did ye read it?"

Ben inclined his head. "Messy business."

"It was."

"And ye handled it exactly the way I would've. I'm proud of ye."

Another even tighter knot of tension unravelled. I'd been fired because of the actions I'd taken last night. I hadn't failed at anything in my life, ever. Not an exam, not my driving test at seventeen, not my helicopter private licence or the extended tests I'd taken earlier in the year to fly commercially. I was driven and hardworking, yet everything I'd left behind felt like a failure.

"Walk me through it. Don't skip a detail," Ben ordered.

As methodically as I could manage, I worked through the events as they'd unfolded, from the minute I'd reached the palace, to when we'd talked on the phone, then the aftermath. The photographer. The drunken friend. The exit strategy.

Ben listened and praised my choices. As the newest member of his team, I still had a lot to learn, but I'd been out with Leo on tour and to high-profile events, and I'd flown as part of that. We had a slick process designed around protecting our principal.

I exhaled frustration. "The problem isn't the fact that she's photographed everywhere she goes. That's unavoidable. It's not even that there isn't the budget for twenty-four-seven protection. It's the fact her team doesn't give a flying crap, and she isn't following any safety protocols, let alone basic ones. Something's going to happen. I can see it a mile off, and any trained person would, too. What the hell is Barrington Bray doing with that team?"

Ben scrubbed a hand through his dark-blond hair, his grey t-shirt displaying our McRae Bodyguards logo. He pursed his lips then picked up his phone. Opening something on the screen, he eyed me. "Only one way to find out."

My heart thumped, but Ben was right. It was no good me complaining to him. He had my back, and the person responsible for that shitshow was the service owner.

"Call him," I agreed.

He dialled. The phone rang.

It kept going, no answer. Then the voicemail service kicked in. Ben hung up and tapped out a text.

"I've asked him to call me back." He set the phone down and steepled his fingers. "I owe ye an apology for that mess."

"No, ye don't."

He trained his gaze on me, his expression telling me I needed to hush. "I agreed to lend a member of my team without doing the legwork to check what you'd be going into. I thought the experience would be good, and I've known Barrington for years so I trusted that his operation would be decent. I believed he'd have his finger on the pulse. I was wrong."

"I didn't mind the work," I slowly gave up. "I would've stayed to help."

"From the picture ye painted of Jared, I doubt he'd listen. No, there's something else going on that we don't know and can't be ignored." He rapped on his desk. "Leave it with me. You're still off the rota for a few more days, so go and chill out, then we'll talk in the morning. Jax is around the hangar somewhere."

He released me, and I slunk outside, lighter than when I'd come in but still troubled. A quick hunt around gave me no joy for finding Jackson, so I shot him a text and let myself drift into the helicopter bay.

This was my happy place. Engine oil and rotor blades.

Near the hangar entrance, a mechanic worked on the

guts of a Sikorsky S-92A, the rescue heli my brother flew in all weathers. Beyond that was a Robinson R44, used by the commercial arm of the hangar to fly private hire. It was cheap and fast, and used to get execs to important meetings and doctors to hospitals. I could pilot both, but it was the Airbus H-125 that was my baby.

I neared my favourite, snug in a bay. I flew it weekly to get Leo to and from meetings and gigs. On his last tour, crowd trouble and a narrow escape left Valentine, another of our team, stabbed in the thigh. As a result, Leo had changed how he moved in and out of cities. No more staying in hotels overnight, no matter the time.

I could fly him to London in an hour and a half. He could perform gigs all over the country then be home and tucked up with his wife and kids before the night was out. It was an arrangement that suited everyone and gave me a role in the service I could be proud of. Something I wasn't exactly feeling after the disaster of the previous few days.

Amid the clatter and clanks of people working nearby, I peered through the window of the heli, checking out the avionics. A quick jaunt skywards would cure my stress levels no end. Flying took every bit of my concentration, and it cleared my mind like nothing else. Then I remembered my promise to Gabe. I couldn't head out in case my sister-in-law needed me.

I was grounded.

A hand seized my shoulder and spun me around.

Jackson laughed and grabbed me into a hug. "Found ye." He pulled back and scrutinised my face. "What's wrong?"

Everything. All of it was wrong.

The fact I couldn't stop thinking about Alex's safety when it was none of my business anymore. The sense of being at home when I should be somewhere else. Ben would address the team issues with Barrington, and that was where my story ended. I needed to get it out of my head.

I mimed shooting myself. "Too much. What are ye doing?"

"We came back from Edinburgh a couple of hours ago, and Ben had us scheduled for a fitness afternoon. Val's out on a trail run, I'm about to hit the weights."

A workout sounded like a very good idea. We had a gym installed in a rear corner of the hangar, past the bunkhouse where air cadets and rescue workers could sleep overnight if needed.

I shoved his shoulder. "I'm down."

He shoved me back, an amused smile curving his lips. "Like that, is it?"

Jackson goaded me all the way to the gym, and our workout turned into a fight. At university, we'd wrestled, and at around the same height of six-two, were well matched. As part of our job, we did high-intensity cardio five days a week and strength training every other day.

It wasn't just the hard slams of combat helping me now.

At a little older than me, my best friend had a world of experience in handling tragedy and pain after the worst had happened to his family. He didn't ask for details of what I brooded over, merely took his position across the crash mat and let me vent my emotions.

After an hour, he had me pinned down, and I finally submitted, smacking the mat. Sweat dripped from me, but at least I could see straight.

Jackson rolled away and lay flat out. "Beer."

I pointed to my phone, left on loud next to the mat. "Can't. Effie duty."

"Steak, then. We'll stop off at the pub and pick up dinner.

The lasses will be happy." He sprang up and offered me a hand.

I accepted and let him haul me to my feet. Then I checked my messages. One arrived in front of my eyes—from my brother, saying he was on his way back and would go home, so he had his wife covered.

That meant dinner alone with my best friend and my sister. I loved them both, but I was still in a shitty mood. The thought of hanging out with an in-love couple was not appealing.

Another idea had crept into its place.

One where I spent time digging around the internet for traces of Alex. Something I'd never admit to my friend.

I regarded him. "Effie doesnae need me anymore. Mind if I rain check dinner? I have something else I need to do."

Jackson tilted his head. "Why do I get the sense you're up to no good?"

"Quit mind reading me. Ye won't like what ye find."

His shrewd gaze followed me back to my car.

For obvious reasons, bodyguards made excellent stalkers, and I was unsure if I could resist trying it on for size.

# 10

# Raphael

Seven AM found me jogging back to Braithar, sweat on my brow from the mild morning and no breeze to cool me off. Scotland didn't get as warm as London, but it was going to be a stunning day.

Shame I wasn't in a mood to enjoy it.

I crushed gravel under my running shoes, rounding the castle to the rear entrance. The imposing and fortified building was owned by Gordain McRae, the original creator of the bodyguard service. His daughter, Viola, had married Leo, our favourite rock star, they had two kids, and all of them lived here. Thus the team had been created. Gordain had worried too much over his daughter's and son-in-law's safety to allow anyone else the responsibility of protecting them.

He offered rooms for a bodyguard to live on-site, and both Ben and Valentine had stayed here before settling in with their lasses. Now was my turn. I'd previously shared a tower apartment with my sister, but since she and Jackson shacked up, I'd given them their privacy.

I prowled the flagstone floor to my doorway, let myself in, then headed straight to the shower. Under the hot water, I rinsed off the sweat and tried to centre my thoughts.

Last night, I'd cyber stalked Alex in a way that had veered far from professional. I'd started off with good intentions, looking for her events calendar and eyeing an upcoming busy week. Typically, she didn't seem to be a working royal, only appearing at large-scale family events, but that had changed recently. Beyond that, I'd quickly found myself deep in gossip. Her dating life. Who her friends were.

I discovered Dori, giving me a full name of Ferdinand Dorian Christian Sonderburg, Count Sonderburg, as he'd informed me, and nephew to both the Grand Duke of Luxembourg and the King of Norway. Both related to monarchs and the same age. Alex had been photographed with him for years, which suggested they had a solid friendship rather than a romantic relationship.

I hadn't found any evidence of a long-term boyfriend at all. Lots of rumoured dates, particularly with celebrities, but any reporting was short-lived and without receipts.

I braced myself against the shower wall. I hadn't meant to go down that rabbit hole. It was none of my business. But since I'd discovered it, I couldn't get the thought out of my head.

Was she single? Why, when any man would be lucky if she even looked his way?

When we'd talked at the base of the palace stairs, she'd told me she was lonely, an emotion I knew all too well. She'd looked like an angel, barefoot, and in a tight dress that I'd wanted to take off her.

She'd gifted me her mask. I'd brought it home. Last night, I'd unpacked my bag and had to take it from the room or I'd stare at it and think of her.

Which meant it was watching me from across the bathroom.

*Fuck.* I stared back through the shower glass, picturing her eyes and the curve of her cheek under the lace. Allowing my mind to wander down that road was a dangerous game. My dick was way too interested in her, and she'd been a client.

The thought smacked into me that right now, she wasn't. I'd been fired. Heat rushed me, and I fisted my half-hard dick, squeezing then stroking myself while keeping my focus on the mask.

Damn, I needed more.

Lurching from the stall, I snatched it from beside the sink and got back under the water. Then I wrapped Princess Alexandra's lace mask around my dick and gave myself a stroke.

Heat and need hit me in a rush. Images filled my brain. The teenage version of us dirty dancing, Alex's hands roaming. Then two nights ago when my arm had been across her body, under her breasts. *Fuck. More.* When she'd brushed a kiss to my cheek.

The deeper I let myself go, the harder I got, picturing every perfect curve with an electric flash of attraction.

The memory adapted to me turning my face to claim the kiss. Her lips under mine...

That did it. My lust for her crashed into me, and I came into the hot water, white lace encasing me and the sensation abruptly, damningly good. A pulsing flood of desperate need followed for a lass who could never be mine, no matter how badly I wanted the opposite.

I wanted her.

Breathing roughly, I let that settle under my skin then opened my eyes, reclaiming logic where I'd temporarily lost my mind. Done. I could manage this thing, whatever it was.

Action was needed that had nothing to do with my over-interested dick. Even if peeling off the mask left a lace imprint I wished would never fade.

*T*hirty minutes on, and with a clear head, I hunted down my boss at the hangar.

In a repeat of yesterday, Ben ushered me into the office. This time, I had better control over myself.

I dropped into a chair. "Something has been playing on my mind."

He made go-for-it hands for me to proceed.

"The bouncer at the club got paid off by the photographer. Alex saw the exchange of money. But she was in disguise and was sure she hadn't been recognised. Her wig and mask were good enough for a casual bystander, so who told him she was there in the first place?"

"Not the bouncer?"

I tapped my finger on my knee, working it through. "Maybe, but a bribe given at that point makes me think it was to turn a blind eye to him taking the pictures. Not to tell him she was there in the first place."

Ben followed my lead. "Because the money would've changed hands earlier at the point the informant had something to offer. If true, that suggests it was someone else. Who do ye think?"

"This is going to sound wild, but one of her bodyguard team. They chose the bar we were going to and also chose to ignore Alex going into the club, even though I told them. It feels too coincidental. I don't know how I'd find out, though. If I track down the photographer, he isn't going to give up a source, and they're hardly likely to admit it."

Ben considered my point. "Perfect timing. I just took a call from Barrington. From Jared, he had a completely different story than the one ye gave."

I snorted. "Naturally."

"He fired him."

I blinked at my boss. "Oh, shite."

"We had a long talk, and let's just say this was the first deep dive he's done into that team since they were set up. Jared and co have had a number of complaints and breached protocol multiple times."

"They cover several members of the royal family. How did no one pick up on this?"

"Barrington might have that contract, but his main focus has been on the city and high-risk London-and-international-based families. Diplomats and ambassadors. Ultrahigh net worth individuals. He took his eye off the ball and has vowed to fix it. He asked for my advice in filling Jared's role. The fourth member of the team is returning next week, but the princess has a series of engagements before then, so he has to hustle to fix this."

For a beat, I held still. Of the three members of the team, there was only one I rated and who hadn't been there that night. "Suggest Riss to manage the team and send me back in temporarily. We'll cope as a unit of four. Jared did nothing useful that I could see."

He watched me for a long moment.

My heart thumped. I needed to convince him. "Leo can spare me, can't he?"

"He can," Ben admitted. "He'll be writing songs all summer and doesn't have another meeting outside of Scotland for three weeks. I was planning training and days off."

"I want to go back. I want to test out how it goes with Jared not there."

"Assuming he was the mole?"

It had crossed my mind. I'd told Johnnie and Will about the princess going into the club. It could be either of them, but it stood to reason that one could've contacted him. Jared felt like the more obvious choice, but I could be wrong.

I swallowed past a lump in my throat. "That isn't the only reason I want to go back. Remember I told ye I knew Alex from my student days?"

"Ye mean Her Royal Highness Princess Alexandra?" He quirked a single eyebrow. "I take it ye know her better than implied?"

"Not exactly. I didn't mean to hide anything. There's more of a personal connection than I expected."

Ben's expression shifted to shrewd judgement.

I worked my jaw. "Don't look for more than there is. I just want to help while I can. Once upon a time, I did her a disservice. I consider her a friend, though she doesnae think the same about me. This will be my way to make it right."

My boss sighed. "I'll make the offer, but it's up to Barrington, and if he agrees, it's a time-limited deal. I'm naw losing ye to his team."

I leapt up. "Loud and clear."

"Fine. Now go do something useful while I make a call. This might be a no, so don't get your hopes up."

Too late. They already were.

*O*ut of the hangar, I drove to Valentine's place, a quick check-in with him and Jax giving me their location. As a team, we weren't often office-based unless we were writing up risk assessments or doing research.

Today was Sunday, though. Not always a day off for us, and even if it was, we often met up for a run or fitness work of some kind.

Or moving furniture, as was apparently happening this morning.

I left my car by Val's and joined the two men who struggled under the weight of a sofa. They carried it from Valentine and Mia's place to the open door of the next cottage.

I raised my eyebrows at Mia who watched them go.

"What's going on?"

She grinned at me. "We bought a new couch. I love that one, but we need bigger. You've seen the size of my fiancé."

Her hand drifted to her belly, and she twisted to answer a question from her little daughter, Tobi. Huh. I hid a smile. Valentine hadn't been shy about wanting to extend their family, and it looked like they were ahead of the game.

It was their wedding in a few weeks. A joint one as Ben, brother to Val, was marrying Daisy on the same day. The whole estate would celebrate with one huge party.

Mia turned back to me. "We've managed to buy a few new things so the place next door is slowly getting furnished, ready for an owner."

"Is there one?"

I loved these cottages. Both single-storey and converted from some previous centuries-old use, they were stone-built, white-painted, and faced another gorgeous view. Val and Mia had made theirs into a snug home. The empty place next door cried out for the same treatment.

Mia tilted her head. "Not that I know of. Valentine was thinking you might want it."

My heart thumped, but I shook my head and gestured to myself. "It's a family home. Resolutely single here."

"That shouldn't stop you having a place of your own. Are you interested?"

Another woman appeared in the doorway behind her, Daisy, Ben's fiancée. She and Mia worked together running a cleaning company, and Daisy had on her branded tabard, but also a panicked expression.

"Oh my God. How do I unsend an email from my phone?"

Mia blinked at her. "I don't know. Why, what's wrong with it?"

"Look!"

Daisy held up the screen. Mia and I leaned in to peer at the email in question.

*Good afterboob,* it started.

I choked.

Mia's hand flew to her mouth. "Afterboob?"

Daisy moaned in horror. "I know. I wished a potential new client a good afterboob. Oh God, he's going to think I'm a lunatic."

Badly, I wanted to crack up in laughter, but that wouldn't help stricken Daisy. "How long ago did you send it?"

"Yesterday. Does that make a difference? Please tell me I can do something."

I tapped through the settings then on the email address. "I'm really sorry, I don't think you can. It's a Hotmail account. You can't unsend to them, which I know because I once tried to unsend something daft."

Daisy took back the phone, clutching it against her chest. "Please tell me it was ridiculous so I can feel better about this."

I grinned. "Actually, it was. At uni, I had to cancel a session with a flight instructor and told him 'sorry for the incontinence' rather than 'inconvenience'. He never replied."

Valentine and Jackson came out of the second cottage, and my best friend smirked.

"I remember that. I've got a better one. I wrote 'you go tit' instead of 'you got it' to Ariel recently. It became a whole thing."

All of us except Daisy burst out with laughter. The woman's shoulders went down an inch, though.

Valentine pointed at himself. "When we were kids, me and my siblings changed our dad's email sign-off. Now, to really set the scene, you have to picture our huge, serious, bar-owning father, and him sending messages that should've ended 'Thanks, Bull' but magically changing to 'Okey dokey pig-in-a-pokey, Bull'."

We laughed harder.

Valentine continued. "The best part is, he didn't notice for at least a week. We forgot all about it until he came home and lined us up to get the culprit. One of his beer suppliers had pointed it out, and he realised all week he'd been sending that out. To his bank, to the doctor, everywhere."

Daisy sighed, still crestfallen but at least slightly entertained. "Thank you all for trying to make me feel better. It looked like such an interesting cleaning job, too. A big house owned by the client's aunt who's gone into a care home. She was a bit of a recluse and a hoarder, according to him, and she's given permission for the place to be cleaned out but said there's an item of treasure hidden in the mess. He didn't know what it was, only that it has to be found and not thrown away with the rest of the rubbish. Isn't that enticing? Now we'll never find out what the treasure is."

Mia gave her a one-arm hug. "Maybe he'll like the boob reference and book us anyway?"

The two lasses disappeared back into the house, and Valentine and Jackson enlisted me to help with the next step of their plan—a bookshelf that needed building and installing. We spent a couple of hours over it, moving a freestanding one to the place next door.

It gave me a chance to poke around and to consider Mia's suggestion. One of the bedrooms had a wide bed in it already plus a bedside table that begged for a lamp. The comfortable sofa sat in the living room opposite a stand for a TV, the bookshelf climbing the wall to the right.

Alone for a moment, I tried to imagine living here.

If I wanted to, Gordain, who owned it and much of the land for miles around, wouldn't mind me moving out of Braithar. But nothing felt simple right now. My mind was only half here, the other half following a certain princess around London.

Committing to a rental agreement came with a reality I didn't like. This wasn't a home for one man on his own.

I wanted a girlfriend.

I wanted the easiness Valentine and Mia had in how they reached for each other, almost without looking. How my sister and Jackson seemed to be each other's missing puzzle piece. How Daisy would go take comfort in a hug from Ben.

In comparison, I felt that gaping hole where my other half should be.

I wanted Alex. The strange and insistent notion took me by surprise. But I was a bad bet with a dodgy past no high-profile person could overlook. My father was a mobster. We'd run from him, but that life tainted my past, present, and future. Even if my brother and sister had no issues with connecting with another person, I still felt unsafe. Alex could never date me. It would be out of the question. She was already in enough danger.

My phone rang, distracting me from my gloomy thoughts, and with Ben's name onscreen.

I answered without a greeting. "What did he say?"

"That Riss took the promotion and you're exactly what he hoped for."

I draped against the doorframe. "I'm going back?"

"You're going back, just to work with Princess Alexandra and just for a week. Pack your bag. You've got your orders."

# 11

# Alexandra

In the pretty receiving room I remembered my father loving, with floral wallpaper and a tea service set out, I regarded the man in front of me. Sir Reginald was private secretary to King Philip, and one of the creepiest men alive.

I couldn't pinpoint what exactly was so off-putting about him; perhaps his soft hands with long fingers, hooked through the teapot's handle, or his pin-neat grey hair, swept to the left at an exacting degree that never changed.

Maybe it was the way he'd treated me since I was a teenager—like I was a piece to be moved around a chessboard and not a human being. Not that my opinion mattered. Sir Reginald was as much part of the fixtures and fittings of Ossington Palace as any other historical item. If ever I needed to talk to the king, I had to go through him first. Even if I texted my cousin directly, Sir Reginald typically answered. Today, though, in between meetings, I'd gone directly to him.

The secretary set down the pot, poured milk into his cup, swirled his tea, then finally raised his emotionless gaze to mine. "What can I assist you with this morning, Your Royal Highness?"

"The list of events you sent me, is there any way we can adapt it?"

Sir Reginald sipped his drink and watched me, as if waiting for me to elaborate.

I rolled my hands. "There are some I'm not entirely comfortable with. I wondered if we could change them."

I was due my period, and a headache panged behind my eyes. I'd sat through two meetings already with charities and organisations, and coupled with the art gallery disaster, all I wanted was to crawl back into bed. On top of that, I'd overheard palace gossip that had sent me fully into misery mode.

Raphael had been fired.

No doubt because of me.

I didn't have his phone number or any way to contact him. Going through his team was a no-no as personal details were never shared. I'd had a quick hunt for him online but found nothing, and desperately, I wanted to hide away with my phone and track him down.

Looming over it was my panic over a specific activity on my calendar which involved public speaking. I just... couldn't.

"Was there one in particular that concerned you?"

I shrank in my seat, feeling like nothing more than a whiny child. I couldn't tell Sir Reginald the truth. He'd laugh me out of town. "It's just a couple of tasks within the overall workload. Perhaps we could take one out, such as the banquet?"

He placed his delicate teacup in its matching saucer and reclined in his seat, taking his time over answering. "When considering activities and events for the royal family, His Majesty is very careful in selecting a balanced calendar that ensures representation across industries and all levels of society."

"I know that—"

Sir Reginald spoke over me. "Of which those allocated to Your Royal Highness are but a small number of the total. I understand that there are other things you might prefer to do with your time. The concept of work is not always pleasant for everyone."

Oh, fuck him. I hid a glower.

"However, the summer break is the only time off of significance His Majesty takes throughout the year and is essential to his well-being and to that of the queen consort and their young family."

My forehead furrowed. "Is there something wrong with him or the family?"

Sir Reginald recoiled. "No, there is not, and you should not suggest such a thing. Are you suggesting I interrupt His Majesty's vital solitude to discuss balancing your calendar?"

Typically, the royal family took the entire summer off. King Philip, my cousin, and his wife and children, their fourth child only six months old, were sunning themselves on a yacht in the Caribbean.

My dad, brother to Philip's deceased father, had always taken two months off as well. Not that Dad did any royal engagements anymore. After my mother left him, he'd suffered a stroke and mostly stayed behind closed doors.

I clamped my jaw. "No, and I'm not trying to shirk my duties, I'm just asking to change a few things this week."

"King Philip prefers the royal family to be visible throughout the year. His reputation as a hard worker is of vital importance, as much as his desire to be a man of the people. If you are not out there representing his interests, we would need to consider an alternative."

"An alternative to me?"

Sir Reginald smiled, the effect deeply unpleasant. "You aren't the only representative of your branch of the family. Should I commence my enquiry?"

A chill slunk through me.

I'd asked for a small change, and he threatened the peaceful life my father lived. In the spring, I'd finished my master's degree, and although my dream had been to spend every free minute painting, I had accepted a request from my cousin, via Sir Reginald, to become part of his royal calendar to cover the gap while he was away. I'd always been photographed anyway, so it made sense to get paid for it. Or, rather, my father was paid as head of our household. The only other member of our branch of the family, as Sir Reginald put it.

I'd received a two-week schedule and had wanted to do well at it. Yet that job, as such, came at a price. After my father's stroke, his removing himself from public view meant that he was no longer working for the royal family. The king, again via Sir Reginald, had made noises about reducing the money that was going his way.

Dad didn't need much. His home, Lancaster House, belonged to the Crown, but he held the lease. Maintaining the huge, draughty building, paying our living costs, and managing his staff, including security, were his only priorities now he didn't have my tuition fees. Was he privileged? Yes. Had he had any alternatives as brother to the king? No. Not that he'd ever found. And now he was unwell, he could do even less. Certainly not attend sporting events and garden parties.

I'd stepped in, and with snake-like precision, Sir Reginald had homed in on Dad as my weakness.

With a stiffened spine, I gave Sir Reginald a single shake of my head. "No. I understand perfectly. Please forget I asked."

"I shall enjoy reading the headlines later."

The secretary rose and left me without another word.

I flopped back on the antique sofa and closed my eyes. My phone buzzed. I found it in my dress pocket and checked the screen.

**Riss:** *I will be with you in a few minutes, ma'am.*

I tapped out a reply, telling the security guard where I was, then thumbed over to the conversation with Dori. Late last night, he'd sent a picture of himself in some club, neon paint daubed on his bare chest and some elaborate drink in his hand.

I called him. He picked up after several rings, a grunt my greeting.

"I think I hate my life."

"Is it spoiled brat day already? It comes around so fast."

I groaned. "You can talk. I tried to change my schedule, and it was like I'd gone full treason."

Material rustled, as if I'd woken him and he was still in bed. "Darling girl, talk to Daddy."

I wrinkled my nose. "Did you just refer to yourself in the third person, and as 'Daddy'? Don't be revolting."

"I wasn't referring to me. Your actual father. You're

stressed out at work. He's been through it all. Surely the old boy would be able to help?"

I sighed. My father's viewpoint was increasingly hostile to the family he'd grown up in. A chat with him usually ended up dwelling on the brother he'd lost too early, the wife who'd been driven away, and the daughter he wanted out of it. But that could never happen, and I'd never tell him why.

"No, I'm currently avoiding him as he hates me being here. Not that he could do anything as that isn't where my problem lies."

"Then where does it originate?"

"With the bodyguard." I winced, but the words were out there.

A pause followed, then interest curled in Dori's tone. "Go on."

"Raphael was fired because of me."

"Use his correct name, will you? Hot Bodyguard has a ring to it. Would telling him about what I'm assuming is at least fifty percent overwhelming attraction assuage the problem?"

"Not if I can't find him."

"Gotcha. Then how about you find him and fuck him? All will be right with the world if he's any good in bed. My guess is he's a giver. He's got that air about him, and he is absolutely into you."

I hissed through my teeth. "If you were in the room, I'd throw something at you."

"I'd catch it. Is fucking him off the table, then?"

"I told you, I have to work today."

"Ugh, the toil. What's the event?"

I filled him in on the afternoon I'd be spending at the Botanical Gardens as well as the outfit I'd chosen, adding, "But my attendance won't be confirmed until I'm there, so it should be low-key compared to the art gallery."

"Sounds boring. Do something bad to make the afternoon more interesting."

"Ooh, I like that idea. A little chaos never hurt a formal event." Plus it could save me from the speech I needed to give in a week.

"Exactly. Send me pictures. Then tonight, when I have had more than an hour's rest, we'll scour the internet to find your man."

"Are you alone right now? I didn't ask." I didn't even know what country he was in.

Dori made a noise of disgust. "I'm going back to sleep where I can pretend the world isn't shit and everything is fine. Night, darling girl. I'll no doubt see your outfit of the day blowing up my phone later."

"Don't hang up—"

He already had, reinforcing what I should've known, that Dori would talk when he was ready and not a second before.

A knock at the door brought Riss into the room.

The new head of my security team, as the last guy had been let go along with Raphael, walked me through the plan for the week. Badly, I wanted to ask Riss what she knew, but she was deep into the arrangements, and I owed it to her to listen.

A gap came in the conversation, and Riss put down her tablet. "That's a wrap. Was there anything which stood out as unexpected or that you wished to bring to my attention, ma'am?"

She'd started ma'aming me in earnest since this morning. I glanced away, trying to be casual. "The team has changed. Can I ask why?"

"I'm afraid I'm not privy to the reasons Jared was let go."

"And the other bodyguard?"

Her brow furrowed. "The temporary team member from last week?"

"Yes, him."

"Raphael Gordonson has rejoined the service and will be present today."

A small gasp escaped me.

Raphael was back. I'd get to see him and give my apology. The hot summer sun shone brighter through the London air.

Riss frowned. "If that's an issue...?"

"No," I squeaked. I went to tell her how I'd once known him but held my tongue, suddenly worried that our familiarity might be another reason for him to disappear. "No issue at all. He'll be an asset to the team."

Her professional smile returned. "If that's all, I'll see you downstairs at one."

She left me, and I let out an excited, if muted, whoop, then trotted out of the receiving room and back upstairs, via Ossington Palace's broad central staircase. Like most royal residences, the building was partially open to the public, but the central wing was entirely private. The king and his family had the main apartments on the second floor, and I had a suite of rooms a fair distance away on the third. I practically danced to it, my heart pounding the whole way.

In my rooms, I locked myself inside.

Between Raphael being here and Dori's challenge to

make the afternoon more interesting, my misery had evaporated. I had to prepare.

# 12

# Raphael

Under the hot sun, we walked the roped line into the botanical gardens. Princess Alexandra smiled and waved at the crowd then shook hands with members of the welcome party.

I scanned the faces, looking for anything unexpected, as well as for the paparazzi from the nightclub. The one good thing was that the princess hadn't been announced as attending, so until the moment she got out of the car, her being here would've been a surprise.

Riss had walked us all through a well-put-together risk assessment and strategy, including an exit at the end of the event into a side street, rather than back into the throng.

With her at the helm, I was a lot more confident in the princess's safety.

Didn't stop my heart thumping every time Alex glanced my way.

When she'd emerged from the palace to meet us at the cars, she'd lowered her sunglasses and welcomed me back.

A damn arrow straight into my heart.

At some point over the course of the week, I would find a way to talk to her. I didn't know how, but if I wasn't getting the cold shoulder for the nightclub overstepping, I had a shot.

We entered the party, passing through a high-ceilinged brick building thick with flowers before heading out into extensive gardens with a marquee at the far end. Tall and elaborate plants bloomed all around, and peacocks strutted their stuff amongst the attendees. The guest list had been provided ahead of time and checked over by Johnnie and Will, with no red flags popping up.

Our job was to keep the princess in our eyeline but stay out of her way, so I took a position beside a stone archway and tried to blend in.

As at the art gallery, Alex sparkled. She had her hair up in pretty ringlets that I'd never seen on her, and a light, floaty white-and-blue dress.

As I stared at her, possibly more intently than I needed to, she reached into her pocket, then scattered something on the ground.

I squinted, wondering if I was seeing things.

She moved on to another group of partygoers and chatted for a few minutes before doing the same thing.

Two peacocks closed in on her and pecked the ground at her heels.

Was she feeding the birds? There was fruit juice and cake available, but she hadn't stopped by the marquee table to get any, which meant she'd brought whatever was in her pocket with her.

I prowled the edge of the party, keeping my distance but laser focused on her actions.

Alex continued on for a while with no further rogue animal feeding, but then crossed a bridge over a tiny stream and scattered crumbs on the other side.

Two small birds I couldn't identify but that were poultry-like pattered after her. The peacocks noticed and scurried over, too.

Riss appeared at my shoulder.

I swung my gaze to her. "Are you seeing what I'm seeing?"

"Is there a problem?"

"No, just a bird invasion."

"They're free to roam about the gardens. Nothing for us to worry about." She held up her phone. "But this troubled me. Unusual activity online. Look at this."

I scanned the status she'd discovered. A royal fashion watcher had shared the website of a clothing designer, stating Princess Alexandra would be wearing their latest line today.

Then I clocked the timestamp. "This was posted before we got here."

Riss gave a single nod.

I worked it through. "Suggesting that this was information provided ahead of time? Is that standard?"

"There is no standard as the princess is new to this role, but I checked, and she did not announce her outfit, and in fact changed her mind when dressing for the event. Whoever told the royal watcher what she was wearing did so between us leaving the palace and arriving here."

That was a narrow window of time. We hadn't left the city.

"Could someone have taken a picture while we were driving?"

"Perhaps. But I can't find any posted, and that's a big ask to work out which frock she has on." Riss skimmed her gaze over Johnnie and Will who were across the gardens.

I followed her focus. In my conversation with Ben, I'd told him of my suspicion about someone on the inside. At that point, Jared had been my main concern. Now, I doubled down on wondering if it was one of the other men.

It was too early to tell the new team leader, though. I'd only been back a day. I needed more to go on if there were genuine threats to Alex's safety.

She pursed her lips. "Stay with the principal. I'm going to make some calls."

"Will do."

Riss left me, and I followed the princess to the table of drinks and food. She picked up a glass and turned, spotting me.

Alex tilted her head. "Want one?" She held out the orange juice, moisture beading on the glass.

"Not while on duty, thank ye." Even if I was hot as hell. Even as I subtly switched off my outgoing comms to allow a private conversation.

Her gaze travelled over me. "I'm glad you're back. I wanted to talk to you."

"I want to talk to ye as well. Obviously not here."

She huffed agreement. "Obviously. Too many ears for what I want to say."

My heart skipped a beat. "Aye, same."

Alex's fingers slid into her pocket once more and scattered crumbs.

I gestured at her action. "What are ye up to?"

She brushed her fingers clean on her skirt and regarded

something distant. "Who, me?"

A robin and two tiny brown wrens flittered to her and pecked the grass.

"That thing with the birds. The big ones will be chasing ye soon."

Something devilish gleamed in her eyes. "Wouldn't that be strange? What an unusual afternoon if all the birds at the botanical gardens suddenly started chasing a guest, let alone a princess who won't be able to make a speech because of it. Wouldn't that make this afternoon the opposite of boring?"

She did a little pretend hair flip that made me grin. And my blood warm.

"You're devious, princess."

"How can I find you online?" she countered.

At the same second, a group closed in on the refreshments table, cutting off my ability to reply.

Alex turned on her heel and stepped away. The little birds followed, and the poultry appeared from under a bush in hot pursuit. More appeared. While the princess sipped her orange juice and chatted with someone who I guessed to be mayor by the chunky gold chain around his neck, the peacocks found her again. Then a flock of white doves descended from a tree.

I choked on a laugh. She was doing this on purpose. At the nightclub, I'd assumed that her friend was the troublemaker. Apparently, both were as bad as each other.

Riss's voice sounded in my ear. "Problem with your comms system?"

Quickly, I flipped my comms back on. "Negative. An error on my part."

"Roger that."

Johnnie's voice followed. "What's with the birds?"

Another laugh threatened me, but I suppressed it while Riss commented on the odd scene. Ahead of us, in the centre of the lawned area, a menagerie of winged animals had gathered. Alex completely ignored them, playing the game so well I barely saw her hand movement, but from the pecking, she was still scattering food.

A uniformed member of the botanical garden's staff edged over and extended a foot to nudge one of the larger peacocks away. It didn't budge, pecking the staff member on the toe instead.

I clamped my jaw tight.

Oh fucking hell. This was ridiculous. She was playing a game to keep herself entertained, and it was so damned delightful I couldn't have looked away if I wanted to.

Alex, the mayor, and another couple of guests were guided into the marquee by the woman she'd shaken hands with outside, presumably the director.

The birds followed, hiding under tables and with two uniformed assistants now in pursuit. There were a number of displays under the huge tent, including local crafts and a series of paintings on easels. Alex's sly hand dropped crumbs in piles here and there.

Yet at the paintings, she balked. It was a small gesture of unhappiness that I couldn't ignore, even if no one else appeared to notice. She liked art, didn't she? I'd assumed so from the art gallery visit.

The group moved on. At the other end of the tent, they exited and emerged once more into the sunshine. The director tapped a spoon against a glass, summoning attention to her. An audience formed in a ring.

"Ladies and gentlemen, I'd like to thank you for your

attendance and support of the botanical gardens annual garden party. This esteemed event...”

She continued on. I stared at Alex. By her tense, amused pout, she was leading up to something but hanging back near the exit to the marquee.

Then her gaze slipped to mine, and the minx tipped me a wink.

The director wrapped up her speech. “Please put your hands together for Her Royal Highness, Princess Alexandra, here with our joint charity ambassador, Lord Mayor Johnson.”

To polite applause, the mayor waved a benevolent hand and beamed.

Alex stepped forward to join him in the centre of the crowd.

From under the tables and the marquee, a rush of birds followed her in a pantomime-like procession.

People squeaked and stepped out of the way of the pecky peacocks. Men danced to avoid the birds underfoot, and the white doves fluttered up in a panic, one tangling in a woman’s frilly skirt. Heads swivelled as others tried to work out what was going on, and voices rose.

A swell of alarm passed over the audience. Some made for the main building.

The director went to speak into the microphone but stumbled over the biggest peacock, narrowly avoiding landing on the bird as she dropped inelegantly to the grass.

The bird pecked the director’s shoulder, and Alex clasped her hands to her mouth, but I knew it was to hide a laugh and not shock.

I narrowed my gaze on the little chaos goblin.

Over the comms system, Riss called it. “Code red. Exit

immediately. Will, ready transport."

My brain caught up, and I instantly got back in the game. Riss was right. The event had descended into a disturbance, and we needed to protect our principal. Even if this was exactly what she'd planned to get out of giving a speech.

We mobilised, forming our protective positions around Alex and moving to the side exit where Will had summoned our drivers. The three cars filled quickly, and I caught Alex's gaze before she disappeared into the central one with Riss.

"Your details," she mouthed at me.

A flood of need chased my adrenaline. She wanted to talk, so talk we would. I just had to find a way to get my information to her that wouldn't make Riss kick me off the team when I'd only just got back onto it.

# 13

## Alexandra

A knock rattled my door.

"Hold on a sec," I told Dori who was on a video call, lounging on an open balcony in what looked to be a night-time mediaeval city.

Riss waited on the other side. She handed me a white card. "Left for you by Mr Gordonson, ma'am. He said you expressed an interest in flying."

I blinked at it. "Oh, right. Thanks!"

I scurried back to Dori with my treasure. For the past hour, we'd hunted Raphael down but got nowhere. Though he was back on the team, I had no idea how long for, and both of us needed to stalk him in detail. Yet we'd failed hard. He wasn't friends with anyone I knew from uni. He wasn't on the student page. The man was a ghost.

"He sent me this!" I squeaked.

"Picture, immediately," Dori demanded.

I obliged, and we both stared at the card.

"It's for a flight school," he observed.

"Do you think he owns it?"

"Why would he be working for you if he owned his own business? Perhaps it's a family company."

"Then he's into flying," I murmured.

"Well, doesn't that just elevate him above the common man. The flight school has socials. Checking them now." He tapped at his screen. "Found him."

My jaw dropped. "What? Where?"

A whoosh brought a link to my phone, then one tap and I was staring at a pilot profile for Raphael. Most of the pictures were of shiny helicopters, but I opened one with him front and centre and sighed.

"Damn," Dori drawled. "Look at that slutty little number where his jumpsuit is open to expose his throat."

I found the picture. Raphael was scorching hot.

"Are you going to call him?" Dori asked.

"I still don't have his number."

"You can ring him through this profile. See, it's at the top."

So it was. A phone symbol to tap and instantly dial him.

Nerves constricted my stomach. "What if I just start with a text?"

"Coward. Though saying that, booty calls generally come about through chat. Sext him up good."

"I'm not going to hit him up for...that."

Dori tapped again at his screen then snorted. "My Alex

alert just got another bird picture of you from this afternoon. That was genius, if I do say so myself."

"Hey, it was my idea."

"Nah, I want at least half the credit. The press has gone nuts."

"I'm going to hang up on you now and think about what to say to Hot Bodyguard."

"Screenshots or it didn't happen."

I disconnected and stared at my phone like it could bite me. Then I pulled on my big-girl pants and wrote out a text from my pseudonym account.

*PennyAllen: How did you enjoy the animal show earlier?*

The message displayed as read almost instantly, but there was a pause before a reply came in.

*Highlandspilot: How do I know who this is?*

Ever the cautious bodyguard. I snapped a picture of my face.

*Highlandspilot: Ah, my regular Disney princess, taming birds with biscuits in her pocket.*

Ha, so observant. No one else had seen me lay my trails.

*PennyAllen: Actually, it was chopped nuts, stolen from the kitchens.*

He was typing, but I quickly fired off another text before I could lose my nerve.

*PennyAllen: Are you busy?*

*Highlandspilot: I have nothing else to do in London except take care of you.*

Butterflies fluttered in my belly, and I took a deep breath, momentarily lost in his interesting choice of words. Then an idea came to mind. A glance out of the window showed me dusk neared on the warm summer evening.

**PennyAllen:** *Can we meet up to talk?*

**Highlandspilot:** *Tell me where to come in the palace.*

**PennyAllen:** *It would be boring if it were that easy. See the location setting on my profile? In twenty minutes, it'll turn on just for you. Find me.*

Then I switched the phone off, bit down on a huge grin, and skipped to the wardrobe to find a wig.

# 14

# Raphael

Goddamn it. My fifth message to Alex went unanswered. It didn't even display as read. I'd even tried calling her but with no reply, and now, I stood outside one of the side exits of Ossington palace, pacing the pavement under the eye of a watchful guard.

If she was going rogue, I wanted to catch her in the act, but the building had multiple exits she could slip out of. I had half a mind to message Riss, except I wasn't sure what Alex was doing. Not enough to involve the whole team.

Plus, I had to confess to myself an alternative motive.

I shoved my hands into my jeans pockets, scowling at a group of tourists who blocked the pavement.

This evening, I'd get Alex alone, even if just for a short while. The thought had my chest tight, and apprehension mixed with a sharp spike of excitement that had me pacing all over again.

It felt like I was going on a date. I'd rapidly changed my shirt and put on aftershave.

I didn't even attempt to process why my mind had gone there.

For the fiftieth time, I refreshed her profile, willing a reply to have come in. Nothing. But then, the indicators changed to show me she'd read my messages. With my heart in my mouth, I tapped the location icon.

It displayed a map with a green flashing dot.

Holy fuck.

I scanned the road names around her beacon with urgency. She was on the other side of the palace and moving quickly. Gritting my teeth, I took off at a sprint and pounded the pavement, hugging the palace boundary and passing the formal frontage.

The armed guards squinted at me as I flew by, but I didn't stop to explain myself.

If Alex was loose in the city, she'd thrown herself into harm's way again, and a wild guess suggested she didn't have another team member with her. I put on a burst of speed and rounded the corner to the exit she'd left, then refreshed her tracker.

Alex was across the road now and further down a wide boulevard that led away from the royal property. She was slower than me, so possibly in a car as traffic crept steadily through the busy city streets, headlights and horns the backdrop of my flight.

Waiting to cross the road was an exercise in torture, but finally I was over and running again. As I did, I placed another call to Alex that went unanswered, for fuck's sake, but at least I could see she was on the same road as me and not that far ahead.

Where was she going? There were countless options in the city. A bar, a friend's house, somewhere private.

On the map, a green space opened up at the end of the boulevard; a large park. Was that her target? I dove between people on the street, outside of busy restaurants and pubs, or wandering in admiration of London's mixture of old and new architecture without looking where they were going.

I dodged and sprinted my way across half a dozen side streets and a long row of shops before closing in on Alex's beacon, right at the end of the boulevard. Across another busy road was the park, the gates still open, though night was almost upon us, and orange streetlamps spilled pools of light on the shadowy path under thick trees.

A woman with short hair passed through a patch of light and peered over her shoulder, her side profile giving me an electric burst of energy. The prey I'd been hunting.

Alex had put on another of her disguises, but even if I hadn't seen her face, I would've known her shape. Warmth flooded me at my success.

It was quickly replaced by fresh concern. If I recognised her, others could as well.

I diced with death to cross the road before she vanished into the park's depths, but as I reached the gate, she was strolling unhurriedly.

I prowled after, catching up to round her with a hand outstretched. "Found ye."

Alex tilted her head. "How long have you been a pilot?"

She neatly dodged my hand and passed me.

I swivelled to keep pace. "Since I was a teenager and decided I had to learn. Why the fuck are ye out in public without security?"

"You're here, aren't you?"

"Because I chased ye across the city. Anything could've happened."

"And if I'd told you where I was going, you would have insisted I took a full team, leaving us unable to talk in private. In this quiet corner of a royal park, where I know the other gates have already been locked so most people have left." She dusted her hands as if winning the argument.

"No, I would've met ye at the palace gates and had a chance to anticipate what we were going to do. Plus ye wouldn't have been transmitting your location to anyone watching." The next words I uttered came out lower and against my better judgement. "I didn't want to be interrupted by others either."

She peeked over at me. Her pixie-cut wig of ruffled blonde hair stuck out at angles, and she'd chosen a long-sleeved top with holes for her thumbs and a pair of ratty shorts for the rest of her disguise. Yet it wasn't that which had me staring at her when she looked away.

The same buzz of something powerful passed between us, just as it had done the time we'd danced together. Alex was undeniably beautiful. She conversed with people easily and handled herself gracefully, even when up to no good. It could have been that spark of passion that ran through her which fascinated me, the one which spilled over into antics that drove the professional version of me crazy. It could have been a lot of things.

In the summer night's air, all I was certain of was the fact I wanted to test how well she'd fit under my arm, should I choose to extend it to tuck her against me.

It took any amount of effort to force my brain to take the lead over my smitten body. "We should go somewhere safer."

"We're fine. I've been coming here at night since I was thirteen. The park keeper will round the lake in a minute and call out that he's locking up. Most people have already gone, but that will take care of the stragglers."

"And if we're shut in?"

"We climb a tree to hop the wall."

I kept my hands loose, watching our surroundings as she spoke. Alex was wrong about the park being empty. There were at least two couples in discreet corners and a small group on a picnic blanket under the trees. No one appeared to be paying attention to us.

She giggled, the sound so pretty. "Besides, you've already catalogued all the dangers, haven't you?"

I rolled my shoulders, still overly warm from the run. "From what I can tell, no one is following ye, and none of the people I spotted are alone. I can have the team here in minutes if there's any trouble, but..."

"You're not going to, because you know I'm right about being safe."

No way I was admitting that.

"What did ye want to talk about?"

She pursed her lips. "Walk me through the flying thing. Not the typical teenage activity. Is the flight school owned by your family?"

"If I talk, will ye answer one of my questions?"

She inclined her head.

"My older brother is a helicopter pilot, and I relocated to Scotland to move in with him when I was fifteen. He has a mentor, a man named Gordain McRae, who gave me a job at his aircraft hangar, and who also created the bodyguard service I usually work for to take care of his famous son-in-law. I did every fetch-and-carry job they needed until I had skills. Then I traded my labour for lessons. After university, I was lucky enough to be sponsored by Gordain to fly commercially."

"Why are you a bodyguard and not a pilot?"

I made a buzzer sound. "Sorry, your turn now. What did ye want to talk to me about?"

"Oh. Straight into the awkward, huh?"

She shoved her hands into her shorts pockets. We'd walked far enough into the park that I could see the lake she'd mentioned. It was silver in the low light and mill-pool calm. To the right was a pontoon with small boats attached, no doubt for hire during the day, and to the left, the path circled under trees.

"I owe you an apology. You were fired because of helping me and Dori at the nightclub. I felt awful when I found out." She peeked up at me. "How come you're back?"

I held my breath for a moment. I didn't like lying. I had an ulterior motive in taking the job, but if I told her, I wasn't sure how she'd react.

The words came out anyway. "I suspect someone is selling information about ye. My suspicion is that they're on your team. Aye, Jared sacked me, but my boss is friends with his, and he heard me out on the shite management of the team. Jared lost his job, and I was offered the chance to return for a week. I took it."

Alex stopped dead on the path and stared up at me. "Whoa."

I winced. "I realise that makes me sound either paranoid or insane."

"No, it doesn't. For a start, you just told me something real. No one ever does that." She started moving again. "Does Riss know?"

Footsteps thumped on the tree-covered path ahead.

I whirled into Alex and spun her away, off the track and around a thick oak. Bracing myself against the tree to cover her, I held her to me and listened hard for whoever was approaching.

"Park keeper," a male voice called out. "East Gate, locking up. Please make your way to the exit, the park is closed."

Night cloaked us in shadows. The man neared our hiding spot, making no attempt to be stealthy with keys rattling and his breathing laboured. I kept my head tucked down and Alex concealed entirely behind my body, my black t-shirt and jeans hopefully enough to disguise us. I was too aware of Alex in my arms, her palm against my chest.

It was a familiar pose, from age eighteen and more recent. I soaked in the press of her fingertips. The warmth of her.

I needed more.

If the park keeper spotted us, he'd throw us out. It wasn't as if we could go to a pub and continue our conversation. I'd have to get a cab to take us back to the palace, where she'd go to her rooms and I'd return to the bodyguard accommodation where I'd been on the edge of my seat, waiting for her message.

Neither of us moved a hair.

Realisation struck in a heady rush. I didn't want this to end. We'd barely started talking, and I had so much more to ask and say.

The man continued on until he was right next to us, close enough for his radio crackle to be audible.

The footsteps passed then died away.

Alex pushed up on her toes, her mouth next to my ear. She spoke in a whisper. "He'll leave by the same gate."

Which meant that as soon as he was out of hearing range, we could make a run for it.

But that thought was entirely buried under my awareness that if I just turned my head a fraction to the right, my lips would meet Alex's. She took a little inhale that sent my blood rushing south, but then grabbed my hand and slipped out of the protection of my body.

"Come on," she breathed.

I had no choice but to follow. Alex darted across the grass with me in tow and down towards the lake. I was snared by the pulse of chemistry from her touch.

Then my brain caught up to where she was leading me. At the lake's edge, she stepped onto the pontoon. The wooden walkway out onto the water was a dead end, only there as a place to moor the boats, so I stalled, not wanting my boots to echo. She shook me off and danced to the end. Then she knelt to the chain that constrained the final boat.

I darted a look back at the darkened path then pursued her. "What are you doing?"

"Hush. This needs to be quick."

"What does?"

"They always leave the last boat tethered but unlocked. I've no idea why, maybe it's a safety thing if someone needs one? But if I just..."

Alex tugged on the chain. It gave, and she let it slither down in the water. She'd untied a boat. I didn't get a chance to tell her to stop as she was already climbing in.

"What the hell?" I bit out.

"Grab an oar. I forgot," she whispered back, pointing at a container full of them.

Cursing under my breath, I snatched a pair and lowered myself to sit on the dock, using my feet to guide the boat beneath myself. I'd spent countless hours messing around on the loch at home, the water icy no matter the weather.

But never with a girl. Never on a warm and romantic night, even if the stars were hidden behind clouds.

Definitely never with a princess.

I handed a gleeful Alex the oars then lowered myself to the boat's curved interior, rocking it with my weight. The waves lapped overly loudly in our stealthy attempt at theft.

When I was settled, I shoved off the dock so we slid away into the water. Then I gestured to Alex. "Row me then, princess."

It wasn't so dark that I couldn't see her grin. She dipped the oars into the water. "I thought you'd try to stop me."

I rested back, not quite relaxed—I never could be in a city—but easier with our situation. At least here, no one could sneak up on us. If we were spotted by the park keeper, we could book it across the lake and run. "I don't want to control ye. Only stop ye getting kidnapped or hurt."

"You think that's a genuine risk, don't you?" She pulled again, taking us out into deeper water.

I lifted my chin. "Kind of amazed ye have to ask. You'd be an asset to a kidnapper. Ye could cause all kinds of mayhem both in the royal family and politically if ye were taken."

She giggled again, and the sound did something strange to my head.

"Perhaps. My father worries a lot and doesn't want me to take on a public role."

"Do ye enjoy the work?"

She made a face. "Let's not go crazy now."

"Then why do it?"

There were other royal cousins in her family, other aunts and uncles who didn't do anything public-facing. From the little I knew about Alex, no matter how good she was at shaking hands and waving to the crowds, I was certain she didn't enjoy a minute of it.

She stared away for so long I didn't think she'd answer. I was right. Alex changed the subject.

"You said you moved in with your brother when you were fifteen. What happened there?"

"My father is a mobster, and I didn't want to join the family business of violence, drug running, and anything else he had in mind for me."

Her mouth hung open. "That's why you're a bodyguard then? To counter what you didn't like growing up?"

"That and the role was there and waiting for me. Leo, our client, is a friend, and the team needed a pilot."

"Leo who? Do I know him?"

"Banks. He's a musician. Currently on album-writing duty, so work is quiet." I posed my own question, just as loaded as hers had been. "Back when we were at university, did ye think I had something to do with the photographer who took our picture? The one—"

"I know exactly which you mean." Alex rested the oars in the plastic loops on the sides of the boat and reached for her phone. The screen lit up her perfectly lovely features as she searched for something. She held it out for me to see.

Onscreen was the photo in question, but not just that. Alongside was the newer one from outside the nightclub. They were oddly similar in the poses, and paired like this, seemed to show a relationship that had persisted for years, though nothing could be further from the truth. The reality was this was almost the sum of our knowing each other.

I gazed between them. "I didn't see the parallel until now."

Alex accepted the phone back. "Dori did. He was delighted to work out that it was you I'd told him about, all those years ago. He calls you Hot Bodyguard."

"Ye never gave up my identity, then?"

"No. Not to anyone. I didn't even discuss it with the friend I went to that party with. Not that she stayed my friend for long. That night changed a lot of things for me. But to answer your question, I didn't suspect you of having anything to do with it."

I watched her. "When I joined your team last week, I got the sense that ye did."

Collecting the oars, I took my turn rowing, as a minimum so I had something to do with my hands and to dislodge a strange ache in my chest.

Alex unpinned her blonde wig and shook out her hair, then leaned forward and wrapped her arms around her knees. Even on the water, there was no breeze, so it wasn't cold that affected her. "If you're such a fan of honesty, I'll tell you. You might not like it, though." At my gesture for her to proceed, she did. "That teenage photograph of us changed the way the media talked about me. According to them, I was running with boys, and my sex life became fair game, regardless of the fact it was non-existent. My reputation as a party princess began the night that picture was taken and shared."

Well, shite. "I had no idea."

"Why would you? And don't you dare apologise. You didn't cause it. You were being kind to me. It's not your fault it turned sour." She sniffed. "Though in full confession, I blamed you for challenging the photographer. I know now that it didn't make a difference. He was going to sell the shot regardless."

A moment passed where we fell silent. My mind churned over what experiences she must have had, seeing herself talked about in the way the press loved to do. The effect that must have had on her.

A darker corner of my mind was hooked on how she'd referred to her sex life and me in the same breath. As if I was part of that life. As if we had a history where we'd been alone together and naked. Where her wandering hands had found their way far beyond the soft touch from our dance.

Christ, but that image was strong.

If she was any other girl, I'd be figuring out ways to ask if I could kiss her. Not that I'd ever wanted anyone as badly as I did Alex. Need burned inside me. I flexed my hands on the oars though I'd stopped rowing.

She raised her focus to me, her lips quirked as if poised to speak. She could ask me anything right now. Any fucking thing and I'd do it.

Instead, she clambered to her feet, toed out of her sandals, tossed her phone to the deck, then dived into the goddamned lake.

"Fuck," I bit out.

It was all I could do to kick off my boots, drop my phone, and jump in after her.

I submerged, leaving the boat rocking. The shock of the cool water displaced the heaviness that had claimed me, and I surfaced to a cackle from Alex.

"God! I never expected you to follow," she crowed, her hair slicked back.

"And leave ye to get a disease all by yourself? What kind of bodyguard would I be?"

She laughed and floated on her back. "I'd tell you I'd been doing this for years, too, but it would be a lie."

"Impulse of the moment?"

"I was overheating. Felt like the right thing to do."

Oddly, I agreed. I had no clue if she felt any degree of the draw that I did for her, but we'd got heavy quickly.

Alex coasted about. When she was ready, we swam to the lake edge and climbed out, dripping but grinning at each other. I'd kept the boat close to us and reclaimed our shoes, phones, and importantly, the wig that was her disguise to get home.

My sodden jeans clung to me. I stripped my shirt and wrung it out.

"If I'd taken a second to think, I would have left this in the boat. At least that way you'd have something dry to go home in."

Alex had gone quiet. I glanced over at where she was on the path, fastening her sandal. Except she'd stopped. Her gaze was stuck on my chest, her mouth open.

I moved in on her and reached to tap her chin. "No eyeing up the staff, princess."

That's exactly what I was. An employee. No matter what that look had told me, I could never be anything else. Just had to tell that to my dick.

# 15

# *Alexandra*

Raphael followed me into the trees to the park's stone wall. He offered a hand, but I didn't take it. In the boat, I'd had the strongest urge to lean in and kiss the man, and it had taken almost everything in me to resist.

The dip in the water worked wonders to cool me off.

I climbed to the first branch.

Raphael watched me, something obviously on the tip of his tongue. He had already given me a game plan for getting back. A taxi would meet us on the road the other side of the wall. Any words we had left to say to each other in private needed to be now.

"At the garden party, I saw ye react to something. I don't want to overstep, but it's played on my mind. I wouldn't be a good bodyguard if I didn't ask."

Right. We'd reverted to our roles, then. "What did I react to?"

"A display of paintings."

Good God. His powers of observation knew no bounds. "I used to paint."

"As of...?"

"A week ago."

"Why did ye stop?"

Another branch and I'd straddled the wall. He tapped my foot to remind me to wait for him there—his solution to not leaving me unprotected on either side.

"Let's just say I discovered I was a terrible artist and it was the wake-up call no one else had the guts to give me."

In a scramble, Raphael was beside me. He scanned the road and came back to me, his eyebrows merged in an expression of concern, and his shirt clinging to that insanely toned body.

We were both soaked. No doubt wearing a layer of grime from the lake as well. I didn't regret it. Not after it had awarded me the sight of him half-naked. That image was branded in my brain, adding to the previous time he'd stripped his shirt for me.

It had the bonus of helping me distance myself from feeling bad about my art.

"How well did ye trust the opinion of the naysayer?"

I tilted my head. "They were strangers."

"Were any a talented art critic?"

"I... I'm not sure."

"So what gave them the right?"

I huffed, trying to pull together the errant parts of my reasoning. "It was an exhibit. Everyone there had an interest in art in some way. The woman didn't know the painting was by me, but she called people over to say how awful it was."

Recognition flared in his eyes. "This was my first job with ye. I saw something happen but couldn't work out what. Ye put a painting in the exhibition? Which one?"

I groaned. "I don't want to tell you."

"Do it anyway?"

My sigh came heavily, and yet I still found my phone and the hidden folder with pictures of my paintings. I scrolled to the right one, and with a tight stomach, offered it out. Raphael's fingertips grazed mine. But it was his rapt attention that grabbed me.

He studied the screen then lifted his gaze. "This is fucking good."

I went to take it back. He pulled his hand away, keeping my phone.

"Can I swipe to see the others?"

"If you must."

His gaze linked to mine. Fresh energy fizzed between us.

"I'll only do it if ye ask."

How the heck did that turn so dirty in my head? Flustered, I gestured for him to proceed. "Please."

Raphael took his time over examining each. He didn't say anything, and with each swipe, I leaned in more, wishing I could read his mind.

At last, that serious brown-eyed gaze was mine again. "You're a damn good artist. If I ever find the people who said otherwise, I'll make them wish they didn't."

A shiver ran over me. I'd needed those words, and in a rush of certainty, I knew I wouldn't have trusted them from anyone other than him. It shouldn't have made sense, except Raphael had proved himself inherently trustworthy, despite the short amount of time we'd spent together. It wasn't that alone. Desire and energy poured into me.

I wetted my lips.

On the wall between us, his phone buzzed.

He glanced down. "Fuck. Car's here."

The moment was over. Raphael became all action, jumping down the wall and helping me to descend after. Then we were in the car and perched on the edge of the leather seats, hoping the driver wouldn't notice we were leaving a water mark.

In minutes, we were outside the gates of Ossington Palace. Raphael flagged down one of the guards to see me inside, quietly telling me I'd be vulnerable the moment I left the car.

I didn't even get to say goodbye.

Inside my rooms, I showered off the lake water, shampooing my hair twice to make sure it was clean. For bed, I changed into my favourite t-shirt, then dropped down onto my mattress and checked my phone.

A message waited from Raphael. He'd sent his number.

**Highlandspilot:** *In case you need to call me.*

I saved him as a contact then replied with mine. Somehow, messaging him properly with real names felt like we'd moved on a step.

**Alex:** *In case you need someone to night swim with in murky lakes.*

**Raphael:** *If ever you want a dip somewhere that isn't going to poison us, I know a place.*

My stomach fluttered with those damn butterflies again.

Logic told me that what I'd felt this evening had been one-sided. Raphael was being paid to take care of me. Therefore I couldn't get any fanciful notions about him wanting to be around me in his own time. Yet this sounded like the opposite. I stuck my tongue in my cheek and tested that water.

**Alex:** *Skinny-dipping potential?*

**Raphael:** *I'm sure that can be arranged.*

He hadn't even hesitated. I stretched out on the cool sheets, sounds of the city coming through my open window along with humidity that stuck my t-shirt to my hot skin. I wanted the previous owner of the shirt here with me.

I wanted a lot of things.

**Alex:** *Talk me through it. Describe the place.*

The dots showed he was typing, then it changed to state he was recording a voice message. Anticipation at hearing him curled my toes. At last, it arrived, and Raphael's low tones filled my room.

*'In a hidden corner of Scotland, there's a loch, surrounded by mountains and high hills. At the west end, a river flows under an arched bridge and feeds the loch from the snow melt and rainfall from the heather-covered slopes. A castle sits on the banks. Kids play in the water, and it's a popular spot for the locals to hang out. But at the eastern end, it's much quieter. There's a wee path down through the forest to the water's edge. We'd need a torch so as not to trip over tree roots. The shore is made of flat rocks that might still be warm from the sun. A good place to leave our clothes.'*

A small moan of need slipped from my lips, and I squeezed my knees together, lost in the scene he was creating. It was a version of tonight where we weren't constrained. A fantasy, because constraint made up my life.

I tapped the voice message button. "Don't stop."

As if waiting on my encouragement, he started recording another. I could hardly wait to play it.

*'Once we've found our way there, we'll kill the lights so we don't give ourselves away. No need to clue any nosy folk in to our fun. But there would be enough moon to see each other by.'*

Damn, this was beyond hot and yet still the tamest conversation.

I replied, my other hand wandering down my body. "So you can see me?"

*'Clear as day, princess. Are ye looking my way?'*

His second sentence came out less sure, as if he didn't know how badly I was into this. Raphael's voice scratched an itch inside my brain. That delicious Scottish accent made every word somehow more vital. Except the waiting between messages was driving me crazy.

My phone buzzed in my hand with an incoming call.

I fumbled it and snatched it up again.

But it was Dori calling. Fuck. I loved my friend, but now was not the time. I dismissed it and tapped Raphael's name to dial him without giving myself a chance to lose my nerve.

He immediately answered. "Hey."

"Hey yourself. Keep talking."

"What do ye want to hear?"

"What happens when we take off our clothes?"

My breathing stuttered. Had I really just said that? I'd lost my mind. But if I had, so had my bodyguard.

"I'd watch the trees until you'd climbed into the loch, then I'd strip and follow ye in. Unlike me, ye don't keep your eyes to yourself. Tell me what ye see."

My fingertips grazed the apex of my thighs. "Strong

shoulders. Your arms out as you swim to me."

"What about before I got into the water? We both know ye peeked."

I touched my clit and hissed. I was wet for him. My legs fell open. "You're hard."

He exhaled. We'd gone there. Past the point of no return.

"Aye, course I am. I've never seen anyone so pretty. When I reach ye, what happens next?"

I knew what he needed. For me to set the pace of this exciting and illicit conversation. But I was out of my depth. I'd never done anything like this. "I...want you in control."

"Ye have it." His voice took on urgency. "I'd reach out, needing ye in my arms like I've imagined too many times. As soon as we're close enough, I claim a kiss. It starts tame, but it can't stay that way. We're naked. Our bodies touch, and though I keep my hands in safe zones, I can feel ye."

The picture he painted had taken over my whole being. I stroked my clit and imagined holding on to him. My breasts against his chest. His lips parting mine in a blistering kiss built up from countless times of imagining it over the years.

"Christ, woman. Your breathing...I can hear how turned on ye are."

"You're making me," I confessed.

"How far do ye want this to go, Alex?"

"Don't stop."

"I won't. Your legs curl around my waist and your arms around my shoulders until there's no space between us. If I'd started turned on, by now, I'm a wreck. Nothing in my head but the feel of your body and the taste of your kiss. The water is deep, but I can just about touch the rocky ground to keep us afloat. My balance lets me use my hands to trace up your spine."

A shiver passed over me. I moved my hand faster. "What if we got out of the loch?"

"Fuck. Aye, we do. I carry ye out, our kiss never stopping. Tell me what ye need from me. Do I offer my shirt to dry off?" He laughed at my whimper. "Then how about my lips travelling down after I place ye on the warm rock?"

"God, yes," I hissed.

I could almost feel him. He was much bigger than me, and I widened my legs further to give him space.

"I kiss my way down your body. You shove my head to where ye need me most. Right between your legs. In a heartbeat, I have your legs over my shoulders and am discovering exactly how hard up for me you've become."

I couldn't answer any more than a moan, my body tight to the point of pain. I drove harder circles over my clit, desperation filling me for what he'd say next.

"The first touch of my tongue to your wet centre has ye bucking your hips to meet my mouth. I die over your sweet taste but don't waste any time because my girl is needy. I lightly lick up and down so I know your shape then form my lips over your clit and suck."

My moan filled the air, echoed by Raphael's groan.

"Lucky for me, you're telling me with those sounds exactly what ye need. How hard. How much pressure. I build ye up and up, toying with ye and loving the game. Except I'm selfish. I want all of it fast, so I push until you're teetering at the edge, pulling away to tongue-fuck ye because I need ye desperate for me. Are ye close?"

"Y-yes. So close."

"Good girl. Feel my mouth and my tongue. The thickness of the fingers I slide into ye so I don't miss a single one of your reactions. You're wild for me. Ye squeeze down on my hand so perfectly then one. More. Suck. And my beautiful girl breaks apart."

My looming orgasm surged and crashed over me, created then released by his words. I cried out and pulsed, dizzying waves of pleasure ebbing through every cell of my body and leaving me boneless. Alone, I could never reach this level of satisfaction. He'd done it over the phone using just his dirty words.

I came down from my high with a blissed-out smile on my lips.

"Still there?" Raphael asked.

"Still here."

"I'm not. I've jumped back in the water to cool off because that was the hottest fucking thing I ever experienced."

My heart squeezed, and I tried to conjure a response. But a check of my phone showed that Raphael had hung up on me.

When I drifted off to a heavy sleep, it was to thoughts of that Scottish loch and him.

# 16

# Raphael

Across the desk in the bodyguard's office, Riss lifted her gaze from her screen. "That's the full breakdown of the timeline. Any questions?"

She'd walked us through the risk assessment for the afternoon's event, a charity football match featuring top-tier members of premier league teams. Alex would be there to show the royal family's support, but her attendance hadn't been announced. A fact I liked, even if my worries were through the roof.

The risk assessment was as good as it could be for a huge public event. The football stadium seated tens of thousands of people, and though searches were done of attendees with bags checked and pat-downs, they weren't rigorous. All manner of dangers haunted my mind.

To my left, Johnnie folded his arms. "Why isn't the princess confirmed as going to this thing today? Wouldn't it be better for people to know?"

Beyond him, Riss shook her head. "That's a bad idea for

many reasons."

"Such as?"

She shrugged. "Riskier to give ne'er-do-wells time to prepare."

On that, we could agree.

I lifted my chin to get Riss's attention. "We know Princess Alexandra has had unusual levels of interest from the press. Should that change our threshold for pulling her today?"

The acting team leader went to answer, but Johnnie cut her off.

"What increased level of interest?"

I twisted to face him. "The paparazzo who hunted her down to the nightclub and sold her picture? The fact someone leaked her outfit before the botanical gardens event?"

His lip curled. "Sorry to tell you this, but that's business as usual. Nothing so dangerous that we'd need to pull her attendance. We already risked embarrassment over whipping her out of the botanical gardens because of the fucking birds."

I gazed at him, a new kernel of suspicion developing. At the start of the meeting, Riss had gone over recent events, covering the two I'd highlighted. I hadn't been sure if she'd talked to Johnnie and Will about the outfit issue, so I'd watched them for a reaction. Neither had done anything except listen patiently.

"Who would be embarrassed?" I asked.

A smudge of red appeared on his cheeks. "The royal family, obviously."

"Nothing appeared in the press about the princess leaving early. That wasn't specifically mentioned. Therefore it's not an issue."

He made a rolling motion with his hands. "Just saying that if you get spooked today, that will be two events she's bolted from in quick succession. It doesn't look good." He switched his gaze to Riss. "Right, boss?"

Riss chewed a lip. "We have a set of procedures and we'll follow them, unless I'm specifically told to adapt them in view of the optics. Even then, I would need a very good reason."

Johnnie snorted. "Other than her being the only working royal right now? We're employed to keep her visible, not bury her because this one scares easy." He thumbed at me. "All I'm saying is we need to be flexible with how we handle these big events or we're going to do ourselves out of a career."

I went to retort but a phone chimed, and Riss stood.

"I hear you both, but it's time to leave. You know the drill."

Leading us, and tightening her braided hair on her stride down the corridor, Riss directed us outside. At the rear car, I stood at the open door, Johnnie's challenge playing over in my mind. The bodyguard team's previous manager, Jared, had been negligent to the point of failure. His bad management outside the art gallery had let the photographer get way too close. Then Johnnie's lack of interest when we'd seen Alex going into the nightclub did the same.

If anything risked his job, it was pulling the same shite. I didn't understand him.

Every thought dissolved as the palace's side door opened and Princess Alexandra emerged. Stepping into the sunshine, she frowned at her phone. Then her focus came to me.

It was a brief touch. Nothing any other person could

look at and discern what we'd got up to last night. Instant heat flooded me once more.

I'd dreamt about her soft sounds of pleasure when she'd made herself come to my words. All morning, when I'd been assigned to the gym for fitness training and she'd been in meetings, I'd thought about her.

Nothing could happen between us beyond this… whatever it was. I'd crossed a line when I'd chased her from the palace, then I'd left it in my dust when I'd got down and dirty talked.

Yet I hadn't been able to stop. Princess Alexandra was in danger of becoming my addiction. I owed her some kind of apology for trying to be hers.

The drivers took us out of the palace gates and into the busy London afternoon. I was alone in the car, Will and Johnnie in the lead vehicle, and Riss partnering up with the princess in the central one.

We tested comms, then my phone buzzed from a different sender. Alex had messaged me. I scrabbled to read it.

**Alex:** *Why so gloomy?*

**Raphael:** *Pretty sure bodyguards are supposed to be mean.*

**Alex:** *Not when you look at me, though.*

I exhaled to control a wave of instant need.

**Raphael:** *I can't look at you like the way I want to in public.*

This was dangerous. If for any reason my messages were read, flirting was grounds for dismissal. Riss wouldn't give me a second chance. Hell, I wouldn't if I led the team. It was beyond a conflict of interest.

Even so, I waited on a reply with barely contained excitement.

The bubbles told me she was typing. The message never came. From ahead, a car horn blared, and my driver slammed on the brakes. We shuddered to a halt inches from Alex's bumper.

"What the fuck?" I snapped.

The driver craned his neck. "Road's blocked. That red Fiesta's facing the wrong way."

Shite. I popped the door and climbed out without registering my actions, my heart thumping and adrenaline flooding my system. A roadblock was a tactic I'd been trained in by Ben, though wasn't a common one we saw in action.

Down the street, Will had also left his car. He called something to the other driver who I could barely make out behind the windscreen.

Riss's voice came over our comms. "Will, report in."

"Just a doddering old gent who's made a wrong turn."

He approached the other vehicle. My level of alarm didn't lower. Not as Will spoke through the window, and not as he went to clear a space in the junction so the gentleman could go the right way.

Alex was just sitting there. Anyone could make a run at her car.

I performed checks in a standard pattern. The nearby buildings, a car coming the other way, rubbernecking but not presenting an obvious danger.

Johnnie should have been out and doing the same, but Riss hadn't ordered it, and the man worked only as much as he needed to.

It was on the tip of my tongue to make the suggestion myself, but just like that, the Fiesta reversed carefully and the road was cleared.

Our lead car cruised on.

For a beat, I stared. I'd expected more. My muscles were loose and ready to throw down, but it wasn't needed.

"Sir?" the driver called.

I dove back inside and fought to calm the adrenaline rush as we caught up with the procession.

Fucking hell. I'd overreacted. Not badly, and probably without anyone else noticing, but I knew the signs that something was off with me. Later, I'd take the time to work up a solution.

If I was at home, I'd head out on a flight. That was my go-to method for stabilising my brain chemistry. I'd never got the chance as I'd jumped straight back into service, but a local airstrip with helis for hire was exactly what I needed.

A little voice in my head told me sex would be better, but that wasn't happening.

I couldn't imagine it. Not on the job.

Definitely not when I was already confusing my motivations in my head.

Thirty minutes on, we arrived at the stadium, our convoy passing crowds in long queues and in bright shirts that announced which team they supported. At a covered entrance, we disembarked and whisked Alex into a lift and up to a busy corridor, the duo of the stadium's coordinator and the director of a charity walking with her.

A conference room with views across the green pitch and tall stands packed with sports fans hosted a welcome party, and we saw Alex inside then took positions in the hall while Riss held a quiet conversation with the coordinator.

When she'd finished, our boss called us in. "Penny Allen was offered the choice of seating between the royal box and another which has been bought for the occasion by the Kensington Hospital Trust."

That was one of the beneficiaries of the match, I'd noticed. I grimaced at the continued use of the same codename Alex had used for years. My suggestion to change it had gone unheeded.

"Which did she pick?" Johnnie asked.

"The charity box. There are some public appearances she said she needs to discuss. I've suggested that she make her first appearance in the royal box, however, for the sake of pictures and the TV crew finding her. We'll cover both."

Riss split our resources, allocating Will and Johnnie to the hospital's box while she checked out the royal one. There was security everywhere, but we had protocol to follow and checks to make.

Protocol which meant Alex needed a bodyguard nearby at all times, and that was assigned to me. Which was perfect as I didn't want to let her out of my sight.

During our team briefing, we'd kept eyes on her through the glass doors to the entertainment suite. I entered the room and prowled the edge. There were maybe fifty well-heeled people in here, with staff circulating with drinks and food.

Alex held court with the group she was here to meet, but her gaze touched on mine.

A smile flirted with her lips.

Today, she was the picture of a working princess. Her purple dress was elegant yet demure, and no doubt chosen because it matched the colours of no team that would be playing today so therefore she couldn't be taking sides. Her heels were mid-height. Her chestnut hair flowed down her back in her classic waterfall style.

But that mouth... It was the curve of her perfect lips that

gave away the real woman under the polished surface. The girl who sabotaged events so she could leave early. Who disguised herself to run through a city and jump off a boat to swim in a lake. One who'd take a late-night call from her bodyguard so he could talk her through an orgasm.

I swallowed a hit of lust and parked myself in a corner where I could simply watch her.

Outside the floor-to-ceiling glass windows, the stadium had filled, and the pitch was being cleared. A quick check of the time told me the game would start soon.

I just wanted it over so we could get Alex out of here.

There were too many people, which had made it impossible to screen them ahead of time. Too many opportunities for something to go wrong.

Alex excused herself from her group and moved over to me. I stood taller.

The princess tilted her head. "Is everything okay?"

"Yes, ma'am."

Her eyes flared. I'd never called her that in public, though I was supposed to.

That twitch of her lips reappeared, and her mischievous expression drove fresh need through me.

She leaned in. "You know, this is a big place. Plenty of corners to hide in."

My heart thumped. Either she was propositioning me or teasing me with a threat to disappear. Whichever was true, we couldn't talk like this. Not now.

Subtly, I gestured to my mic and mouthed, "This is on."

Alex grinned bigger. Then her hand drifted to her belly, and she winced.

That echo of pain across her features snapped me out of

my haze. "Are ye hurting?"

She waved a hand. "Just cramps. No big deal."

Riss entered the room and came to us. "Time for you to take your seat, ma'am. Are you sure which that will be?"

Alex nodded. "I'll do as we agreed. Make an appearance in the royal box to wave to the cameras, then once the match starts, I'll join the charity director. She's been talking about some visit I've not been told about, and I want to find out what's going on."

Riss relayed the instruction to the rest of our team, then we were moving.

When we reached the royal box, Alex entered, and the cameras instantly jumped to display her on the live screens. The announcer called out her presence, and she waved to a cheer from the fans.

I watched the people closest by, scanning for trouble.

Beside the box, a man with a camera craned to get photographs of Alex. A hoodie concealed his head, but I recognised something about him that gave me pause. He lowered the camera, enabling me to see his face.

Holy fuck. It was the paparazzo from the club.

On the pitch, the match started with a huge roar from the fans, but the fucking photographer only had eyes for Alex.

There was no reason he shouldn't be here. It was a public venue, and anyone could buy a ticket. Yet the sight of him sent cold tendrils through my blood.

I went to radio Riss but thought better of it, leaving my position to speak with her instead.

"Malcolm Dennis is a row over in the stands. Perfect vantage point for watching Penny."

Riss's dark eyebrows merged. She knew the man's name as I'd added him to a list of people we had concerns over. "Keep eyes on him. We'll be moving on shortly."

I nodded and returned to my watch.

After another few minutes, Alex stood and exited the box, Riss sticking with her on their path around the stadium to the far side where the charity box was located. Few knew the plan, and to any casual onlooker, they could assume she needed the bathroom or refreshments.

Yet the second she left her seat, Malcolm Dennis stood and abandoned his own.

I watched him trot down the concrete steps and disappear into a tunnel. He hadn't stared after her in surprise. He hadn't craned his neck to see where she was going.

I radioed the change to Riss and pursued my team, catching up with them to take my position. Will and Johnnie formed the sides of our diamond, and I was at the back.

That same sense of wrongness haunted me. Stadiums and arenas were my bread and butter. We moved Leo through them regularly. Yet every doorway and stairwell had me panicked like we were about to be jumped.

On the far side of the huge venue, we safely escorted Alex to rejoin the charity party, and I could finally take a breath.

Riss positioned Will and Johnnie in the hall, taking me with her into the charity box. A wide room held leather sofas and a catering table, opening out onto a private terrace with seats to watch the match. A railing and a drop protected attendees from others, but as I scanned the audience, my heart stopped.

Malcolm Dennis was right there, that little camera in

hand, trained once more on Alex.

How the fuck had he known where she was going?

"Riss, that same paparazzo followed us." I spoke directly to the team leader through my comms, cutting out the rest of the team.

Across the room, she blinked. "I thought you said he was across the stadium?"

"Aye, he was, but somehow he's made it here in the same time it's taken us."

Which only left one conclusion. He'd known exactly where Alex was going to be.

My mind raced to fill the gaps. It was typical for paparazzi to cover all bases and have multiple tickets for an event with segmented locations. That was a common tactic to be sure they could get into position wherever they needed to be, and Dennis could have predicted that his target would be in the boxes on one side of the stadium or the other. But for him to have followed—no, *preceded*—her meant he'd been aware of Alex's movement plan.

The cold crystallised into ice in my blood. How many others knew? Her team, obviously, and the stadium coordinator. Had that rippled out to the wider stadium security team? To the admin or TV crew?

On cue, the cameras briefly trained on the royal box, the huge screens showing it was empty. That was a no, then. The TV crew assumed Alex was still there and had wanted another shot of her pretty face.

Riss appeared beside me and checked out Dennis. Calculation played out in her eyes. "That's unexpected."

"Someone told him where she'd be. Exactly like with the nightclub and with how her outfit was revealed."

I shot my gaze back to the entertainment room behind

the seats. Will and Johnnie were in opposite corners, looking bored. It had to be one of them. There was no other possibility.

"We need to leave," I said.

Riss gave a single shake of her head. "This is unusual, but our principal is not in any danger from one lone photographer."

"No, but she is if her team is selling her information."

The team leader's eyes darkened. "That's quite the accusation to make without evidence."

I bit back frustration. "What is this if not evidence?"

Riss observed the photographer one more time then turned. "I hear you, but a risk event has not been triggered. Therefore, we'll continue as planned. Take a breath, Raphael."

She left me to stew in my own juices. One thing I was certain of was that I wouldn't leave Alex's side. Not while I was the only person who seemed to give the tiniest damn about her safety.

# 17

# Alexandra

Confusion prevented any chance of me enjoying the football match, not that I was particularly a fan of men kicking a ball up and down a field in order to score a goal. More, I was dwelling over the fact that apparently I was booked in for a formal visit at Kensington Hospital which included opening a new wing. A press pack, patient bedside chats, interviews.

All news to me.

Subtly, I'd checked the email Sir Reginald had sent me with the event calendar I'd signed up to. In our conversation, the private secretary had been clear that my work would be limited, and much of it not publicised because he wasn't sure how the public would react to me. Not when I carried the baggage of a party princess.

Yet the hospital's director already had a date in mind and wanted to talk through the finer details. I'd managed to get through the conversation as noncommittally as possible without being rude, but I had a tight belly from worrying over being in the dark. It didn't help my stomach cramps which now panged deep and low.

I just wanted to go home.

When the half-time whistle blew, I took my chance and sidled up to Riss. "What time can we leave?"

"Is something the matter, ma'am?"

"Not really. I'm just uncomfortable."

She checked her watch. "The plan was to leave at the three-quarter point."

I knew that. Royals always left ahead of the rush of people exiting the stadium. It was safer and meant the cars wouldn't get snared up in traffic.

Raphael crossed to join us. "Problem?"

I gave him a half-smile, trying not to betray how the sight of him on full, stern bodyguard duty gave me a fever. "I'd like to leave."

Instantly, he turned to the exit. "I'll check the hall. Will can ready the cars."

Riss muttered something I didn't catch, but it didn't matter. Raphael's readiness enabled mine. Without waiting for Riss, I strode out.

People milled about the corridor, as always, interested glances coming my way. I didn't pay them any mind, happy to be going. In the middle of my protection team, I trotted along, a bounce coming back to my step. Some party girl I was when I had the joy of going home.

Out of the lift, we took on the broad corridor that led to a quieter staff exit of the stadium. But ahead, a side door opened and a rush of people came out.

As one, my bodyguards halted and tightened their huddle around me.

The crowd were from some sort of corporate event from the suits and ties, but many were obviously drunk and laughing loudly. The mass came our way. With our exit beyond them, we had nowhere else to go.

Raphael said something into their comms system I couldn't hear, and Riss replied. We started moving again, and the crowd of people surged around us. The space that was usually left around me condensed until I almost bumped into Riss at the head of our group.

More people flooded out of the room, heading deeper into the stadium.

They were all around us now, the noise deafening with the low ceiling of the corridor.

"It's the fucking princess," someone called.

Dozens of faces swivelled my way, and people repeated my name.

Instantly, I switched on a smile. A sour expression would hit the headlines far faster than any other.

"Oi, oi, princess. Where's the carriage?" a man joked.

"Buy me a pint. You're good for it," added another to a roar of laughter.

My team pushed on, Will and Johnnie on my left and right drifting ahead of me a fraction. It left space for the crowd to get close. Mild panic sank over me. Just like I didn't enjoy public speaking, crowds scared me. There was too much opportunity for individuals to do something rash. To make a play to entertain their friends.

Then sure fingers wrapped around mine, and Raphael brought me against his body. He was much taller than me and broader, so I was instantly surrounded by him. *Safe.* To any onlooker, it was just a bodyguard protecting his principal.

To me, it was doing something strange to my nervous system.

The fear left me. All I knew was his touch.

In thirty seconds, we were through and heading out the doors. That delicious imprint of his fingers on my skin had left a mark, though.

It stayed with me on the drive back through London. All the way through the palace to my rooms.

It doubled down when I stood there, processing everything that had happened.

A knock came at the door. If Raphael had come to me, I'd kiss him.

But when I threw it open, it was one of the palace staff.

"For you, ma'am, as ordered." She placed an item in my hands and turned smartly, trotting off down the hall.

I stared then locked the door and took the offering to my couch. It was a hot water bottle. I hadn't had one since I was a child. Who...? I didn't need to even consider it. I'd told Raphael I had cramps. He'd sent me a solution.

My chest ached at that perfectly lovely little gesture.

Finding my phone, I toyed over what to message him, the hot water bottle warm and doing its job on my belly.

Then I remembered the missed call from last night and jumped to my chat with Dori.

**Alex:** *Shit, sorry! I meant to call this morning, but it's been a day. Can you talk?*

No reply came. I returned to what to say to Raphael.

No matter how I phrased a thank-you in my head, none

of it sounded enough when I typed it out. I wanted—no, needed—to see him. So I sucked in a breath and sent him something else instead.

*Alex: Come to see me? I won't run this time. Staircase three down the hall from the bodyguard office. Third floor. Suite of rooms to the right. The door code to get up here is 74568.*

My hand shook when I tapped to send the message.

Dori still hadn't replied or even opened my text, so I switched over to my email.

A new message from Sir Reginald waited. I opened it with trepidation.

He'd sent a schedule. I scrolled through the activities that spread out through the rest of the year. This wasn't what we'd agreed. He hadn't even mentioned work beyond the couple of weeks we'd talked through when he'd come to me with his proposal. Now I understood where the hospital director had her idea from.

Yep. Kensington Hospital's visit was booked in for October.

My heart sank to the floor.

# 18

## Raphael

*O*ur debrief meetings were typically short, and I was torn between gunning for this one to be over and needing it to play out. Half of my mind was off finding a helicopter and flying my stress away, the rest wanted to nail my team to the floor for what I suspected them of.

"Malcolm Dennis was spotted on two occasions during the match," Riss stated. "First outside the royal box, then on the opposite side of the stadium."

With my shoulders bunched, I watched Will and Johnnie for any reaction.

Neither said a word.

Riss tapped her stylus on her screen. "I've noted him down as a person of concern—"

Johnnie's splutter interrupted her. "On what basis? He's a pap. They're no danger to anyone. All they want is a payday."

Anger tightened my hands into fists. Paparazzi regularly got people hurt or even killed in pursuit of a photo, and yet again, one of the very people who should be interested in this individual was dismissing him.

I was so close to calling Johnnie out, but something held my tongue.

Riss was right. I had no direct evidence. Which meant I needed to get some. I couldn't do that if I challenged him and gave the game away.

The beginnings of a plan appeared in my mind.

"Raphael, you were concerned. Do you have anything else to add?" she asked me.

I managed a shrug to hide my conniving. "Maybe I'm overreacting."

"No kidding." Johnnie folded his arms.

Riss gave me a surprised look but returned to the task of checking through articles about the princess on social media and in the press.

My phone buzzed in my pocket.

I checked it, swallowing a shock of happiness at the name on my screen.

Alex had messaged me. I didn't want to risk reading her words with the team right there, so I stowed the phone and pretended to listen to the rest of the debrief.

Riss wound it up with a parting comment. "Next week, I believe we'll have Toni rejoining us. His mother has made a comeback in her health, and he's indicated he can rejoin the team. I've also been informed of a significant increase to our workload from there onwards."

Both Will and Johnnie grouched.

Toni coming back meant they didn't need me anymore. Tomorrow, we had an evening event for Alex. The two days after were more of the same mixture of meetings and day events, ending with a formal banquet. After that, I was done. I should mind my business, and yet still my mouth was moving.

From what Ben had told me, Alex was only doing public engagements for a short time. She'd said the same.

"Why the increased workload?" I asked.

"The princess's engagement calendar is busy. We're expected to accommodate that. I'll share more when I know more."

I opened and closed my mouth. "I could—"

"It's for me to handle, Raphael. You're all dismissed."

I'd pissed her off by jumping to action the minute Alex said she wanted to leave the stadium, but I couldn't regret that. I also desperately wanted to know the content of the message that burned a hole in my pocket.

Outside the bodyguard office, the two other men headed straight for the exit. I scrabbled for my phone, then died a death when I read Alex's text.

She wanted to see me.

I was moving through the palace with purpose, entering a coded door which gave me access to stairs.

A secret route to the maze of an interior I hadn't known how to access.

Any thoughts I'd had of flying went out the window on my approach to the tall, white doors that I guessed were hers. A voice came from inside. I tapped gently, then the door unlocked and Alex appeared in the frame.

With a phone to her ear, she mouthed to me, "You came."

"Ye asked," I whispered back.

She watched me, beautiful in loose shorts and the t-shirt she'd changed into, and her hair in a messy bun. With her free hand, she gestured for me to enter the spacious living room.

While I locked the door, Alex held up a finger to indicate I needed to wait a second.

Of course I would. I parked myself against the wall and watched her pace as she handled whoever was on the phone. The room reflected the design of the palace overall, with antique furniture and little of the personality of the woman who lived here. It couldn't hold my attention like she did.

On the sofa, the hot water bottle sat in a nest of blankets, though it was a warm enough day not to need them. She obviously felt rough.

"No, I don't want to schedule a meeting to talk about it. Not when that meeting can't happen for three weeks. Please put me through to him now."

She listened then growled in frustration.

"Then tell him this: The answer is no. I don't agree to the list he sent. I won't do it."

She hung up the call then tossed the phone to the sofa, and for a moment, stared at it with an expression of disgust. That melted when her focus lifted to me.

My chest inflated on an inhale. "I take it that's about the work you've been given next week?"

"You know about that?"

"Only that Riss is in planning mode to cover it." I didn't add that I wouldn't be here to guard her. We both knew it.

Alex heaved a sigh. "My cousin's private secretary arranged a whole new set of engagements."

"Without asking? That's underhanded."

"It is, isn't it? I'm not being dramatic?"

I left my position at the wall and crossed to join her on the rug in front of the sofas. "He's not your boss. You're not under contract with him. Every commitment he makes on your behalf is a conversation he owes ye first."

"Yes, but it's complicated because this is my family. As far back as I can remember, we had to do certain public appearances, like at Christmas or the king's birthday. There was never any question about it. The date would be confirmed, we'd be informed of our roles, and we'd show up."

I gestured to her phone. "This is nothing like that. And either way, ye don't have to do any of it. Ye said last night that it isn't fun."

Those brown eyes met mine, curiosity in their depths. "I said a lot of things last night. You did, as well."

The room seemed to close in around me, narrowing so it was just me and Alex in a tight pocket of space. I welcomed the pressure. This was exactly where I wanted to be. This was also the point where I should apologise. I tried to force the words.

"What I said was far from appropriate."

Her gaze clung to mine. "Pretty sure I started it."

"I should've finished it."

"Why?"

My gaze slid to her lips. That forbidden conversation had happened with her in her bed, or maybe on the sofa next to us. My name on her tongue. Her hand between her legs. "I'm under contract to protect ye. It's against the rules."

Alex took a little breath, her cheeks pinkening, and her eyes going hazy. "Got your phone on you?"

I dove my eyebrows together but produced the device from my pocket.

"Set a five-minute countdown."

I did as she asked. "Why?"

"Because until then, you're fired."

Those brown eyes of hers practically begged me, and I dropped my gaze to her lips.

This was the worst fucking idea and everything I needed. I chucked the phone and slid my hand to the back of her head. Dropping my mouth to her, I kissed the lass I'd dreamed about for years.

Our lips met, and lightning struck while the world faded.

Alex pushed up on her toes and kissed me back, her soft whimper of need sending me hurtling down a pathway of no return with desperation clawing at me to get her closer. There was nothing timid to our touch. We clashed. Heat and need and lust swamped me. I'd wanted this so badly. To understand the shape of her lips under mine. To satisfy the constant draw I had to her. We were a ticking timebomb, and I had no choice but to set light to the fuse.

Fuck, did the princess taste good.

Alex pressed tight to me and wound her arms around my neck. On instinct, I grazed down to palm her thighs and lift her so her legs twined around my waist. Then I backed her to the wall, the kiss never breaking but our bodies almost as close as we could get them with our clothes still on.

In my arms, she clung to me. She let me lead. Let me own her mouth and met every surge and fall.

In frantic heartbeats, I knew without doubt this kiss would end me. It already had. I wanted everything. Now. Like she could read my mind, Alex stroked her fingers into my hair, and I groaned at how good it felt to have her touching me. I slanted to take her mouth deeper, hunger driving me on.

I could live in this kiss. My fascination with her only grew stronger the more we were around each other. The chemistry between us was insane. Under her, I was so fucking hard, and I rocked against her, needing more. Everything.

Something beeped in the room.

Neither of us stopped. Despite this being so wrong on a professional level, I couldn't have given it up if I wanted to. This might be the only chance I had to learn the shape of Alex and what she wanted me to do with my tongue. The only moment where the stars aligned and we both let go of all the reasons this couldn't happen.

Alex broke her lips from mine and dropped her head back, panting. "God, yes."

I kissed her jaw. Her throat.

"Get back here," I ordered.

I tipped her chin down to claim her mouth once more. She smiled into the kiss. A bolt of happiness crested over me, matching the insanity, horniness, and everything in between.

The fucking phone kept on beeping.

"Our time is up," Alex whispered against my cheek.

"It's a car horn. Ignore it."

She gave a soft laugh. "Maybe the palace's burglar alarm?"

"Or a police siren. Either way it's not for us. Just kiss me."

She did, the levity leaving us as the passion twisted to becoming darker and more serious as we sank into slow, hot, wet kisses. I'd never known a feeling like this. An absolute certainty in the perfect fit. I squeezed the soft thighs I held her by, loving how my fingers indented her skin. Alex hugged me harder.

A knock rattled the door beside us.

As one, we broke apart our lips and stared at each other.

"Expecting someone?" I dropped my voice low.

She shook her head. "I don't think so."

The person knocked again. "Ma'am? I have your dress selection and the tailor."

Alex groaned softly. "Fuck. That's supposed to be in the morning. It's the eveningwear I need." She raised her voice for the benefit of the people outside. "Just a minute."

I put her down, hating that I had to let her go. It felt wrong. I had no choice.

Alex swayed onto me. I steadied her, and she lifted her gaze to mine, biting back a laugh.

"You made me dizzy."

The feeling was mutual, but our moment was over. I wasn't about to leave without the final word. I kissed her one last time, then broke away before I made things awkward for the listening visitors. From the sofa, I snatched up my phone, the alarm now silent.

I peered back at Alex. "I'll go, and I'll make up some shite about your security schedule as I walk out, but princess?"

She touched her lips, so fucking beautiful in the afternoon light. "Yes?"

"That is going to live rent-free in my head for the rest of my life."

Her lips curved. "Really?"

There was no time to ask how she doubted it. I had to get out of there. I'd wanted to find an airfield to get in an hour's flight. Now, that need was doubled, added to by frustration of an entirely different kind.

# 19

# *Alexandra*

Dresses on a rail were whisked into the room, followed by a stylist and a tailor. They paid no attention to Raphael, but he was all I could see as he stepped out. All I could think about while I tried on the row of sparkling dresses by British designers.

I needed to pick two—one for the gala in two days and another for a banquet in the palace which I could barely think about without nausea. For the latter, I had to give a speech and couldn't imagine causing a bird-related distraction to get out of it.

I settled on an emerald-green satin gown for the gala. It would pop against the venue's red seats and pair well with my dark hair. For the banquet, I let the stylist pick out a formal cream mermaid dress with a modest hemline. I could barely look at it without dread. I even confessed it to the two women, earning grim smiles of understanding.

The next day was the same.

I didn't have to leave the palace, but the meetings went on and on for the whole day, leaving me exhausted.

When the last was done, I holed up in my room and hid from the world.

Something niggled at me.

Dori hadn't messaged or returned my call. I couldn't think of the last time we'd gone this long without contact. I'd texted him again this morning, but no reply had come.

Concern had built steadily through the day.

A best friend hunt was in order. I told him so in a text.

*Alex: If you aren't answering me, I can only assume you're having a good time. Am going to stalk you to find out just how good.*

Yet his socials gave me nothing.

He'd posted nothing new and hadn't been tagged anywhere. That was unusual for my social butterfly friend who delighted in finding me or him online and refreshed his feed more than was healthy.

I clicked through to his liked posts, finally finding something new.

My pulse skipped. Dori had liked a post for the engagement party of a beautiful couple, posted two days ago. I squinted at the caption under the stunning Lake Como picture.

*The happy couple-to-be, Elsie Sale and Victor Vance.*

The woman's name was familiar, though I'd never met her. I mused over it, trying to make sense of the mystery. Her profile told me that she was a musician and her guy was an influencer with a huge following. His page was full of videos and pictures about the relationship amongst brand deals, including a video of his proposal which had millions of views. In contrast, her page was dedicated to her music only.

If Dori knew either of them, he hadn't mentioned it to me.

Nor had this helped me work out where he was hiding. Frustrated, I climbed from my cosy den and slipped on a pair of ballet slippers. I did my best thinking while moving, so I left my apartment to prowl the palace.

After hours, the centuries-old building had a completely different feel to it. Gone were the bustling staff and countless summer tourists, replaced by shadows and spooky long corridors. As a child, I'd only stayed here when my family needed to be in London, but I'd done the same and roamed at night.

It freaked me out back then. At least now I was no longer scared of any ghosts.

I meandered through the hall to the formal staircase and descended. The ground floor might still have staff hanging around, and I found my feet delivering me to the state rooms on the first floor.

Security wouldn't be far, essential as there were paintings by grand masters and other valuables on display, but I was allowed to be here. It was even more fun to give them the slip.

I ignored the picture gallery to enter one of the wide receiving rooms.

A plush carpet muted my footsteps.

Above me, rows of chandeliers glimmered, though none were lit, and an enormous marble fireplace gaped to the side. I padded through patches of light from the tall windows, passing rows of chairs amid gleaming columns. I stepped in and out of the light as I wandered, trying to centre myself but also knowing exactly what had brought me here.

Ahead were double doors to the banquet hall where, in three days, I had to stand in front of dignitaries and speak on behalf of my family. Of all the events Sir Reginald had lined up for me, that one felt like a trial by fire.

That was what I wanted. To look at the space and imagine myself there. To try to picture how I would handle the formalities and the moment I had to rise and address the room. Damn. I wouldn't be able to. The dread I'd felt upstairs returned tenfold. I couldn't move from the spot.

My phone buzzed in my shorts pocket.

I yanked it out, and my heart skipped a beat. Raphael had sent a picture of himself standing in front of a helicopter. Except in the shot, it was daylight, and night had long fallen.

Three dots showed he was typing.

**Raphael:** *Look what you made me do.*

A laugh flew from my lips, and I wrote a reply.

**Alex:** *Did I stress you out so much you flew away? By the way, I love that you can do that.*

**Raphael:** *I need to get you in my passenger seat so you can watch me in action.*

Heat swirled in my veins. It was like he had a hotline to my nervous system.

**Alex:** *Where have you gone?*

**Raphael:** *I'm back already. It was just a little air time.*

Relief chased the desire. Thank heck he hadn't left. I knew he would eventually. Though I barely knew the man, unhappiness tied a surprising knot in my gut at how I wouldn't see him for much longer.

Creeping to the side of the room, I tucked onto one of the uncomfortable seats, hiding in the darkness.

**Alex:** *I'd ask if you needed a copilot, but I'm horrible with directions.*

**Raphael:** *Remind me never to get in a car with you behind the wheel.*

**Alex:** *No problem there, I can't drive.*

He sent back an emoji of a shocked face.

Seconds later, he called me. I took a shuddering breath and answered, my greeting overly loud in the silent mausoleum of the state room.

"How is it possible that one of the most famous women in the country has never had a driving lesson?"

He was outside somewhere, the sound of traffic in the background of the call.

"Bold of you to assume I've never had a lesson. I've had many. Still failed my test three times."

Silence held the other end of the line. I clucked my tongue.

"Go ahead. You can laugh at me."

"I never would. It's a hard test."

I could hear the smile in his voice. "I bet you passed first time."

"Aye, but I was seventeen and in need because of where I live. Nothing beats the confidence of cocky teenagers. Can't ye get a pass for being a princess?"

"I wish. If anything, I think it made the test guys more evil."

He laughed again. "Are ye feeling any better? Dress

picked out?"

I couldn't talk about the clothes. It made me imagine myself in the banquet room, and the panic threatened to take over me again. "You fixed me with your hot water bottle. I was just stalking Dori online as he still hasn't showed."

Down the line, keys rattled and a door clicked, Raphael returning home by the sounds of it. "Strange. Are ye worried about him?"

My gut tightened. Raphael hadn't dismissed me out of hand like I'd done with myself. Then again, he was the one with experience of looking after others. I could barely do that with myself.

"Dori is meant to be my date for the gala tomorrow night. By now, he'd normally be sending me pictures of tuxedos or critiquing the guest list and planning on who he wanted to hook up with or persuade to go to a club with us after. To hear nothing at all is weird."

"One second while I get to my room and we'll talk it through."

I listened as Raphael greeted someone, then stairs drummed and another door shut.

"Is that some kind of bodyguard accommodation?" I sat taller. "Are you in the palace?"

If he was here, I wanted to see him.

"No, princess. About half a mile from ye."

Why did I love the way he called me princess? Like it wasn't my designation but someone dainty and special to him.

Raphael continued, "Will is downstairs. Johnnie and Riss don't seem to sleep here, but there are other palace staff in various flats, too." A mattress creaked, and Raphael continued. "Tell me about Dori. How do ye know each other?"

"Sure you have time for this?"

"Didn't I tell ye I have nothing to do in the city but wait on ye? Plus I called your number. Talk to me or I'll go mad with boredom."

I worked through my history of meeting Dori. "Both of us went to boarding school in Switzerland. Separate single-sex ones, that is. The schools are in the same town, so after hours and on weekends, the girls and boys would mix. There's something uniquely punishing about being sent so far from home, so the kids bonded, fought, and flirted with this edge of desperation. He and I were best friends from the start."

"Did ye date?" There was a funny tone to his voice.

"Each other? Never. We have exactly zero romantic chemistry, probably because we're related through my father's line. Second cousins, I think. I adore him, but it's like he's my favourite brother, if I ever had siblings."

"Sure he feels the same?"

"I am. Why?"

"The last time ye mentioned him, he came up with a nickname for me. I'm naw exactly his favourite person. I wondered if he's jealous and that might be why he's ghosting ye."

*Hot Bodyguard*, that was Dori's name for Raphael. I stared at the pilot picture open on my screen and shivered. "I see your logic, but I'm ninety-nine percent certain he's in love with someone else. He has been for a while, though he's never told me who."

"How do ye know? I'm not questioning it, just trying to get through the facts."

I searched my mind. "He told me he'd met a girl, but it

had to be secret. This was almost a year ago. The breakup affected him big time, but I saw rather than heard about that as he wouldn't say a word. He spills secrets like they're going out of fashion, but for her, he kept it to himself."

"Secret suggesting she's famous?"

Halfway to starting an answer, I stalled, stuck on what I'd discovered with my online stalking. "You could be right. Which is making me join the dots to him liking a post with a celebrity in it earlier. It was her engagement party. I think it said the party had taken place in Italy. I might be reaching, but I've got nothing else to go on."

"Gut instinct shouldn't be ignored. Have ye ever booked a flight for him?"

"That's random. I have, but why?" We'd country-hopped regularly throughout our teens, catching cheap flights between cities and party locations.

"Got his passport number? I can track it for ye. If he's in Italy, that's an answer."

My jaw dropped. "You can do that?"

"We monitor known risks that way."

I jumped to my notes and found Dori's passport details then sent them to Raphael. "This feels very illegal."

"It is. Got a problem with that?"

I smothered a laugh. "No. If I don't criminally cyber stalk my best friend, do I even care about him?"

"Exactly." There was a pause, then he came back. "I've sent off the request. Should have information tomorrow."

I exhaled, feeling lighter than I had all day. A silence drew out between me and Raphael. We'd kissed. Not just a quick peck, but a full-body experience built up of overwhelming need.

I could still feel the press of my bodyguard's lips.

I really wanted to talk about it.

"You kissed me."

His voice returned low. "Seem to remember your hands in my hair, princess."

I was right back there in the scene with his dark, silky hair between my fingers and his hard body crushed against mine.

"Are ye in bed?"

"I wish I was."

"Where are ye?"

I stared down the banquet hall's double doors. "Facing off with demons in the belly of the palace."

A click came from the other end of the wide-open space, and I jerked up with a rushed intake of breath.

"What's wrong?" Raphael asked.

I scanned the darkness and whispered, "I think someone's here."

"Where exactly?"

"One of the state rooms." Cautiously, I stood, peering into the shadows. Nothing moved, yet something had definitely made a sound. It had been a door opening, I was certain.

Raphael's voice returned with greater surety. "This is going to sound crazy, but do me a favour, and go back to your apartment."

He'd told me he was worried about someone selling information on me. I hadn't paid that any mind. Maybe I should have.

"Okay," I breathed.

"Move quickly and stay on the line."

As silently as I could, I left my position and crept along the wall, keeping to the thick shadows I'd hidden myself in. The tall windows on the opposite wall let in enough light to see by, but also for me to be seen.

A creak came from behind me.

I bolted to a side door that opened onto the broad corridor outside, but as I wrenched on the handle, it wouldn't give. Locked.

I cursed under my breath and kept going, glancing over my shoulder. Still, I could see no one, but I could sense somebody behind me.

Passing the fireplace, I dove at the next door. It was also locked.

I let out a whimper, my senses going wild. Whirling around, I stared into the dark. "Who's there?"

No reply came. No one lurched from the depths of the room. Even so, the hair on my neck stood on end.

Again, I picked up my feet, my breathing speeding up. At the head of the room, I rattled the handle to the banquet room. This one gave, and I fell through with barely contained relief.

"What's happening? Only answer if ye can do so safely," Raphael said.

"I'm in the next room along. All the other doors were locked."

"I don't know if that's typical or not. Get back to a main thoroughfare. If ye can't, trigger an alarm. Bring security down."

Rapid movement sounded his end. Then his next words brought a burst of relief to my frightened heart.

"I'm on my way."

"Thank you," I whispered.

It wasn't like me to be scared, but I'd got myself well and truly creeped out by my midnight escapade. Raphael was right, I should get security. But that would mean they'd escort me to my rooms. I wouldn't get to see him.

I backed up from the doors then spun around and took in the room. The banquet hall was huge, with a minstrels' gallery overlooking three long rows of tables. I'd eaten here many times and had seen two kings give speeches. Never once had I experienced any regret that my father was the second-born son. I had no aspirations to be monarch.

But my insider knowledge gave me an advantage if there really was someone prowling after me.

As quickly as I could, I made my way to the back of the room where a hidden set of spiral stairs led up to the minstrels' gallery. At the railing, I crouched, watching the room for anyone creeping in after.

"I've hidden," I told Raphael down the phone. "If someone's watching me, I want to see them."

His boot steps drummed on the pavement. "I'm a couple of minutes out. I need to find ye when I get there."

"You know the staircase I told you to climb for my apartment? If you pass that and keep going, there's a long hall at the end. It goes all the way under the state rooms. Wait at the end. I'll come down when you get here."

Then I waited, listening to Raphael run through the city and with my gaze glued to the space below.

Nothing moved. No further sounds came.

By degrees, my heart rate slowed to normal, and my panic eased. Not my fear, though. That was just as high. I couldn't work out why.

"I'm here," Raphael told me. "I got through. Come down or I'll come find ye."

"I'm coming."

I rose from my crouch, holding the railing, and gave one last look to the room before crossing to the rear of the gallery. From here, a narrow staircase went down two flights, all the way to where Raphael would be waiting. I opened the door and peered into the gloom. No light. God.

I activated my phone torch and went to close the door behind me.

The unmistakable rattle of a handle echoed through the banquet hall. I squeaked and dove down the stairs, descending quicker than I should. At the bottom, I held my breath and turned the door handle, half expecting it to be locked.

Thankfully it gave. I burst out to find Raphael pacing the hall.

He twisted then ran for me. I flew at him.

It shouldn't have been so natural falling into his embrace, but it was. Just like when we'd danced as teenagers. Just like when we'd kissed earlier. One big protective arm curled around my back, with the other hand, he cupped my head, using his body to protect mine.

"It's okay. I'm here."

I'd never felt so safe. I hid my face in his broad chest and fought to get a hold of my emotions.

Raphael brushed the hair from my eyes. "You're shaking."

"I can't believe you ran all the way here. I don't even know if someone was following me. It was probably just a security guard," I babbled.

His watchful gaze claimed mine. "Ye called out a

challenge. They didn't answer."

He was right. Any security guard would have replied to my shout.

I gave a jerky nod. "I should tell someone. I want to go back upstairs first."

"Then that's what we'll do."

Linking his hand with mine, Raphael guided me along the hall and to the back stairs. We ran up them and to my rooms. He didn't let go of me the whole way.

Inside, he locked the door at our backs. "Make the call."

I clutched my phone with the torch still activated.

"Wait."

He watched me. "Why?"

I stepped into his space, palmed his rough cheek, and kissed him. Everything fell away. My fear, the palace we'd just run through. Only him.

Yet too quickly, I had to end it.

"When they come up here to talk to me, there will be a fuss. You'll have to leave when they do. Someone will probably patrol the floor all night. I just had to—"

He touched his forehead to mine. "Never justify kissing me. And don't apologise for bringing me here either."

My heart missed a beat. "Because it's your job?"

"No, princess. Because I wouldn't want to be anywhere else."

Everything next happened too fast. I called security, sending them scurrying. A lead officer and two burly guards came to my door, and I explained Raphael's presence by saying he'd been on the phone to talk about tomorrow's work. Luckily, no one blinked an eye, but the protocols for a potential intruder went into full effect.

Raphael left, escorted out as the palace went into lockdown.

I took myself to bed, and while I should probably have been worrying about a search underway or a stranger being found, all I focused on was a lone text that came in from my bodyguard.

**Raphael:** *Here whenever you need me.*

*T*he following morning was busy with meetings. I had a couple of hours free in the afternoon, but half of that was chewed up with the head of palace security debriefing me on what they'd found.

No intruder had been detected.

There had been no breach of the perimeter that they could discover. Many people had been present in the building, and he gently suggested that I could have encountered someone going about their job, or that creaking old buildings could be spooky at night.

Maybe he was right, but I felt like a scolded child.

This evening, I'd be in my emerald gown with a gala to attend. Hair and make-up on point and a smile at the ready. I anticipated it with the sense that something was wrong, and nothing I did could make it go away.

# 20

# Raphael

"Baby Gordonson is as stubborn as their ma," my brother said down the phone.

A thud sounded, and I released a breath.

"Did Effie throw something at ye?"

"Good guess. Pregnancy hasn't dented her aim."

My smile flickered, and I stared out at the ferry boats cruising along the Thames from the bench I'd dropped onto at the end of my run. My brother chatted on, still with no news about the arrival of my niece or nephew but with plenty to say about where we lived and our friends.

I listened but couldn't help the rising sense of danger whenever I thought about his baby arriving. It had taken a long time after relocating to Scotland for me to feel safe. To some extent, I did, but that sense of security flickered each time we had to encounter our father. He was still in California, still running his Mafia-linked empire. No matter what we had on him, I knew he wouldn't give up wanting us to return. The minute he knew his first grandchild was born could be the moment he decided on a family reunion.

Mentioning this to Gabe was pointless. He knew my fears. He'd damn well counselled me about them more than once, and I wasn't about to dent his joy. So instead, I kept my mouth shut and just listened.

I had to kill time anyway, nothing to do until this evening when I'd be back on duty. I'd tried to sleep in, failing in that, and spent the day working out.

Anything to stop myself from calling Alex.

Two kisses and I was a goner. After her scare, I'd nearly broken my neck to reach her, and ever since, my damn heart hadn't calmed. I didn't understand the overwhelming need I had for the lass, but I was certain I couldn't protect her if I didn't have my head on straight.

"By the way," Gabe continued. "I saw Daisy at the hangar earlier, and she asked when you'd be back. Not sure why."

I wiped the sweat from my brow. "Not sure myself. I'll give her a call."

If anything, I wanted to stay longer. The novelty of being in the city for a few days was fine, but I was over the traffic and the pollution. Over the multiple sources of danger for the woman I needed to protect. In a few days, that matter would be taken care of for me; her missing team member would reappear, and I would no longer be needed. I had half a mind to convince Riss to keep me on.

My phone beeped, and I pulled it from my ear to see the team leader calling.

"I've got another call coming in. Catch ye later," I told my brother and switched to answer her.

Riss's clipped tones had me sitting up taller.

"I read through your message about the incident at the palace last night. I've also spoken to the head of security and had a full debrief. But there's one question I have still unanswered."

I'd tried to speak to her this morning, but she'd been on another job. "Shoot."

"Why were you there?"

"I wasn't. I was talking to Alex when she heard something that made her think someone was near."

A pause followed, and she made a sound of disbelief. "Alex? You mean Princess Alexandra. Why didn't you contact me?"

"We're friends. I was already—"

"Friends? Since when? You're required to disclose that."

I heaved a breath. "We knew each other a long time ago. It wasn't worth disclosing when I started as we weren't speaking. We really only have been for a few days."

"Right. In a matter of days you've moved on to late-night phone calls."

Her disbelief played out loud and clear.

I scowled. "It's the truth. Alex can tell ye the same."

"Her Royal Highness Princess Alexandra," she put emphasis on the title, "requires her team to be above reproach. I can't have someone working for me who's keeping secrets."

"It isn't a secret. I told ye I was there. Ye know everything that happened," I argued, standing from the bench and the shelter of the riverside trees.

"I can't trust that that's true. I head up the team and am responsible for what goes on within it. Do you understand where that leaves me? I have no choice but to keep you on for this evening, but after that, you can consider your temporary position with us over."

I swore under my breath. How the fuck could I argue the point when she was entirely correct? I'd kissed Alex, and that breached any protocol for a bodyguard. At the same point, I couldn't regret it. Not when the memory was tattooed to the beat of my heart.

But fuck it. If I wasn't guarding Alex anymore, that's all our time together could be. A memory.

"I understand. But for the love of God—"

The line went dead. She'd disconnected.

My stomach dropped. I'd meant to say to look for the mole in the team, but I'd already told her this. Tonight, I'd reiterate it, then I'd leave.

This time, it seemed, for good.

**Alex:** *Tell me again why you're worried that someone on my team is leaking my information.*

*S*he was one car ahead and dressed in an outfit that had me wanting to fall to my knees. I'd taken one look at her in her sleek dark-green dress and had to divert my gaze. Straight into finding Riss staring at me.

I'd never had a poker face.

Alone in the last car, I wrote a reply.

**Raphael:** *There's been too many times that the press knew your movements or other details that they shouldn't have.*

**Alex:** *I really hate that.*

**Raphael:** *I'll keep you safe tonight.*

What I'd wanted to do was lay a trap, but with only one evening left with her, time was running out. My resolve returned.

**Raphael:** *Do me a favour? At some point this evening, send a voice message when only Will can hear you. Say that this evening you're going somewhere.*

**Alex:** *Ooh, espionage. I like it. Do I do the same with Johnnie but a different location?*

**Raphael:** *Genius woman. That's exactly what I was going to say.*

**Alex:** *Crack spy team! This will be fun.*

I wanted to suggest she give Riss a third location, but I could only watch one of the places, and Riss would want to accompany her, I was sure.

An incoming call lit my phone, Valentine's name on the screen.

We had at least half an hour left of the journey, and the driver was on a call with headphones in, so I took it, unable to stop a grin.

"Your passport trace came in," he said.

"Ye couldn't just text me?"

"Been missing your voice, fly boy. We all are. Jackson is mooching about all lonely without a bad joke to be seen. Ben's grouchy. The place isn't the same. Anyhoo, the man in question. Want the details?"

"Hit me."

"Your target flew into Milan two days ago. No onward trace discovered, but his passport was registered at a hotel in the city a couple of hours later. Who is he?"

Damn. She was on the money with her Italy guess. "A

friend of Alex's."

"Alex as in the princess? You're getting friendly."

I answered without thinking, lost in the familiarity of my close-knit team that I trusted with almost every detail of my life, and the consideration of what I could do with this information. "Ye have no idea."

Valentine made a sound of interest.

I sighed. "Forget I said anything."

"Ye didn't actually. I'm just inferring a whole lot." Glee filled his voice. "Wait until I tell Mia. She adores the royal family. Give me something juicy. Any lip locking going on? Shenanigans in the throne room?"

"Hanging up on ye now."

"Wait! At least tell me that ye call her 'Your Majesty' when ye—"

I ended the call, my grin spreading.

A new message had come in from Alex while I was talking. My heart thumped as I read her words.

**Alex:** *Thank you for caring. Not many do. Know what I dreamt about last night? Getting the hell out of this city with a certain pilot flying me away.*

**Raphael:** *Would if I could.*

Wasn't that a promise I wished I could keep?

The venue for the evening was a concert hall, some annual charity gala named after a long-dead queen that the great and good attended en masse. I had less interest in the event and a whole lot more in the scale of it. A crowd had formed outside with photographers jostling for position, waiting presumably to spot celebrities who exited a line of cars to a riot of camera flashes.

Our convoy cruised into the queue. As planned, the bodyguard crew exited first to take positions, ready for Alex's moment. My gut tightened with anticipation and adrenaline. Our actions were well rehearsed. We'd analysed the risks and planned well.

None of that eased my spike of intuition that something would go wrong.

Alex's car reached the end of the red carpet, and the princess stepped out. Blinding white lights flickered, and she pasted on a natural smile, posing for a beat with us giving her space so the photographers could get their shots.

With a hand raised to shield my eyes, I scanned the surroundings, my heart thumping. All the fucking lights made it hard to see individuals in the crowd. Anyone could be there. Relief followed fast when Riss gave the signal to close in and get our principal inside.

We jogged up the steps with Alex in the centre of our huddle and entered the wide foyer through tight security, melting to the background while she was greeted by friends and acquaintances. I watched on as she air kissed women in expensive dresses and with what looked like priceless jewels at their throats. I heard her use titles instead of names, and I gritted my teeth when a man kept his hand on her shoulder for a minute too long, only remembering to breathe when Alex laughed with him and pressed up on her toes to whisper something in his ear.

In the centre of her group, she moved up through the theatre building to the box where she would watch the performance.

These were her people, I realised. The attendees were of the same social standing, with their wealth signalled in their fineries and their confidence. Alex had genuine smiles for many, making a point to linger and chat.

There was nothing of the scared girl who'd flown into my arms or the version of her that jumped in a lake. She was in work mode, and I couldn't relate to her. At all. I couldn't imagine being like Dori would've, in a tux at her side, only behind her, watching out for her.

Fuck. Why the hell had my mind gone there?

I needed to centre myself in my role. The concert began with a blare of live music, and all eyes faced forwards.

I tapped my earpiece. "Riss, permission to scope the crowd out front again."

"Granted. Johnnie, go with him."

Alex was safe enough here. I needed to make sure she stayed that way.

I descended the plush stairs, Johnnie a few steps behind. Outside, I prowled the crowd that lingered despite the doors being closed, and making a note of the photographers I recognised. None were Malcolm Dennis, the paparazzo who'd haunted Alex. He had to be here somewhere. There was no way a guy whose main deal was taking shots of beautiful young celebrities would miss an event of this size.

As I searched, my phone buzzed with a message from the princess.

*Alex: I did it! Will is set up to think I'm going to a friend's place.*

*Raphael: Good work. By the way, you were right about Dori. He's in Milan.*

She started typing but stopped, and no reply came

through.

I continued my hunt. Johnnie stayed with me, going through the motions, though I was certain he did it without caring. Once we'd left the crowd to circle the building, he sparked up a cigarette and strolled the alleyway behind me.

"What peril are you expecting down here?" He breathed out a plume of smoke. "The stray cats in the bins looking at you wrong?"

"I'm doing my job."

He released a laugh. "Not for much longer. You're out of here after tonight. I heard Riss tell the big boss."

Shame heated my cheeks. If Barrington knew, Ben probably would by now, too. I'd held out a small hope that I could persuade Riss to change her mind after the gala. But if she'd already set wheels in motion, I had no hope.

Johnnie took another drag of his cigarette. "I feel bad for you, kid. All this constant hassle about danger around every corner has to be exhausting."

"Why wouldn't ye worry? It's what we're paid to do."

"You're young. You've been doing this job all of five minutes. When you're in my shoes, you'll see how badly off your perspective is."

"Is your age the reason you don't give a fuck anymore?" I shouldn't bite back, but the emotions of the night were already high, and he was pissing me off.

"If the first time you see a gun is at the airport on a lads' holiday to Ibiza, then suddenly you think you can be a bodyguard, then yeah, I'll call my age an advantage. Seen and done it all."

Ah, fuck him. "At age seven, I could dismantle a revolver and put it back together with my eyes closed. I'd witnessed more bloodshed and threat before my tenth birthday than you've probably seen in your life. I know scare tactics. I learned them at the hands of men who would make the worst of us shake. Don't think ye know me."

His cigarette hung on his lips, my words making an impact I wished they hadn't. I shouldn't have shared shite, but it was out there now. Johnnie recovered fast and jabbed a finger in my direction.

"Whatever shady background you crawled out of hasn't helped you understand how the game works. The public needs pictures of the princess. The royal family need them to be taken so they stay relevant and in the headlines. She's good at that. All this danger you see is just people doing their jobs. Stop stressing about the photographers when actually, we want them around, and they aren't about to hurt her. Do you get me? If you learn one thing from this job, let it be that."

"What if you're wrong?" I bit back.

Riss spoke over the comms. "The first interval is in ten. On our principal, please."

Johnnie led the way, clearly glad to be going back inside. I followed more slowly, lingering on his words. His attitude was a danger in itself. His challenge about what Alex's role was here didn't resonate with how she saw it. The temporary nature, at least.

My train of thought was interrupted when I passed the theatre's bar. There were few patrons inside, the performance still ongoing, and a group of waiters in black and red ferried trays in and out of the bar room.

One man had his head down, but the shape of him gave me pause. He was familiar.

At my back, a rush of noise came. I glanced around. The interval had started, and hundreds of people were on the move at once.

When I twisted back, the rogue waiter was gone.

Certainty rippled through me, and I was moving. It was Malcolm Dennis. Here, and in disguise. What the fuck was the man doing? He could have bought a ticket as a patron, like he had at the football match. Why would he need to pretend to serve drinks?

A number of reasons crammed into my brain, none of them good. Johnnie had said the paparazzi wouldn't hurt Alex, but there were a hundred different ways they could.

I tore up the stairs, an influx of people coming the other way and blocking my path.

With urgency, I jabbed my earpiece. "Riss, keep eyes on Penny. Don't let her accept a drink."

Her voice returned, faint over the noise of the crowd. "Repeat that."

"Don't let Penny Allen drink anything."

Her reply was lost in a wall of sound. Scrambling through, I made it to the first landing where queues for the bathrooms and for the concessions booth blocked flows of people going either way. Pushing my way through earned me scowls, but I didn't stop. Not until I was on the next more narrow staircase that led through the creaking theatre to the royal box.

Bursting in, I found no one but Will. "Where is she?"

He tilted his head across to the box next to ours.

In the midst of her group of friends, Alex held a wine glass to her lips and took a sip.

"Stop," I yelled.

The boxes were designed for exclusivity over security, with unobstructed views out across the theatre, and high above the rows of people in the stalls below. Leaving by the door and jogging down the hall to the next theatre box would take too long, so with no thought in my head but her, I stormed to the gilded ledge and climbed onto it, stepping over the gap to the opposite ledge.

Horrified stares followed my action, and someone shrieked.

Alex covered her mouth in shock. I jumped down and snatched the glass from her hand.

"Ye can't drink this."

Riss appeared at my shoulder. "What the hell are you doing?"

I kept my gaze on Alex. "Who gave ye that drink?"

Her beautiful brown eyes widened. "A waiter appeared with it a second ago."

"Red and black uniform, cap low over his face?"

"I think so? I wasn't paying attention."

I held it up. "Was that all ye drank? One sip?"

"Raphael, this is out of line," Riss snapped.

At Alex's small nod, I handed the glass to Riss. "Malcolm Dennis is disguised as a waiter. Call the police. That wine needs to be tested."

Her mouth fell open. "Surely not."

My last tether of patience strained to break. In the middle of a dangerous situation, I was yet again being denied. "Do I need to repeat myself or are ye going to take action at last? The photographer we talked about is here and pretending to be a waiter. Your principal is not safe."

Her gaze darted to the door then to the worried faces of the dignitaries and others gathered around us who stared at my theatrics. I had no thought to spare for them.

Alex touched my arm. "What would he do to my drink?"

She believed me. Thank fuck for that. I wanted to pull

her into my arms, but I couldn't. "I don't know. I only know that he's here. Did ye even order that?"

"No. It just appeared." She swallowed, and her gaze left me to find Riss. "I want to leave."

"Ma'am, I really don't think we should jump to conclusions on the hunch of Mr Gordonson—"

Alex held up a hand, her lips in a firm line. "I do."

My temper snapped. "Order the fucking cars."

I was done with this. If I hadn't been fired, this night would have been my last. I couldn't stand by and watch as Alex was exposed to risk over and over again. It broke something inside me.

While Riss reluctantly organised our exit, a stony-faced Will and Johnnie fell in, and I kept at Alex's side, fighting to hide what I was feeling. She'd turned ashen and kept tucked against me. When we hit the foyer and were about to descend the steps, I put space between us, mindful of the waiting cameras.

"Stay with me," she whispered.

"Always."

We jogged down the steps and dove into the waiting car. I slammed the door behind us, not waiting for Riss who could take a different ride.

Only when we were inside did a tiny fraction of my panic ease. I palmed Alex's cheek. "Hospital?"

She took a shuddering breath. "I don't think he'd poison me."

I'd reached the same conclusion. Nothing made better and more sellable shots than a drunk princess causing a ruckus at a formal event, which indicated a party drug or something to lower her inhibitions. But it wasn't my call to make.

I brushed her hair back. "Whatever ye want to do, I'm yours."

Emotion passed over her face. "Take me home. I'll decide when we're there."

# 21

# Alexandra

Our return trip to the palace was short, but the urgency inside me made it feel unending. Raphael coaxed me to drink water from the stash we always had in the cars and checked on any symptoms.

I felt nothing other than upset. Maybe a little foolish. If I'd gone to a club with Dori, I would never have accepted a drink I hadn't ordered. But a waiter handing me one in a situation where that was the norm? I'd never even suspected it.

If I'd drunk deeply, I could be in the grip of a drug right now. Raphael had saved me from that.

Finally through Ossington Palace's gates, Raphael leapt from the car, helping me out.

Riss was already waiting. "Ma'am, I'll escort you inside."

I couldn't do this. If anyone else spoke to me, I'd probably burst into tears.

"No, thank you. Wait for me in your office. See me upstairs?" I added the last part for Raphael.

He gave a curt nod, moving with me through the palace and upstairs. I slammed and locked the door behind us, my emotions boiling over.

"I'm done with this. I'm just…done. A man likely spiked my drink tonight. Why would he do that?"

Raphael parked himself against a wall, his jaw tight. "For a picture."

God. Of course.

I released a breath that was somewhere between a gasp and a sob. Plenty of times, I'd given them that kind of photo opportunity for free. I'd fallen out of taxis, sang while arm in arm with friends as we left a club. Hadn't I given enough?

Raphael's phone buzzed. He glanced at it. "It's Riss. I turned off my comms."

My shoulders sagged. I gestured for him to answer.

He did, listening to his boss. "I'll tell her." He hung up and eyed me. "The palace doctor has been summoned and will be here in fifteen minutes. The police are also on their way."

I managed a small nod.

Raphael dropped his head back against the wall. "What do ye want to do? Because all that's in my head right now is tracking down that bastard so he can never do anything like that again. I also don't want to leave ye. Ye should also know that if I walk out of here, I willnae be able to come back."

"Why?"

"I was fired again this evening. That makes three times. I'm out."

No, no! The one thing I was certain about was how I wanted to be close to him. Even if just for a little while longer. Raphael equalled safety.

"Just tell me what ye need," he asked.

I swallowed my panic. "To get out of here. But I won't be able to. Not if the police are coming. Then palace security will need their piece of me, Sir Reginald, the list is endless."

Raphael's eyes gleamed. "You're telling me that a determined and sneaky princess can't find her way out of a palace with two dozen exits then make a run for it through the city?"

My pulse stuttered.

His next words were the death blow to staying. "I'll get ye wherever ye need to go."

I was already in motion.

In my bedroom, I snatched up my overnight bag and grabbed handfuls of clothes and essentials, Raphael taking over packing duty so I could move quicker. Without thinking, I picked up my sleep shirt, his t-shirt, gifted to me all those years ago, but bundled it quickly into a hoodie and shoved them in the bag, my heart racing.

When I had all I needed, I stood in the middle of the rug. "I need to get out of this gown."

"Not the way I pictured undressing ye, princess."

My cheeks heated, but he was already behind me, and with warm fingers, he unzipped me. A shiver ran down my spine. Raphael grumbled and went to the door. I shot him a grin, excitement hurrying me on.

Out of the dress, I hung it next to the cream one I was supposed to be wearing on the weekend. That banquet had given me nightmares. Now I was leaving, I'd never wear the damn thing. I stuck up my middle finger to the gown, tugged on shorts and a t-shirt, and fitted my favourite short, blonde wig.

In the living room, Raphael shouldered my bag, his eyes darkening as he took me in. "I've left my radio and ID here. Riss has tried calling me twice. We need to go now before she comes knocking. We probably don't have long."

Riss couldn't keep me here. Nobody could. I was a woman grown. But the night would get chewed up with meetings and conversations, and if Sir Reginald put in an appearance, I'd never get away.

Glee chased the last of my upset away. "Let's do this thing."

At the door, Raphael paused to check the coast was clear. In this corner of the palace, I was at the end of the corridor, which meant only one way to go.

"We're good," he whispered.

Without looking, he reached for my hand. My stomach did a funny flip when I laced my fingers with his.

Together, we padded down the hall's thick carpet. The first staircase, the one I'd given Raphael access to, led down to the exit by the bodyguard office. That wouldn't work.

I squeezed his hand. "If we keep going, there's another around the corner, or at least three more further on."

Raphael gave a single nod then stilled, listening. Abruptly, he tugged me against his body and spun to the next doorway, twisting the handle in a fast move that left me breathless. I blinked, and we were inside a darkened bedroom, the door open just a crack.

Still clutching Raphael, I didn't have to ask what happened as sounds from the stairwell clued me in. Riss appeared, talking to someone I couldn't see. Their voices grew louder as they entered the hall.

"Go right, it's the door at the end," she instructed.

Had to be the police as the doctor who came to the palace regularly knew my rooms. If we hadn't hustled, they would've spotted us.

Their noises moved away.

Raphael peered out then glanced at me to mouth, "Okay?"

"This isn't the way I pictured being in a dark bedroom with you."

His expression of surprise at me throwing his words back had me grinning bigger.

We snuck out and crept in the opposite direction. The curve of the corridor hid the others from sight, and I was glad because another look at Riss and I probably would've wanted to talk. She'd been kind to me, but after the last two times of asking her to cut visits short and getting disapproval, something had changed.

At the main flight down, the wide staircase was empty, but a tilt of Raphael's head said to keep going. I agreed. It would be too risky to pop up in the central entrance.

We trotted down a more narrow set of steps at the far end of the palace, pausing to be sure we weren't about to get busted. It had taken long minutes to get this far. Enough for Riss to realise I wasn't inside my flat.

The bottom of the stairs opened onto a ground-floor exit, visible through a porthole in the door. A guarded car park was on the other side, and beyond that, the road and freedom.

I peeked up at Raphael. He'd never let go of my hand. "We can leave this way, but if the guards on the gate recognise me, they might stop me."

"They can't keep ye here."

"They could delay opening the gate if they've been told to look out for me. If Riss is summoned and brings the police with her, I'll have to stop. I don't want to."

Something in his gaze shifted from calculating to a decision. "I'll go out alone. The second the gate is open, I'll stand in it and ye run."

I pushed up on my toes and did what I'd wanted to do all evening. I kissed him, claiming the lips of the man who'd protected and cared about me more than I deserved. I half expected to be pushed away, but Raphael took over. He groaned in need and drove his fingers into my hair to hold my head. Passion exploded through me, hot and needy. Enough to make me want to slide to my knees in the very place I had to run from.

It was short-lived. He broke away, that talented mouth curved in a delicious grin. With one more glance through the round window, Raphael was gone.

I watched him, breathless and ready. He strode out into the night and approached the booth with my bag over one shoulder, raising a hand to hail the guards. They must have said something back as he replied, his smile still in place but fixed now. They weren't opening the gate. Why?

Panic swirled in my belly. If Riss sent out an alert to find me, this was all over.

Raphael patted his chest, like he was searching for something. His pass? He'd left it upstairs.

My heart sank. I'd have to walk out there and demand they let me leave. It might work, it might not. If I failed, it meant the banquet and the speech. It meant not seeing Raphael because the one person I trusted wouldn't be here.

Then miracles happened. The gate shivered then cranked open slowly. Raphael stepped into the gap.

I sucked in a breath and didn't hesitate. Diving out of the door, I sprinted to him, spotting an expression of surprise on the face of the nearest guard. That was all the attention I'd give him. I caught Raphael's hand in mine and ran.

Away from the palace. Away from duty I hadn't asked for.

"Stop," a voice chased us.

We didn't. Not for a second.

When we were streets away, Raphael finally slowed and snatched out his phone. "I'm ordering us a cab. Ye can hide in it while I get my things from my room."

I blinked. "You're leaving, too. It didn't occur to me that meant right away."

He shrugged, stepping into the road so I could stay on the pavement as we passed a couple who were staggering along, clearly drunk. The London streets were as busy as always, and it was barely ten in the evening.

"I was going to head home tonight, but where ye go, I go."

The giddiness in my stomach returned in full force. "You don't have to. You don't work for me now."

His lips curved. "Fully aware. Just tell me where to take ye."

I needed to pick a location. "Home, I guess."

"Scotland?"

I nodded. Dad's house was where I'd spent summer holidays and Christmases, though it never felt like a place of my own.

"Then we're going the same way." He dug his fingers into his hair and raked it back. "Ah fuck. I've had the best idea. Dream come true."

"What is?"

Happiness radiated off him. "How do ye feel about watching me fly?" Whatever expression was on my face made him laugh. "Seems I get ye as my passenger after all."

Half an hour later, we were in a taxi and heading through

central London. Raphael had taken mere minutes to clear his room at the bodyguard accommodation, luckily finding the place empty so avoiding awkward questions.

He'd rung ahead to book a helicopter, and by the time we reached a riverside transport hub with a helipad on the banks of the Thames, one was on its way.

We left the car and entered the building, Raphael talking to a waiting staff member while I drifted to stare from the windows. The city sparkled around us. I trusted Raphael completely.

He came to me. "I have to file a flight plan before the heli gets here. I'll need an address, and ye might want to warn anyone in the house that we'll land in their garden in the wee small hours, assuming that's possible."

I grimaced, imagining the ruckus and second-guessing my excitement. "Can you give me a minute?"

He nodded. I dialled my dad.

The call went straight to voicemail, so I called the landline instead.

"Lancaster House, Perkins speaking. Your Royal Highness, how may I help?"

Perkins was my father's butler and a kind man. "Hi, Perkins, sorry for calling so late. Is Dad asleep?"

"He is indeed, ma'am. I'm afraid he's had a couple of tricky days. Is the matter urgent?"

"What's happened with him?"

"We believe just a cold, but it has tired him out. His sleep has been affected. Nothing to worry about."

Which meant he'd told them not to inform me. I was the worst daughter alive for not contacting him for days. Another fact solidified—we couldn't wake him with the drama of a helicopter landing on his lawn.

With a promise to call my father tomorrow, I got off the phone, twisting it in my hands. I turned back to Raphael. "Change of plan. Dad's unwell. I don't want to disturb him. Even if we landed a mile away, he's a light sleeper and he'll know I'm home."

Disappointment drove over my dreams of escape and squashed them flat. I had friends I could call, but no one all that close. Not anymore. Only Dori would throw open his doors no questions asked, but he was still missing.

Silence played out between Raphael and me. The airfield operative down the room did a great job of looking busy at a tablet screen.

"I think I'll have to go back—" I started.

"Come home with me."

"W-what?"

"I live an hour away from your home. Stay the night at mine and I'll drive ye there tomorrow." His cheeks reddened in the warm office light. "I mean as friends. I wasn't suggesting anything else. Just a place to stay so we don't wake your da. Let me take care of ye."

My breathing stuttered. "The picture you painted, the loch, the mountains, a hideaway, that's where you mean?"

"Aye, it is." Something shifted in his expression. "Say yes, or do I need to kidnap Her Royal Highness to get to keep ye for a little longer?"

I'd never wanted anything more.

"One hundred percent yes."

Raphael exhaled in relief then shifted to action mode. He filed his flight plan then left a voice message for Riss, drop calling her first to chew up the line, then telling her exactly what he saw in quick, succinct sentences.

I did the same, keeping my focus on the view outside the

window to control my nerves. Then at Raphael's request, I switched off my phone. A helicopter landed, rattling the glass. Raphael strode out to greet the pilot then came back for me.

Him reaching for my hand in quiet enquiry would never get old.

We lifted off and sped over the city I'd escaped. It was under two hours' flight time, and I was consigned to the back seat, a requirement of the hire being the other pilot, whose name was Colin, copiloting so he could return with the craft the same night.

I watched Raphael at the controls, performing his checks then flying us with a steady hand. In the low light, I curled up on the seat and just stared. Helicopter flight wasn't new to me; my father used to prefer it, when he'd worked, as it was so much faster than driving or the train. But another part of the evening was entirely novel.

The sensation in the centre of my chest when I caught Raphael glancing back at me. The way I couldn't stop tracing his jaw with my gaze, and the happiness in my soul each time he smiled.

I was in trouble. Not only from rogue photographers who wanted me acting up for their lens, or for fleeing the palace rather than facing the authorities, but because of something else strange and unexpected.

A dangerously warm and generous spark that I didn't even try to stop from catching aflame in my heart.

# 22

## Raphael

At the rumble of gravel under my wheels, Alex stirred. It was after two in the morning, and we'd finally made it home having left the heli at Inverness airport, returning to where I'd left my car, rather than flying all the way home. It meant a drive from there to the McRae estate, but I'd need the car to transport her across the Highlands tomorrow, so I'd told her to close her eyes and sleep. My worries over her being drugged had faded. She'd shown no effects. Getting to her in time had worked, thank fuck.

Tiredness had nothing on me. Throughout the dark drive, I'd buzzed with adrenaline and a deep sense of rightness at what I'd done. At Alex coming home with me to where I could guarantee her safety because I'd be right there with her in my territory, my people around us.

She stretched in my passenger seat and peered out at the towering stone walls of Castle Braithar. "You live here?"

"For the past few months. I used to share an apartment with my sister until she shacked up with my best friend. I gave them space and accepted the spare rooms here.

Gordain owns the castle. He likes to have a bodyguard on-site."

"Gordain. He owns the bodyguard service, doesn't he? You said he set up the team to guard his son-in-law."

"Aye. Well remembered."

"Then this is where the rock star lives?"

I rolled my eyes at her. "Don't tell me you're a fan of Leo's. I'll have to kick ye out."

She giggled. "I don't fangirl over anyone. I was just wondering about showing up unannounced."

"It's late. I'll introduce ye to the family in the morning."

When Alex's curious gaze turned into a nod, I jumped from the car and rounded to open her door, offering her a hand to climb out. Then I grabbed our bags and took the princess home.

My rooms in the castle were hidden away at the back, off a corridor that was rarely used by anyone other than me. I let us in, bracing myself at the strange reality of being here with Alex, then showed her into the big room that was both my bedroom and living space.

Through her eyes, I saw the two-seater sofa and coffee table to the right, and the king-sized bed to the left. On the far wall, a counter ran the length with an office chair scooted up to it and stacks of books and other personal possessions on top. I hadn't personalised it since Valentine had moved out.

I snapped on a lamp. "Make yourself at home. It isn't much, but it's private, and you're safe here."

She slipped off her sandals by the door, her focus skipping over my world condensed down to this space. "You brought me home to a castle. I bet that impresses all the girls."

I entered the bathroom and pulled the light cord. "I wouldn't know. Go ahead and take the first shower. I'll grab a blanket and pillows for the sofa."

She gave me a small smile, took her bag into the bathroom, and closed the door.

For a beat, I stood in the centre of the room, reeling with all that had happened in the past few hours. Getting fired, spotting the photographer, then escaping the palace. I was running on empty. In desperate need of sleep. Yet I still felt as much on edge as ever.

I got to work making myself a bed on the couch. Bringing Alex here was an act of friendship, nothing else. Tomorrow, she'd go home, and I'd have no reason to be around her anymore. I got stuck on trying to persuade myself that we could be friends. We couldn't. An ache formed in my chest at the thought of letting her go. I just needed my body to catch up with what my brain already knew.

Alex emerged from the bathroom in a hoodie and silky shorts. I swallowed then closed myself away to take the world's fastest shower. I'd killed the water and was towelling off when voices filtered through from the bedroom.

"Welcome to our home, Your Royal Highness."

"It's Alex, please. You must be Gordain. Who's this little guy?"

*Shite.* I scrubbed the water from my skin and tugged on a pair of basketball shorts, opening the bathroom door with a t-shirt half over my head.

Across the room, Alex stood in the doorway, grinning, and with Gordain's grandson's tiny hand in hers in a mini handshake.

Gordain's eyes met mine over Alex's head. "I didn't mean to intrude. This one's teething again and keeping his parents up. I saw your car so figured you'd come home and decided to check in on ye." A grin stole over his face. "Didnae realise you'd brought a lass."

"This isn't a regular occurrence?" Alex kept her gaze light.

Gordain snorted. "With this one? Never."

I sighed, because he wasn't going to let me live this down, and swooped in on Torran. "You've already done introductions. C'mere, Tor. Meet royalty."

I swiped the bairn from his grandfather's tattooed arms. Gordain was as fit and healthy as any of us, despite being in his sixties and a man I respected as a father figure.

I hoisted the little boy in the air so he giggled, and we sketched a bow to Alex. She laughed, and Torran flapped his arms. Both he and his older brother, Finn, were our principals, protected along with their parents, and that meant each of us spent one-on-one time with the kids so they knew and trusted us.

"I've naw seen ye in a while, and here ye are, popping out new teeth." I frowned at the bairn. "But what's this about keeping everyone awake? That's no good."

Torran released a string of baby babble, some of his sounds close to actual words but not there yet.

I twisted back to find Alex's gaze on me, her cheeks flushed pink.

She turned to Gordain. "I'm really sorry to show up unannounced."

"Nae bother. You're welcome here. I'm sorry again for the interruption, though I've got to say it was a surprise when a princess opened the door." His mouth fell open in a delighted smirk, and he regarded me. "Trust Raphael to keep me guessing. Give me back the bairn and I'll leave ye in peace."

I guided Alex away from the door. "No can do. We're keeping him. See ye."

I shut Gordain mostly out, and Torran gave a sweet little laugh, peeking through the gap at his granddad. Then he yawned, and I relented, opening it back up to return him. "Think he's tired now."

Gordain accepted him. "Then I'm glad I came down. Night, folks." He gave me one last searching look that told me everything about how he worried for me and whatever the hell I was doing, then left us.

I locked the door. Put my back to it. "I'm sorry about that. I should've messaged him."

"It's okay. Gordain seems lovely, and seeing you with a baby was—" She mimed mind blowing.

"He's like a father to me. Or better. He'd taught me what a father should be. I told ye what my actual dad is like."

Alex perched on the bed and unwound her hair from the complicated updo she'd worn to the gala. Her make-up was gone now, too, and by degrees, she changed from public person to herself.

My stare only intensified when she stripped the hoodie over her head.

She patted the mattress. "Come here."

I couldn't. I was trapped between two opposing forces: wanting her so badly I could hardly breathe, and needing to give her a safe space with no expectation.

"After the night you've had…" I began.

She chuffed an unfunny laugh then reached for her hoodie pocket, extracting a scrap of white lace. "This was hanging on your shower door."

It was the mask she'd worn in Hell. The one I'd used to get myself off to thoughts of her. Heat flooded me.

"I'm not going to ask why it was in there, but I am going to do this."

Alex pushed up on her knees and took the hem of her t-shirt. Without hesitation, she stripped it over her head, discarding it to allow me to stare at her perfect, stunning body.

Ah, Christ.

That wave of heat crashed over and drowned me. In a heartbeat, I knew a truth, that if I did anything more with her, there would be no going back. I couldn't sleep with her and stay sane.

I was fucked. I always had been with this lass.

# 23

# Alexandra

*I* tossed the lace mask and steadied my shaking hand to beckon Raphael. "Don't make me ask twice."

He braced himself against the wall, his gaze glued to my breasts in a way that had me sit taller on his bed. Arch my spine to give him a better view. I was in love with how his chest rose and fell on a heavy breath. Enamoured with the instant tent in his shorts.

His focus returned to my eyes. "Fuck it. Let me make ye feel good."

He released the tight hold he had on himself and crossed the room, kneeling on the mattress to slide an arm around me. His lips took mine, and I melted back onto the sheets with a whimper of need.

At last. I'd wanted this so badly I could cry. His warm fingers on my skin. His lips parting mine so he could taste me. It had been a night of endless drama, and the excitement in leaving had been wrapped up in the man I'd escaped with. I craved Raphael. Needed to feel him all over me.

He needed to touch me, too. I knew from how his hand splayed across my back when our kiss turned hot and heavy. He groaned, and something deep inside me liquefied.

Somehow, we worked together so well. We met and clashed and took in a perfect rhythm that skyrocketed my spiralling need to the point of insanity.

I had to know he wanted me just as much. I reached between us.

Raphael caught my wrist and extended my arm above my head, snatching up the other to do the same so he had both in a light but firm hold against the pillows.

Desperation burned through me. "Don't say I can't touch you."

His focus slid down my exposed skin. "No, princess. This is all about ye. Christ, your body is incredible."

"Please. At least let me see you. Take off your shirt."

Surprise registered in his eyes, but he blinked it away. "Keep your hands there and I will."

I nodded feverishly, and he sat back to strip his t-shirt, dropping it to the floor. Broad shoulders and strong arms filled my vision, while he laid a hungry kiss on my cheek.

"You're still bleeding, aye?"

My mouth fell open. I was on the last day of my period and had a tampon in. I'd forgotten. He hadn't. With a groan of embarrassment, I hid my face.

Raphael caught my hands again. "What did I say about keeping these above your head?"

"But I'm…"

"I'll stay clear of the danger zone."

My surprised laugh changed into a sound of desire as he caught my lips again, one big palm sliding up my rib cage to touch my breasts. *Finally.*

He cupped and moulded me, breaking the kiss to move down my body. If I wasn't imagining things, his hands shook. It only made me burn more for him, my skin electric and my nipples hard. When he encased one in his lips, a burst of relief rocked me. He sucked on me, and I nearly died, my pulse skipping.

"So fucking perfect," he muttered to my chest.

His hand on my thigh eased toward the hem of the small pair of sleep shorts I'd picked out for the warm evening. My knees fell open to give him access. I didn't know what it was about this man. How he had a hotwired path to my central nervous system. But it was real and vivid, and each new place his hands or lips touched drove me that much closer to the edge.

Maybe it was the control he kept over himself. Even now, even with my nipple in his mouth and his fingertips moving to my inner thigh, he was holding back.

I wanted him to break. To fall into the mess of need I was in.

He brushed over my clit through my sleep shorts, and I jerked at the deep pulse of pleasure. Raphael released my breast with a wet pop and sat back, a question in his eyes, and a hand at my waistband.

"Don't you dare stop," I ordered.

"Yes, ma'am."

His smirk turned devilish, and he brought his mouth to mine at the same moment his fingers eased into my last remaining item of clothing, right where I needed them to be. He skimmed over the apex of my thighs as if learning my shape, then cupped me between the legs.

I could have cried in relief. I bucked my hips, and he relented to press a delicious circle into my clit. God, yes, this. Raphael repeated the action. He wound me up in tantalising touches, all the while kissing me with the same dedication I'd seen in how he'd guarded me.

His free hand squeezed my hip then skimmed my waist to work my breasts again. All I knew was him. Every place on my body he touched. All the ways in which he gave me this incredible feeling.

Stretched out under him, I caught alight, an orgasm closing in fast, and moved my hips to chase it against his hand. The steadfast man kept the same pace, delivering exactly what I needed far faster than I believed possible.

It hit me like a wrecking ball, slamming into me so hard I nearly blacked out. I couldn't recall the last time someone else had made me come, but this erased every other memory. Every other touch than his.

I cried out, and Raphael swallowed the sound, an echoing groan faintly piercing my heady state and bringing me back to earth while my body sang with absolute joy.

Nothing had ever felt that good. A fast-delivered orgasm at the hands of a man I trusted more than I trusted myself.

"God," I whispered. "You're so good."

Raphael shivered. If I hadn't been paying him all the attention, I could've missed it. but my words had impact.

He liked the praise.

I might have come, but need still rose in me because he'd been left hanging. I clutched him to me, keeping our kiss going, and loving his fresh burst of energy. He wasn't done. He might've said this was all about me, but that didn't mean I couldn't reciprocate.

Pushing up, I tugged him to lie next to me. Then I straddled him. Urgency sparked in Raphael's eyes, and his hands landed on my hips. I was beginning to get obsessed with how he responded to me. At last, I had his strong body under my hands. I grazed my fingertips over those bulky shoulders, loving the feel of his hard muscles.

"You're beautiful," I told him.

Under me, his dick pulsed. His grip on me tightened.

"I've never come so hard." I traced my fingertips down his abs, loving the flat planes of his tensed belly, and even more how his breathing caught and his eyes shuttered closed.

Praise really did work with him.

How had it taken me weeks to notice this?

"I want to return the favour." I watched him for the expected reaction.

Raphael didn't disappoint. He masked his obvious need and shook his head once, his desperation so close to the surface but held back by rigid control. "I said this was all about ye, after ye were almost drugged tonight and scared out of your mind. Taking pleasure from ye would be wrong."

I ran my hands up my body and palmed my breasts, squeezing them. His gaze followed, and desire practically shone from him. Matching urgency built in me.

"You're trying very hard to be honourable, but that isn't what I need right now. I need you with me, feeling what I'm feeling. Be a good boy and let me touch you."

With a rasp of breath, he threw a forearm over his eyes, his hips bucking into me at the same time. "Just kiss me."

That, I could do.

Leaning in, I brought my mouth to his and claimed his lips, taking the lead on a soft kiss. Raphael let me explore but kept his eyes closed. I could spend days kissing him. Letting the shape of his mouth become the centre of my world. This morning, he'd been clean-shaven, but scruff lined his cheeks now, rough against my skin and delicious.

When I tried to grind on him again, he grabbed my hips to hold me firm. It felt more like the lingering evidence of his restraint.

I didn't want him to hold back when it came to me. I couldn't with him. From the start, from our very first dance, he'd turned my head. Weeks of having him guard me had been a slow and gradual turn-on. Everywhere I looked, he filled my vision. I needed him to feel the same.

"I want to make you feel good, too," I whispered. "Nothing's wrong with me. You saved me from that."

He didn't answer, only giving me an infuriating smirk. "Still needy, princess?"

With a burst of power, he rose and flipped me to my back so I landed with a bounce on the mattress, then he was yanking off my sleep shorts and pushing my thighs apart.

His hot mouth landed between my legs.

I cried out, but there was no pause. No second to wonder over the change. Raphael sucked my still-swollen clit into his mouth and flicked me with his tongue. I keened out and fisted the sheets, lost on the sight of him right *there*, worshipping me. It should've been me tasting him, not the other way around, yet I could barely think around the onslaught of pleasure he generated with steady pressure and generous licks and sucks.

He palmed my waist then eased both hands up to squeeze my breasts. I moaned, rewarded when he squeezed my nipples in time with his sucks. Oh God, he was good.

Good at driving me crazy, good at taking the reins.

Incredible at getting me off.

I shouldn't have been ready to come again so easily, yet he anticipated me and drove to that cliff before launching me over it. I climaxed a second time then sobbed and clung to his head, dimly aware of his low chuckle and one last lick that had my legs jerking.

We weren't done. Not by a long chalk. One night with my hot bodyguard, and it was game over, even if tomorrow I would leave.

When the last of my pulses eased up, Raphael crawled up to hug me, burying his face next to mine. Neither of us spoke. Only breathed together as I came down from my delicious high.

I sensed his frustration. Saw it in the tightness of his jaw.

It was clear as day I wasn't allowed to reciprocate with him.

After long minutes, he reached for my shorts, tugging them back up, then snapped the light off, plunging us into darkness. Raphael kissed me, as if the last thing he wanted to know was the taste of my lips.

Exhaustion and deep satisfaction claimed me. I didn't want to leave him tomorrow. Only this made sense in my world of chaos. Yet in his arms, I settled then finally slept.

24

*Raphael*

I hated the morning light. Usually, dawn saw me leaping up and heading out for a run, happy to start my day and to get to work with my crew.

Not today.

At most, I had a couple of hours left of Alex's time. I'd take her home and drive away. Then probably plot ways to see her again, none of which I could do because she was a princess and I was...me.

She rolled over in my arms, blinking up at me so prettily. "Morning."

I wanted to steal a kiss. Then linger in my bed. Picturing that was an exercise in torture.

Forcing myself to move, I faked a smile and disentangled myself from her to climb from the mattress. Space. I needed space. "Sleep okay?"

Alex tracked me as I crossed the room to tug on my jeans. She didn't speak, so I tried again.

"If you're hungry, I can fetch us some breakfast. Or ye can run the gauntlet and meet Gordain's family."

She unfurled her legs and threw back the blanket. "I'd like to meet everyone. If we have time before…"

"Ye leave."

She dropped her gaze. "Yeah, that. I should call my dad."

"Use my phone. I'll go out into the hall."

"No, don't go."

She accepted the device from me and dialled, her eyebrows pinching in. "No answer. He can't still be asleep. He's an early riser, and it's after ten. I'll try the house again."

She called a second number, and a male voice answered this time. Alex greeted him then frowned. "What do you mean Sarah's there? Was he expecting her?" She listened again, and her gaze shot to mine, incredulity in her brown eyes. "Seriously? I mean, I'm glad he's feeling better, but that's a big surprise."

She pinched the bridge of her nose and closed her eyes. "Okay, no problem. If he surfaces, can you please tell him I'll speak to him later? I'll stay out of his way. On that matter, I'll hide out in the summerhouse rather than take my usual room down the hall. Also, if anyone calls for me, can you say I don't want to talk?"

The faint voice of her father's butler or whoever Alex was talking to made it to me. "Very good, ma'am. I'll ensure the summerhouse is ready and ask that no one interrupt your solitude."

She thanked him, hung up, and gaped at the phone. "Get this. My sick father invited his girlfriend to stay without telling anyone. She arrived this morning, and apparently, he's asked not to be disturbed. He left a message for me saying he's fine. Yeah, sounds that way."

"He has a girlfriend?"

"He's always had girlfriends. This one is a woman he knew from his university days, Sarah d'Farnacee. She was always kind to me when I was little. I like her." She exhaled a short laugh. "He's throwing me over for her."

A rush of hope elbowed its way into my psyche and made a home. "How long does she usually stay?"

"She lives in Portugal with her husband. Yes, she's married. So I can't imagine it would be a short visit. That's why I said I'll stay out of their way and hole up in the summerhouse."

"If he's locked himself away with his lady friend, do ye really want to go there?"

"Not at all."

"Then you're free today."

"I...am."

"Spend it with me." My heart thundered. I'd never wanted anything as much as this. Not for myself. I'd wanted good things for others, often. I worked hard for my pilot's licence and to excel as a bodyguard. But for my heart? I'd never indulged it. It was too risky. But in this moment, the need wasn't mine to own. I was completely in its grip.

Alex's shoulders rose and fell. On my bed, she appeared small. "Won't I be in the way?"

I acted out balling up paper and throwing it away. "That's any plans I had, happily binned off. Tell me, if the week ahead is yours to do as ye want, what does that look like?"

"I suppose I need to tackle what happened in London and with my team. I also want to track down my best friend." Her gaze lifted to mine, something cautious in her eyes. "Top of that list? I like your company."

"I like yours, too." I was first on her list. *First.*

She watched me for a long moment. "You don't have to look after me anymore."

"Then it's your turn to take care of me. It's dangerous around here."

That world-ending smile flickered, returning. "How so?"

It was on the tip of my tongue to say loneliness. She'd been here one night, and the thought of her going away opened up a gaping chasm in my life. One I'd tiptoed around and never acknowledged. I was lonely, even in a house of family, even with the closest of friends. When I closed the door at night, I was alone. For a little while longer, I didn't want to be.

"The dangerous beasts who are going to tease me mercilessly for bringing a princess home."

A beat passed, then Alex's slow smile spread. She was so beautiful my heart ached and ached some more.

"Meeting your friends? I can hardly wait."

Ten minutes on, we were dressed and heading down the corridor to Braithar's interior and into the great hall. Ella crossed the room, a folder of papers in her hand, and her hair frazzled. Like her famous son-in-law, she was a musician and typically distracted by her music.

She smiled briefly at me then stalled, shock registering.

I grinned. "Els, meet Alex. Alex, meet Ella, ma of the house and Gordain's wife."

After a brief chat, where Ella confirmed Gordain was already out somewhere, we continued to the kitchen, finding Viola and Leo at the breakfast bar with their kids.

All fell silent and stared our way, even baby Torran.

Grinning, I again made the introductions and tried not to laugh as the family tried and failed to hide their shock. And to work out how to use Alex's name without some added honorific.

"We've met, actually," Alex told Leo.

The blond-haired rock star blinked and tilted his head. "We have? Oh, wait, I remember. A variety performance?"

"That's the one. My cousin was there, too, so I get why you'd overlook me."

How could anyone not see her, when in any room, she shone?

Leo grimaced. "Shit, sorry."

At the end of the table, seven-year-old Finn picked up a triangle of peanut butter toast and waggled it like it was talking. "Shit, sorry."

Viola growled and poked her husband in the arm. "Quit swearing in front of the kids."

Leo eyed his son. "Like Valentine hasn't taught him a ton of swear words anyway."

"I know, but there's a princess present. Besides, I don't want Torran's first words to be rude ones."

Alex laughed. "My dad swears like a trooper and never moderated his language for me, and he's a prince."

I turned to the second youngest among us. "Finn, what's Val been teaching ye now?"

Finn pursed his lips. He was the sweetest kid. A while back, we'd been supporting Leo on tour, and Valentine had been hurt in the line of duty. Apparently that was the first time Finn had picked up on an adult swearing and decided it was the thing he could do to be grown up.

"If someone does bad driving near us, he calls them a..." He searched for the word.

We all leaned in.

"Fuck nugget."

Everyone cracked up, Viola included. I left Alex at the table to make us breakfast, loving how relaxed she appeared and how easily she got into conversation with the family, picking up a toy Torran threw and making the bairn grin and therefore his parents dote.

I struggled to hold my attention off the lass to cook up bacon for sandwiches.

When we were done, we headed out to my car, the sun high and warming the land.

"I like the people you live with."

"I do, too. Gordain basically adopted Gabe, that's my older brother, then me and Ariel, our sister, when we made the break to get here. His family accepted us just as easily."

None of us had been little kids, but the impact of being around people who actually gave a damn had been a stark change from our violent user of a father.

My heart shrank as a fact made itself clear. I lived under Dad's shadow still, at least partially. I acted in ways that were dictated by what he'd done, and what he still could do. The danger the man presented never left, even if the McRaes opposed that in every way.

Sunlight fell on Alex's loose hair. "Do I get to meet your siblings while I'm here?"

"Maybe. Are ye staying the night again?"

Her flash of a shy smile drove away my gloomier thoughts. We'd reached my car.

"Are you inviting me?"

"If I could, I'd keep ye."

Her cheeks flushed pink, and she ducked inside, hiding her face. "Then yes."

It took everything in me to get in the driver's seat and not just kiss the hell out of her where anyone could see. Inside the cooler interior, I pushed my luck.

"How about a few nights? While the dust settles. If you'd just be hanging out in a summerhouse otherwise, it could be more fun to stay here."

Alex blushed deeper. "I'd feel bad relying on Gordain and Ella's hospitality."

"If that's the only obstacle, I can fix it."

"Then yes, I'd love to."

Didn't that just send my pulse into orbit.

On the road, I left a voice message for my sister. "I'm cooking dinner tonight, either at Gabe and Effie's, or at yours. I'm bringing a guest, so behave."

Alex grinned, her gaze drifting from the gorgeous forest view passing us and back to me. Ariel's reply came in quickly, and I hit to play it so my sister's voice came over the car speakers.

"Oh, I already know. Viola messaged me with a bitch-be-cool warning." A second appeared just as fast. "Also, are you for real? No girlfriend for years then a goddamned princess? Please don't screw this up. The bragging rights are to die for." She laughed. "Though if I know you, you're already head over heels—"

I killed the message and swore.

Alex's grin turned into a giggle. "You can cook?"

"Pride myself on it."

I had to change the subject to save face, but also because with the day spread out before us, I needed to handle the sense of urgency inside me in a way I knew best.

"Quick question, I'm not your bodyguard anymore, so tell me to mind my own business if ye want me out of it, but all the shite we left behind, Riss and the bodyguards, the photographer, the palace, I want to talk to my team and get their take. I tried to do that with Riss and got nowhere, but it's what I know and what works for me. Either way, I need to talk to Ben so he knows I'm back."

"You trust them?"

"With my life."

"Then I trust you. Let's do that first." She took a deep breath. "Plus from all I've heard about Valentine, they're a force to be reckoned with."

She wasn't wrong. I'd set our tracks for the aircraft hangar where I expected my team to be, but when Ben answered the call, he gave another location entirely.

"We have a quiet week. Leo has no meetings and is sticking to the recording studio. I was waiting for ye to come back to start training."

"Where are ye all?"

"Daisy and Mia have a huge house-clearing project on their hands. We're using the downtime to help out. Come to us, and we'll take five for a debrief."

I remembered the cleaning job Daisy was trying to win. I also remembered that she'd asked after me, probably for this reason.

"We'll drive over. Give me the address."

Ben paused. "And by 'we', I assume ye mean yourself and the princess? Explains why Barrington Bray has been blowing up my phone."

"I'll explain everything when we get there."

I hung up, a ping coming in as my boss sent his location, so I turned the car around.

Alex sighed. "I was enjoying trying to forget about the

drama."

I reached for her hand. She laced her fingers through mine.

"One meeting, then we'll forget about it for the rest of the day."

The squeeze of her fingers and the faith she put in me was all I needed to be certain I'd put it all right.

Forty minutes later, we pulled up to the gate of a sizeable house at the edge of a pretty Cairngorms town. Down a long drive, it was surrounded by trees, and private enough that I wasn't going to worry about Alex being spotted. I parked between Ben's and Jackson's vehicles, and a good part of the stress I'd been carrying dissolved. I was a pack animal through and through. I needed my team around me.

Near the front door of the Victorian house was a huge skip, and Jackson and Valentine emerged from the open front door, struggling under the weight of a black bin. They upended it into the skip, the contents clattering down. All around were pieces of furniture in various states of distress and piles of household goods, grouped by type. Glass jars and crockery in a collection, stacks of papers and books.

At our exit from the car, Jackson raised his head and slapped Valentine on the chest in obvious delight. The two jogged over, and I braced myself for hard hugs, thumping each on the back in turn. Then I pushed them away, my grin growing by the minute, and made the introductions to the woman at my side.

"Mia," Val hollered then winced at Alex. "Sorry, but my lass is dying to meet ye."

On the drive over, I'd explained that Mia and Daisy were Valentine's and Ben's better halves, and the two women appeared with Ben close on their heels. While Ben came to me with quiet enquiry in a single raised eyebrow, Alex handled the onslaught of new names and faces well, even complimenting the lasses on their matching blue tabards with *Highland Housekeeping* embroidered on them. The right thing to say.

Daisy preened. "I know it's silly, but this is my little business, and I'm so proud of it."

"No! I love it. You look so smart. Owning your own company is enviable. I've never done anything half so important."

Daisy's eyes widened. "You're a princess," she hissed. Then she clamped her hand to her mouth. "Sorry. You know that. I just mean…"

Mia took pity on her and finished her sentence. "Everything you do is important, right?"

Alex's shoulders sagged. "For other people, maybe."

I side-eyed her, but the moment passed, and Ben fixed me with a stare.

"Debrief, now."

I gave a short nod. "Where can we go that we won't be overheard?"

"Grab a chair and follow me." Ben hoisted up a dining chair from the pile and led us to a shaded patch of the garden, nothing around but shrubs and moss.

With my team gathered, I placed down a seat for Alex and one for myself, looked to her for approval, then at her small but grim smile, launched in. As succinctly as possible, I walked them through all I'd seen and experienced while working on her team. Parts of it they knew, such as the nightclub where she was in disguise yet the paparazzi found her, but other elements I'd only shared with Ben or were new entirely, like her leaked movements in the stadium.

Valentine pointed his hair tie at us, halfway through

pulling his long hair back into a man bun. "Points to inner circle, aye?"

"Got to be." I gave them my lowdown on the other bodyguards. Starting with Jared who'd been fired, then Will, Riss, and lastly, Johnnie.

"Johnnie was pressuring Riss to keep Alex visible and not pull her from events. He also told me last night that Alex's role was for the public to see her, and any antics that caused sensational headlines weren't a bad thing."

Valentine snorted. "On the make, that one. He's parroting someone else."

"That was my guess. What I don't know is who."

Alex raised a hand, speaking for the first time since I'd begun. "What do you mean parroting someone else?"

Ben answered for us. To this point, like Alex, he'd sat and listened. "Any security team worth their salt doesnae give a damn why you're at an event, only for your well-being. We typically clash with organisers and managers who have an opposing objective. They want ye there and visible, we want ye safe."

She followed his explanation. "Then it's Johnnie leaking the information? He's been a bodyguard for a long time, I remember him once saying, so it's not like he's new and getting things wrong."

I nodded agreement. "Probably, but we shouldn't jump to a conclusion yet. And that brings me onto the reason we left London in a hurry last night."

I told them about the photographer disguised as a waiter and how Alex had been delivered a drink she didn't order. The mood shifted across my team, any levity leaving and replaced by a sharper edge.

Jackson looked between us. "That's an escalated tactic.

Work backwards. If we're running with the theory that Johnnie basically confessed to, that you're supposed to be visible and creating headlines, something happened which means they aren't trusting that you'll do it on your own."

Alex paled. "Maybe the fact that my best friend isn't around? Wait, maybe that one of the bodyguards thought I was going to a friend's place after the gala rather than a club?" She hung her head. "Or that I wasn't enjoying the work and wanted to quit? My cousin's private secretary laid it on thick that he needed me picking up the pace or else. I have no clue how I'm going to tackle that."

Without thinking, I reached for her hand, shock stealing over me. "He threatened ye?"

Her gaze clung to mine. "He implied that if I don't step up, my father will have to. Which is ridiculous with how poor his health is."

My thoughts collided, and I brushed my thumb over her knuckles. "That banquet that was stressing ye out, did ye tell anyone that ye didn't want to do it?"

"Sir Reginald. That's the private secretary. I also mentioned it to the two women who came in with my dresses."

Fuck. I shot my gaze to Jackson. The grim set to his lips told me he understood and felt the same.

"What did you just work out?" Alex asked.

"Ye rejected the work then someone followed your steps around the palace, freaking ye out. Ye stopped giving them headlines and they tried to create one."

"You think the private secretary to the king is doing this?"

"What would be his motive? Why does he need ye doing the work in the first place?"

She studied our joined hands. "I don't know specifically.

Other than it's always in the royal family's interest to be in the press."

I forced a soft smile. "Which brings us back to ye creating headlines people love to read. I don't want to jump to conclusions without evidence, but based on probabilities, that feels like a good fit."

I tore my gaze off her to regard my team, Valentine and Jackson both appearing convinced.

Ben studied me and dropped his gaze pointedly to where I still held Alex's hand. "Barrington Bray rang this morning with a demand to talk to ye. I said ye weren't here—at the point of speaking, ye hadn't called so there was no lie. He is adamant that I contact him the moment ye show up."

Alex shivered. "Will you?"

Ben rested his forearms on his knees, his expression one of incredulity. "I don't answer to him. I imagine he's concerned either for your health, and I can see you're fine, or his reputation and his contract, and that's his problem for not managing his team better. However, I get the sense that ye cannae disappear for long without people worrying. Especially not if they are seeking to use ye. That gives us an opportunity."

I sat taller. Ben had a way of pulling together information and creating a plan. I was learning from the best.

"First, we need to put to bed some of these assumptions. By now, the police will have tested the drink served last night. If it was drugged, that shows us the lengths the people behind this are willing to go to."

Alex shivered. "I could call Riss. It means turning my phone back on."

Ben asked, "You've had it switched off?"

"Raphael told me to last night, which I'm glad about or

I'd probably be panicking over missed calls or searching for my name online just to check any headlines."

My boss's lips pursed. "It wasnae for that purpose, I'm sure. Tracking phones is child's play."

She switched her alarmed gaze to me. "You think they'll come after me?"

"Better safe than sorry." I wanted to hug her. Drag her to my side and erase the sadness in her eyes. They'd tried to drug her. Fuck knew what else they'd stoop to.

Jackson pulled out his phone and typed something.

Valentine shook his head. "Don't turn it on. While it's not impossible to track a phone that's off, I'd leave it that way if ye want your peace. We have spare phones. I'll set up a safe one ye can use."

Alex managed a small smile.

"No headlines about the incident," Jackson reported. "Only that ye went to the gala and links to buy knock-off versions of your dress."

She blinked at him. "No one reported the fact I left early? Or the fuss inside the theatre? I don't know if anyone would've overheard, but they definitely witnessed Raphael leap across from the next box to reach me. They would've seen the police turn up, surely?"

Jackson shook his head, though interest shone in his eyes at Alex's reveal of my acrobatics. My best friend slid his phone back into his pocket and tilted his head at me in silent question I knew I'd have to eventually answer.

But my attention needed to remain fully on Alex. "We left in a hurry, and Riss took the wine with us, so the police would've collected it from the palace. At the theatre, I imagine the photographer scarpered, so they might not have carried out a search if they were able to ascertain that, though they would've interviewed staff, surely. Let's find out. I'll speak to Riss. She's rang me several times already this morning so she's obviously desperate."

With Alex's approval and gruff agreement from Ben, I placed the call and put it on loudspeaker.

Riss answered immediately. "Raphael, where the hell have you been?"

"Where do ye expect me to be? I was fired."

"After what happened last night, I need you to be present for the investigation."

"Have the police caught the suspect?"

She clucked her tongue. "I can't answer that. It has been taken out of my hands."

Well fuck. "Who by?"

"If you come back in, you can find out for yourself."

"Not happening. Not when ye and the team think I'm paranoid."

I was winding her in slowly.

There was a pause, then the team leader returned. "You were correct. The wine contained traces of MDMA. That's a party drug. Tell me where Princess Alexandra is."

Every face in our little huddle reacted, Valentine and Jackson grimacing, Ben wincing, and Alex closing her eyes.

I swallowed bile. "Who's taken over the investigation? Someone at the palace?"

"The private secretary to the king. That's how serious this is. He needs the princess back. That's his only priority. Now tell me where she is."

"She told me to take her to her father's."

Riss exhaled a gust of breath. "Thank God. She isn't answering my calls. If you could—"

"I don't work for your team anymore, remember? If she'll speak to me, I'll tell her ye called, but ye let her down. It's too late to be sorry now, and I can't imagine she'd want to chat without there being something worthwhile for her."

A voice sounded in the background, male and angry. "Tell him right now that—"

Alex snatched my phone and hung up. Silence held around us, interrupted only by the chatter of birds in the trees.

She handed it back, pale. "I'm sorry."

"Don't be. I'll take a wild guess at that being Sir Reginald listening in, aye?"

"It was. Then that confirms it. Whoever tried to drug me hasn't been caught, and Sir Reginald, a man who wants me as his puppet, is only interested in tracking me down. Did I get it wrong, or is that what you all heard in that brief conversation?" Alex dropped her face to her palms.

The urge to hold her grew to unbearable proportions.

I fought to stay professional. "You're right. Riss repeated what he's told her to say. Not any update on the paparazzo, but the fact that he needs ye back there."

Opposite us, Ben's expression turned even grimmer. "I suggest lying low for a few days. That will mean calling off the dogs that hunt ye."

Alex nodded without looking up. "Meaning I need to reassure him that I'm out of his reach?"

"Exactly. Text this Sir Reginald and say you're safe but won't be back until the police investigation concludes and the aggressor has been caught. We can operate your phone in a way that it can't be tracked. Then turn it off again so he gets the message that his calls won't get through. I'll talk to Barrington as Raphael's representative and demand he solve the mystery of the leak in the team, as reported to me by the bodyguard I lent to him."

Finally, Alex raised her gaze. "Please say that's enough. I just want to hide."

Ben's eyes showed his determination. "You're the asset. Don't doubt that they'll expose themselves to try to get ye back, and Raphael gave them the opening to do it. All we have to do is sit and wait."

# 25

# *Alexandra*

Thanking Raphael's team, which I immediately trusted far more than my own, I leapt up and stalked to the house, needing to release some of the energy that built up inside me. Thoughts of the palace, and the knowledge that I really had been targeted, had me ragey.

Raphael followed, catching my hand as I stormed up the steps and into...

We both stopped and stared.

The interior of the house was wall-to-wall junk. Piles of boxes, bags, and loose items, with a narrow path carved through.

Daisy stepped down the path with a bulging black bin liner. "Coming through."

We hustled out to let her pass.

She jerked her head at the hall. "Fun, isn't it? That's why I was asking for help. It took a week to get this far inside."

Raphael regarded the sheer magnitude of mess. "This is the afterboob job, right?"

I choked on a laugh. It felt good to think of anything but my situation. "What?"

Daisy tossed the bin liner into the skip and dusted her gloved hands. "The owner of this property is an elderly lady who is in a hospice and very poorly. A hoarder, obviously. She's given permission to her only relative to clear the house, but on the condition that he doesn't throw away a treasure that is somewhere inside."

I hiked up my eyebrows. "What kind of treasure?"

"That's the mystery. She wouldn't tell him. He employed us to tackle the project."

Raphael's hand ghosted over my lower back. "The afterboob reference was a typo in Daisy's email."

Daisy rolled her eyes. "I am never going to get over that. Anyway, I better get back to it. At this rate, it's going to take us weeks."

"Can I help?"

She blinked at me. "I'm sorry, I just hallucinated. Say again?"

"Seriously. I am furious at what I left behind in London. I have energy to burn, and attacking a stack of junk feels like the healthiest way to do it. Put me to work." I swung to Raphael. "Is that okay? Can we stay here for the day?"

I wanted him. I wanted to climb his big body and take out my energy on him in energetic and emotional sex, but I didn't think he'd allow it. Last night, he'd stopped me. He'd lavished attention on me but hadn't let me do the same.

He gifted me a soft smile. "Whatever ye need."

Neither of us were ready for that.

I turned back to Daisy and saw the arguments form in her eyes, but then she registered the certainty in mine and nodded.

"I'd love that. Protective gear is in the back of my car. Masks on inside the house, mandatory. Don't take off your gloves. We have permission to throw everything away but are making efforts to recycle what's salvageable. But the main objective?"

I answered for her. "Find the treasure."

"You've got it."

Raphael ushered me back to the car and helped me find the protective equipment Daisy mandated. When I was kitted out, he glanced around us as if to make sure we had privacy, then bundled me in a hard hug. A fresh burst of emotion sank through me, and I clung on to him. It took a moment to clear, and Raphael just held me.

"I've got half a mind to go back there and track down that arsehole myself."

I inched back to witness the wildness in his eyes. "Please don't leave me."

He brushed his thumb over my cheek. "Okay. I'm all yours."

His gaze locked on mine as if he needed to communicate more than his words. He broke it with a huff of breath. "But there is something I need to go and do. I'll be about an hour. Come with me, or stay here with my team guarding ye while Daisy puts ye to work."

I straightened from the hug and tried to cool myself. "I left my phone in the castle. If you go anywhere near there, could you please grab it and give it to Valentine? He can send the message to Sir Reginald if he doesn't mind. If I turn it on, I'm worried I'll not be able to stop myself from replying to people."

"I'll sort it. Anyone I should look for messages from? Dori, perhaps?"

"Please."

I gave him my passcode, and Raphael escorted me to the door then left me in the hands of Daisy. The blonde business owner directed me into the living room where space had been cleared in the middle, but wall-to-wall possessions crowded in on every side. Cross-legged on the floor, Mia tore off bin liners from a roll.

She handed one to me. "That pile all around the chair is empty food containers. Must've been where the lady ate her dinner. I tried tackling it but kept retching."

I took in the space. "I'm on it. Guts of steel."

Mia's eyes crinkled, and though her mouth was hidden by a white mask, I knew she was grinning. "It's the baby in mine that's objecting."

"You're pregnant? Congratulations!"

"Thank you. It's one of the reasons Valentine isn't straying far from my side. He's doing all the lifting and carrying. I'm being very careful with the dust and gross stuff. Daisy is going to tackle the bathroom and kitchen, when we get to it."

In easy conversation, the three of us got to work. I threw myself into shovelling out food containers by the bag load, throwing them into the skip outside or handing them to Ben or Valentine who were always nearby. Jackson had the task of clearing stacks of books and boxes of paper from the hall then examining them in the light, setting aside anything that he thought Daisy and Mia might need to check in case of treasure status.

I discovered that Ben and Valentine were brothers, though they looked nothing alike, and both Daisy and Mia were getting married soon. They'd had a joint engagement party, organised by their fiancés, and I started to get the sense of the world Raphael lived in.

Not only the clean air and open space, but the good people. The respectful men who worked hard and were dedicated to not just their team but their women, too.

"I was obsessed with your cousin's wedding," Mia told me. "Sorry if I'm talking like I know your family. I just saw it on TV. It was incredible, and their romance was so swoonworthy."

"It was quite the spectacle, and their romance is real. They're the most in-love couple I ever saw." To their twin sighs, I tied off what had to be my fifth bag and dragged it to the door. "It was a long day, though. I was a bridesmaid, which meant being ready with my hair done and gown fitted perfectly by eight a.m. I wasn't allowed to slump in case I creased the dress, only perch on a stool. And eating anything remotely messy was out of the question. I remember being hungry, cold, and desperately wanting to wear a tiara like one of my aunts had from the royal collection."

Turning, I found both women staring at me.

Daisy blinked. "Please tell me you've been able to raid that collection since?"

My mask hid my grin. "Not once. If I'd stayed in London, I mean, I was supposed to host a banquet..." My words dried up so I started again. "One of the royal jewellers would've come to my apartment today with a set for me to try on. A tiara, necklace, and earrings." I wouldn't have had a choice over which. Just another one of the controls Sir Reginald had.

Daisy's eyes were kind. "Why do I get the impression you're better off here?"

"You have no idea." The fact they had no clue why I was a stage-five clinger to Raphael spoke greater volumes over the safety of his team and the information they held.

Mia tilted her head. "Would that be what your wedding is like? All carriages and horses and crowds?"

A shadow appeared in the door. I twisted to find Raphael had returned. Unlike us, he wasn't masked up, so I could see every bit of his frown.

"What's wrong?" I asked.

He shook it off. "Nothing. Message sent. I took the liberty to check Dori hadn't contacted ye."

My heart sank. Through all the running away and delicious hiding I was doing, I still worried about my friend. "Nothing?"

"Sorry."

Daisy stood and stretched. "Coffee break. Good work everyone, especially you, Alex. I can tell you how wonderful, and weird, it is to have the extra pair of hands, but you're really helping."

We headed outside into the fresh air. Raphael snagged Valentine, pulling him over into a huddle.

"New objective," he told his teammate. "The man I asked ye to track down using a passport trace."

Valentine nodded. "Count Ferdinand Dorian Christian Sonderburg. Try saying that drunk."

Despite myself, I laughed. "I call him Dori. Thank you for tracing him."

"You're welcome. Want us to bring him back?"

I blinked, but Raphael was already nodding. "Exactly

what I was going to suggest."

He thought having Dori back would help my sadness. My heart swelled and swelled.

"What have ye tried?" Valentine asked.

I shrugged. "Messaging him, calling him. He's ignoring me. I think he might be hurt over a woman."

Briefly, I gave the background of why I believed Dori went to Italy. "What's north of Milan? Lake Como, where this engagement party was taking place."

"He followed an ex," Valentine surmised.

"Looks that way. I just don't get the obsessive element. He isn't like that. He drops women regardless of if they're hot. He's a loyal friend but doesn't cling to relationships. I've never once in fifteen years of knowing him seen him behave like this."

"Suggesting whatever is going on for him is cataclysmic," Raphael said softly. "People turn their lives upside down when it comes to the one."

Valentine's gaze drifted to where Mia stood at the cars with Daisy. "Aye, they do. Raphael can tell ye about the time I messed up so badly with Mia that I had him fly me across the country to reach her when she needed me. There's no lengths a man won't go to when it's right."

His gaze held Raphael's.

"I just want to help him," I mumbled.

Valentine smirked. "Then let's bring your boy home. Local number trick?"

"Exactly what I was thinking," Raphael agreed.

"Wait, what local number trick?"

Valentine took his phone and opened an app, tapping around in it. "If someone is ghosting ye, dial them from another number. A local one has more chance of being answered, particularly if you're away from home. I can simulate one for central Milan. Ready now?"

My heart thumped. Raphael's hand found mine and held it. I managed a nod and gave him Dori's number.

Valentine called it through his app.

The line clicked, then a sleepy voice answered. "Hello?"

Oh God. It was Dori. He was okay.

For a moment, I couldn't speak. No, more than a moment. My voice dried up completely.

Dori tried again. "Is that the Leonardo? Is there a problem?"

Raphael stared at me then spoke where I couldn't. "Dori, this is Raphael Gordonson, Alex's," he stumbled over the description, "friend."

A pause followed, then Dori swore. "Hot Bodyguard. Fuckkkk."

"Alex is worried about ye."

"She should be. I'm a fucking wreck."

"Let me come get ye. I'll bring ye to her."

Dori swore again, the sounds changing as if he'd gone outside. "Are you in Milan? If so, you've overshot me by a whole country."

"You're in France?" I finally found my voice, my tone coming out as a squawk. "Switzerland? Austria?"

Dori made a sound I'd never heard before. Almost like a sob. Definitely grief. "Darling girl, you're there."

"And worried sick about you."

"I really fucked up this time. Of all the shit I've ever pulled, this was the worst."

"I want to hear all about it. But when we're face to face, and I can see that you're okay. Just tell me where you are."

"Paris," Dori bit out. "With no passport. I can't travel to England."

"That's a good thing because Alex isn't in England," Raphael reported. "I'm going to share my details as a contact, but first, give me the address you're staying at in Paris. We'll fly over and pick ye up."

Dutifully, Dori recited the address of a Parisien hotel. "Do you own a plane, Raphael?"

"Pretty sure that's the first time you've used my name, and no, I pilot helicopters. I'll borrow one to fetch ye."

"The slutty jumpsuit makes sense now, for fuck's sake. By which I mean thank all the angels in Heaven. Alex, can I talk to you in private for a moment?"

I took the phone and moved away, Raphael and Valentine instantly getting into the flight distance to Paris and the logistics of the trip.

"I'm alone," I told my friend.

"I'm guessing Scotland then? I'm happy for you."

"Don't be. Raphael is the one good thing in my life. The rest of it is crumbling to pieces."

"Then we make a matching pair. That isn't what I wanted to say. The king's man has been ringing me. I didn't answer; it's not just you I ghosted, but everyone. I did listen to the last voicemail I got, though. He said I needed to tell him where you were. This was only an hour ago. Darling girl, are you on the run? Did you leave that train wreck of a family behind at last?"

For the first time in what felt like weeks, I took a full and deep breath, the clean Scottish air clearing my brain of the noise that had been building with the pressure my family had piled on me. "I think I have."

"Can't wait to hear all about it. Tell your boyfriend I'm going to sober up. I've been drunk for a week, and travel sickness is a bitch, even in a helicopter. I'll hit the health centre and sweat it out."

"He's not my boyfriend," I said automatically, my gaze on him as he consulted his phone with Valentine and wrote something on a piece of paper.

Dori's drawl of amusement brought me straight back to earth. "Right. Because a man in love wouldn't risk everything, including his pilot's licence, to illegally transport some idiot he barely knows and definitely doesn't like across an ocean, just because a girl wants it. Love you. Hugs soon."

He hung up on me, and I stared at the phone. I had him back, almost, and yet another reason to fall in deep for Raphael.

Yet a small warning played in my head, born from a couple of things he'd said or done, in amongst the hundred others to the contrary. He said he wanted to keep me, if he could, implying it wouldn't be possible, then he hadn't let me reciprocate in bed.

If I was certain of what I felt, of the terrifying, unstoppable want, I needed to get brave enough to ask him the questions that scared me. What about me was making him say no, when more and more, I needed a yes?

# 26

# *Alexandra*

Late afternoon brought an end to the hard work, and Mia and Daisy hugged me, thanking me for all I'd done.

"Come back any time." Daisy slammed the boot of her car, packing away her cleaning goods. "Seriously, you've been amazing."

"Shame we didn't find the treasure."

"There's always tomorrow, and an uncountable amount of personal possessions still to work through." Daisy gazed across the garden, where Raphael, Jackson, and Valentine stood with Ben.

The team leader had been pulled back in to finalise whatever plans they had come up with for Dori. I couldn't wait to hear, and nerves crawled through my belly, not just for my hurting friend, but mainly for Raphael. He was risking a lot. Guilt won out over my emotions.

Daisy continued, "If Raphael is gone most of the day tomorrow, you can come here if you need somewhere to hang out. I don't mean to work. You can just come for the chat."

"I've actually really enjoyed today."

"Really? Want a job?"

I laughed, then Ben claimed her and they left. Raphael returned to me, sweeping his gaze over me in that familiar and reassuring way he did when checking I was okay.

He raised a hand to brush over my cheek, probably rubbing away a smudge of dust on my skin.

"Am I dirty?" I asked.

His lips tipped in a smirk. "You're perfect. Ready to go? We're having dinner with my family tonight, but there's time to change."

The knot in my belly tightened, but I nodded, and we climbed into his car then drove out of the village.

Twisting in my seat, I faced him. "Catch me up on what you've decided for tomorrow."

Raphael tapped the steering wheel. "Ye took the words out of my mouth. For the sake of safety and weather, we're flying out at first light. I've secured a heli, and there's a helipad at Issy-les-Moulineaux in Paris. Should be able to land there. Assuming Dori is waiting for us and we don't need to track him down, we'll head straight back. He's agreed to it all, so I'm hoping it'll be straightforward."

I mangled my fingers together, stuck on the image of Raphael disappearing off across the sea. "Is this dangerous? I don't just mean the flight, but for what you're doing."

He grinned. "You're worried. That's cute. This is what I do for Leo, fly him in and out of cities, bringing him home here. Piece of cake."

His confidence eased some of my concern, but not all. "How long is the flight time?"

"Four hours or so, but we'll need a couple of refuelling stops. Should be home mid-afternoon." He reached for my hand and squeezed it. "The flight planning was a breeze. The bigger issue was who's going with me. Valentine has this irrepressible energy and hates being left behind, particularly as our team is quiet at the moment, but Jackson pulled the best friend card. I think he's unhappy that I've neglected him." He slid a look my way before returning it to the country lane. "I didn't talk to him about ye."

My heart thumped. "You can tell him whatever you like."

His voice returned less sure. "Did ye talk to Dori about me?"

"A little. He called you my boyfriend. I said you weren't."

My whole existence pinned on him correcting me. Or asking the question. The thing between us had happened gradually but surely, and was only growing by the hour. I had no chance of stopping it. I didn't want to.

But Raphael didn't say a word.

His focus was locked on to something ahead, and tension poured off him.

I followed his gaze. Instead of returning to the castle, he'd taken us someplace else, to a pretty hillside where two white cottages overlooked an incredible view. Sunshine spilled over the front gardens where Valentine and Mia climbed out of their car. The door to what must've been their cottage flew open, and a little girl half fell out to reach them for hugs.

Raphael idled the car until they'd gone inside then

cruised on to park outside the next cottage. He killed the engine and turned to me. "I know it isn't a palace, or castle, but I thought the privacy might suit ye better."

I stared from him to the cute building. "We're staying here?"

Colour flushed his cheeks. "If ye want to."

I swung back to take in the building. It was the cutest home, and the view was to die for. I'd been content with the idea of returning to Castle Braithar, mainly because I got to be there with Raphael, but he was right. We had little privacy in someone else's home.

This was...everything.

"I came here earlier to set the place up as much as possible. I installed cameras around the outside. The doors and windows already have decent locks. We only have the basics in terms of furniture, but I stocked the fridge. It'll make a good hideaway."

I'd wondered where he'd gone but figured it was something to do with his job. No. Raphael had yet again been doing something for me. Or for us. The lack of an answer over the boyfriend situation dissolved, replaced by joy.

I pulled back to gaze into his eyes. "You're amazing. I love it."

The corner of his mouth tipped up. "Ye haven't seen inside yet. But even that is going to have to be done in a rush. We need to be at Gabe and Effie's soon."

I was already out the door, on my way to investigate the cottage.

Inside the thick wooden front door, a flagstone floor spanned a generous living room with a kitchen to the left. There was a sofa and a bookcase, and curtains in the windows, plus a wood-burning stove in the corner, the space clean and bright. A short hall held two bedrooms and a new bathroom.

In the main bedroom, I gazed at the big bed, complete with fresh sheets and plump pillows. My bag waited on the bedside table, the only other piece of furniture besides a lamp.

"Like it?"

I twisted around. Raphael leaned against the opposite wall, watching me. The heat in his dark eyes practically scalded me.

"It's perfect. The thick stone walls especially."

In his bedroom last night, I'd been conscious of making too much noise. Castle Braithar was huge, and no doubt with thick stone walls, but I didn't know how close his friends slept or who might wander past the door. Here, we could be as loud as we liked.

His lips curved, but he pushed off the wall and jacked a thumb at the bathroom. "Twenty minutes, princess, then we hit the road again. Don't give me those eyes and make us late. I'm cooking, remember?"

*Right.* Getting my hair and make-up done in that time would be a challenge, but I wasn't going to start without something first. I snagged his hand and stopped him, cupping his neck to bring his mouth to mine for a fast, hard kiss.

Raphael's hand slid into my hair, and he returned the kiss with a passion that gave away how much hid under his controlled surface.

I broke away. "I've never had a place of my own that wasn't just a bedroom. You don't know what this means to me."

Leaving him in my dust, I scrambled to get ready to meet his family. Another first. As far as I was concerned, he could have them all.

Our early evening drive took us through winding roads on the vast estate, and Raphael pointed out houses as we passed, telling me who lived where. There was a real community among the residents, lots of young families, many of them being relatives of Gordain McRae's. Raphael told me how often the locals got together for parties and socials.

"Coming from my background of a broken home and every movement carried out on a public stage, you make me quite jealous," I told him.

We were approaching a new property, clearly modern, but designed to blend into the landscape. He parked up and turned to me. "Most people would assume the opposite about ye. That your life is charmed."

"I should check my privilege, right?"

There was nothing but kindness in his eyes. "That isn't what I mean. Only that I know ye better."

I wanted him to. I wanted to know about him even more.

"I grew up in palaces but with two parents who hated each other and made sure I knew it, then shipped me off to boarding school because that was the done thing for kids like me. My father changed his tune after he was ill, and mourned the wife he'd lost. When drunk, he confesses that he hates the royal family and how it drove Mum away, though he can't really blame it all on the family. He'd cheated on her all throughout their marriage. She did with him as well. Nowadays, I only hear from her if she wants palace gossip, and you know what's happening with my dad."

He watched me in that so engaging way of his. "Then

came me and the university picture which put you in the headlines for all the wrong reasons."

I stared right back, the whole scene shifting in my head. "More and more, I think I got that wrong. I saw it as a curse when it was something else entirely. It brought you into my life."

Another car pulled up alongside ours, Jackson jumping down then rounding to let out a dark-haired woman who had to be Ariel. Our time to talk was over. I hadn't been brave enough to ask Raphael any big questions.

Later, I would.

Inside the oldest Gordonson's home, I was introduced to Raphael's two siblings, and to Effie, Gabe's wife, who was more pregnant than any person I'd ever seen before in my life.

"Almost two weeks overdue," she griped. "And the bairn is an acrobat in the making."

I gave a sympathetic smile. "You're cooking that one up good."

"Which means he or she is going to be huge. I'm so screwed."

She grinned, though it was tinged with a grimace that had her cupping her lower belly while we all moved to the kitchen where Raphael laid out ingredients on the counter. At Effie's request, he was making hot and spicy chicken noodles, and I sidled up.

"Can I help?"

Raphael grinned then gestured for me to take over what he was doing. I rounded to the chopping board then wrinkled my nose.

"This is ginger, right? Don't laugh at me, but what do I do with it?"

Raphael set a pan down on the hob and came over, standing directly behind me with both arms around me to guide my hands. Having him this close heightened my awareness.

Especially when he stooped to put his lips to my ear. "See that teaspoon? Use it to peel the skin off the ginger, then grate it."

I followed his instructions, though my focus was entirely scattered by his proximity.

I giggled. "I'm doing a bad job."

Raphael tutted, joining our hands to show me how to use the spoon. "Can't drive, can't cook. What am I going to do with ye?"

I shivered at his low tones meant just for me. "I can think of a few things."

His grip on my hands tightened, and a thrill passed through me.

"Uh-oh, I was just going to say that Jackson and I will clean up after dinner since you cooked, but I'm going to need to take a picture." Across the counter, Ariel held up her phone. "Permission, please. Not for sharing. I just want to show you what you look like right now."

Raphael gazed down at me, and I gave him a nod. He lifted his chin at his sister. "Take the shot."

She did, then held up the screen to show us. I gazed at our image. Raphael in a short-sleeved black button-up shirt with his dark hair in a tumble over his forehead, bracketing me in the pretty white summer dress I'd worn to impress his family. Both of us were smiling softly under the warm kitchen light. We looked like a couple.

We looked like we were in love.

Ariel grinned. "See? The moment needed capturing.

Raph, I'll send it to you."

She left us, and Raphael released me with a mutter about getting everyone fed so we could leave. I pressed my lips together and got on with wrangling the ginger into shape.

In thirty minutes, we were eating, the conversation flowing about the extreme sports business that Effie ran and Ariel worked for. Like his brother, Gabe was a pilot so had stories of flying and mountain rescue work that Raphael would eventually sign up to as well. I traded their tales for tidbits of royal life, keeping it to the fun stuff, and with no one pushing for anything salacious, like my mother would've done.

Under the table, Raphael held my hand.

This was *nice*. Grown-up. I'd gone from boarding school to uni, with Dori my only real constant, and a party animal attitude we hadn't grown out of.

I'd had my artwork, until I'd quit it like it was a poison. But in this moment, glancing at a happy and relaxed Raphael at my side, laughing at something his brother was saying, I wanted nothing more than to grab a sketchbook and draw him, then commit the moment to canvas.

A groan came from across the table. Effie dropped her fork and clutched her stomach.

Gabe quirked a dark eyebrow. "I'm calling it. It was six minutes ago that ye last did that. It's time." His gaze took us all in. "It is, isn't it?"

Ariel's eyes rounded. "None of us have kids. How would we know? But yeah, get that girl to the hospital. Pretty sure your baby is on its way."

As one, everyone shifted to action, gathering up an ashen Effie and retrieving a bag to go with her and Gabe.

Outside, Gabe carefully helped his wife into the car.

She paused with one hand to the doorframe. "Raph, it's going to be okay."

Raphael schooled his features into a relaxed mask, but I'd seen what was there before, and it surprised me.

Fear.

In the rush to leave, I hadn't noticed anything other than his quick movements and his help for his sister-in-law, but Raphael was scared.

He faked a smile. "Of course it will be. Go have that bairn, and keep us updated."

Effie gave him one last look then let Gabe load her into the car, then they disappeared off into the night, the turnaround so fast it almost made my head spin.

I faced Raphael. His stress had returned, played out on his taut features, his jaw locked and his focus on the retreating taillights of the car. Shadows seemed to crowd around him.

"What's wrong?" I asked.

Ariel twisted around and took in her brother. "Oh no. Stop it."

His gaze flicked to her, but he didn't answer. The siblings glowered at each other, apparently having a conversation without words.

Jackson glanced between them. "No one's going to know. The birth isn't going to be announced or publicised anywhere."

Raphael shook his head once, his lips in a flat line. "Doesnae matter. Ye know the lengths he's gone to in the past. He'll find out."

Ariel scoffed. "And you know what I have on him. What

we all have on him."

Jackson chimed in. "He wouldn't dare."

"He would, or have ye forgotten what he attempted only months ago?"

Ariel's focus came my way with some kind of understanding in her eyes. She spoke again to her brother. "You're displacing."

That comment was about me. "What is he displacing?" I asked.

I was clueless as to what was going on. Why Raphael's mood had shifted so abruptly. All I knew was that I wanted to comfort him from whatever was hurting him. His family knew, and pulling the scant pieces together suggested it was to do with their history, though I had no idea what.

Ariel sighed. "The reason he's a bodyguard, and why he's never had a girlfriend."

Raphael stomped away from her to yank open the passenger-side door of the car, indicating for me to get in. I did, right as he delivered the killing blow.

"And why I never will."

# 27

## Alexandra

In silence, we wound through the dark countryside, back to the cottage, not speaking in the living room where we kicked off our shoes, but moving together, like clouds rolling into a storm front, with lightning crackling and thunder shaking the land.

Inside the bedroom, with the lamp on and the curtains closed, Raphael finally relented.

This was something significant. Some dark secret that was hurting him. I perched on the bed and watched him pace from the window to the wall.

"I'm sorry about that."

I didn't want him sorry. I wanted him to let me in. I stayed quiet.

His gaze flicked to me. "I told ye about our father being a terrible person. In the winter, he tried to kidnap Ariel."

Of all the things I'd expected him to say, that hadn't crossed my mind. "Oh my God."

Raphael dug his fingers into his hair. "Not only that. Jackson, who I'd arranged to protect my sister while I was away at flight school, was injured and abducted by Dad's pet assassin. Obviously Jax and Ariel both survived, but one slight change in history and I could have lost them both. Before that, when we lived with him in California, he regularly hurt Gabe. And me." He added the last two words quieter, as if an afterthought. "He thinks with his fists when it comes to those closest to him. With outsiders, he doesn't hold back on his tactics to intimidate and control."

My heart ached. Of course, I'd suspected something bad of a man they'd run from, but hearing him describe how domestic abuse turned to something deadlier sent a chill down my spine.

"What did Ariel mean that she has something on him?"

"A whole dossier of his backstabbing. If shared, his Mafia business associates will tear him apart."

"You don't think that threat will hold him off." I didn't ask it as a question. The answer was obvious.

Raphael's head slashed once in a *no*. "It has done for a while, but the moment something goes bad for him, what's to stop him thinking 'fuck it'? Where does he turn but to the kids who escaped him? To Scotland, which was his homeland, and his first grandchild who he'll see as the future of his enterprises. He is poison, and from the moment Gabe and Effie announced their pregnancy, the thought has been eating me alive."

I couldn't tell him everything would be okay. My words would be meaningless against a situation I could barely understand. I knew crappy families, though. "Gabe and Effie think the risk is worth it."

"I know. I'm happy for them. I struggle to feel the same. Not while he's still breathing."

"You're doing enough worrying for everyone."

"Who better than a man whose job it is to analyse risks and protect against them?"

Pieces clicked into place. The flying, his strength, his reaction to threat. "You turned yourself into the trained man who can defend against everything your father can throw at your family."

"Because he's a real danger."

Which brought me neatly back to his parting words when we left Gabe and Effie's house. "So you'll stay single forever, when your brother and sister are both happily paired off? While they have kids and settle down, you'll remain alone?"

He scrubbed a hand over his face, his gaze on the floor. "Yes. Ariel's right. I don't have girlfriends. If ever I consider it, I remember the reasons why it's a bad idea. What if he finds out and uses them to hurt me? I'd never forgive myself." His gaze lifted to mine, pinning me with the weight of a thousand sleepless nights he must've had over this. "What if he discovers the famous woman his second son is hanging out with and sees the opportunity of his lifetime?"

I flinched at the description. The easy dismissal of how we were far more to each other than two people hanging out. I hadn't imagined it. The way he looked at me. The late-night chats and the fever in his kiss. Raphael was anything but casual.

"What if that woman is becoming resilient? What if she walked away from people trying to drug her, and a family using her for God only knows what?" I stood from the bed and moved directly in front of him, claiming his gaze with mine. "What if she trusts the guy she's with to keep her safe, always, because she'll do the same for him?"

Emotion brimmed over in Raphael's eyes, so thick it hurt to witness his pain. "What if he becomes the reason for her facing a greater risk than any her family could throw at her?"

With trembling fingers, I reached for his hand, cupping it between mine. I didn't pretend I had an answer, not one that would satisfy him. The one thing I knew and trusted in was the draw between us. The unending, relentless need we had that wasn't one-sided. He wanted me, despite everything he'd described. It wasn't something either of us could stop.

My pathetic need for him to call me his girlfriend fell away, because this was so much greater than that. Raphael stared straight back at me.

I was out of my depth and drowning, and certain I had one chance to get this right. He wouldn't let me touch him, not in the way I wanted. If I told him I had feelings for him, he'd lock down tight and use that as an excuse to walk away to protect me.

"And yet, we have this."

I pushed up on my toes and pressed my lips to his.

He stiffened but didn't stop me from stealing the chaste, warm kiss. It was his slight roll towards me when I pulled back that spurred me on.

Holding his gaze, I commanded, "Follow me."

I turned and walked away, relief fluttering in the beats of butterfly wings when I peeked back to find him following. I knelt on the bed then grabbed one of the pillows, placing it against the base at the end. Then I sat against it with my legs crossed and gestured for him to take the opposite position at the headboard. Slowly, Raphael lowered himself to sitting, his gaze never leaving me.

My white dress had buttons all the way down the front, from the sweetheart neckline to the hem, and I undid the first, holding my breath until I saw the surge of lust in how his focus tracked my movements. "Copy me."

For a beat, he dropped his head back to the wood, gazing at the ceiling like he couldn't look at me. Yet his fingers found their way to the button at the base of his throat, revealing another inch of his strong chest.

I popped the next on my dress. "Your turn."

Raphael followed suit but still didn't look.

I undid the third and fourth, the material opening to reveal my lace bra. "Be a good boy and keep your eyes on me."

He liked praise. Every day, I'd make sure to tell him that he was good. That the choices he made were sound. I wasn't going to leave that out of the bedroom.

As expected, his dark eyes trained back on me, sliding down to my chest.

He didn't need the instruction to continue his slow reveal, but it took him a moment to concentrate, his chest rising and falling.

"All the way off," I instructed. His shirt had far fewer buttons than my dress.

Raphael stripped it and gave me the view I loved. Tonight, he'd described his motivation behind his career choice and why he honed such a strong body. All that power, all that devotion. It made me want to rub up against him like a cat. I carried on, undoing every button down to my waist then lifted my chin to him.

"Now your jeans."

Raphael stared at my body. "All the way off?"

"That's a good boy."

He breathed through his nose but obeyed, settling back on his pillow in just his boxer shorts. "Dress. Gone."

A thrill danced through me, both from anticipation of what I wanted to do and at the fact he was allowing this. Aiding it along. I made quick work of the remaining buttons and peeled back the material, on my knees so the straps could fall down my arms.

We were both in our underwear now, locked away in a secure cottage with one of his team next door and cameras monitoring the grounds. In such a remote corner of the country, I'd never felt so safe. It was all to do with the man in front of me. He'd given me this.

I'd give him a show in return.

Still on my knees, I stroked my hands up my waist to cup my breasts. He tracked the movement.

"I have a problem with you," I said, reversing the direction so I glided down to the straps of my underwear. "I might be semi-clothed, but you've seen all of me naked. You've had your hands and mouth on me. I haven't had the same pleasure. But," I claimed the air before he could interrupt, "I respect the reasons you won't allow this to go any further."

He didn't answer, though one hand cupped the impressive bulge in his shorts.

"Doesn't mean I can't watch," I finished.

Raphael's jaw locked. "Going to need ye to be crystal clear what you're asking."

Always the honourable man and the king of consent. "You won't let me touch you, but I can watch you touch yourself."

He groaned. For good measure, I added my killer blow.

"While I get myself off at the same time."

Raphael exhaled hard then released that perfect control, snapping up his hips to remove his last item of clothing. Shocked, I stared at his sizeable dick, so hard he had to be going insane with need.

He fisted it and stroked himself, reclining with one hand gripping the bed post. Good God, that was attractive. Those abdominal muscles contracting. The way the lamplight showed every strong curve. Need fizzled along my veins, sweat pricking my forehead, my underwear soaked.

There was nothing I wanted more than to straddle him and guide that thick and blunt end to my entrance then spear myself on him. I wanted him inside me. I wanted his hands on my waist and for him to groan my name at the tight fit.

But I'd made a promise, and I was good to my word.

With effort, I held my ground and unclipped my bra. Raphael's lips parted, and when I cupped my breasts, his tongue slid over his lower lip. Again, he stroked himself, his legs apart so I didn't miss a thing of his perfect body.

I was already so into the man. Just being around him all day had me ready and willing, but watching him play with himself while I toyed with my nipples and massaged my breasts for his pleasure had the power to ruin me for good, and I was willing to let it.

The energy in me built and built, so that I tipped my head back and closed my eyes, overwhelmed and so, so turned on.

"Get those off." Raphael's desperate tone returned me to the moment.

I stripped my underwear then lay back, heat burning my cheeks but hypnotised by how his gaze glued to the place between my legs. Slowly, I spread my knees, giving him all the opportunity to look until I couldn't take it anymore and had to touch myself.

At the first glide of my fingers over my wet core, he made a choking sound. I stared at him and how he gripped his dick, not moving.

"Make yourself come, princess. Fuck knows I can't hold off for long. Not when you're right there."

"I'm so wet for you. You do this to me. Only you."

I did as he asked, soaking my fingers to circle my clit. After only a minute, I was panting in need, my body tight and my back arched and my breasts begging for touch. My nipples tingled, my skin was on fire. When I moaned, he seemed to get impossibly harder, his free hand cupping his balls like they ached for release.

I'd wanted to tease him and make this more of a game. For one of us to approach the cliff then fight to hold off while the other chased their pleasure. In my head, I'd drawn it out until we couldn't take it anymore.

In reality, just seeing my beautiful bodyguard sprawled out in front of me with his dick in his hand was enough to chase me over the edge.

I forced my eyes open and my mind to capture the image. The plain need in his eyes and the way he held himself so tight.

"I wish you could fuck me," I blurted, right as my orgasm struck me down. I bucked from the bed then sank into the sheets, satisfied but at the same point desperate for him to fill me and to prolong the pleasure by taking his own and hammering into me.

"I wish I could, too." Raphael growled out a sound almost of pain.

I flew my eyes open. With his shoulders bunched and his forearms taut, he jerked his dick a couple more times, his focus never leaving me. Then, when his gaze touched my face, he came.

Ribbons of cum soaked his chest. I moaned again, fresh heat scalding me at the most beautiful sight I'd ever seen.

I was so screwed over him. So badly from our first dance and every encounter since. More when he recovered and grinned at me, like we'd shared something so delicious and heaven-breaking that his happiness couldn't be contained. That adoration was cemented for good when he grabbed a flannel from the bathroom and cleaned us both up, then killed the light, ushering me beneath the sheets so he could slip in behind.

Definitely when he hugged onto me, growing hard again but not doing anything about it.

Neither would I, no matter how much I yearned for him. Nothing beat how I felt around this man, and though I tried to stay awake and cling to how wonderful it felt to be curled up naked with him, sleep claimed me.

I woke to daylight peeking through the thick curtains in the still, calm room.

Raphael was gone.

# 28

# Raphael

Bright ocean spread out for miles behind us, the sound of the waves lost to the rotor blades that chopped the air overhead. I loved flying. I'd been obsessed with it since I was a child.

Yet I'd left my heart behind in Scotland.

All I wanted was Alex. Leaving her behind this morning had nearly killed me.

"One hour forty," Jackson informed me from the other side of the cockpit.

Never once had he got behind the controls of anything other than a car, but I'd taught him enough about instruments and the panels around us for him to read them. As an unofficial copilot, his main job was to keep me sane on our mission of mercy.

The coast of France flew by underneath us, just north of Le Havre, and countryside with pretty little towns replaced the open water. We'd already made a stop at the very bottom of the UK, in an airfield I'd used many times in the past when flying Leo in and out of the continent, but refuelling had taken forever, and we were behind schedule with over a hundred miles still to go.

"Check in with Ben," I grouched.

Jackson sighed over the headphones but sent the text. He read out his reply. "She's back in the house with Daisy and Mia, throwing herself into cleaning duty. Valentine's with them, and Ben's outside. He's made the point he isn't budging all day and they'll have lunch there. She's safe."

"Any reply from her friend yet?"

"The thumbs-up was the last."

Frustration flickered in my gut. The Parisien heliport we'd stop in had a time limit for how long I could wait. If Dori wasn't there, we'd move to plan B, which was to touch down at an airfield outside of the city, re-strategizing from there. Either he'd come to us, we'd get a second touchdown slot at the helipad, or the last resort was to jump in a car and find him.

Jackson clicked his tongue, staring out of the window to our left. "Clouds are building."

He wasn't wrong. Those dark clouds towered, growing taller as I watched. The reason we hadn't been able to fly overnight was because of the summer storm over the Channel. It had cleared this morning, but the weather forecast for the early evening showed a return. The view from the window and the readings on my instrument panels told me it could arrive sooner.

Cold slid through me.

There were too many risks of delays. Dori not being there. The weather pinning us down. If I didn't get back to Alex today, I'd probably run mad.

An hour and a half on, we'd reduced altitude to come

in over the sprawling city, getting the green light to touch down on the helipad, which was in a fenced-off small field next to a public park.

While I secured the craft, Jackson was readying for his role.

"Clear," I told him.

He jumped out, ducking against the downdraft our vehicle created, and ran for the administration office. In the past hour, he'd made multiple attempts to contact Dori, getting no answer. All morning, we'd only had a single acknowledgement to the fact we were coming in. We were later than planned, too. If he'd struggled to get out of bed, or worse, was still drunk, our delay would have given him more time to reach the helipad.

With the helicopter secured, I was able to take a breather, which usually meant downing a canned coffee to keep me sharp. Instead, I read a text from my brother to say Effie had been sent home from the hospital, apparently not yet in true labour, then climbed out, checking the craft with frequent glances to the office door Jackson had disappeared into. My frustration spiked when he emerged again, his phone to his ear, and his flat expression telling me what I'd feared.

Dori wasn't inside.

Jackson jogged back across the concrete. "He isn't fucking here."

I clamped my jaw then climbed back inside to speak into my radio, asking the controller for a time check of when we needed to vacate.

"Seven minutes, acknowledge," the voice returned.

"Affirm," I replied.

For fuck's sake. The countdown was on.

I relayed the fact to Jackson who tried to call the flighty count again, coming up empty. He then messaged the time constraint in the hope it hurried the man the fuck up.

"I've told him. I don't know what else I can do."

"All we can do is sit and wait."

A quick check back home with Ben told us all was well. I drummed my fingers on my knees, finally snatching up the caffeine I needed. We still had another refuelling stop to carry out. The weather to dodge.

Dori was cutting it fine.

Jackson watched the concourse. "Need to say something. I'm kind of sad ye didn't tell me about Alex when ye returned to London."

I rolled an unimpressed look at my best friend. "Like ye told me about my sister."

They'd started a secret relationship when I'd been away from my and Ariel's tower apartment for flight school, with Jackson moving in so she had someone there overnight. She'd pushed back at my overprotectiveness but had eventually agreed. I'd always thought they would've made a good match. The proximity had brought them around to agreeing.

He pulled a face. "The difference being the whole forbidden-relative deal."

"Ye don't think a princess is forbidden?"

He attempted a smile. It died quickly. For a moment, my friend stayed quiet. "Yet you aren't fighting the comparison. I always knew it would hit ye hard when ye fell."

He tapped his screen to display a countdown timer. We had three minutes.

Pressure closed in around me. All of a sudden, I couldn't stop my words. I'd confided in no one. I'd barely done so with Alex. I trusted Jackson with my life, and he'd been through unimaginable pain in his past. He also knew my history better than most.

"I can't fall for her. She lives in a different world than I do."

"Except for the fact she's living in yours right now."

I scoffed. "Temporarily. That's just one of too many barriers."

He twisted his lips, his dark eyes regarding me. "Name three."

"Only three? My father finding out her identity and using the connection for his own gain. The fact she lost her closest friend and I'm possibly a distraction, only useful until she gets him back. Which could be today, if the arsehole ever shows, and at which point she won't need me anymore. That I'm a convenient safe pair of hands when she's scared."

"Let me guess, ye haven't asked her about those last two points?"

At my headshake, he swore and held up his hand with three fingers raised.

He tapped the first. "Talk to her. Ask if she has feelings for ye, then learn from her answer. Don't guess." He moved on to the second finger. "Give her back her friend then watch how she still looks to ye. I know you're not disrespecting her like that."

I raised my shoulders against the realisation. I had done so, and it was unfair to Alex.

Jackson's steady gaze held no judgement. "Only my best friend would be the engineer of his own destruction. Always putting other people first. It's time we all pulled in around ye. So lastly, when it comes to your arsehole dad, if he dares threaten any member of his family or their loved ones again, which now includes me, we do what we should've done last winter."

"Which is?"

Jackson mimed breaking his last finger.

My breathing stuttered. I'd long wanted my father dead. As a child, I'd imagined it too many times. For myself, I couldn't have done it. If he threatened Alex, the opposite applied.

He held up his phone to display the ticking-down time. "One minute."

My heart thumped at double the rate of the vanishing seconds. Still, there was no movement at the office. Jackson grabbed the door handle.

"Time for one final check." He glanced back at me. "What do ye call the bodyguard who fell for a princess?"

Him and his jokes. I arched an eyebrow.

My friend punched my shoulder. "Royally fucked. You're already in love with her, my friend, and I fucking love being the first to know."

With a grin, he dove out and sprinted for the office.

God, but he was right. I *loved* her. I'd fallen hard to the point it was more truth than any other fact in my life.

Jackson appeared again seconds later with his hands outstretched, right as the controller gave me my takeoff warning.

Fuck it. Fuck all of it.

Without Dori here, we had to extend the visit and move to the secondary site. Waste the time I could be using to get back to Alex.

I crammed every bit of emotion behind my wall of

control, returning my friend's grim smile when he slammed the door and clipped himself back into his seat.

*Thirty seconds.* I worked through the sequence of my preflight checks, ensuring the instruments were operational and the fuel levels were where I expected them to be, and my flight plan was recorded. Once I started the engine, we'd be ready for takeoff in under a minute. I should've already had it underway.

"Stop."

Jackson's tone froze my fingers, poised to flip the switch.

"Fucking hell," he added. "Look."

The door to the office was open, and the tall, blond friend of Alex's wrestled with a uniformed staff member. Dori broke free, swinging a rucksack and falling in his haste to reach us, the picture of elegantly ruffled European royalty.

Jackson swore then exited and opened the rear door, practically boosting Dori into the back of the craft. He strapped him in and tossed him headphones. I could barely hear over the thrum of my pulse.

With Jackson securing the doors and clipping his harness back in place, I checked the clock. Seconds to go.

Over the headphones came Dori's voice, thick under heavy breaths. "I know I'm late. My cab broke down. Gridlock. I had to run the whole way."

I wasn't angry. I was fucking overjoyed. Against all odds and a coming storm, I set our path for home.

# 29

# *Alexandra*

$\mathcal{S}$coop, chuck, scoop, chuck. I filled another bag of rubbish then hollered down for Valentine to carry it outside to the skip. While I waited, I grumpily shook open a fresh bin liner and gazed around the spare bedroom.

Today, Daisy had assigned me to the upstairs room in the hope that spreading us out would give us a better chance of hunting down the treasure. Once we had the item the homeowner needed found, the rest of the clearance would go much quicker. We wouldn't need to check every pile to make sure it didn't contain a diamond necklace or a priceless figurine.

No sound came from downstairs, so I returned to the patch I was working on, where a stack of boxes had been wedged together Tetris-style. Dutifully, I rattled then opened each, checking the contents before discarding them in the bin bag. They were a strange collection of what must've been late-night or impulse purchases. A cleaning product for bathrooms. A mechanical tool for removing fluff from clothing. All examples of an active life the lady couldn't lead. The more time I spent here, the sadder it made me.

Couple that with the mournful sense of loss for Raphael not being here and I was a grouchy wreck, hot under the blonde wig I'd felt safer in wearing today and bothered for other reasons. I'd got used to having Raphael near. I craved him, and the distance between us panicked me. I wasn't sure at what point that change had started, but my addiction to all things Raphael was getting worse.

A figure appeared in the door. Daisy. "How's it going?"

I sat back from the pile and in the path of fresh air from the open bedroom window, where clouds had rolled in to darken the skies, then peeled off my mask. "I was getting a little blue over the state of mind of the woman who lived here. How does someone get like this? Why did no one help her?"

Daisy pulled a pretty grimace and tucked an escaped curl of blonde hair behind her ear. "Her name is Agnes, and her condition is not that uncommon. Hoarding often stems from physical or mental illness or extreme events the mind can't get over. Mia and I did a similar house clean for a woman in Inverness. She'd broken her leg and had other health issues, and over the course of several months, turned from an outgoing and employed woman to a complete recluse. When she came home from hospital, she had a nurse check on her once or twice and a meal service bring her food, but then her employer forced her into early retirement. She didn't have any family and had lived for her job. Her whole community had been at the nursery she'd worked in.

It dented her confidence so much that for three years, she didn't leave the house, which only made her physical health worse. It was only when her power went out one winter that she was forced to allow an engineer inside, and she was so ashamed of how bad things had got. The engineer was kind and had seen the videos I sometimes make of our cleans. She contacted us. We did the job for free."

Daisy moved to where I'd been digging through boxes and picked one up. "I'd say Agnes has something else going on, but I know for sure it isn't our place to judge. Everyone is entitled to a clean home. I consider it a privilege to be able to help with that."

"Kind of judging the guy who employed your company. He's her relative, yet he let her live like this and didn't show any interest until she was near the end of her life."

Daisy took a deep breath. "I wouldn't be so hasty to go after him either. You might be right. He could be completely mercenary and not give a damn about her. He also might be like Ben."

I blinked. "What do you mean?"

She dipped her head at the window. "You might have noticed that my fiancé doesn't come inside this place. His mother is a hoarder. He was forced to live in circumstances like this and couldn't help her. Hers was an extreme case, and I managed to do something to make it better, but not every family is happy and supportive."

I huffed agreement, knowing that well. I'd managed to ignore mine for a couple of days, but every time my brain slid back to the events I'd fled, the more it put my family at the centre of things.

I couldn't go back to them. That much was certain. Even if they somehow tracked me down. It only complicated things with my dad who was the one person I needed to protect.

Daisy continued, "Some people are broken beyond repair or completely alone. The things they bring into the home and the money they spend create glimmers of happiness. In this case, the trash is the treasure for the lady who collected it all." She gave a short laugh. "Though I hope for our sake that isn't the literal truth."

She tossed a box of bathroom tile samples, then found another. A heavier box with packaging I instantly recognised.

"That's oil paint," I told her. "I use that brand."

"I didn't know you were an artist." Daisy offered it out. "Reckon they'll still be good?"

I accepted the unopened box and looked it over, pulling out tubes and brushes. "They haven't been touched. Oil paint lasts for years if it isn't opened."

"Want it? If there's anything usable, I can message the nephew and make him an offer. I already did that with a teapot because I wanted it as a reminder of the woman and her life. He told me to keep it. He'll probably do the same with that." At my nod, she sent a quick text. "He says no problem. Keep them. Oh, there's a stack of paintings with some blank canvases that I stored in the garage. We took them all off the walls on our first visit in case they were the treasure. None were very old, so that was a no, but the canvases can be yours."

Last night, I'd dreamt of painting. I often did. For years, I'd had oil paint smudges on my skin and the compelling urge to return to my work-in-progress. Shutting it down at the point of starting work for my family had been a snap judgement. One I regretted.

"If you think that's all right?" I stood shakily, urgency building in me all over again.

Daisy had already sent a follow-up message. "I'll show you them now."

We descended the stairs to the ground floor and stepped outside where fat raindrops had started falling. Ben was seated at his usual spot at a garden table, but he packed up his tablet and stowed it in a bag, presumably to shelter it from the weather.

Daisy and I entered the garage at the side of the house. The rumbling of tyres chased us.

"Must be Valentine returning." Tugging my mask back up against the thick smell of something rotting, I followed Daisy to a stack of paintings. There had to be thirty leaning against the garage wall in stacks, some landscapes and others I couldn't see. I leafed through the first few, checking what she'd said—that they were modern prints. To the right were three white canvases, still in the plastic wrapping. I took up one, the sense of certainty growing in me to towering proportions.

"Val's still here," Daisy said. "He's round the back, stomping up and down on the garden while talking on the phone."

"Then who just turned up?"

Earlier, Valentine had given me a new and secure phone to use, already programmed with the numbers for the team and for Daisy and Mia. I'd resisted the urge to message Raphael, almost scared to distract him, and relying on the updates Ben and Valentine provided. The last check-in from Jackson told us they'd arrived in Paris, but nothing since. There was no way this could be them.

Without thinking, I moved to the garage door and peered out into the now pattering rain.

Coming face to face with Barrington Bray.

*Oh shit.* I flushed icy cold.

Daisy hissed and circled to block his view of me. "Can I help you?"

"I'm looking for Ben Graham."

"You found him," Ben's hard tone sounded across the garden.

Barrington turned, and Daisy spun back to me, her eyes wide. She ushered me deeper into the garage while Ben took control.

"I didn't think," I mouthed.

She blinked, still appearing in shock, and whispered back, "Do you know him?"

I managed a terrified nod. "The leader of the other bodyguard team. The ones who are hunting for me."

If they found me, my moment of peace would be broken. I'd need to talk to Sir Reginald. I'd have to fight him over his expectations and my work. I just wanted to stay with Raphael and to not be at the centre of that maelstrom.

The storm had come to me.

Daisy's mouth flattened, and she kept her voice low. "We need to get you out of here. Thank God you had your mask and that wig on."

I touched my face, relief spiralling outwards. I had my hair covered and a mask so I didn't breathe in dust. With any luck, it might have been a good enough disguise. Barrington hadn't recognised me. Had he?

I listened hard.

"Ben. You didn't answer my calls. You gave me no choice but to come here."

"I replied and told you exactly what you needed to know," Ben retorted.

"Nowhere near enough. I need to see your man, Raphael. Where is he?"

"I told ye. He's off on another job. What could you possibly want him for? He's not hiding a princess on his person."

His tone held incredulity, but I couldn't smile.

Daisy's hand found mine, and she led me down through the garage, squeezing between a clapped-out car and yet another stack of boxes that lined the walls.

Barrington yelled, "Well, where the fuck is she? She's supposed to be at her father's house, but I've already been there today. They said she wasn't to be disturbed, yet no one's seen her which tells me it's a lie. There's not been one photo of her online in days, and her family is threatening to cancel every contract I have with them. You know what that will do to my business. Tell me she isn't shacked up with your boy because fuck knows where else she could be."

A deadly pause followed. I'd only known Ben for a matter of days but I'd got the measure of the man. He was stoic and calm, but he defended his team to the hilt.

"I don't like being shouted down. I especially don't like a demand being made of a trusted member of my team. Raphael isn't here. He's not even in the country. He's been dispatched on another job, and I can guarantee you," he spoke over an arguing Barrington, "that the princess you lost is not with him. Nor is she at Castle Braithar which is where he's been living. I would know. Can I make myself clearer?"

At the back of the garage, Daisy reached for the handle of the garden door. It creaked, and she shivered then inched it open even slower, dragging it against a pile of leaves. I cringed at the sounds, expecting footsteps at any moment. A hand grasping my shoulder and an order for me to return to England.

None came. We made it outside, and Daisy closed the door so I could stand against it. The overtones of the argument made it to us, though the words were indistinct, and Valentine strode up the garden, a frown darkening his brow as the rain did the same to his shirt.

Daisy beckoned him over, gesturing for him to be quiet. "We need to get Alex out of here. Right now."

His gaze darted from the unseen incomer to me. I set down the oil paints and canvas.

"My car. We'll hide ye inside, but to be convincing when we leave, I'll need to make it look like I'm naw running."

He gestured to his vehicle which was fifteen feet away at the side of the house. It was in plain sight of the front where Barrington could see.

A grin spread over Valentine's face, and he quirked an eyebrow. "Luckily, I'm shit hot at subterfuge. Daisy, go open the boot and make a fuss about some missing item. Something you badly need for work today. In the meantime, I'll get Mia to come down." He came back to me. "Don't worry, princess. No one's taking ye away from your prince today."

Minutes later, Daisy and Mia were deep in a heated, fake argument at the back of Valentine's car, the huge bodyguard wading in to solve the problem.

"Don't sweat. I'll go get it. Not like I've got anything better to do," he griped.

At the other side of the vehicle, I snuck into the passenger-side door, left open by Mia on their pretend hunt. I'd sprinted to the end of the garden then crept back up along the side of a hedgerow, the long grass soaking my shoes. Not that I cared. I only wanted to get away.

I curled into the footwell and made myself small. Still shouting, Valentine dropped heavily into the driver's seat and tossed his jacket onto me. With his window open, he cruised past Ben and Barrington.

"Need to head out for five minutes. Won't be long," Valentine called out.

"Do what ye need to do," Ben snapped back.

"Who's this? What's your name?" Barrington challenged.

Valentine stopped the car. I ceased breathing and held as still as I possibly could, praying that the jacket covered me.

Valentine's reply held nothing but amusement. "Val Graham. Ben's brother. What can I do you for?"

Barrington made a sound of disgust. "Nothing," he muttered.

The engine purred, and we moved on.

A gasp left me the moment the gravel turned to tarmac. Valentine sped up, eating the miles out of town.

He plucked the jacket off me. "All right down there?"

"We're free, aren't we?"

"As a bird. I'll take ye back to the cottage. You'll probably have to stay put for the afternoon, if that's okay? No telling if the arsehole is going to hang around until your boy gets home."

So long as I didn't get whisked back to London, I'd happily stay locked in that darling cottage for the rest of my life.

I gave him a nod of utter relief, and he grinned bigger.

"By the way, Daisy stashed your painting supplies in the boot. Maybe that can entertain ye?"

The idea of taking my feelings out on a canvas had

never been sweeter.

# 30

# Raphael

The rainstorm battered the plexiglass cockpit, and we dropped altitude, the ground seeming to rush up to meet us.

We were heading to a crash, the violent drop almost guaranteed to end us in a crumple of engine parts and a fuel fire. What was it that Gordain once told me? Planes are designed to fly. Cut the power and they'll soar for miles. But helicopters? Those fuckers only ever want to plummet to earth. Our job as pilots was to do everything to prevent that from happening.

Lucky for us I was damn good at my job.

I centred our position and lowered us slowly the last fifty feet, touching down neatly on the McRae hangar's concourse.

Jackson threw me a grin, and I returned it, still buzzing from the fast pace I'd set to get us home, the storm front hard on our heels.

"Christ," Dori muttered. "That was abrupt. Anyone

would think you had a princess to get home to." Despite his tone, he flashed me a smile.

I secured and powered down the aircraft, waving to the mechanic who approached through the storm to take back ownership.

Before we climbed out, Jackson touched my arm. "Ben sent a message when we were in the air. Barrington Bray is around, looking for you because he can't find Alex."

My pulse skipped a beat. "He's here?"

"He tracked Ben down to the house clean. Don't worry, Alex is safely hidden away at your cottage. He didn't get to her, and Ben told him ye didn't have her with ye. But he's sure Barrington is lurking."

I exhaled hard, my brain whirring where the rotor blades had just stopped. "Why didn't ye tell me?"

"It wouldn't have changed our actions in any way. Ben and Valentine handled it. She's safe, and we were flying back at speed. Distracting the pilot is never a good idea."

He was right, but I hated being out of the loop.

"Trust in your team," Jackson warned. "Ben instructed Val to watch Bray. He's across the loch at the village, in the pub, maybe to hide out from the rain."

I swore, jamming my fingers into my hair. "Fine. I'll need to see him. Or for him to see and stalk me. I'll lead him back to Braithar then challenge him. He can search all he likes but he won't find her. Does that sound good?"

"Aye. Pretty much what the boss suggested."

Which meant not seeing Alex. Not getting to witness her face light up when Dori appeared, or to see if she did as Jackson said and still looked to me.

"Can ye..." I jerked my head at Dori in the back.

"I've got him."

I jumped out and opened the door to release the count, rain spattering my face.

"Jax is going to drive ye to Alex. I have something else to do. But keep your head down. One of the people hunting her is around."

Dori tilted his head, his expression shifting to the aristocrat I'd first seen at the nightclub, when he'd been outraged at getting kicked out. "Who?"

"Barrington Bray, the head of her old security team. Have ye met him?"

"Once or twice, so he knows my face."

"Which means you'll need to lie low."

I wheeled around, needing to get to my car and out of here. I was fucking disappointed that I couldn't see Alex. I didn't want to show it.

Dori called my name. "Thank you. I mean that. It's been a shit couple of weeks and I'd be stuck at the embassy trying to arrange an emergency passport if it wasn't for you. You saved my skin."

I had so many questions, but at the same point, they weren't for me to ask. "Just glad to help a friend of Alex's. Again."

On that, I left him to lead a hunter on a wild goose chase.

# 31

## Alexandra

*T*yres crunched on the driveway outside the cottage, and I jumped back from the canvas. All afternoon, the rain had picked up, and I'd lost track of time. But I wasn't about to miss Raphael's homecoming.

I flew to the door and peeked out, careful not to show myself in case of unwanted eyes.

Dori climbed from a car, and I shot my hand to my mouth. Yet somehow, my gaze still clung to the other door, and my heart fell when Jackson appeared.

He gave me a curious look, then Dori was in my face and I was hugging the idiot, urging him inside.

"Oh my God. I was half expecting you to be beat up."

He moved past me and dropped onto the sofa with a

heavy sigh. "Inside bruises don't show."

So dramatic.

I turned back to Jackson who approached the door. "Is he…?"

"Leading Barrington a merry dance. Safer that he doesn't come here until we're sure he's been seen and discounted as having hidden ye somewhere."

But that could take a long time. I managed a small nod, then the bodyguard left us, and I locked the door then turned to Dori.

"You jackass. I'm so happy to see you. Tell me everything about Elsie Sale."

He'd started to laugh but palmed his face. "Shit. You worked it out."

I flapped my hands in a go-figure gesture and took the other end of the sofa, curling my legs underneath me. "You gave me no choice but to go snooping. This is the woman you dated a year ago, right?"

My best friend took a moment, ruffling his fingers through his damp blond hair, seeming to be piecing through what he wanted to say. "Yes. She's the woman I dated a year ago. I fell as hard and as fast for her as you have with your hot pilot."

My heart thumped. "Did you just upgrade him? Never mind. Continue."

"I thought she felt the same for me. In fact, I was certain. I still am. We met at Cano." He used the nickname for an island resort in the Grenadines that his family holidayed in every year. "We spent two weeks together. From day one, we were inseparable. I mean from instant fascination on the first day to complete certainty that I'd found my person by the time we realised a week had passed and all we'd done was hang around each other. We swam in hidden coves and took romantic walks at sunset. We held hands and didn't even kiss for days, because the weight of it felt so fucking huge, it couldn't be rushed. We talked. Endlessly, and we slept hugging each other. With her, I felt like I was breaking apart and reshaping myself piece by piece."

Love-them-and-leave-them Dori had never been poetic, yet his description hurt my heart.

"She was supposed to be relaxing before heading into the recording studio for her next album. Yet she'd taken an acoustic guitar with her and wrote songs while staring into my fucking eyes like I somehow inspired her."

He made a sound of disbelief and tipped his head back. "She said she was single but that she'd been on a few dates a month earlier with this man." He spat the word. "An influencer her manager set her up with for the sake of good optics."

"You didn't tell me any of this."

"I couldn't. Not only for the fact that Elsie is intensely private, but because it scared the hell out of me. I imagine you know the feeling. Is he your boyfriend yet?"

I heaved a sigh. "Working on it."

"Good. That boy has wife-me written all over him." He found his phone. "In fact, hold still." Dori took a shot.

"What are you doing?"

"You have a smudge of paint on your cheek and down the side of your hand. Love that he's got you painting again."

A whoosh sounded.

"Did you just send that to him?"

"Part payment for the helicopter ride. Your hair is a little messy, too. A man in love is going to go nuts over that shot."

My cheeks warmed. My canvas and paints were in the spare bedroom, hidden away where no one could see. "Back away from my love life and return to yours. What broke you and Elsie up?"

Dori sobered. "The holiday ended, and she returned to the US. I had commitments elsewhere, but we spoke almost constantly when she wasn't recording, and I was due to fly back to see her in two weeks. I would have changed everything for her. Where I lived. My whole shitty personality. She is so real. So fucking talented. She told me she adored me. Missed me every minute. That she needed me back. How could that not be love if she was blind to all my faults?"

I sensed his pain like it was a monster in the room. "Then how the hell is she marrying some guy who looks like a complete tool?"

Dori's lip curled. "He live-streamed his proposal two days before I was due to fly over. She said yes. On air. Millions saw that video. Must've made him a killing."

I reached for his hand. He gripped my fingers, emotion flushing his cheeks.

"I'm so sorry," I said. "I saw it. She seemed flat. Did you talk to her?"

"I got a single message from her official social media account. Here."

He picked up his phone again and thumbed to a page then held it out. I read the message.

*Ferdinand, sorry, but I won't be able to see you as planned. It was great hanging out, but I'll be busy for the foreseeable future. Thanks for all the support! Elsie.*

I handed it back, wariness descending over me. "There's no way the woman you described wrote that. It's so clinical, and I can't imagine you had her use your first name. No one does."

"Never. She doesn't run that account either. Her publicist does. She joked with me that she doesn't even have the password." He flicked to a different account. "This is hers."

I examined it. This version of the musician had thirty-five friends and shared real pictures of her life. Pretty ones, but informal and far more personal.

"The account's been dead since that last post," Dori added.

It was a picture of a couple beside a tropical lagoon, white sand, tan lines, and nothing but love in their eyes. Her and Dori.

My heart ached all the more.

He took back the phone and tossed it into his bag on the floor by the sofa, emotion visibly rocking him. "I tried to walk away. She's an adult. She made her choices. But then I saw the engagement picture and just...flipped. There was evidence that built up and up in my head until I couldn't ignore it. If there was any chance I was wrong, I had to take it."

"What evidence?"

"Not only her expression in that video, but the fact it took eleven months for them to have an engagement party which was only a few weeks before their wedding. Why would that be if she wasn't pushing back? The other thing was her music. She wrote two songs with me. Both were killer. Neither made it to the album she's releasing in September. Hints have been dropped for every track, and none are those."

"So you flew to Milan."

"Yes, super sleuth. I found out where the party was happening and hired a car then drove out to the lakeside hotel. The influencer's brother and a posse of hangers-on met me at the gate, as if they'd guessed I'd show. I never even saw Elsie."

"They kicked you out? Wait, your passport. Did they mug you?"

"Two held my arms while the brother found my wallet. They kept that and my passport, luckily I'd left my phone in the car, and told me that Elsie had forgotten all about me and I needed to learn a lesson about staying out of other people's business."

I narrowed my eyes. "Interesting choice of words."

His gaze distanced like he was right back in the scene at that lakeside hotel, close yet so far from the woman he loved.

I squeezed his hand. "Did they hurt you?"

Dori snapped back to the present and centred on me. "Not any more than I already was, and it's obvious I was way out with how much I thought she cared about me. Fuck the whole situation. The important thing is I'm with you here now. So, let me say I'm sorry for dropping your calls. I was humiliated. I still am. You've been through shit, too. Tell me everything."

We weren't done with handling his situation, but I could tell he needed a moment of distraction, so methodically, I worked through all that had happened to me.

As I did, I led him into the kitchen and made us a sandwich each, earning a comment that this was the first meal I'd ever prepared in my life. Sadly, he wasn't far off the truth.

Though we'd talked for a while, there was still no sign

of Raphael.

Dori got more outraged the more I went on. "One part of that, I can explain. Sir Reginald called me."

"What? How does he have your number?" I'd wondered that since we'd got back in touch.

"I figured you'd given it to him? It wasn't the first time. He said he needed to know what designer you were wearing to the botanical gardens bird extravaganza. You'd told me, so I passed it on. Thought it was the right thing to do."

My mistrust grew. Not for Dori, but for the private secretary. "That detail was almost immediately revealed on a gossip site. If it wasn't him who leaked it, it was a member of his staff. And I never gave him your number."

"Shit, sorry."

"Don't be. If someone from your family rang me and asked for something as innocuous as that, I'd have told them."

He scoffed. "Like anyone in my family has ever given a damn what I'm doing."

"I need to share this with Raphael. Would that be okay?"

Rain hit the windows behind the closed curtains, the light around them muted. I hated the thought of him being cold and wet.

Dori stretched out his limbs, rocking his kitchen counter stool. "Knock yourself out. If anyone has a hope of solving our problems, it's him."

"Back off," I teased. "He's mine."

Dori heaved a sigh. "I hope he is. You need someone like him. Listen, I have to find a hotel for the night. Feels kind of remote out here so I don't want to wait until dark and get stranded."

"You can stay here."

He shot me an incredulous look. "And listen to you and hot pilot go at it all night? Our friendship is in recovery, darling girl. Let's not make things awkward. I'll stay close by. We can talk tomorrow, but my head is pounding and I just want to curl up somewhere and sleep. Feels like I'm running on empty."

I managed a nod. I had my friend back. He was more than a little broken, but he was here, and I'd help him work out what to do next with his musician.

Earlier, when Valentine had dropped me off, he'd asked me to message him with anything I needed. I shot him a quick text now to ask if there was anywhere local Dori could stay that would be out of sight of Barrington, should the man still be around.

A minute later, and there was a knock at the door, followed by the bodyguard's cheerful voice. I let him in, disappointed again that Raphael wasn't with him.

Valentine tugged down his hood covering his topknot of hair and regarded Dori. "How fussed are ye about luxury?"

Dori raised a single shoulder. Exhaustion hung heavy on him. "So long as it's clean and the door locks, I don't care."

"The aircraft hangar has a bunkhouse, used for pilots staying overnight and sometimes the mountain rescue crew. I stayed there for a while after relocating here. It's basic, but it's free."

At Dori's agreement, the two of them readied to leave.

I caught Valentine's sleeve. "Any update on Raphael?"

"He sent a message a few minutes ago that Barrington had pursued him all the way back to Braithar and he'd challenged him as planned. Barrington took off in his car.

We tracked him heading out of the estate, so with any luck, he's history. Best to still stay out of sight until we're sure."

My heart leapt. "Then I can see Raphael?"

"Drop him a line, honey. Watch how fast he races back now he knows you're alone."

With a final hug of my friend, I let them go, then ran for the bedroom. I'd hidden too much of myself from Raphael. He never knew the depths of the effect he'd had on me, even back when we were teenagers. I fished the possession I'd been searching for out of my bag and smiled.

Tonight, I wanted nothing between us but the truth. I'd fight for him. Even if the fresh drama made him feel I was even harder to reach, I'd prove I wasn't. It was the only way.

# 32

# Raphael

In Braithar's cool corridor, I stared out of a narrow window at the dusk and the rainstorm that battered the estate. From further inside the castle came the sounds of a happy family evening, someone strumming a guitar, kids laughing.

Alone in the dark, I thumbed to a message on my phone.

*Jackson: It was you she looked for, bro.*

God, I'd needed to know that. Just as much as I'd needed the image Dori sent.

I'd dealt with Barrington, proving as much as I could to him that I hadn't hidden Alex anywhere around and reiterating that she was at her dad's. Gordain had even come out of Braithar to challenge the man, at which point he'd driven away. Even though we'd tracked him leaving the estate, he knew my car now. I couldn't drive to the cottage and park outside.

Another message arrived on my phone.

*Valentine: The count is at the hangar for the night. Repeat, the count is off the premises. Coast is clear, my friend.*

Then a third nearly ended me.

*Alex: If it's safe, please come to me.*

I was already moving. Tugging up my hood, I snuck to a side exit of the castle and plunged out into the dark. Rain battered me, and I sprinted for the trees on the far side of the clearing.

I couldn't drive to Alex, but a little rain never hurt anyone.

The cottages were a good hike across the Scottish landscape, but I knew the estate like the back of my hand. Through the woods, I stormed, steering clear of the road and using animal tracks. Thick clouds hid any moon, and the summer undergrowth had me saturated quickly. It didn't stop me.

I didn't slow until I was closing in on the cottage, the warm lights visible down the hill.

Hunkering down, I watched for several minutes then took out my phone and shot Alex a quick message.

*Raphael: Unlock the back door. Stay out of sight.*

My hair dripped water on the screen, and I shut it down then waited until faint movement at the back door showed me she'd done as I asked.

I could barely catch my breath.

Only when I was certain that nothing else moved in the rain-strewn night did I release my energy and storm through the dark, down the slope and to the door. Without missing a beat, I twisted the handle and ducked inside, closing and locking it at my back.

A hitched breath had me turning to face Alex, waiting for me in the darkness, wearing only a shirt.

*My* t-shirt. The one I'd given her when we were at university. Recognition nearly knocked me out.

In that moment, my life changed. I was done. Done waiting, done holding myself back. From the emotion in Alex's eyes, I wasn't the only one locked in this insanity.

She was mine now. And I'd do everything necessary to keep it that way.

# 33

# Alexandra

Raphael regarded me, the faint light from the bedroom gleaming on the wet strands of his dark hair. I couldn't hold back. Even if he was going to tell me no again, I needed to be in his arms.

I flew at him, and he caught me up in a fierce hug, his skin cool to my touch and his damp shirt blotching mine.

I couldn't speak, so I did the next best thing and kissed him.

Raphael returned my kiss with hunger, one hand sliding to my jaw to position me perfectly, and the other skimming down my spine. If his actions shocked me, I had an answer that would shock him. He reached the hem of the t-shirt and slipped under, so his fingertips touched the bare skin of my thigh.

Raphael stilled and eased those fingers up to the curve of my backside. Then under to find me wet and ready. I electrified at the touch. He groaned against my lips, then with one hand lifted me into his arms, still kissing me, but moving down the hall with purpose.

A thrill drove away all but one thought. That I didn't want conversation. I didn't want him to feel he had to explain himself. I only wanted him.

"Stop."

He obeyed me, pausing ahead of the entrance to the lounge. On the other side of the hall were the bedroom and bathroom doorways, but here was just as private. We didn't need a bed or a mattress in this moment. Not after he'd spent an entire day fighting for me. Just like five years ago when he first showed me how much he cared.

I palmed his cheek, easing back in his arms to put space between our bodies. Then I flattened my palm to his chest and grazed down and down until I reached his waistband. Holding his gaze, I undid his jeans button.

It was a question or maybe a demand.

Wildness flashed in his eyes. It gave me hope. Raphael dove in for another kiss, moulding his lips to mine and taking what he needed in desperate swoops. God, he wasn't stopping me.

I found the zip of his jeans and lowered it, slipping my hand inside to find him already hard for me. I cupped him through his boxer shorts, and Raphael made a sound of need that crashed heat through me with the realisation that this was happening.

At long last, we were doing this. Right here, right now.

Raphael spun around so my shoulders hit the wall between two doorways. One hand supported my bare ass, and the other touched my face so he could claim my gaze. Still, I didn't want to speak. Instead, I bypassed his boxer shorts to take him in my hand and squeezed then stroked him. His eyes slammed closed. His chest rose and fell. The first time I'd touched him like this, and I was already addicted.

I was also very naked under this t-shirt. And hot. My skin burned though the summer night was cool. Sitting forward, I stripped the shirt and dropped it, leaning back against the wall so he could see me. The invitation was clear. If he wasn't inside me in seconds, I'd probably die.

He didn't keep me waiting. There was no hesitation this time. No second-guessing or delay. Raphael fully freed his dick then brought it to my centre, sliding up and down me and getting himself wet. With the way he held my weight, he had complete control. Lucky for me, his had apparently gone.

It was so sweet being right.

Raphael notched himself to my entrance and at the same time locked his lips onto mine and thrust home.

My cry was smothered by his mouth. He was so thick that it took several strokes until he was fully seated, and all I could do was hold on and try to breathe. The sensation of him inside me spiralled brilliant pleasure out from the places we were joined. And holy cow was it towering.

Instantly, I loved this. We fitted together perfectly, and I wanted to spend the rest of my life doing nothing but this. We'd wasted so much time when he could've been inside me multiple times every day.

Raphael withdrew his hips and punched forward, filling me and lighting up multiple pleasure centres at once. He did it again, and I moaned, so turned on it was almost unreal.

His hand landed on the wall beside my head, and

Raphael braced himself, changing the angle so he could stare down our bodies.

He made a sound of urgent need and fucked me faster, his forehead to my collarbone. All I could do was take it. Absorb every blow and let him burn up his passion in my body as he coaxed out mine. It would take almost nothing for me to come. From the second I'd got his text message asking me to unlock the door, I'd become alive with need for him. Desperate for this.

Reaching between us, Raphael felt over where we were joined and slowed his pace, focusing on hard, repeated hits and with his fingers shifting to my clit. The added attention had me closing my eyes against how good it felt. I clutched on to him, lost in anything but the feel of what he was doing to my body. I loved the image of us. Him all in black and soaked from the storm, and me completely naked in his arms, the power that was burning between us almost ready to explode.

He stroked me over and over, timed with his hits. My orgasm closed in, charging towards me with a pace made of how well he could play me. He knew the rhythm that would work. The steady delivery of devastating pleasure. In seconds, I was rocking on him and gasping as a world-ending climax threatened to strike me down.

Just a few...strokes...more. I clamped on to him in a series of pulses, losing my mind of everything but him. All I wanted now was to keep him with me. To take this as far as it could go.

I needed him to come, too.

Raphael slowed his movements on me, and when my head had cleared from the dizzying waves of happiness, I caught his cheek and had him look at me.

"Go faster."

His eyebrows dove together, but he kissed me and did as ordered, stoking the fires inside me all over again at a punishing pace. Raphael unleashed was like nothing I'd ever witnessed. Every muscle was tightened to an extreme. Every inch of him was focused solely on me. I'd asked for faster and he delivered because he'd only ever been all about me. Just like I wanted to be for him.

Inside me, he thickened, and I cried out, a second orgasm chasing the first just as fast. He muttered something I couldn't understand. My blood rushed in my ears, my only certainty now that I needed him to feel what I was feeling. Not to stop or do the honourable thing or to withdraw. But to keep going, to fuck me until we both broke.

He pulsed again, and slowed. I gritted my teeth.

"Don't stop."

Raphael swore but obeyed. I knew he was close. We'd danced around each other far too much for this to be anything other than explosive, and I needed him to slip. I needed that trigger to be pulled and for him to stay with me throughout.

Through hazy vision, I connected our gazes. I showed him in my expression everything he made me feel. It was too easy not to hide anymore. He kissed me until I was breathless, so close to that edge again and solely focused on that plunge in and out of my body. It was tearing me apart in the best possible way. Ruining me.

When he'd pushed me back to the edge, I gritted my teeth so I didn't fly over it alone. I felt the urgency in every punch of his hips and in the tight grip he had on my body.

"Alex," he begged. My name a prayer on his lips.

"Be a good boy and come with me."

Surprise flared in his eyes, yet he didn't stop. He didn't

slow. I'd given the permission he'd needed, and now he only needed to take what was his to claim.

In the darkened hallway, against the wall, my bodyguard thrust into me over and over again until I was lost for anything other than this. The cottage could've collapsed around us, and all I'd know was how he filled me so sweetly.

Then I was coming again, but clamping down my jaw in desperate need for him to get there, too.

I spasmed around him, and Raphael made a choked sound and slowed, thrusting a couple more times which was all I needed to launch into heaven. Then he came inside me, his arms clutched around me, and his breathing ragged. When my climax finished rocking me, emotion rushed in its place.

I'd never known anything like this. I'd never met anyone like him. I'd do everything to keep the thing we'd found because there was no other option but us.

# 34

## Raphael

Fucking shaking, I staggered with Alex in my arms, into the living room and down to the rug. I wasn't done worshipping her. Not by any measure. Still inside her, and still half hard, I knelt over her and pressed a kiss to her waiting lips.

"You're so beautiful."

She smiled into my kiss. "I finally have all of you."

I inched back to connect to her gaze. "Ye always have."

That smile got bigger, and emotion crinkled her eyes. "I've worn your t-shirt almost every night for five years. You were the one man I could never get over, even if we had nothing but that dance. For all these years, you were my ideal, and now I have you. Oh—now is probably a good time to tell you I'm on the pill."

My brain fritzed. My jaw unhinged. "I...fuck, I didn't think."

"Neither did I. I don't care either. And that is the last

outside world thing we're talking about tonight. The rest of it is locked outside the cottage."

She mimed closing a lock, and I collected the pretend key from her fingers and tossed it.

I was down for that. All we'd done was handle problem after problem. More than ever, I needed space with her so we could just be us, no matter how short that time had to be. And I was far from done with her.

The thought of what we'd done, the no-condom deal, settled over me. Fuck, that was hot.

Alex wriggled into me. "You're hard again."

I trailed my lips from one cheek to the next. "I'm inside ye. Chances were slim of my dick ever going down."

Her peal of laughter was like silver bells. "There I was, wondering if it was the idea of knocking me up."

I groaned. "Don't. Just the thought is making me crazy."

"Oh my God, you're for real. I could just ditch the pill tonight, really send you insane."

I stole a kiss to stop her teasing. Urgency commanded me to make the most of this moment. To claim her and keep her here. I sat up and ripped off my shirt, but undressing fully meant withdrawing from her perfect body.

I tapped her hip. "Don't go anywhere."

She giggled, and both her hands slipped to between her legs when I jumped back to rid myself of the rest of my clothes. Then I returned to kneel at the cradle of her hips and collected her wrists to reveal what she was hiding.

I was leaking out of her, and that image would never leave my brain.

Alex's cheeks reddened, and she tried to close her knees. I gripped her wrists and stretched her arms above her head, and at the same second, fitted myself between her legs and thrust home once more.

She tipped her head back on the rug, and those legs fell open again for me.

"There's my dirty princess. Wanting her bodyguard to put a baby in her and spreading her legs for him."

Alex bucked onto me.

This time, I had the opportunity to do more than just fuck her into the wall like an animal. She was slick with my cum, and I withdrew enough to capture some of the mess on my fingers and rub it over her clit. Fuck it. I needed to claim her completely as mine. I wetted my fingers again and daubed her chest and both breasts before wiping the last on her lips. She sucked my fingers, and heat surged through me.

"You marked me," she said.

"I want to live here, just like this."

Something flickered in her eyes, and she took a shaky breath. "Us in this cottage?"

I'd meant in her body, but the second the words were past her lips, I could think of nothing else. Us living here. That baby a real part of our future together.

Yet I couldn't answer. She hadn't known me long enough, not in any real terms. I hadn't thought it through or planned or prepared. Yet from the very bottom of my soul, I knew this was what I wanted. What I'd always wanted.

She was the girl I'd fallen for after just one dance. Princess or not, my heart had claimed her as mine.

"Ye kept my shirt. Now ye have somewhere to hang it up." I kissed her cheek and her throat, keeping those hands pinned so I could move down her body. She had the most incredible curves, and I'd spend the night showing her so.

Alex arched into me when I took her nipple in my mouth and toyed with her. She'd liked that before. I was enjoying learning her one action at a time. Palming the other breast, I gave up my hold on her wrists so I could play. Instantly, her fingers were in my hair and grazing my scalp in a way that had me pushing up to continue the contact.

"I crave your touch," I confessed.

"I need yours," she swore back.

They were the only words either of us said for a long time. I fucked her on the rug, collecting her legs to lie flat against my body so I could use them as leverage. Then, when I'd made her come for a fourth time, I flipped her over onto all fours and chased my pleasure with her incredible backside in my hands, giving me clear sight of my dick disappearing into her body. Nothing could beat that. Whatever we had been to each other, it felt like it was changing. I could only hope for the better. I'd permanently altered to fit to her. Nothing would ever be the same after tonight.

Alex peeked back at me then dropped her upper half so only her backside was raised. "I need you to come again."

Fucking hell. It took all my concentration *not* to come.

"Going to need one more from ye, princess."

She clucked her tongue. "Always the bodyguard, giving me orders."

I laughed then groaned as her fingers sought the space we were joined underneath her, then played. She found her completion quickly, and I followed her over that ledge and emptied into her a second time in the space of an hour. Coming inside her was addictive. We were messy and new, and I'd never wanted anything more than Alex.

I gathered her in my arms and carried her to the shower, still breathing like I'd run a marathon. Under the water, we shared wet, open-mouthed kisses while we cleaned each other, finally making it to bed to realise something.

The storm outside had stopped.

While ours had only just begun.

Alex yawned and rolled to give me space to join her. I pulled her into a hard embrace, her back to my front, relaxing to enjoy the stretch of her naked body and how she hugged my arms.

My dick, of course, didn't stand down.

She writhed onto me. "Slide inside me again."

"Tell me about painting."

"I did some. I loved it."

"Can I see?"

"Nope. Well, maybe tomorrow. Are you going to do as I asked?"

I kissed her shoulder. "Had the thought I should let ye sleep."

"Sleep like that. In me. I want to."

Without giving up the close hug, I angled to slide between her legs then inside her. Both of us groaned, settling into the sensation.

"Good boy," Alex murmured.

I pulsed, thickening more.

It was dark in the bedroom. In the hall and the living room, we'd explored each other by lamplight. Now, in the all-encompassing dark, and with exhaustion wrapping around me in a warm hold, the frenzy left me. But not the need to claim her. That would never go, I was as certain of that as I was my love for flying.

"Just so we're clear, there is no chance of me sleeping now," I said.

Alex exhaled a shaky laugh. "God, same. Go slow until we're done. Then maybe we can rest."

I eased in and out of her, just an inch or two, the sensation of deep need stirring and spreading over me. Likewise, Alex shifted in a slow rhythm, working me like I was her. I had no idea how much time passed, only how the desire built and built. It wasn't a hard taking now. Only soft and all-encompassing.

I was so gone for her, that when she came, triggering my orgasm instantly, I nearly told her. I nearly said the words that couldn't be taken back. My heart thumped the message instead.

It said I loved her with every single beat.

# 35

## Raphael

That same heavy heart woke me hours later, darkness thick and Alex sleeping across my chest. For her, I needed to change. Myself, as a minimum, but also my ideas.

As carefully as possible, I eased out from under her, settling her back down in the warm patch I'd left, then stole away to the living room.

Spying on my father would be best not done naked, so I dragged on my boxers and took my tablet to the sofa, logging on. For a long while now, we'd monitored him. Anything urgent would prompt a notification, such as his private jet leaving the States, or mass movement of his associates, say, if they'd left him to burn, but all had been quiet.

Methodically, I worked through the various traces. Dad owned a transport company, and we had access to numberplate recognition software that told us his trade routes. I scanned the data.

Nothing new. He was operating as normal.

Nor had he strayed outside of California, which was reassuring. In addition to our tracking, his second wife had sworn to report back to us if anything went wrong with him, but it didn't help me feel safe.

It should, yet I couldn't shake the sense of impending danger. Maybe it was to do with the trauma my brother gently tried to talk to me about, of witnessing extreme violence from a young age and having no method of processing that. I'd confided once in Gordain, and he'd suggested therapy, but I'd found my peace in the skies and in having an escape method like nothing else could provide.

Under the tablet's blue light, I sat back and considered what I'd done. Far more dangerous than my father was the fact I'd fallen in love. I'd let down my defences, and somehow that felt like every single other protection I'd had in place had been destroyed.

"Raphael?"

Alex peered around the doorframe, her expression hesitant, like she was worried at disturbing me.

My errant pulse skipped at the sight of her. "Come here."

She slipped into the room, and, ah fuck, she was still naked, but sadly not for long as she snagged my t-shirt and pulled it over her head. The moment she was in reach, I tugged her to my lap, discarding the tablet. Her knees slipped to the sofa cushions either side of my hips, and I held her waist.

"I woke and you'd gone." She tilted her head.

"Not far."

"What...? Never mind. It isn't any of my business."

Under her, my dick pulsed, getting hard already, despite my mood. Alex took a sweet little inhale.

"I won't hide anything from ye, and ignore my dick. It

isn't like he's been neglected." I collected the tablet up again and showed her the screen. "Data tracking my father."

She studied it. "You do that?"

"It's a method to help us feel safe from him."

"What are you looking for?"

"Changes to his patterns. The only protection we have is Ariel's dossier of evidence. If he goes ahead and betrays the people he's working with, that's of no help to us anymore."

"Did you find anything?"

"No."

Her gaze left the screen and returned to me, curious, and with something resembling sorrow in its depths. "Does midnight research work when you're stressing out?"

"Usually."

"But not tonight."

Ah fuck, she knew already. The connection between us had been strong from the start, and it was only growing. I'd found my person. My heart told me so. From the first, I'd wanted to protect her, then I'd been dying to take her home. Now I had her here, she was showing me just how much she wanted to understand me right back.

It was a startling, beautiful realisation, and I couldn't answer her from the strength of it, but I didn't need to. Alex pressed her lips to my cheek.

"I'm assuming you don't want to talk about it?"

My dick throbbed again, my blood pumping faster. "Not now."

"I hate you being sad. I can't do anything about that, but I can do this."

She stripped the shirt and moved my hands to her breasts while she kissed me, then shifted her position to free my dick, stroking me from root to tip.

I groaned, loving the feel of her touch and happily distracted from my thoughts.

But this wasn't going the way I expected. Alex broke our kiss, gave me a pretty smirk, and climbed off my lap to slide down my body. She knelt on the floor between my legs and fitted her mouth to the end of my dick.

I tipped my head back at how fucking good that felt. Her hot mouth. The light suck she gave me as a warm-up. I couldn't stare down at her clever tongue in action or I'd come in under a minute.

My princess wasn't having it. She came off me. "Watch me blow you."

Damn, fuck, God. I obeyed her and enjoyed the image of the stunning woman sweeping her silky dark hair to one side and gliding her mouth over me.

On her knees, Alex drove me crazy. I speared my fingers into her hair but fisted the sofa back with my other hand to stop from grabbing her too hard. She tongued, sucked, and teased me, cupping my balls and running her thumb over them until I bucked into her mouth and cried out.

My breathing had turned ragged. She owned not only my heart but every single part of my body.

Though I fought to control myself, I throbbed in her mouth, and Alex came off me, her hand replacing her mouth, working me faster.

"Be a good boy and stop holding back. Come for me."

Her mouth returned to encase my desperate dick, and one more suck and I came, nearly losing my mind. That praise thing she'd worked out? Fuck did I need that so badly.

She drank me down then grinned at her victory, leaving me a panting, sweating mess, with no other thought in my head but her.

Her victory, in that respect, was sweet.

Sunlight spilled around the curtains of our bedroom, and in my arms, Alex stirred. She kissed me, and we moved together in slow lovemaking that felt like we'd never stopped. Insistent, demanding presses of our lips, and our hips working together. She clung to me as she came. I said her name like a prayer when I fell after.

This. I wanted this forever.

The decision had been made and tattooed to my soul.

Alex climbed from the bed and slid my shirt over her head, disappearing for a moment then returning to the doorway. "Up. You showed me yours last night, I want to show you mine."

I followed her into the spare bedroom. As far as I knew, there was nothing in this room, but the collection of items in the corner showed me that had changed. A canvas. A piece of board with smudges of paint. Tubes, brushes, and more.

Alex hugged her arms. "We found most of it at the house clean. Valentine lent me his daughter's easel."

My focus locked on the painting itself. I'd guessed from Dori's shot that she'd done something artistic, but we hadn't gotten around to discussing it. Her surprise broke new happiness over my heart.

The subject? The profile of a man's face. Light lines to

show the features. A well-defined mouth. *My mouth*. She'd drawn me.

"Is he turning away or towards the viewer?" I asked.

Her beautiful eyes held mine. "Towards, at last. It's you, five years ago, back when I should've done what my instincts demanded and brought you near. I've thought about you so much since then. This is the view I remembered of your face as I looked up when we danced. Is that okay?"

I backed her to the wall. Claimed her lips again. "It's incredible. You're painting again. Fucking love that."

She smiled into the kiss.

"Eyes on me," I murmured, stealing her words from in the night, and ready to tell her how much more I loved than just her art.

Someone hammered on the front door, the sound ricochetting through the cottage and shattering the calm. We stared at each other, and my hackles rose. Nothing good ever came from an early morning wake-up call like that.

All that fear from in the night rushed back.

"Stay here."

In the living room, I went to the door. "Who is it?"

"Valentine. So sorry, but there's some shite going down. It couldn't wait."

I swung open the door, blinking at the bright sun. "Talk to me."

He indicated his head to the room beyond. "I'd better come in. Ben and Jax are on their way."

The warmth from spending the night twisted up with Alex left me fast. Peering around to make sure she wasn't in sight, I let him in, then held up a finger to pause him and snatched up our remaining scattered clothes. In our bedroom, Alex was already pulling a fresh outfit from her bag.

"I heard," she said.

I offered a grim smile. When dressed, we returned to the living room.

Valentine was staring at his phone. "I've been monitoring the news and alerts for your name, Alex. This appeared ten minutes ago."

He held up the screen to display a headline.

*Concerns at the Palace Over Princess Alexandra's Whereabouts.*

Alex recoiled. I took the phone and read aloud.

"A source at Ossington Palace reports that the royal family is deeply worried over wild child Princess Alexandra. Last seen several days ago, the princess has been rumoured to be in the company of an unnamed man previously in the employ of the palace." I raised my head. "What the fuck?"

Valentine's forehead creased in deep lines of concern. "Another appeared shortly after, presumably a gossip rag hustling to make up a story and steal the clicks. It's on the next tab."

I jumped to it then swore.

***Sexy Lexi:*** *Stalking Studs and Spiralling?*

Alex gritted her teeth. "'A palace source' is code for the office of the private secretary. It means it's real. This is what they resorted to? The lowdown, dirty-tactic-using bastards. I won't talk to them and they decide to get every person in the country tracking me down?" She paced away then swung back. "That's it, isn't it? They can't get me to make scandalous headlines so they invented one? I haven't even thought about how to tackle that mess. I've barely caught my breath."

I wanted to tell her it was all going to be okay, but something gnawed at me. I faced Valentine. "Why did ye call in the team?"

We could use their advice, sure, but for him to do that before talking to me was odd.

He worked his jaw. "The speculations started almost immediately."

"Meaning what? How are they speculating?" Alex swung her gaze between us.

Another knock rattled the door. Valentine backed up to it, still watching us. "Next tab, Raph. The identity of her mystery man."

I thumbed to the following page, the headline more of the same but the picture below startling and bold.

It was of me, body blocking Alex at the stadium event when we'd been surrounded by a crowd. A bold red circle showcased a feature on the photo. Our joined hands.

Something inside me crushed.

It was over. The secrecy and anonymity we'd shared here. Alex's safety and place of calm.

Alex's breath stuttered. "I'm so sorry."

"Who is it?" Valentine challenged the person outside.

Ben called out a reply, "It's me plus Jax."

"Dori, also," a second voice called.

Valentine let them in then succinctly caught them up, taking back his phone for show and tell.

Jackson palmed his jaw. "I don't get the claim you're missing when you're supposed to be at your da's place."

Alex's shoulders rose. "Dad's people would never give up information on me, not like the Ossington Palace staff. Not a peep. Not even if Sir Reginald called himself."

"So they're having to smoke ye out by using your boyfriend," Jackson concluded. "I don't like this. It smacks of 'by any means necessary'."

I stared at my picture reveal, still open on Valentine's phone. "Enough people know where I live to send them right to us. The press are probably already on their way."

Ben nodded once, his powerful arms folded. "To Braithar. We'll have longer until anyone looks for ye here. No one on the estate will talk." He turned to Val. "Has Raphael been named yet?"

"No. I have an alert out for that, too."

Alex made a sound of frustration. "This is such crap. What could they possibly need me for that's so important? I missed the state dinner, sure, but did that make headlines? No. Did the fact someone spiked my drink garner the interest of the press? Nope. I bet it never even got reported because one of them is paying off that photographer." Her eyes flashed with anger. "Dori, tell them what you told me last night."

Her friend's gaze darkened. "Sir Reginald got my phone number from somewhere we don't know and called me a few times. On the day Alex went to the botanical gardens, he hit me up for her outfit choice. I gave it."

"Which then got leaked, proving he's part of it." Alex looked at me. "Undeniable evidence. I hate it."

I felt the same. "We need to get to the bottom of why he's doing it. Time's up whether we like it or not."

She blew out a shaky exhale, her hands balled into fists, and pink spots formed on her cheeks. "And in the centre of it all is you. I wouldn't blame you if you wanted nothing to do with me. They'll be evil if this story takes off. They'll dig into every part of your life. I didn't even consider that until now because there was no risk of it. No risk to you."

Her voice caught at the end.

I bundled her against my chest, my heart beating too fast.

Dimly, I was aware of Ben marshalling the others into the kitchen and saying something about making coffee. I didn't pay any more attention to them. I needed to make Alex understand. She thought we were over because of this.

I laid my lips to her hair. "I'm not going anywhere."

"You should. I'm toxic to be around. One of the reasons I don't have close friends besides Dori is because they get sick of seeing themselves in the press. My best friend at uni, the one you met? She got upskirted by a newspaper shortly after the picture of you and me and never spoke to me again. My own mother left my dad because the shit they printed about her eventually got too much."

"Why are you giving Hot Pilot reasons to quit you?" Dori queried from the kitchen. "He isn't like them."

I tipped up her chin and made her look at me. "He's right. I'm not. However this goes down, we face it together."

Her gaze clung to mine. "It might get worse."

"Then I'll handle it."

"Even if they share your name? Even if this can't be managed and goes global?"

The strain in her voice told me she'd realised what I'd already leapt to—that my father might see the pictures and hear the rumours. If it happened, that was my problem to solve, and though Jax's murderous remedy had stuck in my mind, there had to be other options.

I cared about her too much not to try.

Though it scared the fuck out of me, the issue in hand was her family, not mine. If that flipped, I'd take care of that, too.

"Whatever they throw at us, we'll be okay."

"Us," she repeated, her voice small, then with a nod to herself as if confirming something, she cupped the back of my neck and pulled me in for a kiss. "That's probably the most romantic thing I ever heard."

"Same," one of my team called from the kitchen.

I smiled against her lips and caught her hand to lead her with me to join them, buoyed, because *us* meant fighting this together.

At the kitchen table, I looked to each in turn. "What are we thinking?"

Ben lifted his chin. "Moving quickly to control the damage. I've already sent a request to my legal guy to get him to request a takedown of your photo from any major sites, and a pre-emptive one if you're named. It's been posted on the internet which means it's forever, but we can limit visibility. I don't have the approval to act for ye, Alex. I wish I did."

She gave him a grim smile. "I wish I'd known that your team existed and I had hiring power."

He shrugged. "Say the word and we're yours to employ."

My heart hurt. I fucking loved my team. They'd teased me but also accepted Alex with no hesitation, working with me in what I wanted to do. They understood without me needing to ask or say a word. I had no idea how lucky I'd been to land on my feet with them, but I'd never take it for granted.

Alex swallowed. "I can't pay you. I don't have any income or access to royal bank accounts."

My boss's smile remained kind. "Raphael is already firmly on your team. What's a few more of us? Sign us on and we're yours to instruct. Leo pays us fine and doesnae need us right now. He won't mind. The alternative is lending my crew out to other teams, and we all know how that went."

He held up his phone with a pro-forma contract.

"It's as easy as that?" Alex signed her name with her finger.

"Done. I'll get onto the lawyer to try to manage the media circus that's bound to follow." Ben strode back into the living room and made a call.

Valentine took over his role. "That handles your protection and the shite online. Now we have to address the immediate concern. People will be on the hunt. Ye don't wait around for them to come to ye."

Alex shivered. "Which means we need to leave."

"But not in Raph's car." Jackson held up his keys. "Mine's outside. Have at it."

I accepted them with a nod of gratitude. "Next, do we hide elsewhere or make a stand and face them?" That question was for Alex alone.

She chewed her lip. "I'm supposed to be at my father's house, so if I'm there, the search is over. All I have to do is show myself and the speculation is done. Will you come with me?"

My lips twitched. "Asking me to meet your da already. I'm down."

She laughed, then her eyes widened. "I've had an idea. We wanted to test out the theory that one of the bodyguards was selling information, right? That's what started all this. It's got to be linked."

Valentine inclined his head. "It absolutely is. Whoever's paying them off is behind this. You're thinking it'll help us get to that all-important why."

Alex grinned agreement. "I'll call each in turn and ask

them to secretly come to me at a different location in Dad's grounds. We can have people watch out. Then if unexpected bounty hunters or press arrive, we'll have the proof with the side benefit of bringing the cameras to the site while I handle my family."

I tried to picture what she'd described. "How many different locations are there that this will work?"

"At my dad's estate? It's massive. Tens of thousands of acres. There's a café, a place outside the gates that does tours of the grounds, even one wing of the house that's open to the public and has a gift shop. They're each a fair distance apart."

We all stared at her.

Dori blew on his nails. "Stop flexing the princess shit."

Alex waggled her phone. "Got their numbers? Let's get them all to Scotland."

Rapid fire, she left voice messages for Will and Johnnie, asking them to meet her in the afternoon. "Lastly, I'll call Riss and tell her to come to the main gates because I need guarding. She won't say no. What happens when she arrives will speak volumes."

I watched her. "Ye suspect her, too?"

"No, not really. But she's in the thrall of Sir Reginald, and he's the one pushing me to work more. He also made a comment once about anticipating the headlines I'd create. He'll show up at Dad's, and we can have it out in private. Several birds, one stone." Her shoulders slumped, but she sent the final message.

"Sir J is creepy." Dori shuddered.

I squinted at him. "Don't ye mean Sir R?"

"He's been on the palace scene for as long as I've known Alex, and back when we were teenagers, he was introduced to me using his full name. I think of him as that."

A warning played out in my head. "What does the J stand for?"

"He's Sir Reginald Jessop," Dori supplied.

"Like Jared Jessop, the old head of your team?" I asked Alex.

Her brow furrowed. "Maybe? I don't know the surnames for any of my bodyguards. Only you."

Valentine was already on his phone, typing, Jackson doing the same on his own.

Valentine held his up in a flourish. "Father and son, if this old picture is the right people."

Alex's frown morphed into surprise. "It is. They're related?"

I swore. "No wonder Jared had a chip on his shoulder. He thought he was untouchable. That's probably why Barrington is working so hard now to not lose the contract. He already had to let the boss's son go. I wonder if he knew."

Ben had returned and leaned against the kitchen entrance. "My guess is not or he'd never have done it. But what a sneaky move on Sir Reginald's part, planting his useless son on your team. Fingers in every pie and corrupt from the start. Even more, we need that paparazzo guy to tell us who paid him off. If we're right about Sir Reginald, his pet photographer will show up today, too. Who wants to nab him?"

Valentine cackled. "At last, a little action. Jax and I will. Up for a jaunt to a palace?"

Jackson added his approval. "Hell, yes."

Dori pressed both palms on the table and looked like he had something to say. "Can I help? I have zero experience in security work outside of being guarded when I'm doing royal shit myself, but I'd know Malcolm Dennis in the dark. He threw a punch at me, and I wouldn't mind seeing him stepped on. Let me? Fuck knows I have energy to burn."

Jackson tilted his head. "What royal family are ye?"

"Norway and Luxembourg medley."

Alex pursed her lips. "Just imagine Dori's family tree growing out of piles of gold rather than earth and you've got him."

My two coworkers regarded each other.

Valentine quipped, "Not it if he gets bashed."

Jackson shrugged at Dori. "You're in."

The count almost smiled then coughed into his fist to hide the emotion.

Valentine turned to Ben. "What do we do to motivate the fucker?" He made two hand gestures simultaneously, fingers rubbing together to represent cash and a fist to show pain.

Ben twisted his lips in consideration. "Whatever works. They're playing dirty, so we will, too. Today is going to bring many truths to the surface, I feel. Alex, they might not all be nice ones. They rarely are when people pull moves like this."

She sighed but kept her chin up. "I don't care. I'm out. They can't make me go back. Whatever they throw at me, I'm ready."

As was I, in front of her or by her side. However she needed me.

# 36

# *Alexandra*

By air, we travelled to Lancaster House, Raphael touching down in a clearing in the thick private woods behind the mansion. I'd rung ahead to Perkins, and Dad plus his lady friend were expecting me.

He hadn't heard my news yet. It was still early enough not to have made the mainstream headlines he might see, and for that, I was glad.

Nothing about this was good, but fear built inside me in anticipation of my father's reaction and the resulting stress making him sick again. Maybe if I'd followed Dori's advice and talked to him earlier, none of this would've happened, but hindsight didn't help me now.

I had to explain this to Dad in person, taking all the care

Perkins that there might be press hunting for me, and he'd talked to the security who patrolled the estate, texting me during the flight that none had been seen yet, and they'd close the gates.

Good. We'd beat them here, which meant there was time to do all I wanted in the right order.

Most people travelling up from London would take several hours on an airport hop, and could go to Raphael's home first, if they knew his name, and Raphael's team plus Dori would be an hour by road in their own vehicles. Valentine's early action meant we were on the front foot at last.

When we left the helicopter to climb into a waiting Land Rover, my father's groundskeeper behind the wheel, nerves over a new realisation cramped my stomach.

Raphael claimed my hand across the seat. "Okay?"

"Why is it in the middle of all the drama, the one thing I'm fixating on is introducing my dad to you?"

He sat up taller. "Now I'm second-guessing what I'm wearing. Should've brought a smart jacket."

I glanced over at him and shivered. Raphael was in his standard wear of black jeans and a t-shirt. We hadn't lingered in the cottage after making our plans, and he matched my casual vibe. He was so perfect, and all I'd ever brought him was hassle.

"That isn't what I meant. What if you meet my father and want nothing more to do with me? He can be eccentric." I'd already explained that he was frail and his hands shook. If he was tired, the evidence of his stroke would be in his face, too. But I hadn't shared his mischievous side and how he loved to tease.

Raphael laughed and stroked my knuckles with his

thumb. "Not happening. Your exploits didnae scare me off, so nothing will."

"Exploits?"

"Leading me on a run around town, jumping in a lake, charming birds into a riot. Ye know, the typical princess-and-bodyguard dating scene."

I laughed, but my amusement didn't hang around for long.

Out of the woods, we zoomed up to the crenelated entrance to a private wing of the house, surrounded by an extensive lawn and tall hedges. The entrance hall was four storeys high with a narrow tower abutting one corner. It was the prettiest house, yet never truly my home.

Raphael's gaze travelled over the eighteenth-century stately home, constructed by an ancestor in the romantic style of much older buildings. "No wonder your da likes it here."

"It has everything he needs, including a dungeon he regularly threatens to lock people away in."

Someone cleared their throat, and my father's manservant regarded us from the doorway.

Perkins bowed his head. "Your Royal Highness. Sir, welcome to Lancaster House."

He made way for us to enter the cooler interior. Dad liked things kitsch and had had the house done out in the family tartan. That plus the deer heads and abundance of weaponry on the walls made it a true Scottish retreat. One he hadn't left in a long time.

With the door firmly closed behind us, Perkins, who was nearing eighty if he was a day, straightened his lapels and gave us a critical but professional once-over. "Ma'am, you'll find your father with Mrs d'Farnacee in the East breakfast room. He's waiting for ye. Sir, if I may."

He stepped to a tall cupboard and flipped through hangers until he extracted a tartan jacket, handing it to Raphael.

My boyfriend, because I was running with that now, slipped it on. "Perfect fit. Thank ye. Please call me Raphael."

Perkins bobbed his head. "Very good, sir. I'm sure you'll find His Royal Highness more amenable to a young man already dressed in his colours." His eyes twinkled, and he indicated for us to follow.

If I'd been alone, Perkins would still have taken me to my father. Things were done a certain way at Lancaster House and had been so for decades. That familiarity gave a small degree of reassurance though did nothing to replace my worry.

Through the house, we climbed a flight of stairs, and outside a pair of tall double doors, Perkins halted and knocked. Dad called out an answer, and Perkins marched in, the sound of laughter and conversation finding us in the hall.

Raphael dropped my hand and swallowed, staring straight forward but not moving.

I nudged his shoulder with mine. "Breathe."

"Never met a girlfriend's parent before."

"So, we're dating then?"

He jerked his gaze to mine. "Of course we are. Aren't we? I can't believe I'm asking that in a palace to a princess."

I preened. "Now who's nervous?"

"He's your father. Wait, do I bow?"

"At the neck, and call him Your Royal Highness the first time you address him and then sir after. And yes, I'll be your girlfriend."

His heated gaze touched mine, but we could do nothing to celebrate the moment. Not now. Later, I'd make him ask me again when I had the chance to show how it made me feel.

Perkins announced us. "Her Royal Highness Princess Alexandra and her companion Raphael Gordonson."

"Alexandra," Dad boomed. "Come in, child."

Raphael straightened his shoulders, and we entered the bright breakfast room. At a small table in front of open French doors, my father set down his teacup and watched our approach, his dark-blue smoking jacket wrapped tight around him despite the warm day. At his side, Sarah d'Farnacee rose gracefully and curtsied to me, her cloud of blonde hair and make-up perfect as always and her smile soft.

I greeted them both, noting that Raphael sketched a perfect bow. It had never occurred to me until now that it could be seen as strange that we did this, but my father preserved all manners of respect, and I'd been taught to from as early as I could remember. As always, Raphael rolled with the punches.

"A pleasure to meet ye, Your Royal Highness, Mrs d'Farnacee," he said.

My father made a small shooing gesture to Sarah, and she rounded the table to stand in front of Raphael. "Mr Gordonson. I find myself in need of a strong young man to assist me down to the patio. Would you mind?"

Raphael shot me a surprised eyebrow rise but offered his arm to Sarah, then escorted her out of the French doors and down the stairs, their footsteps disappearing.

My father watched them go. I waited for his judgement.

"Smart young man. I take it you bringing him to me and Perkins stuffing him into our tartan is of significance?"

I was too nervous to sit, so held the back of a sturdy and ornate dining chair. "Yes, Papa."

"Let's hear it then. How long have you known him?"

"Five years."

He sipped his tea. "His family? Perkins looked him up but found nothing."

"He isn't titled."

"Then he wants one?"

I made eyes at my dad. "He's a pilot, actually. He works hard and is self-made. He flies and drives, unlike either of us."

My father appeared unconvinced but picked up the last bite of food from his plate and finished it. He was eating well, then. There was colour in his cheeks, and he had a snarky attitude about him that suggested he was in better health.

"Self-made or not, he'll need to change his game in order to marry you, Alexandra. In the old days, he'd need a title."

I resisted a disrespectful eye roll. "He hasn't asked, so don't jump the gun. Plus he doesn't need to change anything. It isn't necessary. All that matters is that he's important to me, and I wanted you to meet him, among other things. Stop making wedding plans."

My father hummed. "Well, I suppose he's a better choice than that nephew of Norway you run around with. I confess I'm relieved it won't be him who will come to me for permission."

My nerves left me, and I rounded the seat to drop into it. "You love Dori. He's on his way here, actually."

Dad brightened. "Is he? Think he'll join us at whist?"

My mind slipped to the mission Dori had taken on with Raphael's team. To the whole drama that brought me here. I stiffened my spine. "Perhaps. There's something I need to talk to you about. You have to promise not to rage about it."

"Well, spit it out, then."

"Over the summer, the king asked me to step in to carry out some public appearances while he was away."

Dad's lips thinned. "The nerve. Off sunning himself while he set you to task. No, no. I never wanted that for you. You have your art, plus you always hated public speaking. No, Alexandra. Absolutely not."

"Calm or I won't continue." My throat clogged at his referencing my art and my aptitude. I never knew he'd noticed.

My father reached for a plastic pill dispenser on the table. He popped one of the compartments, extracted a small yellow pill, displayed it to me, then swallowed it. "Proceed."

This was the hard part.

I couldn't do it. I couldn't tell him about the security leaks or the danger I'd been in with the drink spiking. Though Dad looked well, another stroke could ruin him.

I dropped his gaze and half of what I could've said. After our conversation, I'd go out and make the appearance that would make the press lose interest in me. Dad didn't need to be any the wiser about that. The only part I couldn't handle myself was Sir Reginald's threat to put my father to work or defund him.

"They want me to do more, and I don't mind helping out our family, but there were concerns over how it was being managed..."

"What kind of concerns?"

"Raphael's team are bodyguards. Their advice was for me to stop. But if I'm not the one doing it, it was suggested that you—"

"Perkins," my father bellowed. "Fetch me my telephone."

Perkins stepped through the door. "At once. Please be advised that we have another guest arriving. I'm informed a second helicopter recently touched down."

My father grouched about who that might be, but I was already on my feet. With any luck, my lure had worked, and I had to get in there first to control this mess.

# 37

# Raphael

*A*rm in arm with the prince's girlfriend, I crossed the lawn outside the palace in no particular hurry.

I kept my gaze on the hedgerows. "What are my chances?"

"Of winning Alfred's approval? I'd say fair. Perkins already briefed him on what little he knew about you, and the prince enjoyed the fact that your private life is not visible online. If he didn't like the idea of you, he would have kept you in the room to make sure you knew it."

I chewed on that. "So sending me out so he can talk to Alex in secret is a good sign?"

"I believe so. Alexandra is the apple of his eye, even if he is a terribly neglectful father. He'll like you if the princess tells him to. Have you met the mother? An absolute troll. I assume that Alexandra hasn't been in touch with her recently, though she's clearly in crisis?"

I didn't answer, and Sarah arched an eyebrow.

"I'll take that as a yes. I don't mean to pry, only to point out how neither parent is very present. If you do have to meet her, I'd recommend taming via a tray of baked goods and gossip."

I held in a laugh. "Noted. I appreciate the advice."

A beeping sound came from somewhere on Sarah's person, and she released my arm to pat her pockets. "Please excuse me. Ah, it's my daughter. She texts as if I have eyes to read that tiny screen without the glasses I left upstairs. Could you, please?"

She thrust the phone at me. I read aloud.

"Mother, when are you coming home? There's no food in the fridge, and the help is too busy cleaning up after Laurie to go shopping."

Sarah grumbled. "Text back that she should go herself, though I'm sure she'll complain about it."

I did, making it a suggestion rather than a demand. "How old is she?"

"Twenty-seven. Laurie is her six-year-old, my grandson. She had a fight with her husband and moved in with me rather than work it out."

"That sounds rough." I tried to be sympathetic, but my mind was still in the upstairs room with Alex.

"It's rough for me. Why do you think I'm here? Their argument was over her laziness. I'm with the husband."

I burst out in a genuine laugh. "Shite, sorry. I can't relate. I fended for myself from my teenage years. Time on her own will do her some good. Maybe give the help she referred to some time off?"

Sarah brightened. "Genius. Hand me back that phone."

She squinted then dialled a number and strolled away.

I took a moment to check the messages in my team's

group chat. They'd all arrived on-site. I scrolled down to the last.

*Jackson: The café is thick with reporters and armchair detectives. Johnnie leaked big time. No sign of the photog.*

It didn't surprise me. Johnnie's attitude had given away his intent without him having to say a word. It pissed me off that I hadn't acted faster, though. I could've done more.

Another message sprang up on a different chat, one for my family.

*Gabe: At long last, let me introduce you to the newest member of our family. Our lad, born half an hour ago at a hefty nine pounds four ounces. Mother and baby doing fine. Effie's relieved it's over. We're both instantly in love.*

He attached a picture of a wee scrap of a dark-haired bairn, bundled in a white hospital blanket and with his eyes closed.

Instantly, my sister was typing.

*Ariel: Oh God! The cuteness. Got a name for him?*

*Gabe: Not yet. We had one picked out, but it doesn't suit him. Back to the drawing board.*

I sent my congratulations, waiting for the familiar wave of fear to swoop in on me, as it had done every time I'd thought about our father interfering with his grandchild's life. It didn't come. Perhaps it was the high energy of the day. Maybe later I'd lose my mind.

Still walking with me, Sarah chatted on the phone in a language I didn't know, and I took a moment to centre myself, skimming over the perimeter of the private lawn and up to the gate.

A furious-looking grey-haired man stormed up to it.

He hit a buzzer on a keypad and waited, his gaze locking on to the house. Sir Reginald. I'd only seen his picture this morning, but there was no mistaking the haughty stance or the malice in his eyes.

Good. I had a few choice words to say to the man, and fuck was I letting him near Alex. In case this took a minute, I wrote a quick message to Jackson. If he was free, he could step in for Alex. I had a private secretary to take down.

The gate buzzed open, and he strode in, making a beeline for the house. I had a chance and had to take it.

"Sir Reginald Jessop," I shouted.

Sarah blinked at the incomer and flitted away.

The man's attention shot to me. "Raphael Gordonson, I presume." The hostility in his expression shifted to calculation. He rerouted to bear down on me, his lips curved in a cool and unfriendly smile when he reached me. "The bodyguard."

I tilted my head. "The underhanded, scheming palace insider."

The smile dropped. "I have something to say to you. It will be brief. Follow me."

He turned and stalked across the lawn, heading towards a distant building on the other side of a wide pond. At a guess, I assumed it to be Alex's summerhouse that she'd planned to stay in.

The man didn't say a word until we climbed the steps and he'd thrown the door open then closed it behind us. The bright room was warm. The polar opposite to the iciness of the man in front of me.

Anger brewed in my gut. If we were right, he'd done any number of things that could've got Alex hurt. Drugging her could've killed her. But there was the outside chance that he didn't know what was going on, so I needed to walk a line.

I held up a hand. "I'm going to make this really simple.

You can't make Alex come back."

"Why, because you say so?"

I shrugged. "No, I'm naw her keeper. She won't return because she doesn't want to. But if we're getting personal, ye can't make me give her up either. You've wasted your time in coming here."

He tutted. "Make you? No need. You'll do it yourself."

"How do ye figure that?"

"Because you are not part of her world and you never will be. I manage her affairs now."

Annoyance swarmed in me. "She manages herself, and we all saw what happened when shite employees don't give a damn about her safety."

He sighed. "I don't have time for this."

"Why, when it was your useless son leading her team?" I watched for a twitch or some sign I was on the money. It didn't come, so I pushed harder. "Is that how Jared persuaded Johnnie to turn rat? A quiet request from the boss with insider connections and a bribe or whatever ye did to keep control. What I don't get is how ye have the nerve to endanger her life then stand there like ye still have the upper hand."

My words bounced off Sir Reginald like they were rubber. He didn't even flinch.

Then he smiled. "I know who you are, Raphael West."

*West.* I stilled, my blood turning icy cold. I hadn't used that surname in almost a decade. I'd given it up when we came to Scotland and adopted a surname to honour the man who'd taken us in. Gordonson was mine by law now, on my driving licence and passport. The very few people who knew about the change would never have said a word.

*West* meant Sir Reginald knew that history. *West* meant

he might know about my father, just as my brother's baby had come into the world.

"How?" I managed.

Sir Reginald continued, "You ran your mouth to Johnnie, claiming you were The Big I Am, and while he thought you were full of yourself, I suspected different. I was right. The rest is irrelevant, as is your presence here, so you will listen to me carefully, then you will leave this place and never bother Princess Alexandra again. Am I understood?"

# 38

# Alexandra

Footsteps drummed Lancaster House's wood-panelled entrance hall, and I spun around, relief filling my heart. Raphael hadn't answered my call, nor could I find him. After leaving Dad, I'd searched outside, but he was nowhere in sight.

But it wasn't Perkins returning him to me. Instead, he brought Jackson.

I stared wide-eyed at Raphael's friend, like he could produce my boyfriend from his back pocket. "Do you know where he is? I've been trying to find him."

"Not sure. All I know is he assigned me shadow duty."

"I thought you'd be hunting down the photographer?"

He fell into step with me, and we made for the arched

exit. It felt strange for Raphael to have just disappeared. Definitely for him to not answer his phone. I didn't like it. Pausing before we went outside, Jackson explained the crowd of people who'd arrived at the café which was to the far south of the grounds.

My shoulders sagged. "Then it was Johnnie."

He pulled a face. "It feels too easy. I saw him there, sitting in the middle of it. He was brazen. I've only seen pictures of the man, but he was easy to identify. Like he didn't care if he was seen."

His phone buzzed, and both of us jumped. He snapped to answer.

"Wait. I'm going to put ye on loudspeaker. Alex is with me."

He tapped the screen then held it between us.

Valentine spoke. "The gift shop is packed, and your man Will is here."

My mouth fell open. "Both of them? They were both in on it?"

Another call flashed on Jackson's screen. A group call from Ben. Jackson switched to accept, keeping it so I could hear.

"Dori and I got the photographer. Straight outside the front gate."

"Oh my God." I clasped my hands to my mouth.

Dori chimed in. "I had him on the ground with a knee in his back. For good measure, I shoved his face in the mud. After what he put you through, I wanted to do more, but Ben said I had to chill."

"What are you going to do with him?"

Ben answered. "He's broken the law. We'll keep him until

the police arrive."

Perkins morphed out of the shadows. "May I suggest your team bring the infidel inside? I have a solution."

Ben agreed, but a cacophony of sound built around him. "Alex? There's a real crush going on out here. Sorry to say your team leader is in the middle of it."

"Riss as well? They were all in on it?" I'd expected her to turn up with Sir Reginald, but what were the chances those photographers were at those gates when others had followed real leads elsewhere?

Because they'd been told. By her.

The events of the past several weeks took on a darker hue. Every member of my team had been conspiring against me. All of them in the pay of who could only be Sir Reginald and for reasons I couldn't even guess at.

Then the other implications hit home. A crowd outside the gates meant someone would eventually tell my father. I'd left him to make his phone call in private, while I'd tried to find Sir Reginald, but I needed to handle this. I just wished I had Raphael with me.

"I'm going to go out and do my public appearance now," I told the team. "Jackson, can you come with me? I'll make it brief so they go away."

"Actually, I don't think you will." A figure stepped into the open doorway, his face shadowed until he shifted into a patch of light.

Sir Reginald had found me.

Jackson muttered something into his phone but didn't budge from my side. Shock stole my breath. I'd wanted him to come. Riss being here should have been indication enough. Anger cramped my belly.

"You have some nerve talking to me like that," I bit out.

"You endangered my life. You paid someone to drug me. Was it also you who scared me in Ossington? Why bother?"

He dipped his head. "No, Your Royal Highness. You misunderstand. I have merely arrived with your team to return you safely to London."

The three corrupt bodyguards at different corners of the estate had been my idea, but under his control, it looked like a sting operation so I couldn't leave.

"Then it's true. Why on earth do you think I'd go back?"

"Come, come, your holiday is over and your boyfriend has walked away."

I stared. "Raphael? No, he hasn't."

Jackson's expression of incredulity backed up my thoughts. Raphael would never leave me. But where was he?

Sir Reginald continued. "It has always troubled me when members of the family do not pay the appropriate respect to what they owe the Crown. King Philip entrusts upon me a great deal, and I do not take that lightly. If we need visibility throughout the year with trivial headlines of a princess in a frock to keep the attention of the British public, then that's what we shall deliver." He angled his head like a snake about to strike. "What you'll deliver. I believe I've made my position clear."

I took a step, furious. "You're deluded. Dangerous. When my cousin finds out what you've done—"

"Oh, your cousin won't care about that. Only that we get the results, which means you getting back in the fucking helicopter with me and doing as you're told." His eyes gleamed as he delivered his killer blow. "Or your ex-boyfriend's real name gets splashed all over the afternoon news, and your father loses his home. Can I speak plainer?"

Perkins recoiled in shock.

I swallowed a bitter sense of loss. He had no remorse and complete certainty over what he'd come here to do.

At the doorway, Ben marched in with Dori and Valentine, the latter holding a photographer with his wrists caught behind his back. Sir Reginald's eye bulged.

At once, several people started speaking.

But it was a booming voice at the top of the sweeping staircase that silenced us all.

On the first landing, my father stood, resplendent in his blue smoking jacket and with antlered stag heads on the wall either side of him. "Alexandra, I assume this is the new security team you've appointed? Perkins, would you assist them in locating the brig?"

The brig was my father's dungeon, used in previous centuries to house local villains.

"At once, sir." Perkins bowed his head and indicated for Valentine to follow him. Then he paused and gestured at a now-silent Sir Reginald.

Of all the people in the world the private secretary was afraid of, there were only two. The king, and the king's uncle.

"That one, too, sir?" Perkins asked.

My father gave a ratty tap of his toe. "Obviously. Lock them both up until I'm ready to deal with them. I have other business to attend to and do not expect to be disturbed."

Sir Reginald squawked in protest, but Ben was already on him and strong-arming him after Valentine and the photographer.

I squeaked in shock and got out of their way, Dori coming to my side and Jackson staying with me as I restarted my heart and followed them to another staircase and down.

Perkins took a set of old, thick iron keys off a hook on the wall and unlocked two stone-walled rooms with barred doors. Ben and Valentine thrust one man in each, and Perkins twisted the keys in the locks.

Sir Reginald flew at the bars of his cell, spittle forming around his lips. "You cannot keep me here."

Perkins didn't flinch. "Actually, His Royal Highness is designated Constable and has the power of arrest. Ye committed a crime, as did your friend." He addressed the sullen photographer who hadn't made a peep. "Your brazen confession enabled your arrest. If ye have a complaint, take it up with the police when they arrive."

He pocketed the keys then ushered us all out.

I wanted to laugh, or to enjoy Dori's story of his exploits in tackling the photographer. But more, I had to find Raphael.

# Raphael

The door to the gallery swung open, and the prince burst through. Alex's father eyed me then jerked his head for me to walk with him again.

After talking to Sir Reginald, I'd returned to the house to find Alex but stumbled in on the prince alone in his breakfast room. I'd cursed myself for breaching no doubt multiple protocols, but the man had waved me in, finishing up a phone call. Shortly after, he brought me here, to what he'd called his exercise room, the portrait gallery that smelled of beeswax and hundreds of years of history.

Shouting had reached us. He'd told me to stay put while he investigated.

Turns out I was a royalist. Not only was I in deep with a princess, but I obeyed princely orders without question.

Being alone for a minute had given me time to think.

All about my life and my response to threats. The dangers I anticipated, and those which hadn't happened yet still scared me enough to put up walls around myself. Walls a princess had scaled without even trying.

Alex's da commenced our stroll again down the long gallery, the gold leaf on the paintings either side of us shining. He pointed at one. "That is Alexandra's great aunt who she is named after. Can you see a resemblance?"

I took in the portrait of a woman in a shepherdess outfit complete with sheep at her feet. "I'm not sure."

He snorted in amusement. "Neither am I. I have no eye for art, unlike my only child. I like that you didn't pretend for my sake. Most would."

I wasn't sure how to answer that, so I stayed silent.

He walked on a few steps then wobbled. Unthinking, I caught his arm, and the man grouched but straightened, patting my hand.

"Everyone here protects me. Or perhaps I live in a bubble of my own making. It appears that I have entirely missed out on a very real threat to my daughter." He swung his attention onto me. "Tell me, Mr Gordonson, do you love her?"

Fucking hell. I swallowed. "With the greatest respect, the person who should hear that first is Alex."

He watched me for a beat then smiled and continued walking. "Good. You're the one she turned to. It's your team downstairs taking care of her, and your men standing by her when those of her own family did not. I have ignored what Perkins saw coming, choosing only to warn her of what not to do, neglecting to give her the tools or the time to handle this when it became a real issue."

"I'm not sure what you mean."

We reached a brocade settee beneath an enormous painting of a hunting scene.

The prince sat heavily and gestured for me to take the

other side. "I want to know everything that has gone on with Sir Reginald, the workload he gave to my daughter, and how it was handled. Tell me now. Do not miss a thing."

"I will. If ye don't mind me telling Alex where I am." I found my phone. I should've done this already, but I'd been stuck in my thoughts and drowning. I also had to check she was okay with me sharing. For all I respected her da, this was her call, not mine.

"Go ahead. She's quite safe. I've locked the bastards up. I never did like that private secretary. Obsequious, backstabbing toad."

Surprise stole the last of my reserve. Seemed I wasn't the only one with a story to tell.

His eyes gleamed. "I mean to clear this up myself. And I've already set in motion how I'm going to do it."

# 40

# *Alexandra*

I started at the message landing on my phone and jumped to read it.

**Raphael:** *Okay if I share the full story with your da? He's demanding answers. Happy to tell him no if you don't want it.*

A sob flew from my lips.

**Alex:** *You're still here? Of course you can share.*

He might as well. Dad had already ordered two men locked up and would need to talk to the incoming police. I hugged my arms. Raphael hadn't left me. Yet another reason to hate Sir Reginald.

**Raphael:** *Where else would I be? Didn't I tell you I wanted nothing other than to be around you?*

He'd adapted the words he'd gifted to me in London.

Upgraded us once again.

"Alexandra?"

I lifted my head to Sarah's quiet enquiry.

Raphael's team were in deep conversation across the entrance hall. From a relieved look Jackson shot me, Raphael had messaged him, too.

"Lunch," Sarah decided. "Perkins has arranged for us to eat indoors. He is making a suggestion, which comes from your father, I believe, that you do not go outside for a little while."

"Did he say why?"

"Something about long lenses and the right moment."

She directed me into a dining room where a buffet was being laid out by more of my father's staff. We took a plate each, though I wasn't sure I could eat. Not until I had Raphael back with me. Sir Reginald had threatened him. I couldn't get that out of my head.

"I'll be staying here, you know," Sarah informed me. "It suits me to be away from home, but I also wanted you to be reassured that your father is well taken care of. He asked, and I finally accepted."

That...was good to hear. "You're serious with him?"

"I always have been. My marriage has long been over. I stayed for my children, but I don't think I'm helping them by being so on-hand now."

"Will you marry my dad?"

"Gosh, no. Can you imagine what they'd dig up on me? How simply awful to be the subject of that attention."

Sarah lifted a hand, and one of the waiting staff brought a bottle of wine and filled up her glass. I refused the same. It was barely noon, not that I was judging.

My father's companion took a healthy sip. "You don't have to do that either. Have your relationship, but don't feed your man to the wolves. I like Raphael. Seems a steady and serious sort of boy. It would be a shame to see him shredded in the same way others have been. That can be wearying as an individual, let alone in a relationship where one party brings incomparable baggage."

She was right, but sadness trickled through me. One day, I wanted to be married. Not in the way my cousin had been with a royal procession, crowds lining the streets, and a huge cathedral. But in a private ceremony like Daisy and Mia had described. Something personal and binding, with a moment where I got to tell the people who mattered about the man I loved and make promises and get them back in return.

I picked at my food until Perkins appeared beside me.

"The police are here, ma'am."

"I'll talk to them, and they can take the photographer away. I'd like a minute alone with Sir Reginald."

Perkins raised a white eyebrow. "Someone else does, too."

I cocked my head at him. "Why are you being so mysterious today?"

He didn't answer but instead led me back into the wood-panelled hall.

In a side room, Ben was already deep in the debrief with the attending officers, sticking with me while I gave them my statement. The rest of the bodyguard team were absent, but I soon worked out why when they reappeared with Riss, Johnnie, and Will.

I didn't even acknowledge them.

The photographer was escorted away, and in the midst

of the fuss, I snuck down to the cellar and prowled on to the second cell.

Sir Reginald perched on a stone seat, his chin still held high.

I watched him through the bars. "Why did you do it? What was in it for you?"

"Any action I took was signed off by His Majesty King Philip. Is that what you want to hear? Whatever you think you're doing now, it doesn't change the fact that you cannot run from your responsibilities."

"But if I return, you'll step back those threats?"

His beady eyes trained on me. "Get back to work, and I'll forget everything I discovered about Mr West. Likewise, your father can continue his indolent isolation here."

"Raphael's surname is Gordonson."

"If you say so. The media might disagree when I talk to them. Make your choice, Alexandra."

He'd print Raphael's old name? To this point, my boyfriend still hadn't been named in the press. Now I knew why. Sir Reginald was holding that string. I swallowed, hating the man beyond words.

A strident voice filled the narrow corridor. "You forget yourself, sir. Do not command my cousin in that way."

I jumped. Sir Reginald leapt to his feet, the colour draining from him. He fell into a deep bow. Almost as quickly, I sank into a curtsy, my heart thumping.

King Philip left the cellar stairs exit and strode down the corridor. I hadn't seen him since Christmas, and while he was tanned from the summer, he was a little thinner. His hair, the same shade as mine, had a greater peppering of grey at the temples. The man appeared exhausted.

Two figures were close behind him, my father, with

Raphael helping him down.

I forgot all about the king and swept my gaze over Raphael with urgency.

He was okay. Though he'd messaged me, I'd still imagined the worst and panicked over not having him near.

My father passed me to join his nephew outside of the cell, then Perkins and two police officers followed, the latter gazing in awe at the king they were pursuing. Perkins unlocked the cell and ushered Sir Reginald out.

Raphael came to me. Unconcerned over who was looking on, he wrapped both arms around me, and I sank into the hug.

"I missed you," I whispered only for him.

He kissed my hair. "Same. Your father and I get along fine, though, ye might like to know. We had a long chat, then his nephew arrived and that conversation got extended again."

I took a shuddering breath.

Down the end of the hall, the king addressed his private secretary. "Sir Reginald Jessop, I entrusted you with the care of my household and my personal affairs. In turn, you lied and cheated out of greed. Can you deny it?"

"But, sir. You don't understand. With all you were suffering, I did what was necessary," Sir Reginald spluttered as he was put under arrest.

"Silence. The evidence against you is damning, and I have heard more than enough from the witnesses called in," the king continued.

"What's happening?" I asked.

Raphael put his mouth to my ear. "A conspiracy. His son, Jared, and Barrington Bray are co-owners of the bodyguard company, and it is failing. Their solution was to engineer high-profile action to generate business, which I believe is why they endangered ye. Jared messed with the team; Barrington sold your exploits to corporate partners to prove their company could manage even the most difficult client."

I worked it over. It made sense why Jared never cared, even about being fired, as it was a farce. He was arrogant. Probably thought the work was beneath him considering his father's position. Then Barrington had come all the way to Scotland to hunt me down. What had Jackson called it? Desperate? They were at risk of discovery or maybe bankruptcy. It made sense, at least partially.

Raphael went on, "Ben spoke to your other team member, Toni, who was happy to spill what he knew, then Riss crumpled and helped fill in the gaps. My team brought her, Will, and Johnnie in to stand in front of your father and cousin and explain themselves. They folded like a deck of cards. She's guilty of taking a bribe, but she also regretted it and discovered the connection."

"I'm glad to have it all out there, but he threatened you, though."

I glared at Sir Reginald as he passed, his head hanging down. He didn't look at us.

From behind, someone offered their opinion. "I may have an answer to that, if you'll join me upstairs?"

It was the king, and there was no chance either of us would disagree.

Back in the entrance hall, King Philip switched his gaze between me and Raphael. "I owe you both an apology, but first, Alexandra, would you take a walk with me? I'm informed that a public appearance is required. Down to the gates and back should do it."

On his arm, and feeling like I was in an alternate universe, I stepped out of the house. We strolled down the long gravel track that led to the main entrance where a hubbub of reporters and the public had gathered. King Philip chatted about his children while I stayed perfectly silent, letting the long lenses take their fill before we turned and walked back up.

"Thank you," I managed at last when we reached the house.

The king released my arm. "It is the minimum owed, along with an explanation."

Upstairs, in my father's favourite drawing room, which had an expansive view down to the same gates that were now clearing of the crowds, I took a seat between Raphael and my dad and waited on the king to speak.

I couldn't remember the last time I'd sat down with any degree of privacy with my cousin. Probably never. He was always surrounded by hangers-on, or we were at a large-scale family event where he'd sit at the distant end of the table with fifty people between us. His packed calendar meant he flew from location to location, always in demand. It was why I hadn't minded helping out over the summer.

My cousin rubbed the space between his eyes and sighed heavily. "I fear this is my fault. Earlier this year, I asked Sir Reginald to make suggestions for how we could expand the royal family's visibility. I did not give him permission to act on any of his recommendations, however, nor did I check in with him. I have been distracted, which stems from another direction entirely. For that, I offer my apologies."

"The source of your distraction, is that anything we can help with?" my father asked.

King Philip worked his jaw then answered. "I'm surprised you don't know already. Enough of my household is aware, and secrets do not remain so long in the palace, probably because people like Sir Reginald barter in them. My hope is this particular matter will not become public knowledge."

His gaze searched us.

Dad and I murmured a promise, but Raphael leaned in.

"I'm a stranger to ye, but I know well how family secrets have to be managed and how they have the power to destroy. Ye can be assured of my silence."

King Philip took a deep inhale and nodded. "In March, not long after our fourth child was born, Helena informed me that she wanted a divorce. This was not from a lack of love, but from the pressure and intrusion from the press that was relentless. Every photograph of her analysed the natural strain of motherhood, and this last pregnancy had been her hardest. She couldn't cope, and could not thrive as a parent or just simply as a woman, none of which, to my shame, I'd understood until she told me. My shock was all-encompassing. To this point, I'd celebrated how well she tolerated the constant invasion of our privacy, and it had made me complacent. I could not lose her."

Emotion rolled over his tightly controlled façade, and I felt the recoil in a wave of sadness. They were divorcing. That was the tragedy of a century. Their love had been everything. My inspiration and childish dream. For that to have been destroyed by others was horrible.

"I'm so sorry," I said.

King Philip tried to smile. "Not all is lost. I have spent the past five months in desperate search of a solution. With time, therapy, and significant change, I'm very glad to say Helena has given me a second chance. She will be withdrawing from public life for some time with my approval. It can be forever, if she prefers. The press can do with that what they like. I see the damage that happens when we try to lead them, but far worse, the damage that can be done to individuals if we indulge them."

I hated what the queen consort had suffered. The king,

too. If Sir Reginald knew some part of this, or suspected it, no wonder he was so desperate to keep another member of the family in the headlines.

A memory hit me. Back weeks ago when we'd spoken, the private secretary had reacted when I'd asked if there was anything the matter. He'd picked on me as a solution to his son's problems and the king's. What an asshole move, but at least now I understood. The queen consort's news would go live eventually, and my drunken, or drugged, exploits would've been the perfect foil.

The king settled his gaze on me. "I apologise for what Sir Reginald attempted in order to distract the press from my side of the family. It was unthinkable and not done with my approval. I would never have ordered that, and the threats he made about defunding your father's living are meritless."

Dad huffed. "I could've told her that. I have never taken from the family coffers. Nor were you ever a burden, daughter."

I gave them both a tight smile.

The king turned to Raphael. "I understand a threat was made against you, which must have been a deeply unpleasant way to familiarise yourself with our family. I have spoken to Sir Reginald's team. They researched you and discovered a name change via restricted deed poll records. Not normally accessible to most, but the word of the king goes a long way, and Sir Reginald abused that in order to do his digging. Beyond that, he did not go. I can assure you of that team's discretion ongoing."

Which meant they didn't know about his father. I wilted. Raphael's hand claimed mine.

"Thank ye for the explanation, Your Royal Highness," he said.

"Philip, please. My uncle informs me that you will join

the family in due course. I'm glad we haven't put you off."

I glared at my father whose eyes gleamed at the tease. Raphael half crushed my fingers.

King Philip braced his hands on his knees. "I'll take my leave now. Alfred, thank you for contacting me and allowing me to put right what my office got so badly wrong. Alexandra, I'll no doubt see you at Christmas. Raphael, I appreciate your understanding. Next time we meet will be under better circumstances, I am sure."

We all stood as King Philip did. He walked to the door which magically opened, Perkins and other courtiers waiting just outside and armed guards visible beyond them.

Raphael ran an arm around me. "Did that really just happen?"

I shook my head in bewilderment. Sir Reginald and the photographer were in the hands of the police, Barrington's team in tatters, and the threats to us were over. The mysteries had been solved.

An idea jumped into my mind, and I took a breath. "Philip, one more thing," I called, then I came back to Raphael. "I want to ask him a favour, but it means sharing information on you. Is that okay?"

Raphael's dark eyebrows merged, but he nodded, that trust right there in his eyes.

I ran for the door. Outside, the king had paused. He lifted a greying eyebrow at me, and we stepped into a quiet space in the hall.

"The threat Sir Reginald made to Raphael was to use his birth name as blackmail, though he didn't know the impact that would have. Raphael's father is a dangerous man. A criminal. Raphael escaped him with his brother and younger sister, but he believes that one day the father might come after them. Now I'm on the scene..."

I chewed my lip, wondering what the heck I was asking.

My cousin tilted his head. "Did you know that Helena's uncle is in a maximum security prison?"

My lips parted. That gossip had never hit the tabloids.

"Like this father of Raphael's, he was an unsavoury element who threatened his niece after she became associated with me. We ignored and monitored, then one day he came to Ossington Palace. Armed."

I clapped my hand to my mouth.

"It turns out he'd hurt and made threats against a lot of people and was poised to sell his story to the highest bidder. His idea of storming the palace was to get the attention of the press. Unfortunately for him, he'd also left explosives in his car which blew up outside an embassy, with no injuries aside from a hole in the road, I'm glad to say, and neatly branding him a terrorist. He's now safely tucked away at my pleasure in prison and unable to menace anyone else."

The king's people had done that, I was almost certain if I read between the lines. Sir Reginald's actions weren't in isolation.

The king smiled at me. "If this father who does not deserve the name comes calling, let me know. I'm sure we can arrange similar for him."

He exited, taking the noise and fuss with him.

Raphael found me. "All okay?"

"Can you take me home now?"

"I thought you'd never ask."

# 41

# Alexandra

After saying goodbye to my father and Sarah, who was now back at his side where it seemed she belonged, we returned downstairs. Raphael's team talked to the police, Riss, Will, and Johnnie sitting in a row and looking forlorn. Riss gave me a sad smile, but I couldn't return it. If she'd suspected anything at all, she should have told me. Instead, she'd taken the money then acted after. I couldn't forgive that.

Raphael checked in with Ben that we weren't needed, but Ben shook his head. "Barrington is in custody after they nabbed him elsewhere. The picture of ye, Raphael, has been taken offline, and your name never appeared. The latest headlines are the shot of the king with his cousin, but the press is hustling to present the news in a different way.

All the other articles about ye, Alex, are vanishing. They're offering it as a rare glimpse into the close royal family with two of the younger generation spotted out for a stroll. They're commending the king for visiting his elderly uncle. No hint of 'find the princess' now. You're exactly where you're meant to be."

Another knot of stress dissolved. Perhaps the last one. Today had done a number on us all.

Ben waved us off. "Go on home. We'll handle it from here."

The release we both needed.

In what felt like no time, we were in the air and flying to the McRae estate. On the flight, Raphael had me unlock his phone to see the picture of his new nephew.

I gazed at the gorgeous swaddled cutie. "He looks just like you."

"Do you think?" At the aircraft controls, the landscape flew by behind Raphael. "I always thought this baby's birth would terrify me. That feeling hasn't hit yet. I don't know if I'll ever feel safe from my father, but I'll do everything I can to make sure that bairn is. And ye. So will my team."

"So will my family. I asked the king for a favour."

I told him what I'd said and what King Philip had confided in me.

Raphael's eyes widened. He swore, his grip on the helicopter's controls tight. "I can't believe ye did that for me."

"This thing between us? It works both ways. I get to protect you, too. And if that means calling in all the king's men to put your father in jail the second he steps foot on this island, then so be it."

He laughed, relief obvious on his features. "Aye, princess.

That helps. Fucking hell, that's the best thing I've ever heard."

That was more than good enough for me.

Back at our cottage, Raphael locked the door then brought me into his arms and just hugged me. The afternoon was at an end, though the sun was still bright around our closed curtains. Enough to make our hideaway even cosier.

His low, beloved voice rumbled in his chest. "So apparently I'm marrying a princess."

I pushed at his chest with a laugh. "Don't. I can't believe my father's meddling. At least it means he likes you."

He didn't let me go. "I like him, too. I'm in love with his daughter."

My protests faded. I gazed up at him in happy shock.

He brushed over my cheek with reverent fingertips. "I'm pretty certain I've been in love with ye since that first time we danced together. Ye stole my heart when your palm slid under my shirt to lie on my chest. Ever since then, you're the only person who could ever have got in, despite the obstacles I put between us. Ye were already there. You've shown me what it is to want someone so badly that nothing else matters. Only ye. I'm in love with ye. Completely, wildly, and in over my head."

My fingers trembled, but I laid them down in the place he'd said, where the steady thump of his heartbeat underscored his words.

It was my turn to speak. "I thought I'd lost you today. I thought enough had happened to drive you away from me. I should have trusted this because I feel it, too. I've never loved anyone else. I've never even tried. Yet I'm so, so in love with you."

Emotion crinkled his brow, but he smiled. "Our hearts

knew before we did. Be mine, princess."

"Always." I pressed up on my toes and kissed him.

Raphael returned my kiss with urgent energy that spilled into pawing at each other's clothes. We didn't even make it into the bedroom, dropping to the sofa then the rug to forget the craziness of the day on each other's bodies and celebrating all we'd found.

I loved him. He loved me. I'd show him every day how much that meant.

Later, in our little kitchen, as the sun set, Raphael cooked dinner for me. I was sure to praise every bite.

Then after, he bundled me into his car for a drive out onto the estate.

We had the windows down to the warm night. It was nearing the end of summer, but right at the beginning of us.

"Where are we going?" I asked.

He smiled across the car and used our joined hands to change gear, not giving up an answer. I found out soon enough.

We left the car behind at a dark track then set out on foot. The lapping water clued me in.

"We're at the loch?"

"When I brought ye to Scotland, ye asked me if everything I'd described on our late-night phone call was real. This was on your list."

We emerged from under the cover of trees to the flat rocks he'd told me about in his skinny-dipping story. The one where we'd stripped and swum together. And after, got down and dirty on the banks.

I shivered in anticipation and danced ahead, slipping my sandals off at the water's edge.

"I want to ask ye something," Raphael said.

I twisted to face him. He was already out of his boots, his t-shirt discarded, too. I loved that view so much. I'd never get over his muscular forearms and broad shoulders. He was too perfect for words.

"Ben and Valentine's double wedding to Daisy and Mia is next week. Will ye be my date?"

Coyly, I tugged the hem of my top to reveal my belly, extending my arms up and up. "Sure you want a mischievous princess around? Last I recall, you told me you'd keep me if you could. Has that changed?"

His focus slid up my body, lingering when I discarded the shirt.

"How about I keep ye for good?"

I kicked off my skirt then reached for the fastening of my bra, pausing. "Is that a formal offer for me to move in with you?"

Slowly, he nodded then shucked his jeans, his shorts already tented.

I pointed at them. "Off."

This corner of the loch was all he'd described. An isolated inlet where no one could see us. I had no fear anymore.

He obeyed me, and my bra went the same way as his shorts, then I drew my fingers down to the line of my underwear, the last remaining item of clothing between us.

Raphael cupped his dick and watched me. "Move in with me, please."

I whipped off my underwear and threw them at him. Then I carefully descended into the cool water, shivering for more than one reason. "You'll have to catch me first."

He made a break for it, and I squealed as he splashed in

beside me. I swam, but he was right there, capturing me in his arms, just like I'd imagined when he'd talked to me on our late-night dirty phone call.

"Yes, I'll move in with you. There is no place I'd rather be than at your side."

Raphael kissed me.

We made love on the banks of the water, and it was every bit as incredible as I'd imagined.

# 42

# Alexandra

An engine purred outside the cottage, and I lifted my head from my sketch. "Are we expecting anyone?"

Raphael poked his head out of the kitchen. He had been baking, and the place smelled amazing. "I might have plans for us this afternoon."

We'd spent the morning locked away, starting a conversation about what we needed to live together. Furniture. Our clothes. All in good time.

Outside in the fresh air, Gordain climbed out of a small blue car, Finn with him, the boy scampering to Valentine and Mia's door.

Gordain grinned at us, his gaze taking in Raphael in what I now realised was a checking-in method the son had learned from the adopted dad. "Your ride, Alex."

I blinked at it. "What do you mean?"

He gave me the keys. "This is Viola's, but she never uses it, so I keep having to take it out to keep the engine alive. You'll be doing us a favour if ye use it for a wee while."

I crushed the keys. "I can't drive it, though. Gears freak me out. I'll mess up and crash it. I can't do that to your daughter's ride."

Raphael guided me to look inside and pointed. "It's an automatic. It has go and stop. Ye can't go wrong. Learn in this and get your licence for an automatic only. It'll be far easier, and you'll have your freedom."

I climbed in. It had never occurred to me to do anything other than the full licence, but why the heck not?

Outside, Gordain clapped Raphael on the shoulder. "You'll teach her, aye? I did with Ella what feels like a hundred years ago."

"Don't think I knew that," Raphael replied.

I poked my head out. "This is so kind of you. I don't know what to say."

Gordain's smile was soft. "We're just glad you're both happy. It's all that matters."

I leapt back out to give the man a hug. He let me, then waved to Valentine who'd come from his cottage with Finn over one shoulder, his daughter, Tobi, under the other arm.

Raphael claimed my hand in his. "Want to go for a drive?"

"I think I do."

Being with Raphael was making me brave as, although I sweated over backing out of the parking spot, the go-and-stop nature of the little car took out well over half of my driving anxiety, leaving me able to concentrate on the road.

I even enjoyed it. That was a crazy thought.

After navigating all the way around the estate to near the aircraft hangar, Raphael had me pull over to the side of the road. "How about we head out to the villages? It means a busier road."

"I can handle it." With him, I could do anything. "Ooh, we could go visit Daisy and Mia at work. Can we go pick up Dori first? He'll lose his mind over seeing me driving a car."

My friend had stayed in Scotland, content to sleep in the bunkhouse and apparently becoming friends with Jackson. Or maybe it was more that he didn't want to go out and face the world. Despite his role in the drama at my father's place, Dori was still flat. I needed to work out how to fix that.

With Raphael's directions, and an indulgent smile at my excitement, I got us to the bunkhouse and added Dori to our day trip, grinning at his bafflement with me behind the wheel.

Steadily, and kinda slowly, I drove us out to Daisy's house clean, leaving the car in the middle of the drive as risking either of the other cars here by parking was not on today's menu. As per usual, Ben was seated outside and doing something on a tablet. Raphael went to talk to him, leaving me with Dori.

I waved to Daisy who was in an upstairs window then nudged my friend with my shoulder. "I'm staying in Scotland."

"Thought you might. I like it here. It'll be no hardship visiting."

"Even if you're sleeping in a bunkhouse?"

He stuck his hands in his pockets and kicked a pebble. "I thought I'd miss our partying, but honestly, I'm over it. I want to grow up, too."

"Thought any more about—"

I'd been about to ask after his musician, but Daisy hollered a greeting from the doorway.

I joined her, eyeing the cleared hallway at her back. "You've done so much!"

She sighed, her hands on her hips. "I don't know. It still feels like a marathon, and the weddings are in just a few days. We'll be stopping for three weeks. I wish we'd at least found the treasure so that it was plain sailing when we returned."

"Darling girl," Dori called. He'd mooched off to the garage.

I trotted over, Daisy coming with me and Mia bringing up the rear. Dori stood at the paintings, halfway through the stack with a canvas revealed.

"Isn't this familiar? Like that artist you admire."

I took in the portrait then sank down in front of it, Dori picking up and removing the dozen that had blocked it from view. And protected it. The mastery of light, the pale precision of the impressionist art, I knew it so well as I'd studied this artist with adoration.

I exhaled a shaky breath. "This is it. The treasure."

Daisy stared. "Are you sure?"

A laugh flew from my lips. "It's a Cecilia Beaux. Dori, you've been here ten seconds and you walked straight up to Agnes's secret hidden treasure. You're amazing."

This, at last, brought the slightest smile to my best friend's lips. It failed quickly enough, but in that second, with a celebrating Mia telling the others about the discovery and Daisy on the phone to the homeowner, I set my gaze on my best friend.

I'd fix him. I wasn't sure how, but I'd do everything I could to make him as happy as me. Luckily, I knew a team of bodyguards who might want to help.

# 43

## Raphael

A tired-looking Gabe opened the front door to let us in, a tiny wail chasing him. He and Effie had brought their son home yesterday, but neither had slept for more than a few hours together in days, so we'd given them time before visiting.

Ariel and Jackson had already arrived, so when Alex and I entered the living room, we tucked up next to them on the sofa, all gazes on the wee scrap of a bairn in my sister's arms.

Ariel's eyes were lined with tears, which said a lot as she never cried. "He's perfect, Effie. So beautiful. Look at what you made!"

Effie curled in an armchair with a blanket over her and her dark hair tied up. My sister-in-law had been the image of a hardened athlete, and motherhood had softened her. "We agree. I can't stop staring at his face."

"Luckily, he looks just like his ma," I told her, saying the only thing that should be told to a woman who'd just undergone days of labour.

Ariel passed me the baby, and I tucked him on my arm, tracing and memorising every little feature from his button nose to his wisp of dark hair. Alex took a photo and stroked his cheek, and at long last, I realised my fear for his safety had gone.

All I felt was a rush of love so strong it could have floored me.

"Okay there, uncle?" Gabe said softly.

"Hush it," I said back but with a smile. "Do we have a name yet?"

The couple glanced at each other, and Effie spoke.

"Nope. He's still just Baby Gordonson. Originally, we wanted to go with something that represented his role in our lives. More specifically, in your lives here in Scotland, and in the freedom ye found. His birth represents so much. Ye both," she indicated to me and Ariel, "were young teenagers when ye first came here. I didn't know then what you'd become to me, but I knew ye needed family. People who'd love ye. My husband was the same, even if he gave me the runaround."

She grinned at Alex. "Did ye know I had to basically torment him into loving me? Gordonson men are tough nuts to crack."

Alex curved an eyebrow at me. "Sounds familiar." She returned Effie's smile. "We need to compare notes. I want all the stories."

Effie smiled, and her gaze dropped to her son. "That need for freedom and a new lease of life is in the past, though. We are living it now, so naming a child to represent anything to do with your shared history just didn't hit. We couldn't do it. He's his own person. He'll grow up without the tyranny of his grandfather. We're not tying him to that."

Gabe heaved a sigh. "Which takes us back to the drawing board. Any and all suggestions, throw them at us. We'll see if anything sticks."

Jackson and Ariel began name generating, the new parents hearing and shrugging at most. I stared down at the bairn then ran an arm around Alex.

"Got any ideas?"

She sucked in a breath. "I wouldn't want to make a suggestion. I'm brand-new to this family."

"Yet the promise ye extracted from your cousin was done to protect us all, including this wee one."

The room fell silent.

"Uh, maybe explain that?" Ariel asked.

Quickly, I outlined what had gone on. I hadn't told any of them. Not that I shared my troubles with them in general, but with my sister-in-law in labour, a family meeting had not been on the cards. They didn't even know my picture had appeared online or connected with Alex's.

When I was done, all stared wide-eyed.

My brother was quickest to recover. "The king offered us his support?" He uttered a laugh. "Makes sense now why that haunted expression has gone from your eyes, Raph. Thank ye, Alex. I refused to live a life in fear, but I've got to say that helps a lot."

Effie watched her baby and tilted her head. "What if we stop looking for big meaning in the name? We just pick something that suits him."

Gabe's eyebrows rose. "Where's the list of names we liked?"

She found her phone and opened her notes. "Xavier—"

"That's perfect," Gabe said.

Effie blinked at him. "I put that on the list because it's the name of the snowboarder I admire, but more because I think it sounds really cool. Xavier Gordonson is a badass name for when I take him out on the slopes."

"Xavier Gordonson." My brother tried it on for size. Then he smiled. "Welcome to the world."

$\mathcal{B}$raced by Jackson at my side, I moved in on Dori. The count, invited by Alex to ours for dinner, lifted his head at our approach, his posture stiffening. Throughout the evening, Alex had tried to get him to talk, but he was muted. Nothing like the man I'd met in a nightclub when he'd sprayed champagne, jumped on a table, and caused a ruckus. She had the feeling she might be the blocker, so this was our alternative plan.

"This is the firing squad? Put me out of my misery," Dori said sardonically.

I ducked my head at the door. "Up and out. We're taking ye for a walk."

He sighed but stood. "Maybe a quick dip in the loch. Don't let me surface."

Outside in the fresh night air, I led the way, strolling out into the lane that led around the hill and in the direction of Braithar, Jackson keeping pace. "You're unhappy. Alex hasn't told us your story, but we know the basics and want to help."

"My heart's broken. Nothing any of you can do about that."

Jackson palmed his shoulder in a friendly gesture of solidarity. "Tell us the story. Maybe we'll have some ideas."

Dori relented, probably because of the alcohol Alex had plied him with, but the words came thick and fast. His falling in love with his musician. Their romance. The way he knew to the bottom of his soul that she was the one for him, but then her agreement to marry another.

At last, we got the details of why he'd lost his passport and had been avoiding Alex.

Jackson gave me a look behind Dori's back. Neither of us liked the sound of what he'd told us.

"So you see, she made her choice. I should never have gone to find her."

"Have ye moved on?" I asked.

"What the fuck does it look like?" He hauled in a breath. "I don't mean to snap at you. But no, I haven't. I can't."

"Because ye haven't heard the words from her lips," Jackson said.

Dori swung his gaze up. "Exactly. That's why I went. It felt off. It still does. But what am I supposed to do? I don't know where she is. There's no way her management company would tell me—I know, I tried. I can't call or text her any more as my number was blocked. The one place I can still see her is an account that she doesn't use anymore."

"Have ye tried messaging her there?" I asked.

"Yes. No reply."

The conversation had taken us all the way through the woods so we were above Braithar.

Jackson planted his hands on his hips. "What if someone else tried to get in touch with her?"

Dori shrugged. "She knows about Alex, but I can't

imagine she's going to reply to her. Not when she ignored me. Why would she?"

"What if she can't reply? What if ye were right all along and she's somehow restricted and her comms are being controlled?"

Dori didn't answer, but emotion brewed just under his surface. He hadn't given any part of this up.

"One of the things Ben trained us to do is think outside the box," Jackson continued. "To get ye to answer the phone, Valentine used a local number trick. We could do similar with Elsie."

"What are ye thinking?" I asked.

"Leo. He can approach her. With his star power, there is no way she'd ignore the contact. Especially if she has a new album coming out. Her record company would bend over backwards at the hint of him helping to promote her. We can try it. Even ask her to come here for a recording session if we think she's being manipulated and needs a way out."

It was a good plan. I turned to the count. "Ye knew her, Dori, even if ye think those two weeks were a fever dream, there was a connection. Believe me, I fell in love in a shorter time than that and would move mountains for Alex. Tell us to do this or tell us to mind our own business. Either way, we're friends and we don't want to see ye down."

The count looked between us. Surprise shifted to certainty in his eyes. "You really think this will work?"

"Only one way to find out."

"Do it."

We half ran the rest of the way to Braithar and hunted down Leo. As an old romantic, he needed no convincing to join in our conspiring, directing us into a music room to plot.

In thirty minutes, his friend request to Elsie's private account had been accepted. That had been our first plan of attack, the record company approach a second. Good to know we didn't need it. The greater the privacy the better.

"Okay, to the DMs. I'll ask if we can discuss cowriting a song," Leo said.

Dori swallowed and nodded.

Leo sent the message, and we all stared at the screen, waiting on her reply.

*Elsie: This should really be approved by my manager. My contract is pretty tight, and I get no say, which I know sounds ridiculous. I only accepted this request because I respect you as a musician. How did you even get this account name?*

*Leo: A mutual friend. If you're by yourself, can I call? I'll explain it better.*

A long several minutes passed. We'd scared her off. She wasn't going to reply.

Leo's phone rang with a video call.

He answered it, careful to keep the background behind him a wall of guitars and not the rest of us. "Elsie?"

A small, tentative voice filled the air. "It's me. It's nice to meet you, Mr Banks. Who did you mean by a friend?"

"Are you alone?" Leo checked.

"I am."

"I know him as Dori."

The room held its collective breath. With the phone at an angle, I could just make her out. She had her blonde hair down in soft waves around her heart-shaped face. The picture of her and Dori together on her account had been of a happier-looking woman.

"Dori?" she breathed. "I'm shocked that he still thinks

about me, let alone to recommend me to you."

"Why's that?" Leo asked.

"That's highly personal, plus ancient history. How do you even know him?"

Leo's gaze held Dori's, who practically vibrated with how rigid he held himself.

"We're friends. I don't think you're ancient history as far as he's concerned."

She made a sound of frustration. "I don't know you to have this kind of discussion, and if I'm overheard... Listen, whatever he said is a lie. For the sake of setting the record straight, he broke up with me by a single message while I was in the middle of the toughest and most gruelling album recording sessions you can imagine. He shattered me, then blocked me, and left me no method of contacting him. Since then—" Her voice strained, and she stopped.

Dori burst off the wall and snatched the phone, carrying it off down the room. Wild-eyed, he held it up so Elsie could at last see him. "That was a lie. I thought you'd blocked me. I couldn't get in contact with you at all. I tried every way possible. When I couldn't get through on your phone, I called your management team, your publicist, all of them. You'd gone ahead and got engaged, and the way I found out was that video appearing online."

Dead silence filled the line, then a sob. "No, that isn't what happened."

"It is! Believe me, I bled to see you. I came to your goddamned engagement party to reach you just to be sure—"

"You did what?"

Dori slid to his knees on the music room floor. "You didn't know?"

The three of us made to leave. The contact had been made, our job was done.

Something sounded her end of the line.

Elsie spoke in a rush. "The engagement was fake. I only agreed to it as a publicity stunt because I was upset over losing you. Your breakup message had come in that morning, and I was broken. I mean destroyed. But it went too far, and now…"

Voices sounded on her end of the line, abruptly cutting off her speech.

Her voice was the only clear one, with the emotion completely gone from her tone. "…Leo Banks. We're talking about a collaboration. Why would you need…Victor!"

Dori scrambled up and tossed the phone to Leo who caught it and centred his face on the screen, right as a man appeared behind Elsie in the frame. The influencer she was engaged to. He took in Leo then walked away.

"Don't be long," he told her. "We have shit to do."

Dori took the phone back but stayed with us. He touched his gaze on each of us, and I gave him a nod, sharing the sense of something being badly wrong here.

Elsie watched her fiancé leave, and her throat bobbed. "He's gone."

"You're in trouble," Dori said.

She took a breath. "It's complicated."

"Or, it's simple. You've been lied to and kept away from me. Did anyone tell you I'd asked to speak to you?"

"No one. You even spoke to Misty, my manager?"

"Even her. She told me you were too busy to talk and that she'd pass on my name but I shouldn't expect shit back."

"She lied. Oh God. Why did she lie to me? She knew how

hurt I was. Dori, please, the breakup message wasn't from you?"

Dori crumpled. "No. I never would've. I got one, too."

The two of them watched one another, and the emotion fucking choked me. It felt intrusive to witness, but I also knew Dori needed us. Like Alex, even in the middle of a wealthy family and castles for days, he had next to no true support. He needed a team around him.

Like he'd read my mind, Dori centred himself. He panned the camera to show me and Jax. "I have bodyguard friends here who can get you out. I don't know what's going on there, but I'm certain you have to leave now."

"I can't. I'm under contract. It's tied up so tight."

Leo chimed in. "Let me help with that. My mother-in-law employs the best entertainment lawyers and would love to tear up whatever they had you sign."

The woman on the phone screen paled. "Is this even happening? Dori, please."

"All you need to do is tell us yes." He gripped the phone tight.

The desperation in her features bled into her voice. "Yes."

# Epilogue

## Raphael

A short while on and we were celebrating again, this time at a boozy party following a double wedding. Ben and Daisy, and Mia and Valentine had been married in simple ceremonies back to back. Neither bride had wanted a huge fuss, and according to Ben, chose to spend their hard-earned money on their honeymoons.

Not that the party was in any way slacking. The copious amount of alcohol had been provided by Gordain and his older brother, Callum, and the food brought by every invited household. The venue was Castle Braithar's hall with a friend of Leo's playing DJ and every face a friendly one.

We were well into the evening, with ties loosened and more than one overtired child asleep on a chair and ready to be carried to bed. The happy couples danced in the middle of the floor space with the older generations smiling on, and the teenagers from the newer generation stealing drinks and trying to appear grown up.

At a round table, I enjoyed a beer with Jackson, my lass and my sister dancing together like they'd known each other for years. In a corner, Dori danced with Elsie. Like Alex had been, the musician was in hiding here, but none of us would give her up. We'd helped her escape, which was a story for another day, and she was working on getting out of her predatory contract. Dori didn't stray far from her, and from the looks of things, she only had eyes for him.

All had come good for everyone.

Mathe, the son of Effie's brother, Artair, had been sitting with us, asking question after question about our bodyguard work. At thirteen, he was nearing six feet tall, but with a grandfather closer to seven feet, had some distance to go.

He was a determined kid. Serious about jumping into work as soon as he could.

Satisfied with our answers, he left us to go hang out with his gang of cousins. The next generation of McRae kids would be a force to be reckoned with. They were already a tight group with all the love and support they could need. I loved that my nephew, Xavier, would join their clan. My own kids, too, if Alex wanted any.

She danced back over, landing on my lap and stealing a kiss.

I hugged her to me. "Just a random question, but if your father gets his way and marries off his daughter, what kind of ceremony does that look like?"

Alex rested her head on my shoulder, her focus on the room. "Most of my family enjoys the spectacle. Or maybe are forced to endure it. The public expects a royal wedding to be a huge deal. There's something magical about a prince or princess finding love."

Her fingers interlaced mine, and she squeezed. "I can't think of anything worse. I want this. The real magic of a quiet ceremony with no strangers. No fanfare, no photographs sold to national papers. I wouldn't even want the media to know because it would be none of their business. I don't know how possible that will be; I can't ignore my relatives completely. Dad would probably want to come."

Her lips curved, and I couldn't resist stealing a kiss.

"Other than that, I'd just want to be married more than have a big wedding."

I couldn't have said better myself. When the time was right, I would get down on one knee and beg for my princess's hand. After, of course, asking her da first, because I knew she'd want me to. After that, and for the rest of our lives, I'd get to keep her.

### The End.

To read all about Dori's rescue of Elsie, download the free bonus epilogue here!

https://dl.bookfunnel.com/3ayh683a96

(There are lots of free bonus epilogues for my books. Downloading any adds your email to my reader list, which is super helpful for me as I can tell you about news and new releases. You can unsubscribe at any time with no drama. Thanks for loving the McRae universe as much as I do!)

# ACKNOWLEDGEMENTS

Dear reader,

We've reached the end of the McRae Bodyguard series! Raphael and Alexandra have found each other, and all is right with the world. We have every member of the team paired off, and even wedding bells and babies on the way.

Do you love the world of the McRaes? Are you feeling mild panic about this being the last book after four series set in this lovely part of Scotland? Tell me who you'd like me to write about next, if we were to stay here. A third generation? Another business or team on the estate? I'm always ready and willing to write what you want to read.

SECRET CODES

There is a secret code in each *McRae Bodyguards* book, and the answer is given at the end of this section. Not only for *Keep Her from Them*, but also for *Take Her from You*, the previous book in the series.

**Keep Her from Them's code:**

Alexandra gives Raphael a code to get into a back staircase of the palace.

That number is this book's hidden code.

Go find it then use your phone's alphanumeric keypad (i.e. 2 = ABC, 3 = DEF etc) to turn the numbers into letters. One letter per number. In order, they show that Alexandra has been thinking of Raphael.

--

Big thanks go to my readers whose love for the McRae clan never fails to inspire me. To Liz, Elle, Zoe, Emmy, Sara, Katie, Lori, and Shellie – you're the best and I couldn't get anything done without you. To Cleo, you make such pretty graphics and beautiful formatting. To Lisa, Kale, and the team at Audio Sorceress, the audio is fabulous. To my ARC and Street Team, plus everyone who does this outside of my teams, your reviews and posts make my day so much brighter.

Love to talk about my books with likeminded readers? Add yourself to my Facebook *Jolie Vines's Fall Hard Reader Group*

Or join my newsletter list here https://www.jolievines.com/newsletter

Lastly, as always, I thank N&M who are my whole world.

Jolie x


--

**The secret code answers (spoilers if you haven't worked them out yet)**

Take Her from You:

His smirk increased. "Ye trust me, aye? My bank account number is forty-six, thirty-three, thirty-nine, sixty-eight."

Decoded answer: I NEED YOU


Keep Her from Them:

**Alex:** *Come to see me? I won't run this time. Staircase three down the hall from the bodyguard office. Third floor. Suite of rooms to the right. The door code to get up here is 74568.*

Decoded answer: PILOT

# ALSO BY JOLIE VINES

**Marry the Scot series**
1) Storm the Castle
2) Love Most, Say Least
3) Hero
4) Picture This
5) Oh Baby

**Wild Scots series**
1) Hard Nox
2) Perfect Storm
3) Lion Heart
4) Fallen Snow
5) Stubborn Spark

**Wild Mountain Scots series**
1) Obsessed
2) Hunted
3) Stolen
4) Betrayed
5) Tormented

**Dark Island Scots series**
1) Ruin
2) Sin
3) Scar
4) Burn

**McRae Bodyguards**

1) Touch Her and Die

2) Save Her from Me

3) Take Her from You

4) Keep Her from Them


**Body Count**

1) Arran's Obsession

2) Connor's Claim

3) Riordan's Revenge


**Standalones**

Cocky Kilt:

a Cocky Hero Club Novel

Race You:

An Office-Based Enemies-to-Lovers Romance

Fight For Us:

a Second-Chance Military Romantic Suspense

# ABOUT THE AUTHOR

JOLIE VINES is a romance author who lives in the UK with her husband and son.

Jolie loves her heroes to be one-woman guys.

Whether they are a brooding pilot (Gordain in Hero), a wrongfully imprisoned rich boy (Sebastian in Lion Heart), or a tormented twin (Max in Betrayed), they will adore their heroine until the end of time.

Her favourite pastime is wrecking emotions, then making up for it by giving her imaginary friends deep and meaningful happily ever afters.

Have you found all of Jolie's Scots?

Visit her page on Amazon and join her ever active Fall Hard Facebook group.